～THE～ PARISIANS

ALSO BY MARIUS GABRIEL

The Ocean Liner
The Designer
Wish Me Luck As You Wave Me Goodbye
Take Me to Your Heart Again
The Original Sin
The Mask of Time
A House of Many Rooms
The Seventh Moon

THE PARISIANS

MARIUS GABRIEL

Text copyright © 2019 by Marius Gabriel
All rights reserved.

Published by Lake Union Publishing, Seattle

www.apub.com

Amazon, the Amazon logo, and Lake Union Publishing are trademarks of Amazon.com, Inc., or its affiliates.

ISBN-13: 9781503905047
ISBN-10: 1503905047

Cover design by Debbie Clement

Cover photography by Richard Jenkins Photography

Printed in the United States of America

THE PARISIANS

One

Olivia Olsen had never felt further away from Lindstrom, Minnesota, than on this hot summer morning in Paris, 1939. The lightest of breezes rustled in the leaves of the trees. The sky was a blue mixed by Monet, the passers-by had been painted by Renoir. All along the banks of the River Seine, Parisians sat fishing with the earnestness of men who had been tasked with supplying the Sunday lunch. And Olivia, too, had laid out her bait.

She had stationed her easel with a view of the Pont au Change, the stone bridge whose arches bore the proud capital N of Napoleon, with the towers of the Conciergerie prison beyond. She had rendered the scene with dashing Impressionist strokes, in rich colours; but there was a blank space in the centre of the canvas, as though a figure had yet to be painted there: and indeed, as the sign she had attached to her easel explained, for three hundred francs, Mademoiselle Olivia Olsen was prepared to put you in the picture, giving you the perfect souvenir of Paris to take home.

To complete the image of the Parisian artist, Olivia was wearing a beret and a spotless artist's smock, garments she never wore in her studio when doing her real work. Not that this wasn't important. It might not be serious artistically, but if she failed to get a client today, the consequence was that she wouldn't be able to buy herself any dinner.

Her finances were very rickety lately. She had tightened her belt to the point where no more notches remained.

She usually managed to get at least one commission every Sunday, and if her luck was in and she started early, sometimes two or three. Until her real work began selling, this was what kept her from starving, and reminded her to stay alert and smile prettily at anyone who lingered to look at her painting.

With hair the colour of ripe wheat and blue-grey eyes that were wide and fringed with thick lashes, she had the colouring of her Swedish ancestors, who had emigrated at the turn of the century, escaping Scandinavian famine and flood for the land of plenty in the American Midwest. From them, too, she had inherited her tall and sturdy body, with its robust good health and its capacity for hard work. She had a short, straight nose and a full, pink mouth, and more than one saunter-ing promenader paused to look at the artist rather than the art.

One such person was leaning against the balustrade beside her now, watching her closely. Her customers tended to be plump, pros-perous tourists. This fellow was young and slim and unquestionably Parisian, with his bamboo cane and carefully curled blonde beard. He was extremely handsome, perhaps even too much so; but Olivia's obser-vant eyes had noted that his clothes were rather worn. A student, she guessed. He met her eyes and raised his hat.

'May I ask, Mam'selle, why you're dressed up as Henri Matisse?'

'I might ask you,' she retorted, 'why you're blocking my view?'

'I'm waiting for you to start painting me,' he replied calmly.

Olivia tapped the little card attached to her easel. 'Have you got three hundred francs?' she asked sceptically.

'I was hoping we could negotiate.'

'My terms are not negotiable.'

'That's very unreasonable. How long will it take?'

'About two hours now. Then I'll take the painting back to my stu-dio, dry it, varnish it, frame it, and you can pick it up in three days.'

'Three hundred francs is your last word?'

'My last three words, to be accurate.'

He sighed. 'Very well then. I agree to your terms.' He propped one elbow on the balustrade and struck a debonair pose. 'You may proceed.'

Olivia was irritated. 'I don't believe for a minute that you've got three hundred francs or anything like it.'

He rapped his cane on the ground. 'What effrontery. Are you demanding payment in advance?'

'My terms are half now, the rest when you pick up the finished painting next week.'

'You call for a lot of trust.' He took a leather wallet from his pocket and carefully counted out a hundred and fifty francs in notes and coins. Olivia couldn't help noticing that the wallet was very thin after the money had been removed. She doubted whether there was anything left in it at all.

'Are you sure you want to do this?'

'As sure as these stones under our feet.'

'Then at least keep still.' Olivia was already sketching busily, blocking in the young man's slim figure and bearded face, trying to capture the insouciance with which he faced her.

Having caught his outline with swift strokes, Olivia began colouring the sketch with oil paints from her palette. She diluted her colours with turpentine and cobalt, not only for economy, but to make sure they would dry quickly.

Her subject was wearing a suit that had once been expensive, but had faded with age. He had probably picked it up in a pawnshop, she thought. He had an aquiline nose and a high forehead. His hair was too long for her taste, curling over his collar in heroic style. The removal of the beard, manly as it undoubtedly was, would make him even more handsome, since he had an excellent mouth, which seemed to hover on the brink of a smile without ever quite getting there.

He had been inspecting her with similar concentration. 'Do you bleach your hair?' he asked.

'Absolutely not,' she said in a clipped voice.

'I ask because so many American girls do.'

'In your vast experience?' she enquired, even less pleased that he had identified her as an American so quickly – she was rather proud of her fluent French.

'And because your eyebrows and eyelashes are so dark,' he continued, unperturbed by her frown. 'Not that this is in any sense a defect. To the contrary. The contrast is very striking, ensuring that your beauty cannot possibly be missed.'

The compliment hadn't mollified Olivia. 'Would you mind keeping quiet while I concentrate?'

'Your French isn't bad. How long have you been in Paris?'

'Since last December,' she admitted reluctantly.

'And you're still struggling?'

'You ask a lot of very personal questions,' Olivia said.

'You would hardly be hawking sketches on the riverbank if you had countesses lining up with their offspring for you to paint. And yet one can see that you have some talent.'

'How kind of you to say so.'

'What you are doing there is just a pastiche of Monet and Renoir, of course.'

'Oh, really?'

'I have a very good eye for art.'

'You certainly have a very high opinion of yourself.'

'I value myself for what I am. Everyone should do the same.'

'If everyone were as insufferable as you the streets would run with blood.'

'As a matter of fact, the street where we stand did once run with blood, and not so long ago. The guillotine stood close by.' His eyes sparkled. 'And France was healthier for it.'

'I suppose you're eager for another revolution,' Olivia retorted, stabbing paint on the canvas with her brush.

'I hope to live to see another one, yes.'

'Are you a Marxist or something of that sort?'

'I am a man with a brain.'

'And until the revolution you spend your Sundays sauntering around annoying honest working people.'

'How is the painting coming along?'

'I'm surprised it's turning out at all, the way you're annoying me.' She studied the painting critically. It was indeed coming along better than she'd anticipated. 'Could you possibly keep quiet for the next hour? I've never known anyone talk as much as you do.'

The smile that hovered on his lips almost materialised. 'You don't like to talk?'

'You're here to amuse yourself, but I'm here to work. I can work or I can talk. I don't like to do both.'

'Well, which would you prefer?'

Olivia sighed and laid down her paintbrush. 'What I'd *really* like is a cigarette.'

'Why didn't you say so?' He produced a silver case and offered her one.

She took it gratefully and cupped her hand around his as he flicked a battered silver lighter into flame. 'Thank you.' She exhaled a plume of smoke upwards, watching it catch the bright sunlight. A wave of dizziness washed through her brain, and she held her brow with her free hand.

'What's the matter?' he demanded.

'Just a bit giddy. This is my first cigarette in three days.'

'Had you given up?'

'No. I just couldn't afford any.' She inhaled again, feeling the nicotine percolate through her bloodstream, a pleasurable poison. 'Aren't you going to join me?'

He showed her the empty case. 'It was my last one.'

'Sorry.' She held the cigarette out to him. 'Share?'

He accepted the democratic proposal graciously, inhaling and then passing it back to her. They smoked in companionable silence until the oddly intimate but all-too-brief luxury was over. He pinched out the stub and put it carefully back in the case, where it would no doubt serve to make another smoke later on. The gesture didn't escape Olivia.

'This is silly,' she sighed. 'You obviously don't have a bean and nor do I. Why are you wasting three hundred francs on a painting?'

His eyes opened wide. 'Wasting? Not at all,' he replied seriously. 'At three hundred francs, the privilege of your exclusive attention for two hours is very cheap.'

Despite herself, Olivia smiled. 'Well, I hope you're getting your money's worth.'

'The experience has been a little up and down so far,' he said wryly.

'Sorry if I was grumpy. I was dying for a smoke.' She picked up her palette and resumed painting.

'I've seen you here before.'

'I come every weekend.'

'Yes, I know. You do very well with the American tourists. Especially motherly ladies.'

'It seems to me,' Olivia said, brushing ultramarine into the shadows of his jacket, 'that you know an awful lot about me. But no more talk, please. I'm doing your face.'

Surprisingly, he kept quiet, though she could see the suppressed amusement in his features making his eyes sparkle. This self-confident young man was annoying, she decided, but likeable. And he had shared his last cigarette with her. 'It's so peaceful when you stop talking,' she said at last. 'All right. I'm nearly done. I'll leave it as it is for now and finish it later at home. Can you come on Wednesday?'

'I'll be there.'

She gave him her address. In exchange, he took out a little card case, and passed her a business card from it. She examined it. On it was printed simply the name Fabrice Darnell and the outline of a quill pen. Olivia looked up. 'You're a writer?'

He bowed slightly. 'I am an essayist. My work is not fiction. It is directed at achieving social justice and liberty for the individual in modern society.'

'That sounds like fiction to me,' Olivia said dryly.

'May I see the painting?' He studied it. 'You're very good. You've captured something of me in a few strokes. I just wish you had spent more time on the details.'

'My style is Impressionist.'

'Meaning you make a virtue of sloppiness.'

'You'd just stopped annoying me. Now you're starting again.'

'The truth is seldom popular.'

'You can go now,' Olivia commanded, covering the canvas with a cloth.

'Is that all?'

'I think you've had your money's worth.'

He looked downcast. 'Can't I stay and continue our conversation?'

'No,' she said firmly. 'You'll keep my customers away. I need another fly to fall into my web.'

Her tone was decisive, and he seemed to accept his dismissal. But at last, the smile that had been hovering on his lips arrived. It was a very sweet smile, tinged with wistfulness, lighting up his face. 'Very well. I will see you in three days. Goodbye, Mademoiselle Olivia Olsen.'

'Goodbye, Monsieur Fabrice Darnell.'

He raised his hat to her and walked away without looking back. She followed his figure with her eyes until it vanished among the crowds strolling along the banks of the Seine.

Two

A mile or two from where Olivia had set up her easel, Antoinette d'Harcourt was watching her friend undress. Arletty, reaching behind her back with her long arms to unfasten her brassiere, caught Antoinette's eyes on her.

'Why are you looking at me like that?' she demanded.

'Can't I look at you?'

'Yes. But you were frowning. What were you thinking?'

'I was thinking how little grace you have.'

'Oh, well, thank you. That's very flattering.' Arletty hung her bra on the chair and rubbed the creases the straps had left on her small breasts, with their erect brown nipples. 'I'm glad I asked.'

'Don't pretend to be offended. You know how beautiful you are.'

'But I am only a daughter of the people. And you, as all the world knows, are a duchess.'

'And as all the world knows, a film star is far more important than a duchess these days.'

'Even a graceless one?'

Antoinette stretched back on the bed, smiling. 'Don't twist my words. You're a miracle. You're skinny—'

'Thank you again.'

'Gangly—'

'Better and better.'

'Gawky, not to put too fine a point on it—'

'Please don't put too fine a point on it, my dear.'

'—and all Paris is at your feet.'

Arletty kicked off her heels and inspected her narrow feet. 'I don't see all Paris.'

'At any rate, *I* am at your feet.'

'How confusing. A second ago you were at my throat.'

'I adore you.'

'After all those insults? Permit me to doubt your sincerity, Madame d'Harcourt.'

'You light up every room you enter. The dullest film becomes fascinating when you are in the scene. You are the wittiest, cleverest, handsomest woman in Paris. And I love you madly.'

Arletty put her head on one side. 'And now you expect me to forgive you?'

'I *beg* you to forgive me.' Antoinette held out her arms.

Arletty clambered on to the huge bed beside Antoinette. The hotel suite was furnished in shades of cream with gold accents, exquisite rooms designed to please a woman's taste. They had been meeting at the Ritz for some months in order to be discreet; they could lunch together under the eyes of the *beau monde* and then slip upstairs to their room without being noticed. They shared the bill between them.

Antoinette wrapped her arms around Arletty. 'You drive me mad.'

Arletty turned her face away from Antoinette's hungry mouth. 'Scraggy as I am?'

'I didn't say you were scraggy. I said you were gawky. And you know yourself it is true.'

'I think you're growing bored with me.'

Antoinette's face twisted. 'Oh, darling. How can you say that? My deepest terror is that you will grow bored with *me*. I couldn't bear that. I think I would die.'

'Don't be silly.'

'I'm so plain and dull, and you're so beautiful.'

Arletty could hear the genuine pain in Antoinette's voice. She lowered her lids and suppressed a half-smile of triumph. It was gratifying to have a duchess so infatuated with one, even in these times when (as Antoinette had just said) having starred in a few films counted for more than a family line a thousand years old. Besides, at forty-one it was a coup in itself to be so passionately desired by anyone. Arletty knew that, beautiful as she still was, there were now crow's feet appearing around her celebrated eyes and ironic lines bracketing her generous mouth; and her body, which had never been remotely voluptuous, was now starting to appear frankly thin.

She was cool and remote through the intimacies of love. Where Antoinette grew flushed, her lips and eyelids swollen, her breath rushing in and out of her lungs, Arletty was almost silent, her face retaining its mask-like immobility, as though to keep to herself whatever pleasures she felt.

Afterwards they propped themselves against the feather pillows and ate chocolate *gâteau*. The sun was slipping down over place Vendôme, ushering honey-coloured spectres into the beautiful rooms.

'I'm going to leave my husband,' Antoinette said.

Arletty glanced at her quickly. 'Is there some difficulty?'

Antoinette made a face. 'You know very well what the difficulty is, my dear.'

'Don't do it on my account,' Arletty said sharply.

'I can't continue with the charade. I've given François twelve years. It's enough. The marriage was a formality to begin with.'

'You have two young children. They are not a formality.'

'François doesn't love me. I don't love him. There is nothing more to say.' She lifted another piece of *gâteau* into her mouth on the silver fork. 'I'm not speaking of a divorce, of course, or of a public separation. We shall simply each go our own ways. The boys will remain with him. They need their father more than they need me. You say nothing?'

'I have said what I think.'

'I'm in love with you, Arletty.' Antoinette looked at her friend for a response but got none. 'Your face is so hard sometimes.'

'And I am gawky and skinny and all the rest, yes. You've told me.'

'I meant all that in the most loving way.'

Arletty had eaten no more than a mouthful or two of the *gâteau*. Strictly disciplining her appetites had been a habit since her childhood, a childhood that had been tough and constrained by poverty. The woman beside her, born to riches and privilege, could not imagine such a life. Nor had Arletty ever spoken of it to her. She had only come to the attention of people like Antoinette d'Harcourt when she'd risen to fame; and that fame had come late in life, when she was already a woman in her mid-thirties.

How spoiled they all were! Complaining that they were not free – they who had never known a day of hunger in their lives!

It was too late for her to become like them. She would never be like them. Although she was now the darling of the powerful and the high-born, she was not herself powerful or high-born. They all called her by her stage name, Arletty. A director had christened her that, saying that her real name sounded like a chambermaid.

But she was, and always would be, Léonie Bathiat, born in Courbevoie on the left bank of the river, among the railway sidings and the factories; a *gavroche*, a scrambler, a climber, an alley cat, skinny and gawky. When Antoinette made jokes about her lack of grace they stung, though she kept her mask in place and her claws sheathed.

Antoinette had been born wealthy and aristocratic. And her husband, François-Charles d'Harcourt, was the scion of a family that had led the Norman conquest of Britain. Abandoning him could not be done without a scandal.

Arletty's amber eyes took in the glowing room, where even the dust motes that drifted in the air were flecks of gold. 'We have all this. We see each other several times a week, eat together, make love, go to all the smart places. What more can you want?'

'I want to be yours completely.'

'You can't be. Don't leave François on my account. If you leave François, you will see no more of me than you do now. In fact, you will see far less of me.'

'Why?'

'Because I can't afford a scandal.'

Antoinette laughed. 'I don't care about a scandal.'

'But I do. I have a career. You do not.'

'That's a cruel thing to say.'

'Yes, you have your poetry, and very pretty it is. But if you could no longer publish your slim volumes, you wouldn't suffer the slightest inconvenience. You possess a fortune. I can't afford to lose my livelihood.' Arletty's face could be grim, as it was now. 'And if I were to be compromised sexually and mauled by the gutter press, I would find it very hard to get work.'

Antoinette, always prone to emotion, went red. Her eyes filled with tears. 'I didn't know you thought of me as something disgraceful.'

'That's not what I said.'

'You can be very *petit bourgeois* sometimes, Arletty.'

Arletty turned away wearily. 'Well, we can add that to my other faults.'

'Really, you're in a strange mood today. You're upsetting me terribly. I had no idea you were ashamed of me.'

'I'm not ashamed, but I am sensible. In times past, actresses compromised dukes. Nowadays it is the duchesses who compromise the actresses.'

'Do you think any of our friends care what we do?'

'None of *your* friends care,' Arletty said impatiently. 'But then, your friends are all lesbians.'

'And you aren't?'

'No, I'm not.'

Antoinette uttered a short, painful laugh. 'You say the most extraordinary things.'

'My dear Antoinette, I assure you that the codes of the little people are far more rigid and unforgiving than those of your own class. And it is the little people who buy the tickets to my films.'

Antoinette leaned forward and grasped Arletty's wrist in her hot, damp hand. 'Listen to me. I have a fortune, as you say. If you lose anything because of me I am prepared to repay you handsomely. Double. Triple. You never need to be afraid of that, darling. I will support you.'

Antoinette was foolish enough to think that was an inducement to a woman who had climbed her own way up the ladder. Arletty disengaged her wrist from Antoinette's grasp and looked at her watch. 'It's late. I have to go.' She swung her long, slim legs out of the bed and began to pull on her stockings.

Antoinette watched her with swollen eyes. 'You've made me very miserable. I thought you'd be pleased about my leaving François.'

'I'm sorry, but I'm not.'

'I'm leaving him, whatever you say. I've made up my mind. I can't keep on living a lie. I have to do it for my own sake.'

Arletty said nothing but finished dressing and then went to the mirror to brush her hair. The face that looked back at her was cold, almost perfectly symmetrical and almost perfectly untouched by the afternoon's emotions. The hardships she'd been through had taught her self-discipline and, above all, to look out for herself. Nobody else would look out for her, whatever promises they made.

She applied lipstick to her mouth, emphasising the curves of her top lip, as the fashion of the day demanded. Snapping the gold tube shut, she touched her eyelids with her little finger, separating some of the long, curved lashes that had stuck together. On the bed behind her, Antoinette was crying silently but steadily.

'Why do you make yourself unhappy?' Arletty asked quietly. 'You have everything you want, including me. Your husband gives you all the freedom you require. It's not necessary to make any dramatic gestures. Just enjoy the life you have.'

'I'm not like you,' Antoinette said, blotting her eyes with a lace handkerchief.

'No, you're not.' Arletty turned to face her friend with an ironic smile. 'I worked my way up from the bottom. You want to work your way down from the top. Take my advice, chérie. Enjoy what you have and be thankful for it.'

Antoinette held out her arms imploringly. 'Come back to bed and take away the hurt.'

Antoinette was like a child at moments like this, Arletty thought. It was time to make a graceful departure. She shook her head. 'I have my lines to learn. We start filming in the studio tomorrow morning at eight.' She gathered her things and went to the door. 'Remember to wait half an hour before you leave the suite.'

'I can't bear to part on bad terms.'

'We are parting as we always do, like friends.'

'Don't leave me like this!'

But Arletty was irritated with Antoinette and already had her fingers on the door handle. She blew Antoinette a kiss, not wanting to smudge her lipstick, and let herself out.

It was a relief to be out of the cream-and-gold room. She was not a devotee of emotional scenes. She avoided the elevator, where one inevitably had to wait, and then likely be imprisoned with some bore who would want to ask impertinent questions. Besides, she enjoyed walking down the magnificent spiral staircase of the Ritz, its ornate wrought-iron balustrades and its tapestries lit by the crystal dome high above.

The great hotel was bustling. The boutiques beside the elevator were thronged with customers eager for costly Paris trinkets to take home:

diamond jewellery, silk scarves, tortoiseshell vanity cases, inlaid bijoux of all kinds.

A crowd of new arrivals lined the reception desk, matching sets of monogrammed luggage trailing behind them on gilded trolleys. American, British and German voices rang out. Arletty negotiated a path through the crowd without being accosted by fans. The doorman tipped his hat to her with a smile. He, like most of the staff of the Ritz, knew all about her assignations with the Duchess of Harcourt. One could not keep secrets from hotel employees. But the great thing about the Ritz was that secrets were preserved faithfully, never sold, never betrayed. It was the mark of a really top-class establishment.

She walked out into the wide expanse of place Vendôme, Paris's most fashionable public space. From the top of the towering bronze column at its centre, Napoleon looked down, the globe of the world in one hand, the other hand on the hilt of his sword. Shading her eyes with her palm, Arletty glanced up at the distant greenish figure. It was a fine thing to be up so high, she thought. But it was a long way down.

Three

On the long walk home to Montmartre, Olivia thought about her only client of the day and his amusing way of talking. It had been a lonely Sunday, and he had provided the brightest part of it. She was looking forward to seeing him again and crossing verbal swords with him. And his hundred and fifty francs, tucked safely away in her pocket, promised a decent restaurant meal tonight, and maybe a consoling glass of *vin ordinaire*.

Her apartment was at the top of a rickety building on a very steep street in the Artists' Quarter. It was neither comfortable nor cheap, but she occupied the entire top floor, which commanded a view of an actual vineyard – said to have been planted to keep the city at bay – which sprawled untidily down the hillside between rows of quaint and crooked houses.

Entering the building, however, meant negotiating the Scylla and Charybdis of her landlady and her landlady's husband, who had been separated for years, and who lurked behind opposite doors in the passageway. Olivia tried to creep silently between them, but her luck was out today. Both doors burst open, and angry faces appeared to port and starboard.

'Things can't go on like this,' Madame de la Fay hissed. 'You owe me two weeks' rent, Mam'selle.'

'Today is Sunday so it's three weeks,' her husband added from the other side. The de la Fays hated one another, but were united in their even greater detestation of defaulting lodgers. Madame de la Fay had a face like a vulture, Monsieur de la Fay's breath was like acetylene gas. 'We are not running an almshouse, Mam'selle. You cannot stay here for nothing.'

'I'm terribly sorry,' Olivia said, squirming. 'I had to buy paints and canvases—'

'Your domestic economy is your business,' Madame de la Fay snapped. 'I must insist that you pay your rent or pack your bags tomorrow. I have other applicants waiting for your room.'

Olivia thought of the money in her pocket and the other half to come on Wednesday. 'If you could just give me a couple more days—'

Madame de la Fay folded her brawny arms. 'No more days.'

Her husband was examining Olivia's baggage with sharp red-rimmed eyes. He pointed at the canvas accusingly. 'You've had a commission today.'

'Yes, but—'

'She's had work,' de la Fay spat at his wife. 'She has money!'

'I must insist.' The landlady had her palm outstretched, blocking Olivia's escape. 'Pay up or pack up.' Her face was implacable.

Olivia's heart sank. She realised that there was no way out. She dug in her pocket for Fabrice Darnell's money. 'It's only a hundred and fifty francs—'

The landlady pounced on the handful of coins and crumpled notes. 'This will pay one week. Have the rest by Friday or out you go.'

It was useless to ask for any more concessions. The doors banged shut, leaving her in the dark passage. Now penniless, Olivia trudged up the stairs to her attic. She was very gloomy. The good meal and the glass of wine had vanished. And there was no doubt the de la Fays would pounce with equal swiftness on Fabrice Darnell's second instalment on Wednesday. His arrival could hardly be hidden; she didn't get many visitors. If she didn't start selling her work soon, her sojourn in Paris would come to an untimely end. And hard as the past months had been, the thought of abandoning Paris broke her heart. She had come to love this ravishing city where it was so hard to survive.

She let herself into her room, a high-ceilinged space that was crowded with canvases on three walls. The fourth opened out on to a narrow balcony, little more than a ledge, from which she had a spectacular view of the vineyard, the innumerable smoky chimney pots of Montmartre and the distant dome of Sacré Coeur, now silhouetted against a golden sunset.

That view was the great attraction her lodgings possessed. The bare floor was splintery, the skylight above let in the rain (as well as the precious light she needed for her work) and the bed supplied by Madame de la Fay was a very squeaky iron one, which had surely been used as a street barricade in the Revolution. She had a table, a couple of chairs and a basin – cold water only – in one corner. The bathroom was one flight down, and dingy, though equipped with a huge bath on ball-and-claw feet.

In this warm weather, the old iron stove remained unlit, so Olivia made her supper by heating a can of beans on the little spirit stove that she also used for melting the dammar crystals with which she varnished her paintings.

She took her meagre meal, still in its saucepan, out on to the balcony, not only to enjoy the sunset but also to escape the atmosphere of linseed oil, turpentine, beeswax, varnish and canvas that pervaded the attic. The de la Fays were not ideal landlords, but at least they tolerated the pungent aromas of her trade, which not all proprietors did. They were smells dear to her, though to few other people in her life.

Hungrily spooning up the beans, Olivia reflected, as she had done that morning, that she had come a long way from Lindstrom, Minnesota. She had certainly eaten better – and more regularly – there. But it was hard to stay gloomy with all of Paris at her feet.

Paris! The word had exerted an almost mystical pull on her from infancy. And the fault lay largely with her mother, who had filled her head (as the rest of the family never tired of saying) with foolish romantic nonsense.

Most of the family had arrived in the 1860s, when Sweden had been struck by crop failures. They had settled in sturdy little communities, regarding themselves as quintessentially American, yet remaining true to their heritage. What they valued was hard work, hard-headedness, piety and a complete lack of imagination.

But she needed more than that to feel that she was really, truly alive. Her mother was the only person who understood that.

But then her mother, Gitte, was the only Olsen who had ever been to France; had been, moreover, to visit Claude Monet's famous garden, with its lily ponds and its Japanese bridges; a visit, made before Olivia's birth, which was commemorated in Olivia's peculiar middle name, Giverny.

Olivia had tried to be a good Olsen: cheerful and up-to-the-minute American by assimilation, cow-dung Swedish by descent. But she had wanted more, and she had saved up for another life.

The setting sun had turned the Paris evening into a sea of crimson, washing out everything that was sordid and colouring everything with glamour. She sat there, lost in the glory of it all, until the crimson faded into night.

Olivia was awakened on Wednesday morning by a knocking at her door. Much as she had been anticipating the delivery of his hundred and fifty francs, she was not very pleased to find that it was Fabrice Darnell.

'It's not even nine o' clock,' she complained, pulling her worn kimono around herself as she peered round the door. 'Go away and come back in an hour.'

'Your landlady is waiting downstairs,' Fabrice replied. 'She's already tried to get your money off me.'

'Give it to me.'

'I haven't seen the painting yet.'

'Don't you trust me?' She held her hand out for the money. He counted it into her palm reluctantly. She gave him ten francs back. 'Go to the corner shop and buy a small packet of coffee. Come back in an hour.' She shut the door in his face.

By the time he returned, she had made herself presentable and had opened the windows on to a bright, soft morning. He had brought not only the coffee she had requested, but a bag of little sweet brioches as well, which inclined her to forgive him for the rude awakening.

She had put his painting on an easel in a well-lit corner of the studio. He inspected it now while she made coffee on the spirit stove.

'You've worked on it a lot,' he commented.

'Do you like it?'

'Very much.'

She had worked from memory, using the shadow of his hat brim to give his face an air of mystery. 'I told you that you could trust me.'

'I take back all my reservations.' He accepted the strong cup of coffee she handed him and wandered around the studio with it, examining the paintings that were stacked, in some cases three and four deep, against the walls. Without being invited, he turned around the ones that had been condemned to face the wall. Olivia doubted whether he had the money to buy anything else, but there was always hope, so she tolerated the intrusion. At last he said, 'You have real talent. These views of Montmartre are very original. And the paintings of the vineyard are enchanting. The contrast between the leafy vines and the drab brickwork – sheer genius.'

Olivia smiled. 'It's one of my favourite subjects.'

'I can see that. Your love of Paris shines through in every painting. If you're not selling, it's because your work isn't getting enough exposure.'

'I hawk my stuff round all the galleries,' she said, 'but they'll scarcely look at it. Paris is full of students trying to sell their work.'

'You're more than a student.'

'I'm not even that,' she said ruefully. 'I've been studying under Laszlo Weisz since I first arrived here. He's an old Hungarian who's been in Paris since the last century, and he's a wonderful teacher. But the idea was that I would support myself by selling my paintings, and I haven't managed that very well.' She sighed. 'I'm going to have to give up the lessons. I can't afford them any more.'

'I'm sorry to hear that.'

Olivia shrugged sadly. 'It's a cliché, isn't it – hopeful artist comes to Paris, starves, gives up, goes back home and joins the real world.'

'You're not thinking of giving up art altogether, are you?'

'If I don't sell a few paintings, I won't have much choice. You haven't eaten any of these brioches.'

'That's because you've eaten them all,' he pointed out.

She saw that it was true: she was just finishing the last one. 'Oh, I'm so sorry. I was starving.'

'Yes, I can see that.'

She licked the last traces of sticky sugar off her fingers. 'You wouldn't happen to have a cigarette, would you?'

He produced the old silver cigarette case. 'I suppose you haven't smoked since last Sunday?'

'My landlady waylaid me when I got back and pocketed your deposit. I owe rather a lot of rent. I'll give tobacco up one day. I can't afford luxuries.' Olivia exhaled gratefully. She had noticed the monograms on the silver case and lighter. 'Did these belong to your father?'

'Yes. He died when I was seventeen.' He waved away her conventional phrases of sympathy. 'I was lucky to have him as long as I did. Now, tell me the truth. Have you eaten anything at all since Sunday?'

'Of course.'

His warm hazel eyes were focused on her. 'What?'

'I always have a supply of beans in my pantry,' she said, indicating the wobbly shelf where her provisions were stored.

Fabrice glanced briefly at the scanty larder. 'You'll come to my place for a home-cooked meal tonight,' he said decisively.

'Very kind of you, but I'm not in the habit of visiting strange young men's homes at night. Nor,' she added, raising her hand as he began to speak, 'of selling my favours for a bowl of soup.'

That almost-smile hovered in the depths of the golden beard. 'Your virtue is safe. I live with my mother. She will cook the meal. I restrict myself to opening and pouring the wine.'

Sorely tempted by the thought of a decent meal in comfortable domestic surroundings, Olivia wavered. 'Well—'

'When I left the house this morning, she was preparing a nice, plump chicken for a casserole,' he said suavely. 'Perhaps even *coq au vin*.'

Her mouth watered. 'Oh, gosh.'

'It's not far from here. I'll walk you over at seven tonight.'

'All right. But no monkey business.'

'Do I look like a monkey?' he asked, preparing to leave.

'No comment. Don't forget your painting.'

'Thank you. My mother will be very happy. It's a gift for her. You haven't signed it,' he pointed out.

'Oh, I forgot.' She picked up a brush and added her usual signature: O.G. Olsen.

'What does the G stand for?' he asked.

'Giverny.'

'As in—'

'My mother corresponded with Claude Monet as a young woman and went to visit him before she got married. She never stopped talking about his garden.'

He looked at her with interest. 'I need to hear more about that.'

'After supper.' She tied a sheet of brown paper around the frame to protect the painting from dust, and saw him out. Since he had praised her work, she was feeling warm towards him. She watched him going down the stairs almost fondly. In fact, the prospect of *coq au vin* – or perhaps it was the cigarette he had given her – was making her quite giddy.

The Darnells lived, as Fabrice had promised, just a few streets away. The house was tall and narrow, squeezed in between larger dwellings on either side. As soon as he ushered her inside, however, Olivia felt herself enfolded by a welcoming homeliness. There were no signs of wealth, but everything was comfortable and spotlessly clean, and the aroma of chicken cooked in red wine brought on another attack of giddiness.

Fabrice's mother emerged from the kitchen to meet Olivia, drying her hands on a striped apron. She was a trim, energetic woman in her fifties, who shook Olivia's hand in a firm grip. Fabrice had obviously inherited his good looks from her; she was handsome, with a long nose and a flashing smile that showed her lower teeth in a way Olivia thought very glamorous. Her manner was friendly but brisk, and her eyes – hazel like her son's – were sharply intelligent.

'Your painting of my son is charming,' she said to Olivia. She had hung it in pride of place in the little salon. 'I must thank you.'

'Please don't thank me, Madame. It was a commission. Even if the subject is a very distinguished one,' she added with a smile.

'You will call me Marie-France,' she replied, with the same decisive manner as her son, 'and I shall call you Olivia.'

Dinner was a happy occasion, and not only because the meal Marie-France had prepared was a delicious one; since leaving America, Olivia had sorely missed being enveloped in the warmth of her family, and although the Darnells were a tiny family, they made her feel that she completed the circle. The absent member presided over the table from a framed photograph above the sideboard.

'My father was a great man,' Fabrice told her. 'A great thinker, a great humanitarian. Those are his books over there.' He indicated a shelf of some five or six volumes under the photograph, which showed a bearded, melancholy man with lowered eyes, looking as though he regretted having written so many serious books and would rather have liked to have had some fun.

'What did he write about?' Olivia asked.

'He was an anarchist.'

'I'm afraid I'm not quite sure what that is,' Olivia said apologetically.

'It's a belief in the fundamental goodness of man.' As he'd promised, his role in the dinner so far had been restricted to opening and serving the wine, which he did with all the ceremony of a top sommelier. 'Anarchists believe that there is no need for violence or compulsion to organise society. No governments or police are necessary, simply a voluntary cooperation between citizens and complete freedom for the individual.'

'Are you an anarchist too?'

'Of course. I write for the leading anarchist publications.' He took a newspaper off the sideboard and showed it to her. 'They publish my articles every week.'

Olivia examined the newspaper, which was called *Le Libertaire* and had staring black headlines and dense columns of print, but few photos. Fabrice's name appeared on a long article on the second page, entitled 'War on Tyrants!'.

'You don't throw bombs, do you?' Olivia asked.

'I restrict myself to the pen. Throwing a bomb may get rid of one tyrant – but a stroke of the pen can slay hundreds.'

'In theory, at least,' Marie-France said. She was looking at her son with an odd mixture of pride, love and sadness.

'They will all meet their match. Hitler, Mussolini, Franco—'

'Don't say those names,' Marie-France said. 'They are too hideous.'

'Hideous as they are,' Fabrice declared, 'their nemesis will come, and their heads will roll.'

Olivia had been aware of the constant talk of war in the newspapers over recent months; there had also been fretful references to it in her letters from home, but she had been involved in her own affairs and had paid little attention. 'It's too horrible to contemplate,' she said. 'After the last war, surely nobody wants another bloodbath?'

'Tyrants feed on blood,' Fabrice said.

Marie-France laid her hand on her son's. 'I think we need another bottle of wine, my dear.'

'Of course, Maman.' He went out to get it.

In his absence, Marie-France turned to Olivia. 'You are a very talented artist.'

'I'm making progress. Slowly.'

'Fabrice tells me you had to suspend your lessons?'

'I couldn't pay for them any more,' Olivia said frankly. 'I expected to be able to sell my work more easily.' She sighed. 'I was doing all right back home. I guess there's more competition here.'

'It was very brave of you to come all this way to a strange city in a strange country,' Marie-France said gently.

'Blame my mother for that.' Olivia smiled. 'She's been telling me stories about Paris since I was a child. She came here as a young woman, and she made it sound so magical. But it's been a struggle.'

Marie-France's wise eyes flicked to the portrait over the sideboard. 'In Fabrice's case, the delinquent parent was his father. He filled Fabrice's head with high flown ideas. And Fabrice, too, has found his path in life a struggle. He almost died of tuberculosis as a child, and he seems all the more passionate about politics because of that. Life isn't easy for young people nowadays.'

'No, it's not.'

'Fabrice doesn't earn very much with his writing,' Marie-France went on. '*Le Libertaire* pays him a few hundred francs and that's about it. But luckily, I have a steady job. Has he told you what I do?'

'No.'

'I am a housekeeper at the Ritz hotel.'

'That sounds like hard work.'

'The work is hard, yes, but the pay isn't bad. And there are generous tips, if one is lucky. And then, if one is luckier still, there may be parcels to take home from the kitchens.' She hesitated. 'I don't wish to offend you, Olivia.'

'What do you mean?'

'For a woman in need of money, there are worse ways to earn a living. Business is good lately. The hotel is always full. They are looking for an extra chambermaid.'

'A chambermaid? You're suggesting I apply for a job there?'

'I've worked at the Ritz for almost twenty years. With my recommendation, you would be taken on. There are girls applying all the time, but the Ritz is special. They won't take just anyone.' She studied Olivia frankly. 'But perhaps you'd consider the work beneath you?'

'Oh, no. I've helped my mother in the house all my life, and I don't mind hard work. But – I wouldn't have time to paint. It would mean giving up my dreams, silly as they are.'

'Well, perhaps not giving them up,' Marie-France said sympathetically, 'just setting them aside for a while, until you find your feet again. You won't have much time for art, certainly. But at least you would be able to pay your rent – and eat – and afford a few luxuries. Am I being very tactless?'

'I can see that Fabrice has been talking about me.' Olivia smiled ruefully. 'No, you're not tactless at all. You're being very kind.'

'It's just an idea. Think it over. If you're interested, come to the Ritz and ask for me at the staff entrance on rue Cambon.'

Fabrice came back in with a fresh bottle of wine, and the conversation moved to other topics.

As Fabrice walked Olivia home at midnight, she was pleasantly sleepy, relaxed by the wine, her stomach fuller than it had been in many days. The warmth of the night added to her feeling of well-being.

'Did my mother mention the vacancy at the Ritz?' Fabrice asked delicately.

'Yes, she did – and thank you for telling her I was a starving waif.'

'I hope you're not offended.'

'Of course not, silly. It was very kind of her to offer to help.'

'Naturally,' he said gravely, 'I've never approved of her working as a slave for the rich and idle, who are too proud to make their own beds or wash their own clothes.'

'But when she puts a plate of hot food in front of you, you're able to suppress your scruples?'

'It's her decision. All actions must stem from individual choice. That is the essence of anarchism.'

'It sounds a very convenient philosophy.'

His face stiffened. 'I'm grateful that she supports me. I just hate to see her exploited and selling her labour in a cynical capitalist market.'

'Well, I might just be prepared to sell my labour to the cynical capitalists if it will ensure a steady supply of chicken stew.'

Fabrice glanced at her. 'Are you going to apply for the job?'

'I'm thinking about it. It would be better than starving.'

'I'm very glad that we're going to be seeing a lot more of each other.'

'Oh? Will that be necessary?' she teased.

'Absolutely.' They had reached her lodgings. He put his hands on her shoulders and kissed her with complete naturalness on both cheeks.

His beard was somewhat bristly. If they were to see more of each other, it would have to go, she decided. In the dim light of the street lamp outside Madame de la Fay's house his eyes were warm, looking into hers fondly. 'Good night, my dear. May I see you tomorrow?'

'Much too soon. Tongues will wag.'

'Friday, then?'

'If you bring cigarettes. American cigarettes.'

'You drive a hard bargain.'

'I'm a hard woman.' She smiled at him over her shoulder as she let herself into the silent house.

Four

With her back against the silk-framed windows of her permanent suite at the Ritz, Gabrielle Chanel, known to all the world as Coco, was displaying her famous silhouette to perfection. She was wearing one of the flowery afternoon dresses that she had made all the rage in this perfect summer of 1939. Her close friends, the two Jeans, Cocteau and Marais, watched her quick nervous movements as she took a cigarette from a platinum case and fitted it in an amber holder. From deep in the bowels of the hotel, a hammering thudded into the room, which was exquisitely decorated to the exacting requirements of Madame Chanel herself.

'That noise is rather tedious,' Marais commented. Known as the handsomest man in France, and the athletic star of a swashbuckling film directed by his lover, Cocteau, he had shed his virile public persona in this congenial setting of luxurious fabrics, morocco-bound books, African masks and exotic bric-a-brac of all kinds. He was curled up against Cocteau on Coco's velvet sofa, a glass in one hand, the other laced in his own blonde hair. 'It's giving me rather a headache.'

'They're extending the wine cellars,' Cocteau said, kissing Marais' temple tenderly.

'No, they're not,' Coco said briskly. 'They're building a bomb shelter.'

Cocteau chuckled. 'You are funny, Coco.'

'I'm not funny in the slightest. That's exactly what they're doing. It's going under the back garden. Reinforced concrete walls a metre thick.'

'How depressing,' Cocteau said, his smile fading. 'That means there really will be a war. The management of the Ritz know everything.'

Coco lit her cigarette. 'Perhaps it's not such a bad idea.'

'The bomb shelter?'

'The war.'

'You can't be serious.'

'There will be a temporary inconvenience, but at least it will sweep away the Bolsheviks and the Jews once and for all.'

The two men simultaneously exclaimed in horror at this sentiment. Coco turned her back on them and looked out of the window. It was not agreeable to watch her old companion Cocteau, now fifty and looking distinctly withered after decades of drug addiction, draping himself over Marais, a boy of half his age.

She had meant what she'd just said. After three years of terror and chaos, she had decided that war was inevitable. It would be a relief. The Bolsheviks and the Jews had already turned Paris into a battlefield more than once. She had seen her beloved place Vendôme littered with burning barricades, fogged with tear gas, the scene of pitched fighting between police and striking workers raging to slaughter the Deputies in the government.

And among that bloodthirsty mob had been hundreds of her own workers – women to whom she had given employment, upon whose tables she had put bread! They had turned against her, their minds filled with communist rubbish, as though she had not risen from far greater poverty than they had ever known – as though she had not been born the illegitimate child of an itinerant peddler of underwear, educated in an orphanage, forced to earn her living with the skill of her fingers from earliest youth!

Did they know how she'd dragged herself up from the gutter? How hard she'd worked, the sacrifices she had made? Did they think it had come easy to her? That Coco Chanel had been born rich? She'd had many things in her mouth, but never a silver spoon. She'd whored and clawed her way to the top. Nobody had given her a damned thing.

And there might be other benefits, greater benefits still, to the coming war. The Nazis knew how to treat the Jews. She had observed with much interest Hitler's efficiency in recovering the wealth the cunning devils had hoarded, forcing them to make restitution for the underhand plots by which they had enriched themselves so obscenely.

Her partners, the Wertheimers, had bought a majority share in her perfume company, long before she'd realised just how valuable Chanel No. 5 would become. Her friends pointed out that the Wertheimer company paid her millions each year, making her fabulously wealthy; but she could never be happy, getting only ten per cent of the profits from her own perfume. Ten per cent! Why, it was daylight robbery! If the Nazis could offer her a way to get back what was rightfully hers, then she would be a Nazi, jackboots and all.

Against such potential gains, the war would indeed be little more than a temporary inconvenience. There would scarcely be a war, with luck. France, with its weak socialist government, would yield like butter to the German knife.

She would see it out right here, in the Ritz, lapped in luxury and safety. It wouldn't touch her. And when it was all over, there would be a new world order; and those who had been so shabbily treated – herself, her friends the Windsors, all those who had the courage to speak out against the Jews and the Reds – would enjoy the place in the sun they so richly deserved.

She heard Marais giggling and looked over her shoulder. 'What's so funny?'

'You're muttering to yourself,' he replied, 'like an old woman.'

Coco drew her brows down darkly. 'An old woman?' The boy was too callow to know when to hold his tongue. If he had not been the darling of Cocteau, she'd have administered a stinging rebuke. She had just celebrated her fifty-sixth birthday, and though she declared that age meant nothing, she was aware that the shadows were lengthening. She turned back to the view of place Vendôme, upon which the sun was pouring down like honey. 'I talk to myself when I have nobody sensible to talk to.'

She could hear whispering from the caramel velvet sofa. After a while, Marais said in a subdued voice, 'I apologise if I spoke out of turn.'

Coco puffed cigarette smoke without replying.

Cocteau added his voice. 'I have some nose-powder,' he said in a conciliatory tone.

Coco plucked the cigarette out of the holder and tossed it into the square below. 'It's a little early in the day,' she said. 'Besides, didn't you tell me you were finished with all that?'

'But I haven't touched opium in months,' he replied. 'Not since I met Jean. And you seem depressed, Coco. It'll cheer you up.'

She gave him a hard look. 'I'm an old woman who needs cheering up, am I?'

He smiled. 'If there's to be a war, we'll all need cheering up.'

She studied his hollow eyes and cheeks. She had paid for him to be cured, and he had sworn that he was cured; but she knew he would no more ever be cured than she herself would. He had his four or five little pipes a day, she her nightly injection of morphine, without which she could not sleep. But he was right: she was nervous and depressed, and in need of stimulation. 'Well?' she said. 'Where is it?'

Cocteau produced an enamelled silver box. 'I get it from a friend at the dental hospital. Medical grade. Come.'

They sat close together on the sofa. Cocteau tapped a little mound of the white powder on to each of their wrists with a tiny spoon. They snorted in unison, then a second time, into the other nostril.

Coco felt the rush of optimism and confidence surging through her brain. That was better, much better. Her anxiety had vanished.

All challenges dwindled. She felt her creative urge, the daemon that had made her among the richest women in the world, awakening. She laughed out loud and jumped to her feet. The rooms, exquisite as they were, were too small to contain her now.

She threw open the doors to the balcony and went out into the afternoon sunshine. The noise of motor and human traffic rising up from place Vendôme was like a symphony in her ears. The two men joined her, in similarly elated mood, but she hardly noticed their chatter beside her. She stretched out her arms to embrace her city, her Paris.

Olivia followed Marie-France down the narrow corridor. She had presented herself at the staff entrance on rue Cambon, as Marie-France had told her to, and had stated her business to the concierge there. Within a few moments Marie-France herself had materialised, and had led her into the world behind the public areas of the Ritz.

Dispensing with gilding, satin and marble, the back end of the hotel was all business. There was a pervasive and not altogether pleasant smell compounded of stale cooking, boot polish, old wine bottles, lamp oil, damp wool and dying flowers. It was also dark, crowded and noisy.

Serious men and women in a variety of uniforms squeezed past each other, each intent on his or her own task. In the bustle, Olivia sometimes got separated from Marie-France, and had to find her by following the jingle of the great bunch of keys at her waist.

Indeed, everywhere were keys, keys, keys. Every functionary seemed to have his or her own set of keys in this world, ringing at a belt or clicking in the locks of doors, which swept open to give her glimpses of sub-worlds – kitchens seething with chefs in white hats, storerooms packed to the ceilings, sweltering laundries.

Marie-France Darnell, too, was all business. She was wearing a severe black uniform with black stockings and a lace cap. 'The place is in an uproar because of the bomb shelter they're building. There's dust everywhere.' She said very little else to Olivia until they had reached a door bearing a brass nameplate on which was engraved *Claude Auzello, Directeur*. She turned to Olivia.

'He'll ask you a few questions about yourself. Answer promptly. Don't be nervous.'

This last injunction was somewhat superfluous; Olivia was already nervous. In the past twenty-four hours, she'd come to realise that she wanted this job very much. Not just wanted it – needed it. The world was still in the grip of what people were calling the Great Depression, and work of any kind was hard to come by. And although it had seemed a wonderful idea to dash off to Paris and be an artist, she saw now how foolish the venture had been, and how kind of Marie-France it was to put her forward, a complete stranger, for this job.

'I'll do my best.'

Marie-France nodded and knocked on the door.

Monsieur Auzello was a stern-looking man with a proud, hooked nose, busily writing at a desk. He rose from his chair, straightening his old-fashioned morning coat, which had tails that hung almost to his heels.

Marie-France nudged her forward. 'This is Olivia Olsen, Monsieur Auzello.'

He gazed down on Olivia from his considerable height, like an eagle. 'Your age?'

'Twenty-two, Monsieur.'

He held out his hand. 'Your *carte de séjour*.'

She handed over her residence permit. He inspected it. 'You are Swedish?'

That was what it said on her *carte de séjour*, because a careless clerk had scribbled her nationality as *Suédoise*, and then had refused to correct it. 'Well, actually—' she began, but he interrupted her.

'Previous experience in hotel work?'

'None.'

He put on his spectacles to look at her in astonishment. 'None at all?'

'No, sir. But—'

He held up his hand with a frown. 'But you know how to make a bed. Yes, yes. There is more to this work than that. Turn around, please.' She pirouetted slowly, feeling absurdly like a ballerina on a musical box. Auzello's wintry-grey eyes surveyed her from head to foot. 'You are presentable and clean. That is something. But there is much to learn, and the work is hard.'

'I'm willing to learn, and I don't mind hard work.'

'What languages do you speak?'

'English, French and Swedish.'

He folded his spectacles back into his pocket. 'What do you know about the Ritz?'

Olivia hesitated. 'I've been told it's the best hotel in the world.'

'That is correct.' He indicated the photograph that hung on the wall behind him, showing a Victorian gentleman with mutton-chop whiskers and a handlebar moustache. 'My late employer, César Ritz, who founded this hotel, was nothing short of a genius. It is now my privilege to continue his tradition.' He spoke in a clipped, military way. 'Let me ask you: who do you think is more important – me or you?'

'You, of course.'

'You are wrong. We are of equal importance. Each time a guest interacts with an employee, he interacts with the Ritz hotel as a whole. In everything you do, you represent César Ritz. If you fail in your duties, the Ritz fails. If you excel, the Ritz excels. Do you understand?'

'Perfectly.'

'The tradition of the Ritz may be summed up in two words. Absolute luxury. And where does luxury begin, young woman? It lies in having what one wants. Always look for signs that a guest may need something. A good hotel is one in which a guest has everything he asks

35

for.' He raised his bony forefinger, exuding a smell of cologne. 'A great hotel is one in which a guest never needs to ask for anything.'

'Yes, Monsieur Auzello.'

'I would not normally consider someone with so little experience. However, the majority of our guests are English-speaking. Your fluency in that language will be an advantage. And the recommendation of Marie-France is, of course, inestimable. I am prepared to give you a trial.'

Olivia's heart leaped up. 'Oh, thank you!'

'You will work without salary for a month. If I am pleased with your progress, you will be taken on, and given a year's contract. If not, you will leave the hotel without a penny. Do you accept these conditions?'

Olivia tried to hide her dismay. 'Yes, sir.'

'Marie-France will show you your duties. Do exactly as she instructs you.'

'Yes, sir.'

'A few points in advance. Do not engage in conversations with the guests, other than to greet them politely. Always smile. Never say "yes". The correct formulation is, "With the greatest of pleasure." Do not say "sorry". The phrase is, "Please accept my sincerest apologies." And never say "no" at all.'

'Got it,' Olivia said faintly.

'I hope so. Exceed expectations. Don't get in anybody's way. You are dismissed.'

And that was that. Outside, in the busy corridor, Olivia hugged Marie-France. 'Thank you, thank you! I won't let you down,' she promised.

'I knew he would like you,' Marie-France said with satisfaction.

'He thinks I'm Swedish.'

'Just as well. His wife is American, and they don't exactly get along. He thinks American women are far too modern. You just keep being Swedish.'

'I don't mind that. But a month without pay!' Olivia said ruefully.

Marie-France snorted. 'Do you know how many girls are applying for the job? Half of Paris would give their eye teeth to be in your shoes. Don't worry, I'll make sure you don't starve. Well, you may as well start right away. Let's get you a uniform.'

The uniform was a dark-blue dress with white cuffs and collar and a white pinafore tied with a fetching bow at the back. A starched white cap went on her hair, which had to be tied back in a bun. Olivia put it all on with great satisfaction. It was, frankly, far better quality than any of her own clothing, and she got two of everything, which it was her responsibility to keep clean and pressed.

Marie-France smiled at Olivia's obvious pleasure in the garments. 'The novelty will wear off, I assure you. For the next couple of days, I'm going to pair you with somebody experienced. You'll go around with her, helping and learning. Let's see who's available.'

The person Marie-France chose for Olivia was a German named Heike Schwab, who had been at the Ritz for a number of years. She was a heavy, surly-looking woman who did not seem very pleased at being burdened with an apprentice. She shrugged her square shoulders when Marie-France introduced them and set off down the corridor without a word, pushing her trolley.

'Don't be put off by her manner,' Marie-France murmured to Olivia as she prepared to follow her new mentor, 'she knows her job and she's a hard worker.'

Olivia followed Heike Schwab into the first room. She couldn't help exclaiming at the beauty of the apartment. It was her first glimpse of the legendary accommodations at the Ritz, and it didn't disappoint her. The room had been decorated in shades of gold and cream. The damask wallpaper was old gold and silver, the bed canopied in heavy

bronze silk, the furniture honey-coloured with gilt fittings. It was palatial, yet it enveloped one in instant warmth. 'What an exquisite room!'

'Look at the bathroom, the waste baskets and the sheets before you
call it exquisite,' Heike said grimly in her heavy German accent. 'People
are dirty. The richer, the dirtier. Take off the sheets.'

The bed was certainly not fragrant. The occupants had made love
in it and then had their dinner in it. They worked in silence. Olivia
estimated Heike's age at around forty; she had a heavy jaw to go with
her heavy presence, powerful body and short-cropped black hair. But
for the large bosom that strained her uniform, she was man-like. The
few questions Olivia asked were answered with monosyllables.

While they were emptying the waste baskets, a cheery young valet
in a striped apron came into the room, carrying the now-gleaming shoes
that the occupants had left to be polished. He surveyed Olivia with
appreciative eyes. 'You're the new chambermaid?'

'I'm only on trial,' Olivia replied.

'With a face like that, you can pick up plenty of tips. Even the
ugly ones make fifty francs a day. Eh, Heike?' He grinned, preening the
sideburns budding among his pimples. 'If you need any help, just ask
me. My name's Victor. Me, I like blondes.'

'I'll bear that in mind,' Olivia said ironically.

'Haven't you got work to do?' Heike rumbled.

The young man flipped Heike a salute of the sort they'd all seen
from the newsreels. *Jawohl, mein Führer!*

After he'd left, Heike put her fists on her hips and glowered at
Olivia, her face mottled with anger. 'Easy to see how *you* got this job.'

'What do you mean?'

Resentment seemed to have been simmering in Heike like the contents of a volcano, which now burst out. 'You walk in off the street and
get the job, just like *that*.' She snapped her fingers in Olivia's astonished
face. 'You don't even know how to do the work. You think I'm blind?'

'I don't know what you're talking about.'

Heike showed her teeth in a mirthless smile. 'A few minutes on old Auzello's desk did the trick, eh?'

'What?'

'*Oh, ja.* Up with your skirt and it's all yours. And while you play the princess, the German mare must pull the plough.'

'That's not what happened!'

'No?' Heike swept the roses from the bedside vase into her trash bin and turned back to Olivia, her jaw set. Her eyes were like wet black pebbles. 'Then explain to me why better women than you were turned away.'

Olivia felt the blood rush to her cheeks. She knew that she'd only got the job through Marie-France's recommendation – and that Marie-France had recommended her only because Fabrice had urged it – and that Fabrice had urged it because he was sweet on her. There was enough truth in Heike's accusation to sting.

'I know how lucky I am,' she said, 'but I didn't sleep with anyone to get this job, and I'm prepared to work as hard as anyone.'

Heike sneered at her. 'Enough talk.' She held out a toilet brush. 'You know how to use this, at least, I imagine.'

There was no point arguing any further. 'Yes, I know how to use that.'

'Then get on your knees.'

Under Heike's stony eye, Olivia set to work in the bathroom. Heike clearly took pleasure in keeping her on her knees and insisting that every nook and cranny of the lavatory and sink be scrubbed, but Olivia kept her annoyance out of sight. If Heike thought she was playing the princess, she would show her otherwise. But nothing she did seemed to please the German woman, who made her redo every task, and the atmosphere remained heavy.

The routine was brisk: the sanitary ware had to be left spotless, the towels changed, any used soap replaced. The bed was stripped and remade with fresh linen. Clothing scattered carelessly around had to be gathered, brushed and carefully folded. The carpet was vacuum-cleaned with an up-to-the-minute American machine, which was also used to dust the drapes.

'You are too slow,' Heike told her. 'We have eleven more rooms to do.'

'If you didn't make me do everything three times, we'd get it done faster.'

'If you did it correctly the first time,' Heike said angrily, 'I would not have to ask you to repeat.'

'There's nothing wrong with the way I'm doing it. I've been cleaning house since I was a child.'

Heike rounded on her, holding up a large and very hard-looking palm. 'If you answer me back, I will give you this across that pretty face.'

'Don't you dare touch me,' Olivia shot back, her heart starting to race.

Just at that moment, Marie-France came into the room, carrying fresh flowers for the vase. 'Everything all right?' she asked.

'This girl is lazy and insolent,' Heike snapped. 'Why must I be saddled with her?'

'Because you're one of the best,' Marie-France replied soothingly, beginning to arrange the flowers in the vase. 'And it's her first day. Be patient with her.'

'She argues with me to my face!'

Marie-France glanced at Olivia. 'Do as Heike tells you. You can learn a great deal from her.'

Had Marie-France given her the ghost of a wink? With an effort of will, Olivia swallowed her anger. 'I'm sorry, Heike.'

Marie-France left them to it, Heike glowering and Olivia tight-lipped.

It was not a very good start to her working career at the Ritz, or a particularly happy day that followed. The work was indeed hard, and being put in harness with a woman who obviously hated her on sight didn't make it any easier. Chambermaids, Olivia learned, worked a twelve-hour shift and were expected to service twelve rooms in that time, as well as perform any other duties the housekeepers allocated them. There was a lunch break in the canteen, a spartan eating area where simple and not overabundant food was served from a staff kitchen. Otherwise, the entire day was spent in a hurry, racing to get those twelve rooms done.

By the time her shift was over, she was tired. This was a lot more demanding than painting. Her hands were dry and stinging from detergent and her back was aching. She was sturdily built, but keeping up with the much stronger Heike was demanding.

Marie-France left the hotel with her and showed her where to catch the tram back to Montmartre, slower but cheaper than the Métro. They clung to the rail on the upper deck, which was crowded with workers heading home.

'You're tired,' Marie-France said with a smile.

'I'll get the hang of it.'

'Yes, you will. You've learned a lot today.'

'I'm not really "lazy and insolent", you know.'

'I do know that.'

'You gave me a hard taskmistress,' Olivia said wryly. 'She doesn't like me very much.'

'Heike had a friend who was dismissed. You took her place.'

'You didn't explain that!'

'She deserved to be sacked. She was a thief. Heike knows that perfectly well.'

'Heike doesn't seem like a woman who would have many friends.'

'Unfortunately, she's not. She was a very successful athlete when she was younger. She won gold medals. I think her life has been a disappointment after that. But I hoped she would take to you. Be patient.'

'I know you're helping me because of Fabrice.'

'I'm helping you because I want to. A young woman on her own in the world needs friends. If my daughter had survived, she would have been just your age.'

'Oh, Marie-France. I'm so sorry to learn that.'

The tram swung around a curve, pressing the two women against each other for a moment. 'She died of croup at three months. Fabrice was only two years old – he doesn't remember. I'm very happy that you and he have become friends. He's never had a close friendship with a girl before.' Marie-France paused. 'I don't put any pressure on you, Olivia. I ask only one thing – that you avoid breaking his heart.'

'I'll never do that,' Olivia exclaimed. 'I like Fabrice very much. I think he's the cleverest person I've ever met.'

Marie-France smiled tenderly and a little sadly. 'Oh, yes. Fabrice is very clever.'

'It's too early to say how things will turn out. But I promise I'll never lead him on or give him encouragement if I don't mean it.'

Marie-France laid her hand on Olivia's for a moment. 'Then we are in agreement. You'll come to us for dinner tonight?'

She was about to refuse. But the canteen meal had been hours ago, and her stomach was growling; and cans of baked beans were all that home offered. Olivia nodded. 'Yes, please.'

Five

Sunday was the day for her lesson with Laszlo Weisz. It was to be her last, and she had to brace herself to tell her old teacher that she couldn't continue with him. He had been a father figure to her since arriving in Paris, and she was going to miss his friendship as much as his teaching.

He arrived promptly at two, as always. She couldn't help noticing that he was looking frail. Despite the fine weather, he was wrapped in a shawl, as though needing the warmth. He was in his seventies; every ounce of spare flesh seemed to have dropped from his frame.

'Why are you looking so sad?' he immediately asked in the heavy Hungarian accent he had never lost.

Olivia made a wry face. 'I'm giving up painting, *maître.*'

He raised his bushy eyebrows. 'What the devil are you talking about?'

'I can't keep going like this, broke all the time, selling nothing.' She drew a breath. 'And I'm going to have to give up my lessons. For a while at least.'

Laszlo took her hands in his urgently. 'No, Olivia. You mustn't do this. You have so much talent!'

'I have to face facts, *maître.* I can't feed myself on my talent alone.'

He squeezed her hands with his paint-stained fingers. 'My dear, I will give your lessons for free. You can pay me when you are rich and famous.'

Her eyes stung with tears. 'That's so kind. But you'd wait a long time to be paid. I'm going to get a real job.'

'What does this mean, please?'

'A friend found me work as a chambermaid at a big hotel. I won't have time for painting.'

Her old teacher's face was furrowed with sadness. He released her hands. 'I see.'

'Oh, Laszlo. I'm so sorry to let you down.'

'You have not let me down. But it breaks my heart to see a gifted young artist forced to give up.' He looked around Olivia's studio at the paintings that were stacked against the walls. 'This is truly a very stupid world, which cannot understand beauty when it sees it.'

'Nobody wants to spend money. People are saying war is coming.'

Weisz nodded slowly. 'I believe it is coming again, the madness of 1914. Truly a very stupid world. Perhaps you are doing the right thing. Perhaps you should leave Paris altogether.'

'I don't want to leave.'

'I would go back home, except Hitler will swallow Hungary too. Already he is hammering on the door of Poland. If they don't stop Hitler, all of Europe will go up in flames.'

'Nobody wants war.'

'Hitler does. He is armed to the teeth, and he has an old score to settle with France. Don't forget, the treaty he hates so much was signed at Versailles.'

'Hitler says he wants peace.'

'He says one thing and does another.' Weisz stroked his tangled white beard. 'As a Jew, I have a particular reason to fear them. But they threaten every civilised human being on the planet.' He smiled wearily. 'And you are one of the most civilised persons I know. You do not belong anywhere near him. If you are giving up painting, then you should go home. Risking your life for art is one thing. Risking your life to be a chambermaid is quite another.'

'I'm not leaving Paris,' Olivia said.

'You could continue to paint there. And you'd be safe. Roosevelt will not let America be dragged into another European war. He's said so.'

'If I'd wanted to be safe, I'd never have left Minnesota. I'm staying. Even if I can't paint any longer. I love Paris too much to go home.'

'Even if Paris hasn't been kind to you?'

'Paris has been wonderful to me. It just doesn't buy my paintings.' She paused. 'Except for one nice young fellow.'

Laszlo sighed. 'Aha. And he is the reason you don't want to go home?'

'I didn't say that.'

'Your face says it. Is he handsome?'

'Very.'

'And rich?'

'Unfortunately not, *maître*. He's anti-wealth. An anarchist, in fact.'

'Nobody's perfect. But he loves you?'

'He admires me. Or so he says.'

'And he is the one who got you this hotel work?'

'His mama. As a matter of fact, it's at the Ritz.'

The old man shrugged wryly. 'Well, at least you are leaving art for the best hotel in Paris. Now, if this is to be your last lesson, then let us begin.'

He was the best kind of teacher, gently encouraging her but firm in pointing out her mistakes. She was going to miss him painfully. He looked at her latest paintings, offering thoughtful comments, and guided her as she put his suggestions to work on a fresh canvas. Sitting side by side at the easel, with Laszlo occasionally taking over her brush to illustrate what he meant, they lost themselves in a world where there was no crisis and no shadow of war, only beauty.

All too soon, the two hours had passed, and her last lesson with Laszlo was over. She made him a mug of tea to warm him up, and then walked with him back to his flat on the rue Lepic.

Taking her arm in his, he asked, 'Tell me more about this young anarchist of yours.'

'There really isn't much to tell.' She smiled. 'We're just friends at this stage.' But Laszlo was not content with that, and answering his fatherly enquiries about Fabrice, she was aware of a growing warmth in her heart. If she was not in love with Fabrice just yet, she felt that she soon would be. There was a kind of inevitability about it. 'It just feels right,' she said at last. 'I don't know if it will really go anywhere, but so far it just feels right.'

The old man nodded, as though she had told him what he wanted to know. 'I wish you joy,' he said quietly. 'You'll be a fine artist one day. Never give up your dream. But promise me that if you ever feel the wolf's breath on the back of your neck, you will go straight back to America.'

'I promise, *maître*.'

She said goodbye to him in the warm glow of a purple evening and walked back home sadly, feeling that her life was changing for ever.

※〜

She worked alongside Heike every day that week. Olivia prided herself on being a fast learner, and tried to avoid mistakes; but there was no easing of tension between herself and the German. If anything, it got worse. Heike criticised everything she did. Nothing was ever to her satisfaction. That heavy antagonism never lifted.

Nor was it mitigated by the tendency of male staff to seek Olivia's attention. The older men were fatherly, the younger ones flirtatious. She felt rather like a spoonful of honey surrounded by bees. It embittered Heike against her even further.

Olivia had never been in an environment of this kind before, with so many men around. Her family had more women in it than men.

She'd been educated at an all-girls institute for the daughters of farming folk. The proximity of dozens of males was a new experience.

Marie-France's eyes were discerning. 'You're not used to men, are you?' she said one day.

'Well, not in such numbers, at any rate.'

'You have to learn how to keep them at a distance. Not all the offers of advice or help are altruistic, you know. Some men assume the chambermaids are fair game. And the guests can be troublesome too. Don't get caught alone in a room with any man, employee or guest.'

Olivia was discovering the power – and danger – of her looks. But with a month in which to prove herself to Monsieur Auzello, she was determined not to make any mistakes. Following Marie-France's advice, she remained determinedly cool, Scandinavian and aloof.

Her sorrow at having to give up painting (even if it was, as she told herself, only a temporary renunciation) was acute. She kept a little sketchbook in the pocket of her pinafore, and whenever an opportunity presented itself, she would take it out and make quick sketches with the stub of a pencil. One day, she hoped, she would be able to work these rough notes into full paintings.

The Ritz, she discovered, was a complicated universe made up of two worlds. In one, the guests lived charmed lives, surrounded by beauty, untouched by want or anxiety. In the other, the staff toiled day and night to ensure that this state of affairs continued undisturbed. As Marie-France put it, 'The Ritz is a place where two hundred poor devils work themselves to death in order that two hundred lucky devils can live in luxury.'

The chambermaids moved between these two worlds constantly, emerging from glorious suites, which they had left spotless and fragrant, and plunging into the nether darkness of labyrinthine corridors, heavy with the smell of food and sweat and lye soap.

And though she'd been inclined at first to think chambermaiding a humble occupation, she soon saw that there were far worse jobs: such as that of the cooks, cursing and dripping sweat as they slaved over the furnaces in shifts that sometimes lasted twenty hours; the laundrywomen, whose arms were boiled crimson, their hands swollen and white with the bleach; the scullions, armpit-deep in stone sinks, scouring copper pans with sand, surrounded by mountains of greasy crockery; the old women who scrubbed the marble floors on their hands and knees at two in the morning, their joints swollen like camels'.

By contrast, to work in airy bedrooms was a privilege. You could throw open the windows on to the place Vendôme and see the blue sky. You dealt with crisp linen and fresh flowers. When no one was looking, you could dance around the magnificent beds for a moment and pretend all this was yours alone.

The Ritz was an easy place to get lost in. The hotel was composed of several buildings, connected by labyrinthine passages and winding staircases, and nowhere was there a helpful sign to point the way. It took Olivia weeks to work out the layout.

While she was on probation, she ate supper with Marie-France and Fabrice every night. Marie-France even advanced her the money to pay her rent, ensuring she was not thrown out by the de la Fays before she got her first wages. She was growing very fond of Marie-France, one of the most practical people she'd ever met. There was much to admire in her: frugal but generous, upright but tolerant, Olivia was willing to accept her as a second mother.

Fabrice was the joy in her life. He was charming and funny in public; and in private he was tender and loving. She had told Marie-France the truth when she'd said she'd never had a boyfriend. You couldn't count the callow boys who'd walked her home from church, or the farmer (sixty if he was a day) who had blurted out a proposal of marriage and had wept openly at her astonished refusal.

Fabrice was a man she could respect. She loved his sense of humour, his good looks, the way he moved, his self-confidence. They went to the art galleries or took walks together through Montmartre or along the

Seine, talking non-stop. He was sensible enough not to lecture her on anarchism or socialism; but they discussed every other subject under the sun, especially art. And they arrived at their first kisses.

Seeing each other every day wasn't enough. They began wanting to be private together, up in Olivia's studio. Madame de la Fay turned a blind eye to these visits, so long as the rent was paid. Here they would sit together on Olivia's squeaky bed, kissing, gazing into one another's eyes and aching to go further.

'I want to be sure,' he said one day, 'that you don't care for me just because of my mother.'

'She does make a very good *coq au vin*,' Olivia replied solemnly.

'That's true.' He put his arms around her, his face serious. 'But I've grown very fond of you, Olivia.'

'I've heard more romantic speeches than *that*,' she snorted.

'All right, I'm crazy about you. You know I am. I used to watch you every Sunday at the Pont au Change and dream that you'd be mine one day. It took me weeks to get the money together to ask you to paint me.'

'Skinflint.'

'I don't want to lose you.'

'I'm not going anywhere,' she said, smiling.

'Even if war breaks out?'

'If war breaks out, I'll fight on the barricades with a saucepan on my head.'

He kissed her, laughing. 'You are never serious.'

'I'm serious when I say I'm crazy about you too,' Olivia replied. 'And though I'm also crazy about your mother – and her *coq au vin* – and Paris – and France – it's for your own sake, and not for any other reason.'

Fabrice kissed her. 'You know how to make me happy.'

'Would you like to know how to make *me* happy?'

His eyes sparkled. 'I've been trying, but you won't let me!'

'Not *that*. It's your beard. It has to go.'

'But chérie—'

'Yes, I know it makes you look like Ulysses, or your hero Bakunin, or someone of that sort, but now that we're on smooching terms, it's giving me an awful rash.' She displayed the pink curve of her cheek. 'Look what you do to me.'

Fabrice fingered the tawny curls on his chin regretfully. 'What if you don't like what's underneath?'

'Is there any hideous scarring? A tattoo of a naked lady, perhaps?'

'No.'

'Then I think you're safe.'

'It means extra expense, you know. Razor blades, a brush, soap. Shaving is no joke.'

'I shave my legs. You're not getting any sympathy from me.'

'Very well. Next time you see me I shall be a beardless youth again.'

'I like it when you're obedient.' She narrowed her eyes. 'Shall we have one more smooch in the shrubbery before it goes?'

'As you command, milady.' He took her in his arms. Their kisses were growing hotter and more daring. Sometimes they were so passionate, and lasted so long, that they broke off gasping with desire – and lack of oxygen – only to resume again a moment later. This was one of those times. They kissed with open mouths, exchanging those caresses of the tongue that were so thrilling. The difference was that it swiftly made them both frantic for more.

Fabrice was so urgent that Olivia was pushed back on to her bed. Nothing reluctant, she pulled him on top of her. They had experimented with this a couple of times before. She loved his weight on her. He pressed his hips against her, his arousal thrusting against hers, to the point where she began to feel the rippling contractions of a climax that could only be avoided by hastily pushing him off again. But this time she held on tight and let it happen. It came from deep inside her, swelling deliciously until it burst like a ripe melon, flooding her with pleasure.

It was her first climax with another person, and she felt absurdly pleased with herself as her body relaxed into blissful limpness.

Fabrice looked down at her face, which was now flushed and heavy-lidded.

'Did you—?'

'Yes,' she said contentedly.

He looked extremely proud of himself, as though he'd done something tremendously clever. 'I wish it was as easy as that for me!'

'Perhaps you're not trying hard enough.'

'I'm very hard, believe me,' he said ruefully.

'I noticed!'

'When will you let me—?'

'By and by,' she said, sitting up and arranging her hair.

'When is "by and by", if you please?'

'When I'm being paid. Then I won't feel like a kept woman.'

'I don't know about kept. You're certainly a very difficult woman,' he said, shaking his head.

'I know what I *can* do to give you great relief,' she said.

He brightened. 'Yes?'

'Let's go out and buy you a razor, and I'll help you shave off that beard.'

Arletty had fallen in love with the car at first sight. It was a dark-blue Packard convertible, a huge thing with sweeping wings and a white leather soft top, the sort of automobile that a film star ought to have. And she *was* a film star now, no longer a player of comic roles or bit parts. With the release of *Le Jour se Lève* a few weeks earlier she had entered the ranks of serious actresses playing serious roles. No matter that she had played a cynical mouthy Paris *canaille* – or that so many of her new and swanky friends apparently thought that was what she really was, and viewed her with voyeuristic fascination – the important thing was the pay cheque she had received for the film: a cool two hundred and fifty thousand francs.

That was serious money to go with the serious roles. In two years she had hauled herself from obscurity to become the highest-paid actress in the French cinema. And for the first time in her life, she had begun to feel safe.

The Packard was her reward to herself. And what a car, a massive hunk of American prestige. She walked slowly around the machine in the hushed automobile showroom, watching her own reflection in the gleaming paint and chrome. It was the best mirror a woman could have, a mirror of power, glamour, progress.

The grille was a gleaming snarl of chrome fangs, framed by head-lamps the size of buckets. She touched the hood ornament with a gloved hand: a naked, winged woman with backswept hair, hurtling forward with outstretched arms. That was what she herself was, poised on the tip of the wave.

The salesman opened the driver's side door for her and she slid behind the wheel. The seats were sumptuous red leather. The ones in the back were cramped jump seats: she was not planning on carrying many passengers.

Arletty took the ivory wheel in her hands. If anything said that she had arrived, it was this moment. She drew her breath and held it in her lungs, revelling in the raw feeling of being alive.

'Mam'selle Arletty?'

She let out her pent-up breath and turned to smile at the showroom manager, who was bowing unctuously. 'Yes?'

He held out a portmanteau. 'The papers are all completed. Everything is in order.'

She took the portmanteau. 'The car is mine?'

'Of course, Madame. And may I wish you every enjoyment with it. We can have it delivered this afternoon.'

'No. I'll take it now.'

'Of course, of course, as you please.' He snapped his fingers impatiently at his staff, who hurried to set about the business of moving other cars out of the way and opening the glass doors on to the street. 'Would Madame prefer the roof down or up?'

'Down.'

They unfastened the soft top and slid it back over the tonneau. The doors were now open and the way was clear. The manager began to explain a few last details concerning the brakes and the headlights, but she cut him off impatiently. 'I'll attend to all that later.' She put on her dark glasses. The showroom staff applauded spontaneously as she started the car and drove out into the sunlight.

The manager must have spread the word, because a cheering crowd had gathered in the street outside, including pressmen with their cameras at the ready. They shouted for Arletty to stop, but she had no intention of stopping for anyone right now. Waving one hand, she sailed past them and, finding the back street empty, floored the accelerator. The Packard's engine responded with a roar, pushing her back in her seat. The sensations of power and freedom were heady. The gleaming prow flashed in the sun, the winged woman cleaving the air. Not bad for a *canaille* from Courbevoie.

It was to Courbevoie that she was now headed. She drove fast, barrelling alongside the river, passing the barges and the bridges and the rows of unemployed men staring dully into the grey water, oblivious of the sun overhead.

The suburb where she had been born was little changed since her childhood. In the shadow of these factories, whose brick chimneys were like tall crayons smudging the blue sky, she had learned to skip and dance. By this overgrown canal, where boats moored for decades rotted half-submerged, she had listened to the older women talking about men as they did their washing, had smoked her first cigarette, a thin, silent, knowing girl; between these rows of grimy houses she had picked up the *gouaille*, the sharp Parisian repartee that had become her trademark, and which her smart new friends found so screamingly funny.

As always, a feeling of melancholy nostalgia washed over her. This grey, working-class *banlieue* would always be home to her. Childhood guilt and childhood joy were inextricably mingled here. It would always be a part of her, and she would always be a part of it.

Oh, but it was grand to drive down the streets of her youth in this magnificent car, with the wind in her hair! Already, she had gathered a gaggle of street children, who ran after the Packard, screaming, 'Arletty! It's Arletty!'

She parked in front of a drab house, half-hidden behind a myrtle hedge that badly needed clipping. The children caught up with her and surrounded her, chanting her name and scrambling on to the running boards of the car to peer inside and whistle in admiration.

'Hey. If you scratch the paint, I'll give you this,' she snapped, showing them the palm of her hand. They laughed, but scattered nevertheless. They knew she was serious. One of the older boys made a pistol out of his finger and thumb and shot himself in the heart, crumpling to the pavement in imitation of Jean Gabin in the final scene of *Le Jour se Lève*. Arletty put her hands on her hips. 'You're a comedian, eh? Keep these little bastards off my car and there'll be five francs for you when I come out.'

He jumped to his feet with alacrity. 'Sure thing, Arletty!'

'Don't you Arletty me. I'm Mam'selle Bathiat to you.'

She pushed past the overgrown hedge and knocked on the peeling front door. After a long while, it opened to reveal a woman drably dressed in a housecoat, her sagging face tightened by disapproval, as though by invisible threads. 'Well?'

Arletty took off her dark glasses. 'Hello, Maman.'

Her mother looked her up and down, taking in the dark-red dress, the jewellery, the smart black hat and heels. 'Is this how you come to see your mother?'

'How should I come to see you?'

'I suppose I should be thankful you're wearing any clothes at all.'

Arletty laughed shortly. 'Oh, Maman, please.'

Her mother did not respond to her smile. Her eyes focused over Arletty's shoulder to the Packard, with its buzzing circle of street children. 'Is that yours?'

'Yes. I've just bought it. Isn't it beautiful? I thought you might like to go for a drive this afternoon.'

'No, thank you.'

'Why not?'

'I would be ashamed to be seen in such a thing.'

Arletty grimaced. 'All right. Are you going to let me in? I have something for you.'

Reluctantly, her mother stepped back and allowed her into the front room. Arletty leaned forward to kiss her, but her mother pulled away before Arletty's lips could touch her cheek. Hiding her hurt, Arletty spoke gaily. 'I'm making a new film, Maman. *Madame Sans-Gêne*. It's great fun. A part just made for me.'

'Another tart, you mean.'

'Well, that's putting it uncharitably. She's a woman who doesn't care about the conventions.'

'And will you take your clothes off again?' Before Arletty could say anything, her mother went on in a hard monotone. 'It's not enough that you have to play tarts and trollops, is it, Léonie? You must show your skeleton to all the world – and at your age!'

'At my age?' The brief glimpse of her naked breasts in the shower in *Le Jour se Lève* had been cut in most cinemas, but had been seen by enough people to cause excitement, and had contributed materially to the success of the film. 'I am not so bad for my age,' Arletty said coolly.

'You should be married by now, if any decent man would have you. You should have used your breasts to feed an innocent child, instead of showing them to the world.'

'I don't want a husband, and I certainly don't want a child, thank you.'

'You don't want anything that's decent, or natural.'

'I suppose it's too much to expect you to be proud of what I've achieved,' Arletty said wearily.

'Proud, you say? Your name stinks, my child.'

'Not so I've noticed. I'm the most invited woman in Paris.'

'Oh, yes. The sort of persons who invite you are amused by your affairs with men. And not only men,' she added bitterly. 'I never thought I would live to hear such things said about my own daughter.'

Arletty felt the heat rise to her cheeks. 'What things?'

'You are not only corrupt. You've become a corrupter.'

'And who am I supposed to have corrupted?'

'You know very well. You've seduced the Duchess of Harcourt.'

Arletty laughed briefly. '*Au contraire*, my dear mother.'

'Perhaps you think it funny to have stained one of the greatest names in France.'

'You're such a snob,' Arletty drawled. 'I assure you, she didn't need seducing. If anything, she seduced me.'

'Do you expect me to believe that? A woman of that family!'

'Her family is no better than ours. And her tastes were established long before she met me.'

'I don't want to hear the details of your unnatural relationships,' her mother cut in angrily. Now in her mid-sixties, she looked ten years older. After the death of her husband in 1916, she'd gone to work in a munitions factory to support the family. The years at a lathe had made her old before her time. Arletty had started in her teens as a stenographer, but the life hadn't suited her. She'd been drawn to the bright lights, and her tall, slender figure had given her an entrée into modelling, and then acting. It had taken her twenty years to get where she was now, but the gulf that had opened between herself and her mother seemed to have yawned wider with each of those years. It cut her deeply that her mother despised everything she had achieved, but she knew that her mother's narrow working-class prejudices were never going to change.

'Let's not quarrel,' Arletty said, lowering her voice. 'I am the way I am. You are the way you are. We can still be friends. Look. I've brought you something.' She held out the envelope.

Her mother took it and extracted the contents: a cheque for ten thousand francs. She stared at it blankly. 'What's this?'

'It will help you live a little better. Buy a few luxuries. Perhaps get some help in the house, so you can take it easy.'

'I don't want this.'

'Don't worry, I can spare the money.'

'I don't care what you can spare. I don't want it because of the way it's been earned.'

'Maman, don't be melodramatic. I earned that money honestly.'

'How dare you try to buy me off?'

'I don't need to buy anybody off,' Arletty snapped. 'It's a gift. I thought you would be grateful.'

But Arletty hadn't grasped how angry her mother had become. 'Grateful? *Me*, grateful to *you*?' She tore the cheque in half and threw the pieces in her daughter's face. 'There!'

Arletty took a step back, astonished. 'You're mad. What have I done to you?'

'*Madame Sans-Gêne*,' her mother spat. 'That's you, all right. Madame care-for-nothing, Madame ashamed-of-nothing.'

'If you're stupid enough to tear up ten thousand francs, then too bad. But you don't need to insult me.'

'You insult *me*!' She gestured at the photograph on the mantel. 'You insult *him*. What do you think he would say to you?'

'I don't know. He would probably be too busy beating you to care.'

'How dare you!'

'Oh, in your determination to turn him into a saint, have you forgotten all the black eyes he gave you?'

Marie Bathiat's cheeks were white with rage. 'You're no better than a public whore. And now you show up here in that strumpet's chariot, wanting to parade through Courbevoie with me at your side! Haven't you brought enough shame on us?'

'I think I'd better leave,' Arletty said, her throat closing tightly.

'Yes, go. Get out. Get out of my house!'

She met her mother's hot eyes. 'I won't be back.'

Her mother turned away. 'So much the better.'

Arletty was trying not to cry as she slammed the door. She was trembling in every limb with shock and anger. She walked swiftly back to the Packard. The children fell silent as they saw her face, parting to let her through. Putting on her dark glasses, she got behind the wheel. The boy she'd appointed to guard her car appeared at the window. 'I didn't let any of them touch it, Mam'selle Bathiat.'

She dug in her purse for the coin. 'My name is Arletty,' she said thickly. 'There is no Mam'selle Bathiat.'

He shrugged. 'Whatever you say.' He held out his grimy hand.

She gave him the money and started the car. With the shameless, winged figure before her, she drove swiftly past the grimy houses, the smoky factories, the stagnant, rotting canal.

Six

It had been a terrible day. At lunchtime almost the entire workforce of the Ritz had crowded into the canteen, where the senior staff took their meals, to listen to the radio. They had heard the British prime minister announce from London that the Germans had not responded to the noon deadline he had issued, and that, consequently, Great Britain was at war with Germany.

Abandoned guests clamouring for food, drink and service had called them back to their duties. The afternoon had passed as though in a bad dream. They all knew that the French deadline would expire at five p.m., and that after that, France would join Britain at war against the Germans. The Ritz staff, who came from at least ten different countries, went about their work with sombre faces, occasionally forming little knots to whisper hastily and then hurry off.

Olivia, whose probation was now over, and who was a full-time employee of the Ritz, was working with Heike, who was even more sullen than usual. Some of the staff, especially the French, had made insulting or threatening remarks to Heike. She was among the last Germans still working at the hotel; in the past weeks the others had discreetly melted away, going back across the Rhine in preparation for a war they thought was inevitable.

To almost everyone else, however, the eve of war had come as a shock. It was here suddenly, the thing they all dreaded but had not wished to look at, like the monster that lurked under the beds of children. Now, with terrifying purpose, it had clambered out and proved itself real after all.

The older men and women, who remembered the last war with Germany, were gloomy. The younger ones were ebullient, as though at the start of a football match. But this would be no football match, Olivia knew that.

She wondered what was going through Heike's mind. Heike was ominously silent as they worked. There were not even the usual criticisms and rebukes. Olivia was shy to ask her how she felt, but she felt a kind of pity for this hulking woman whom so few liked, and who was so evidently unhappy. What would she do now?

As they were finishing off a room that the occupants had vacated late, the pimply valet, Victor, came in. With his fists on his hips, he whistled a few bars of the 'Marseillaise' and then grinned impudently at Heike.

'It's five o'clock,' he announced. 'We're at war with you.'

Heike paused in what she was doing. 'Now,' she said quietly, 'you will learn to fear us again.'

'I'll never fear *you*,' Victor retorted, 'you ugly, fat Nazi bitch.'

Heike covered the ground between herself and the valet with astonishing speed. She slapped him across the face with such force that Olivia thought his head was going to come off his shoulders. He staggered against the wall, clutching his cheek, and then – although he was eighteen at least – burst into tears like a child and ran out of the room.

Heike turned to Olivia, her eyes glaring blindly. For a moment it seemed as though Olivia was going to get the same treatment; then Heike picked up the sheet she had dropped. 'Take the other end,' she commanded. Olivia obeyed, and they started work again.

'He shouldn't have spoken to you like that,' Olivia said after a pause.

'He will learn,' Heike replied in the same quiet way. 'All of you will learn.'

Within ten minutes of this incident, Monsieur Auzello strode into the room. He looked down at Heike from his considerable height. 'Mam'selle Schwab,' he said in a sharp voice, 'you are dismissed. I must ask you to quit the hotel immediately.'

Heike made no reply, but very deliberately finished arranging the silk canopy around the bed. She smoothed the coverlet with her large square hands, watched in silence by the crowd that had gathered at the door of the suite. Then she pushed her way through them into the corridor. Nobody spoke; but Victor, his eyes swollen, spat at her as she passed him.

'Get back to your duties,' Auzello commanded. The staff moved off, muttering. Auzello turned to Olivia. 'You will work late today if necessary, to make up for Schwab's absence.'

'Yes, Monsieur Auzello.'

She continued to work alone. The great hotel was oddly silent, as though the events of the day had stunned both staff and guests alike. Even place Vendôme was unusually empty; Napoleon on his column had the late afternoon sunlight to himself as he contemplated yet another war with bronze eyes.

Victor returned excitedly. 'There were two gendarmes waiting for Heike in rue Cambon! They've taken her away.'

'What will happen to her?'

'She'll be locked up.'

'She didn't do anything!'

Victor examined his face in the ornate Empire mirror and touched the red imprint of Heike's hand, which was stark on his cheek. 'You call this nothing? They're rounding up all the Germans in Paris and sending them to internment camps in the Pyrenees. They'll be cold and hungry up there, believe me!' He grinned at Olivia. 'Don't look so worried. This war will be over in a year. Our army is twice the size of theirs.'

Olivia thought of Fabrice. The rituals of lovemaking, which had been so new to her at first, were now a vital part of their lives together. She had been almost a virgin, if there was such a thing, when they'd met, her experience limited. With Fabrice she had entered fully into the religion of sex, with its incense – hers warm and dark, his sharp and bright – its half-stifled hymns, its sacred dances. His body, lean and yet strong, delighted her. He was elegant in his lovemaking, as in everything he did, and he gave her joy. She knew that he adored her in return. The difference in their origins and upbringings only intensified the attraction between them.

They had been talking of marriage. Fabrice, ever the anarchist, laughed at her desire for a ring and a marriage certificate, but was prepared to humour her. They took minimal precautions and Olivia, in some almost-negligent way, had supposed that one day she would wake up and find herself pregnant; and she had supposed that then they would marry in some registry office (for Fabrice would not enter a church) and that they would slip out of this enchanted backwater and enter the great stream of human life.

But the stream of human life had grown turbulent, and she was now afraid of what lay just beyond the enchanted backwater. She was afraid that the mighty flood would tear them apart, pull them down, crush the fragile thing that they had.

※

The outbreak of war had made her concerned for her old teacher, Laszlo Weisz. She decided to visit him on her way home, and show him the sketchbook she always kept with her at work.

Laszlo lived in the rue Lepic, where the street market was held. Rue Lepic was cobbled and steep, still littered with the discarded cabbage leaves and carrot tops of the day's market. His apartment was at number 17, a narrow doorway sandwiched between two shops. She rang the bell, and he came trudging down. Peering through the grille, he seemed not to recognise her at first. Then his eyes lit up.

'My little Olivia! Come in, come in!'

His first-floor apartment was chilly, and crowded with canvases and small sculptures, as always. He made her a cup of tea and then leafed through her notebook.

'They're just quick sketches of people at the hotel,' she said apologetically. 'I don't have time for anything else these days.'

'You have such an eye,' he said, shaking his head. 'You capture the essence with a few pencil strokes. Everything you draw has life. It's a great gift. Promise me you will keep drawing, Olivia. Never give up.'

'I'll try not to,' she promised. She couldn't help noticing how unkempt her old teacher was looking. His white hair was hanging over his eyes and his beard straggled across his frayed shirt. 'Have you got a pair of scissors?' she asked.

He produced them and sat tamely while she draped him in a towel and gave him a haircut and trimmed his beard. 'You're so kind, my dear.'

'You told me there would be war, and you were right. At the hotel they're all saying that it will be over in a few weeks, and that the French army will thrash the Germans before the winter.'

'There is no hope of thrashing the Germans,' he replied quietly.

Olivia paused in her snipping. 'Don't you think we can win?'

'Not this time. France has no stomach for a fight. We will be lucky to last a month against the Nazis.'

'Don't say that, *maître*!'

'They will not invade this year. The declaration of war has taken them by surprise. They were planning their war for next year. Now the weather is starting to be bad. They will wait until the harvest is gathered in next summer, and then they will come.' He spoke with sad certainty. 'It will be quick and brutal. Like everything they do.'

She knew that Laszlo was a pessimist, and prone to melancholy, but his words still filled her with unease. 'Isn't our army much stronger than theirs?'

'You are too young to remember the last war, my dear. Strength lies not in numbers, but in determination. And the Nazis are filled with a terrible determination. We are weak and afraid. A hundred sheep are no match for five wolves. Get out of this, Olivia. Go home.'

'I'm in love, *maître*,' she said with a smile. 'I told you it felt right. Fabrice and I are going to get married.'

He patted her arm fretfully. 'Mazel tov. But getting married won't stop the war, my dear. And this will not be like other wars, fought on faraway battlefields. It will be a war in which machines will rain bombs down on defenceless cities, on women and children.' Weisz took her hand. 'I am afraid for you, my dear. An old man like me is just a bundle of rags. But you – you are young. Go back home and paint in Minnesota.'

'And leave Fabrice?' She had finished cutting his hair. He looked a lot better now. She got a broom and swept up the snowy clippings on the floor. 'I can't. I'm making my life here, *maître*.'

He sighed heavily and began crooning something in Yiddish, his rheumy eyes half-closed. When she offered to cook him a meal, he just shook his head without interrupting his song – or perhaps it was a prayer.

She put the broom in the cupboard and went home to Fabrice.

Montmartre was hushed when she got back. The convivial groups at the pavement cafés were absent. The waiters were already stacking chairs; curtains were already being drawn. The old man who gathered the refuse trundled his stinking cart past Olivia, calling out in a doleful voice, '*C'est la guerre, Mam'selle, c'est encore la guerre.*'

A golden harvest moon was rising over the higgledy-piggledy rooftops as she climbed the steep hill to her lodgings. Fabrice was waiting for her. She caught the glow of his cigarette in the shadow of the door-way. He came out to meet her, and they embraced tightly.

'What a day,' she said ruefully, her mouth muffled against his shoulder.

Upstairs in her studio, sitting beside him on her bed, she told him about Heike and Laszlo. He had spent the day at *Le Libertaire*, preparing a special edition to mark the start of the war. And he had other news.

'It's not enough to write. Now is the time for action. I'm going to join the army.'

'But your chest, Fabrice—'

'They'll find something for me to do. They need every man they can get.'

They hadn't turned on the electric light. The full moon, shining in the open window, provided all the illumination they needed. Now clean-shaven, he seemed to Olivia like some handsome doomed god. She saw that it was useless to try to argue with him. All over France, millions of young men were taking the same decision.

She rose and undressed, laying her clothes over the chair. Naked, she got back into bed, and held out her arms to Fabrice.

'Come.'

As soon as she saw Paul, Arletty knew what he had come to tell her.

Her brother was a quiet man who had never shown the slight-est interest in her career. Their lives had diverged in their teens, when Arletty had begun acting and had left Courbevoie. He had chosen to remain, working in a local factory and staying close to their mother.

'How did it happen?' she asked in a dry voice.

'The doctor says it was a stroke,' Paul replied. 'We were eating sup-per. She suddenly fell forward with her face in the plate. She was dead in an hour.'

'Do you think she suffered?'

Paul shrugged. They knew each other well enough for her to understand that shrug – Marie Bathiat's life had contained little but hardship.

In the Packard, driving back to Courbevoie, he laid his hand gently on her shoulder. 'It wasn't your fault, Léonie. You mustn't think that.'

Her throat was choked. 'We had a terrible argument—'

'I know. She told me. Arguments don't kill people. Or she would have died thirty years ago. You can't blame yourself.'

She just shook her head by way of a reply, determined not to shed the tears that threatened to shake her icy composure.

There were crowds of people in the house, including the little redhaired priest, her old enemy. If Paul didn't blame her for her mother's death, the priest certainly did. His sour face said it all. He refused to shake her extended hand. 'I always knew how things would end up with you,' he said, turning away.

Her mother had been laid out in the front room. The dead woman's face was rouged and unexpectedly bloated.

'The undertaker pushed cotton wool into her cheeks,' Paul murmured with a grimace. 'He said it would make her look happy.'

The expression on her mother's face was not happy. There was no forgiveness in the lined features, no tenderness in the worn fingers that were locked together on the thin breast. The undertaker's rouge looked like a flush of anger. Arletty kissed her mother's cold brow, watched by everyone.

Her mother's life had been so devoid of love or warmth. Why had she been so maddened by her daughter desiring those things? Had she really wanted Arletty to stay chained to poverty and grief all her life? She'd raged at Arletty for her immorality, because she had flirted with men, because she had shown her body – a scrawny thing, God knows – to the cameras. Had morality really been the issue? Or had there been a bitter rivalry? The jealousy of an unloved woman for a beautiful daughter?

She stood by the coffin, receiving the condolences of half-remembered people from her childhood. The cramped, dark house looked and smelled the same as it had done for forty years. The look and the smell were of hardship cherished and daily polished until it had attained the dull glow of martyrdom. The Christ hanging on the wall had been burnished year after year until the salient points of his body had lost their paint and showed through like bone; the patterns of the upholstery had faded almost to invisibility. On the mantelpiece stood no ornaments, only the photograph of her father, crushed by his own tram decades ago. There was no hint of comfort or frivolity anywhere.

Yet despite her father's casual brutality, she had once been a happy child in this house; until, that was, his death had tipped them from poverty into destitution, and her mother's bitterness had turned on her, destroying the bonds that held them all together. That had been the end of her youth.

The expressions on the faces that came up to her were mixed. Some were in awe of the great Arletty. Others showed envy, disapproval, simpering admiration.

An older woman, beside whom she'd worked in the laundry as a teenager, eagerly clasped both her hands.

'Your maman is in the arms of God, Léonie,' she said, her eyes brimming with tears. 'She is in Heaven. Console yourself with that, my dear.'

'The disadvantage of being an atheist,' Arletty said, disengaging her hands from the other woman's hot grasp, 'is that I do not believe in Heaven. The advantage is that I don't believe in Hell, either.'

The woman gaped at her. 'Léonie!'

Arletty had had enough of condolences. She turned away and went out into the garden to smoke a cigarette. There was a crowd of children in the street, some gawking over the gate, others hanging around the gleaming car. Arletty was trembling all over. That damned fight over the Packard! Why had she walked away from her mother? Why hadn't she gone back, apologised, asked for a reconciliation?

But she knew the fight had been over far more than the Packard. And that there would never have been a reconciliation.

Paul came out to join her. She gave him a cigarette and they smoked together for a while.

'You're too thin,' he said at last, glancing at her sideways.

'I'm a hundred and three pounds, five foot eight, the same as I always was.'

'You just look smaller.'

'That's because we're orphans now.'

'Yes, we're orphans.' He cupped his cigarette in the palm of his hand. The black workshop oil could never quite be scrubbed out of the seams of his knuckles or from under his nails. 'She loved you, you know.'

'No, she didn't.'

'She did. She was just terrified of losing you.'

'She said dreadful words to me.'

'You shocked her. The things you got up to.'

'I had to escape from here, Paul. You know that.'

'I don't blame you. I'm not saying that. She wanted to keep us both.'

'But you stayed.'

'I'm a tame bird. You're a wild bird.' He dropped the cigarette and crushed it out under his boot. 'So there's going to be another war.'

'Yes. As if the last one wasn't enough.'

'I'm not complaining. I'm too old to be called up, and it means extra work for the factory. We'll all keep our jobs for a year or two.' He looked at his sister. 'We have to go back inside. They're waiting. Rub your eyes, Léonie. Make it at least look like you've been crying. Or they'll talk about it for weeks.'

She laughed shortly. Then she didn't need to rub her eyes, because the scalding tears were pouring down her cheeks.

Seven

Coco Chanel rattled the telephone at her bedside furiously. 'Hello? *Hello?*'

The nervous voice of the Ritz switchboard operator came on the line. 'Mam'selle Chanel?'

'Get me a line, you idiot,' Coco demanded. 'I'm trying to call London.'

'I'm so sorry,' the operator stammered. 'But the lines – the lines are all down.'

'What do you mean, "*down*"?'

'There are no lines, Mademoiselle.'

'No lines to London?' she asked incredulously.

'No lines anywhere. Not even in Paris. They say the Germans have cut them all.' Her voice was tearful. 'They are only seventy-five miles from Paris!'

Coco slammed the receiver down, trembling. She fumbled the bedside drawer open and took out the silver case. It was beautifully engraved with designs of poppies, and it held everything: three syringes, spare needles, vials of morphine. She took out one of the syringes, and hesitated with the needle an inch from her vein. She needed this every night, to stave off the terrors that came with darkness. But to start during the day—

She would end up like Cocteau or Christian Bérard, screaming in the addicts' ward of the Pitié-Salpêtrière.

With a quivering effort of will, she put the morphine away and lit a cigarette instead. She went out on to her balcony and gripped the wrought-iron railings with both hands, the cigarette clamped between her dry lips. The sky was dark, though it was mid-afternoon. Black smoke blotted out the sun. It rolled in from the industrial areas, where deposits of oil were being burned to keep them from the advancing German tanks. The stink of it was everywhere. Below Coco, the place Vendôme was as empty as the stage of a theatre, waiting for a new cast to emerge from the wings.

A year had passed since the declaration of war. And what changes that year had brought.

In the space of that year, the army of France had been routed. Not defeated in battle, because the Germans had not presented themselves at the heavily fortified Maginot Line, where the great siege was supposed to take place. After months of waiting, which had grown so tedious that people called it the Phoney War, as though they were disappointed by it, the Wehrmacht had struck at dawn on the tenth of May. They had thrust into Belgium and Holland, completely bypassing the Maginot Line; and from the high forests of the Ardennes, they had poured down into France like the Huns of old.

Dazed by the screaming Stuka dive-bombers, outflanked by tank battalions executing brilliant manoeuvres that had been meticulously planned months ahead, the army had for the most part been forced to surrender without a fight.

Hundreds of thousands of captured soldiers were being herded into camps as prisoners of war, and were now hostages, their lives dependent on the subservience of their families to the new overlords.

A wave of despair had swept through France. The cities had emptied. Millions of refugees were streaming south through the countryside, sleeping in hedgerows, besieging the ports, the railway stations and any exit that could be found. Roosevelt had declined to help. The British had fled, having had to be ignominiously rescued from the beaches of Dunkirk in a flotilla of fishing boats.

The government had abandoned Paris, declaring it an open city: there would be no defence of the capital against the approaching Germans, despite the mountains of sandbags that had been piled around the great monuments, or used to barricade the streets.

The city lay deserted now. There was not a car to be seen, not a taxi to be had. Chanel herself was marooned here: her faithful chauffeur had been called up, and she did not know how to drive her sky-blue Rolls-Royce. She had to get out of Paris. But now, with the telephones dead, she could not reach her powerful friends in London.

Thank God the Ritz had not closed. Old Madame Ritz, who lived in seclusion on the fourth floor, had wanted to shut down and lock up, but they'd persuaded her that if the Germans found the hotel empty, they would simply commandeer it, and it would be lost. A far better idea would be to rent rooms to German officers with a taste for luxury. There would surely be plenty of those.

Something settled on the sleeve of Coco's blouse. She brushed it away, but it left an ugly black smear on the white silk. With a sharp cry of dismay, she realised that flakes of soot were raining down from the sky, covering everything.

She hurried back inside and tried to rescue the blouse, but it was irreparably stained, ruined. She tore it off and flung it across the room. Catching sight of herself in the mirror, she saw a skinny old woman with tangled hair and glaring eyes, her face shrivelled with fear and anger.

Her rooms were in disorder, the bed unmade, clothes draped over every piece of furniture, newspapers scattered where she had tossed them. Her two chambermaids, Germaine and Jeanne, had abandoned her days earlier, scuttling back to their village, rats fleeing the sinking ship. It was insupportable. She hurried back to the telephone and snatched it up.

'Send someone to clean my room at once. Do you hear? At once!'

Marie-France caught Olivia as she was stuffing a pile of dirty sheets into the laundry chute.

'They want you to go to Madame Chanel's suite right away.'

Olivia heaved the obstinate bundle of malodorous linen through the hatch. 'She has her own maids.'

'They've run off, and she's in a rage. I'm sorry, chérie. I know you have enough on your hands, but there's nobody else I trust.'

It was stiflingly hot, and Olivia mopped her brow. During the past year, the staff of the Ritz had shrunk from several hundred to a few dozen. The men had been called up, the women had fled Paris. Only the old and infirm remained, yet the exacting standards of the Ritz had to be maintained. It was small consolation to find that she was now, as the fittest of the remaining chambermaids, indispensable to the hotel: the huge amount of extra work had not been matched by any raise in salary. The days were long and exhausting, the responsibilities heavy. 'I still have five rooms to do, Marie-France!'

Marie-France touched Olivia on the shoulder. 'I'll find someone to help, I promise. Go to her now, before she has a fit.'

Tired and in a bad temper, Olivia collected her trolley and made her way up to the second floor, where Chanel – alike called Madame or Mademoiselle, since she had vowed never to marry – had her personal suite. She knocked, and receiving no answer, let herself in.

She was astonished to find the sumptuous rooms in disarray, and even more astonished to find Chanel herself dishevelled and quite alone among the disorder.

Olivia had glimpsed her many times in various parts of the hotel, always surrounded by chattering groups of friends and clients, always impeccably dressed, the very essence of chic. What she found now was the great couturier huddled in a chemise, her lean arms wrapped around herself as though it were midwinter, rather than a summer afternoon, looking half-crazy.

Chanel's black eyes flashed at her. 'You took your time,' she spat. 'Look how they've left me!'

Olivia gazed around. Plates of congealed food lay on chairs or the floor, where they had obviously been abandoned for days. Dirty clothes were strewn everywhere. The bed, with its embroidered eighteenth-century canopy, was a tangle of sheets, a large wine stain like dried blood on a pillow.

And now she saw that two tears were sliding down Chanel's cheeks. Dismayed, she went over to her, and sat beside her on the velvet banquette, putting her arms around the thin shoulders. 'Madame,' she said gently, 'don't cry.'

Chanel stiffened, evidently not in the habit of being embraced by chambermaids; but she allowed herself to be comforted, shedding a few more sparse tears. She was shaking. The sunken look of her face, Olivia realised, was due to her not having any teeth. She also noticed that the older woman's hair looked like a bird's nest, and smelled like one too.

'Let's get you tidied up and dressed,' she said. 'Then I'll do what I can with your rooms. Shall we wash your hair?'

Chanel allowed Olivia to lead her to the bathroom. She certainly lived in eye-popping splendour; the bath was solid marble, the taps golden swans. She made a pile of the dirty towels, which were embroidered with Chanel's initials in purple, and found clean ones. Among the cut-crystal bottles of perfume and toiletries that cluttered every surface, she found shampoo; and with Chanel hunched obediently over the bath, every knob of her spine showing, began washing her hair.

'They've all run away,' Chanel blubbered under the stream of water. 'Cocteau, his boyfriend, my staff, everybody. They ran like rats and abandoned me. I'm the only one left.'

'Everything will be all right,' Olivia said soothingly. Chanel seemed part child, part crone.

'Are the Germans in Paris yet?'

'Not yet,' Olivia replied. 'They say they'll be here in a day or two. But they've promised there will be no shelling or bombing.'

'I thought the war would last longer.'

'We all did, Madame.' Olivia rinsed foam from the lank, brown hair, and wrapped it in a towel. 'Have you got a hair dryer?'

Chanel gestured at a cupboard. 'In there. How old are you?'

'Twenty-three, Madame.'

'Why are you still in Paris?'

'My fiancé is here.'

She showed her gums in a snarl. 'My God, are you such an idiot?'

'It's my choice.'

'And if the Germans kill him?'

'He tried to enlist, but they turned him down because he had TB as a teenager.'

'He was lucky.'

'I agree, but he doesn't think so.' She found the hair dryer, a gleaming new American appliance, and set about trying to style Chanel's complicated system of curls.

Half an hour later, with Chanel calmed, dressed in a grey suit, decked with a fabulous set of pearls, and her teeth inserted, Olivia tackled the rooms. It was a job for at least two people, but she did the most important things, clearing away the dirty crockery, making the bed with fresh linen, gathering the soiled clothes for the laundry. From the velvet banquette, Chanel watched her. Olivia found her glittering black eyes somewhat malignant in their unwavering gaze.

'You're a pretty thing,' Chanel said. 'What do they call you?'

'Olivia, Madame.'

'Tell them always to send you from now on. I don't want anybody else. Understand?'

Olivia's heart sank. The last thing she needed was a demanding personage of the status of Madame Chanel to look after, in addition to all her extra duties. 'Yes, Madame,' she said reluctantly.

'You don't want the work, eh?' Chanel picked up the telephone. 'This child you've sent me,' she said sharply into the instrument, 'the handsome blonde, you know who I mean? No, no, she's satisfactory.

I've no complaints. But I want her from now on. Yes, every day, until my two come back. You can put it on my account.' She replaced the receiver and showed Olivia a beautiful blouse covered in soot. 'Look! Ruined. One of my favourites. I made the lace collar myself when I was your age.'

'I'll get it clean. I know how to wash silk.'

'Is there no end to your gifts?' Chanel asked dryly.

Olivia gathered her things. 'That's as much as I can do for now, Madame. I have five other rooms to finish this afternoon.'

Chanel grunted as she opened a newspaper and peered at it through her glasses. She had a cigarette hanging from her lips with an inch of ash ready to drop off. 'You can come back this evening and finish off.'

'But Madame—'

'I'll be waiting.' The ash fell on her lapel. She brushed it off in a gesture that also dismissed Olivia.

Olivia pushed the squeaking trolley, loaded with Chanel's dirty linen and crockery, down the corridor. Working at the Ritz brought you into contact with a lot of famous people, but what it almost always meant was more work.

As she rounded a corner, she was confronted by a group of guests making their way to the elevator. She pushed her cart against the wall to allow them to pass. One of them, a heavily built man in a dark suit, paused.

'You're the Swedish girl, aren't you?'

She recognised the rubbery face and clipped moustache as belonging to the Swedish consul in Paris, Raoul Nordling, who was a frequent visitor at the hotel. 'I'm American, Monsieur Nordling.'

He nodded. 'Yes, but your family are Swedish, aren't they?'

'Yes, sir.'

'You speak the language?'

'Yes.'

'What are you doing here, girl? You should be on the first boat home. If you're looking for adventure, this is not the time or place.'

'I'm staying.'

Excusing himself from his companions, Nordling took a notebook out of his pocket. 'Then we're going to have to do something about you. Give me your details.' He wanted to know her full name, address, date of birth and height, recording everything methodically in the notebook. 'Get a photograph taken tomorrow and bring it to the consulate. I'll have a Swedish passport for you in twenty-four hours. You know where the consulate is?'

'Yes, sir – but I already have an American passport.'

He didn't answer her smile. 'You never know what is going to happen, young lady,' he said. 'The Nazis will be in Paris by the weekend. Get it done.'

He hurried off to join his friends and Olivia went on her way. The Ritz was in an extraordinary state, to match the extraordinary state of the country; in defiance of the general exodus, the rooms were nearly all full. Most of the guests belonged to neutral or Axis nations. Many were correspondents reporting on the war, a few were intrepid tourists, eager for a big experience. The American contingent, like Olivia herself, was relying on Franklin Roosevelt's determined non-interventionism. So long as America stayed out of the war, they occupied a privileged, protected position. If that changed, her situation would be very different.

Her parents had written frantic letters, begging her to come home. But she was passionately in love, and the man she loved would not consider fleeing his city or his motherland. So here she remained.

The truth was that she felt little sense of danger. There were reports of Stukas strafing the defenceless columns of refugees that straggled along every country road in France; but by and large, the conquest was eerily peaceful, even surreal. They had seen photographs, perhaps propaganda pictures, perhaps not, of French villagers greeting the Germans warmly, of Wehrmacht officers smiling with groups of civilians. The

Nazis couldn't be so bad if they would pause in an invasion to play football with French schoolchildren, surely?

People said that after the armistice, life would go on very much as normal. Perhaps, under the efficient Germans, who had made their own trains run on time, and built magnificent new autobahns, life would go on even better than before. That was something Olivia wanted to believe.

But perhaps Nordling was right, and it might be prudent to have a passport from another neutral country, just in case.

She did not leave the Ritz until very late. Madame Chanel had insisted she stay, ostensibly cleaning the suite, but in reality (Olivia suspected) providing some human company, until almost midnight. She had been rather shocked to see Chanel inject herself with morphine and grope her way into bed, sinking almost at once into a dead sleep.

There were no trams, so she took the Métro home. The carriages were almost empty. The few passengers avoided one another's eyes. Olivia slipped the little notebook from her pocket and made a quick sketch of the melancholy, chiaroscuro faces. These days, she had to remind herself to keep drawing. She had almost forgotten what it was like to call herself an artist, to be mistress of her own time, to express herself in colour and line.

Montmartre was a ghost town, many of the boarding houses empty, the windows battened and the doors stuck with paper seals, as though that would keep the Germans from requisitioning the premises.

Fabrice was waiting for her in her studio. Their domestic arrangements had settled into a routine that suited them all: Fabrice spent three nights a week at her studio, four with his mother. Twice a week they all ate together at Marie-France's house. It was, as Fabrice put it, an anarchist *ménage* with its own morality. He had brought a covered plate of food prepared by Marie-France hours earlier. He was in a state of great agitation.

'I'm ashamed to be a Frenchman,' he muttered, pacing up and down as Olivia devoured the cold food hungrily. 'You've read the reports? Our soldiers ran like rabbits. My God! How could they be so faint-hearted?'

'They were badly prepared,' Olivia said with her mouth full.

'It's more than that,' Fabrice replied. 'France is morally and spiritually bankrupt. The humiliation! Thank God my father isn't alive to witness this!' He was wringing his hands. Olivia knew that his rejection by the army had inflicted a deep wound. The night it had happened, a friend had had to bring him home in a wheelbarrow, dead drunk. But the record of his childhood tuberculosis was enough to rule him out immediately, even before the physical.

The injury to his pride had been festering for months. It had been agony for him to sit the past year out, unable to do anything but produce a torrent of newspaper articles exhorting his fellow Frenchmen to arms against the Fascist enemy. The police had eventually seized all the copies of the radical papers, and shut the presses down. He had been effectively silenced. And now, watching the mighty army of France crumple without a fight was driving him mad. For her part, she was just glad that he was a non-combatant, and not in danger of being killed or captured, but she couldn't say that to him. He didn't see it that way.

'They say the Germans are seventy-five miles from Paris,' she said, pushing the plate away at last. 'I met Raoul Nordling at work. He wants to issue me a Swedish passport.'

'You must accept. And if things get too bad' – he sat opposite her, looking at her with hollow eyes – 'you must leave France.'

'I'm not leaving you, Fabrice.'

'And I won't allow you to stay if there's danger.'

'It's quite touching, this idea of yours that I'm obedient to your whims.'

'I'm serious. You don't know what the Nazis are capable of.'

Eight

The arrival of the Germans in Paris provided a spectacle that Josée de Chambrun was eager to describe in great detail to Arletty and Antoinette d'Harcourt.

'My dears, you've never seen such discipline, such *order*. A sea of tanks, all the way up the Champs-Élysées, and not one out of line by so much as a millimetre. I doubt whether such a parade has been seen since the war chariots of the ancient Romans. And all our great monuments draped in huge German flags, red and white and black: the most extraordinary spectacle you can imagine. You would think one would feel sorrow at seeing the Tricolour hauled down and the swastika go up in its place. But no. One felt something else altogether.' She paused to stir her cocktail reflectively. The three women were sitting in the drawing room of the de Chambrun mansion, the curtains discreetly drawn; at a time like this, smart women did not drink cocktails in public. 'One felt a *thrill*, deep in one's marrow. One felt a surge of *renewal*. The sense of a new era dawning, of the old cobwebs and rubbish being swept away by a powerful new hand. And the German soldiers – imagine! They have the most beautiful blue eyes!'

Arletty and Antoinette listened in silence. The only daughter of Pierre Laval, the foremost politician of the era, and the wife of René de Chambrun, an aristocratic, French-American financier, Josée Countess de Chambrun stood at the very apex of Paris society. In 1931, at the

She took out her notebook and flipped through the pages. 'Loo these are some of the sketches I did today. This is Coco Chanel. I dre her when she wasn't looking. It's quite good, don't you think?'

'I'm not interested in Coco Chanel. I'm only interested in you.' Fabrice pushed the sketchbook aside. 'I'm worried about you.'

'I'm more worried about *you*,' she replied seriously, looking into his eyes. 'The Germans won't be very pleased with all those articles you've written about them.'

'They must take me as they find me. I can't unwrite them.'

'You're the one who should be leaving France, my darling. All your friends have.'

He shook his head. 'If you won't leave, I won't leave.'

'And if you won't leave, I won't leave.'

'I feel ashamed that you should witness my humiliation, Olivia.'

'Don't say that!'

'And I feel ashamed that you should have to humiliate yourself to the Nazis.'

'Monsieur Auzello specifically forbids any of us from being servile. When they arrive, we are supposed to treat them like any other guests.'

'But they aren't any other guests, are they? They have their heels on our necks.'

'It can't last for ever. Monsieur Auzello says——'

'Damn Monsieur Auzello,' he cut in. 'Monsieur Auzello and his lot capitulated. His words are empty.'

'He did his best,' Olivia said. 'I know how you feel, Fabrice.'

'God, I need a cigarette.'

They had both given up smoking, partly as their contribution to the war effort, partly because the price of tobacco had risen sharply. He put his head in his hands, looking stricken. She felt desperately sorry for him. There was always one thing she could do to comfort him. She took his hand.

'Come, darling,' she said gently. 'Let's go to bed.'

age of nineteen, she had switched on the first floodlight illuminations of the Statue of Liberty in New York. *Time* magazine had called her 'the most elegant Frenchwoman of our time'.

Everything in her life since then had been touched by the same magic. Now very rich, pro-Nazi and adaptable, Josée was a lively Latin beauty who rustled in silks and delighted in the Parisian arts of discovering people and putting them together.

She had scooped Arletty out of obscurity a few years earlier, charmed by the actress's acid, working-class wit, and had introduced her to all the best people. Indeed, Josée was the woman who had presented Arletty and Antoinette to one another, at an unforgettable New Year's Eve party, an introduction that had had far-reaching consequences – for better or for worse.

'Yes, my friends,' she went on, glancing from Arletty to Antoinette with her brilliant smile, 'a new day has dawned. There's no need for these long faces. We mustn't think of this moment as a defeat.' She indicated the black Chanel suit Antoinette was wearing, as though in mourning. 'It's the greatest opportunity we've ever been given. An opportunity to put things right in France.'

'To put things right?' Arletty repeated quietly.

'Yes! Oh, darling, I know you're a woman of the people, but life has detached you from the people. You belong with us now. And we have so much more in common with these Aryans than we do with the mongrel socialists and communists who've been trying to drag France down for decades.' She leaned forward, her lustrous eyes wide. 'Papa says it's inevitable that he will come to lead the new government. Of course, it's a delicate moment, and he needs to play his cards well. But he has a very good hand – and you know how clever Papa is at cards!'

'You mean he's willing to be the Nazis' stooge,' Antoinette said bitterly.

'That is not the way I would put it,' Josée retorted. 'Power is a thistle, beautiful but spiky. It has to be grasped with courage.'

'How botanical you are.'

'Papa is the only man qualified to lead France into the future. Pétain is gaga, no more than a figurehead. Hitler needs to be able to rely on someone with real experience and ability.'

'Forming a government under the Nazis is simply collaboration with the enemy.'

'Talk of collaboration is absurd, under the circumstances. France must be governed, and it must be governed by the French.'

'A velvet French glove to wrap around the iron German fist?'

Josée laid her hand on Antoinette's. 'I understand how you feel.'

'Do you?'

'You're depressed and upset. But you'll come around. You'll see things our way soon enough.'

Antoinette pulled her hand away. 'I hope not.'

'You are going to have to adapt to the new circumstances, Antoinette.'

'I don't know how you can sleep at night. At least I did my part. I didn't rush out to embrace the enemy.'

Josée smiled charmingly. 'Your little women's ambulance service? Something of a social club for ladies with certain tastes in common, wasn't it?'

Arletty, who was beginning to fear that an argument was brewing, gathered her things. '*Madame Sans-Gêne* has work to do, even if you two great ladies do not. It remains to be seen whether our new masters will allow us to finish filming. But one must have hope.'

Her farewell kiss from Josée was warm, but the countess and the duchess bade each other the most frigid of goodbyes, their lips inches away from each other's cheeks. Arletty took Antoinette's arm as they emerged from the house and walked down the street. Arletty's spanking new Packard was safely out of Paris, garaged in Lyon, so they were heading for the Métro station. 'Josée's right. You're going to have to learn to adapt, my dear,' Arletty advised her friend.

Antoinette made a gagging sound. 'I nearly vomited when she went on about the German soldiers' beautiful blue eyes.'

'I don't object to a pair of beautiful blue eyes myself.'

'Women of your class don't have the same loyalties as women of mine.'

'Thanks awfully.'

'You know it's true. You come from the revolutionary class. You're only loyal to yourself. You don't think in terms of the state, the monarchy—'

'The *monarchy*? My dear Antoinette, have you forgotten the guillotine?'

'—but Josée should know better,' Antoinette went on, ignoring her. 'It makes my gorge rise to hear people like her already picking over the bones of our poor country. After the collapse of our armed forces, it's the ultimate degradation. And how dare she sneer at our women's ambulance service!'

The women's ambulance service in question, run under the auspices of the Red Cross, had been widely accused of being a coterie of upper-class lesbians, but Arletty didn't think mentioning that would be helpful.

'Well, watch your step. Here come some of Josée's perfectly aligned war chariots.'

They stopped at the edge of the road. The vehicles in question were not tanks, but a column of German trucks, marked with the black-and-white cross of the Wehrmacht, packed full of soldiers in field-grey, holding rifles between their knees. Seeing two beautifully dressed women on the sidewalk, they started wolf-whistling. Arletty stared back impassively, but Antoinette made an obscene gesture. There was laughter, raucous but good-humoured. They could afford to be tolerant. Antoinette's gesticulation was probably the only resistance they had encountered since crossing the Marne.

Impulsively, Antoinette threw her arms around Arletty and kissed her passionately on the mouth in front of the Germans. Arletty struggled free from the feverish embrace. 'Are you mad?'

'I love you! I can't live without you!'

'Nobody is asking you to,' Arletty said angrily, hotly aware of the cat-calling soldiers. 'You don't have to make a spectacle of yourself in public!'

'They'll drive us apart,' Antoinette wailed. 'They'll take you away from me!'

For the first time, Arletty saw how glazed Antoinette's eyes were, how white her face. 'Have you started taking opium again?' she demanded.

'I need something. I can't bear this.'

'You promised you would stop!'

'How can I stop? It's all falling to pieces.'

In the middle of the convoy were trucks of another kind, open to the sky, unsheltered by canvas. These were crammed with captured French soldiers, evidently being paraded through the capital as an object lesson. Their uniforms in disarray, bareheaded and disarmed, they slumped in the wooden seats, the picture of dejection. A woman ran up beside one of the trucks, holding out a baguette. The men snatched at it eagerly, and without a word of acknowledgement, tore it apart, cramming chunks into their mouths.

Antoinette burst into tears at that. With no way of comforting her friend, Arletty stood watching the trucks that rumbled past, crowded with the gaunt soldiers who would meet nobody's eyes.

Place Vendôme was a roaring traffic jam of German armoured vehicles and staff cars, all flying the swastika on their aerials, pumping diesel fumes into the square and all but blotting out the sky above. The whole of Vendôme was cut off to civilian traffic. Rue Cambon was blocked too. The Germans had set up a barricade at the entrance to the smart, narrow street behind the Ritz, and Olivia was confronted by a German guard post when she tried to get in.

The sentry who demanded her papers was young and stern-faced, his eyes shaded by his steel helmet. Olivia looked covertly at his grey uniform, shiny boots and gleaming machine-pistol as he flipped through her passport. She was carrying the Swedish one that Raoul Nordling had issued her, which gave her surname in the original Swedish spelling, Olsson. He had taken her American passport and had locked it in the consulate safe. She would get it back if necessary, but from now on, the Swedish passport was the one she carried.

In the passport, her place of birth was given as Stockholm, her nationality as Swedish. Her heart was pounding against her ribs. It was one thing to read about the Germans in the newspapers, quite another to be faced with a real one, six feet tall and holding the power of life and death in youthful male hands glittering with blonde hairs.

The passport passed muster, and her name was written down in the sentry's ledger. But when she tried to slip into the staff entrance of the Ritz, another checkpoint awaited her. Two soldiers examined her papers thoroughly, writing her name down yet again and searching her bag. Their faces were cold and hard.

Within, all was tumult. The corridors were crowded with officers, barking commands in German or accented French, their baggage piled up in every available space. They had brought with them a particular smell, of machinery, male sweat and cologne; and they had also brought a huge logistical problem.

'Olivia, hurry.' Marie-France seized her arm and pulled her into the melee. 'They're turning out all the guests on the Vendôme side. The rooms have to be emptied and made up as soon as possible.'

'*All* of them?' Olivia gasped.

'Even Madame Chanel. Even Mrs Corrigan. We'll have to start there. Field Marshal Goering is taking her suite, and he's expected at any moment.'

For years, Laura Mae Corrigan had occupied the grandest rooms at the Ritz, the Imperial Suite, a palatial apartment with fittings to rival Versailles. The widow of a Midwestern steel magnate, she enjoyed an income said to be over a million dollars a month.

She stood now outside her quarters, a forlorn little woman with a beaky nose, weighed down with pearls. 'Please be careful with that mirror,' she was begging the two elderly men who were manoeuvring a majestic Empire console out of the doorway. 'It's awfully old.'

'Oh, Mrs Corrigan, I'm so sorry about this,' Olivia said impulsively, appalled at the chaos in the Imperial Suite.

Mrs Corrigan turned to Olivia. Her eyes were the washed-out green of a distant prairie. 'It's quite all right, dear,' she said with simple dignity. 'Only, I want them to be careful with my things.'

'I'll see to it,' Olivia promised.

In charge of the removal was a German officer in the light-grey uniform of the Luftwaffe, the German air force, who was barking commands, using a riding whip for emphasis. The remaining staff of Ritz porters consisted of old men, who were struggling with Mrs Corrigan's collection of furniture and art.

Seeing Olivia come in, the Luftwaffe officer pointed his whip at her. 'You are the chambermaid?'

'Yes, sir.'

'These apartments are filthy,' he shouted. 'Disgusting! Dust and cobwebs everywhere! Everything will have to be spotless for the Reichsmarschall. Do you understand?'

'They will be,' she replied. It was useless to point out that Mrs Corrigan had stuffed the apartment with so many bizarre objects, some of them rubbish, some priceless, that cleaning the rooms had been a nightmare.

Monsieur Auzello arrived. He had been called up in 1939, and had spent a year in the army, where it was said he had behaved heroically, and had been broken-hearted by the armistice. He had returned to the Ritz thinner and greyer, but his moustache bristled with defiance. 'What is going on here?'

The German officer swung on him. 'These men are too slow.'

'They are taking the proper care.'

The German used his whip to contemptuously flip the Great War medals pinned to one of the old men's chests. 'They are old fools. I will delegate a squad of my own men to complete the removal.'

'Quite impossible,' Monsieur Auzello replied briskly. 'I cannot permit that under any circumstances.'

The German loomed over Auzello. 'Do you know who will be taking these rooms?'

'Yes, of course,' the managing director replied. 'Reichsmarschall Goering made the reservation himself.'

High-ranking German officers were being given a ninety per cent discount at the hotel, and had their pick of the rooms. All along the corridors, similar scenes were being played out as guests were suddenly finding themselves homeless, in most cases having to lug their own suitcases out under the hard eyes of German guards.

The Luftwaffe officer's cheeks were now flushed. 'Do not take an obstructive attitude, or the consequences will be severe.'

The room had fallen silent, all activity ceasing, all eyes on the two men.

Auzello did not flinch. 'Pardon me, Monsieur, but the Reichsmarschall was most insistent that I supervise the preparation of the suite myself,' he replied in the same implacable way. 'My staff know their work. I cannot permit the intrusion of unskilled workers.' He met the German's eye squarely. 'Should something be damaged – or stolen – the Reichsmarschall will be extremely displeased. He will want to know who was responsible.'

Not for nothing had Monsieur Auzello risen to directorship of the best hotel in Paris. This cunning reply baffled the Luftwaffe officer. He slapped his palm with the whip. 'See that it is done quickly, then.'

'It will be done in good time,' Auzello replied with a bow.

The German pushed his way out. There was a silent but perceptible sigh of relief as he left. Monsieur Auzello turned to face the staff. 'The Germans have won the war,' he said in a clipped voice. 'But here in the Ritz, they are our guests, not our masters. If I catch any one of you fraternising with these invaders – or behaving in a servile fashion – I shall dismiss you instantly. Service, and nothing more! Is that understood?'

There was a murmur of assent as the director's steely eyes swept the room. 'Yes, Monsieur Auzello.'

'Our beloved France has seen worse moments than this, and France has always risen triumphant. This is only the beginning. We shall return to the battle – and we shall be victorious. In the meantime, get back to your work, and keep your hearts high.'

Faces around the room brightened. 'Yes, Monsieur Auzello!' came the reply.

'He's right about one thing,' Auzello said quietly to Olivia. 'There are cobwebs everywhere. Goering is on his way. See to it, Olivia.'

'Yes, sir.'

Single-handed – Marie-France and the few remaining chambermaids had their hands more than full – Olivia tackled the mighty task. She asked the porters to leave one of their ladders so she could reach the moulded ceilings and the chandeliers. Running a hotel of this size with a skeleton staff was exhausting for everyone concerned, including Olivia, even though she was by now hardened to the work. But by the end of the day, the magnificent apartment was reasonably clean, all poor Mrs Corrigan's effects had been removed, and the windows had been thrown open to air the rooms. Tomorrow she would make up the beds and put out towels. The Reichsmarschall had not yet arrived, but when he did, he would find his quarters at least mouse- and spider-free.

She made her way home wearily in an evening drizzle. Fabrice was in his usual volatile mood.

'Do you know who has been in Paris today?' he demanded as she was pulling off her raincoat. 'None other than Adolf Hitler himself.'

'We heard nothing about it,' Olivia said in surprise.

'I wish I'd been there.' Fabrice's eyes flashed. 'My God! If only I'd known, I'd have been waiting with a pistol in my pocket and put a bullet through his brain.'

'I'm glad you didn't,' Olivia said practically, inspecting her cold dinner. 'They'd have strung you up on the nearest lamp post.'

'If only I'd known,' he kept repeating as he paced around the table while she ate. 'My God! What an opportunity! If I'd been there with a pistol – or a knife. By God, I'd have seized him by the throat with my bare hands and choked the life out of him!'

'What good would that have done?' she demanded. 'They'd have killed half of Paris in reprisal. And somebody worse would take his place. You have to stop thinking like an anarchist, Fabrice, and start facing reality. This is not a time for being stupid.'

'We're going to start an underground newspaper, supporting the Resistance.'

'Fabrice, please don't,' Olivia said in alarm.

'We're going to set up a printing press in a cellar,' he went on, ignoring her agitation. 'We can't stay silent while they strut around Paris in their jackboots. We have to respond, even if it's with pen and ink!'

Olivia put down her knife and fork and went to him, grabbing his arms. 'Fabrice, I forbid it. It's a crazy idea. You're in enough danger as it is. If the Germans find out the things you've been writing, you'll end up in a Gestapo cellar.'

'Look around you,' he retorted. 'France is one huge concentration camp. We're all prisoners, Olivia.'

'What use are more words, Fabrice?'

His beautiful hazel eyes flashed. 'Then I'll get a gun and shoot one of their generals.'

'You know what they do in Poland,' she said urgently. Stories had been emerging from Poland of civilians being rounded up and shot in reprisal for attacks on German soldiers, of houses and villages burned to the ground to punish any sign of resistance.

'Perhaps we need something like that here to shake us up.'

'I can't believe you can even think of it! What if it's your mother they shoot, because of some stupid damned thing you cook up? Or me, for that matter?'

'Better to die free than live a slave.'

'That's empty rhetoric,' she snapped, exhausted with arguing.

'We have different ideas,' Fabrice said hotly. 'I can't lick the German boot the way you and Maman do.'

'That's a horrible thing to say,' she retorted. 'Women have fewer choices than men.'

'What does that mean?'

'It means your mother and I don't have the luxury of lounging in cafés all day, talking nonsense. We have to work and bring home food.'

'I would rather starve than eat the food you bring home.' And with that he got up and walked to the door.

'Fabrice, don't go like this,' she called after him. But he did not turn back.

Nine

She arrived at the Ritz to find the German annexation – or infestation, as Monsieur Auzello put it – almost complete. They were everywhere in the hotel, calling for champagne and hot baths, sending piles of clothing to be laundered, drinking at the famous bars, stuffing themselves on Escoffier's legendary dishes in the restaurant.

'Make the beds up in the Imperial Suite,' Marie-France said as Olivia tied on her pinafore in the cramped little room where the chambermaids dressed and ate. 'They say Goering may arrive at any minute.'

With the morning sunlight streaming in and sparkling on the crystal of the chandeliers and glowing on the polished marble, the apartment was like a beautiful stage set, waiting for the actors to arrive. Carpets and drapes were lustrous, the silk-upholstered furniture shimmering. Oil paintings of princes and princesses from past centuries looked down approvingly.

Olivia was especially fond of one of the bedrooms, which had been modelled on that of Marie Antoinette at Versailles. She thought it enchanting, with its pink crystal chandelier hanging low over the little gilt bed draped with heavily embroidered curtains.

As she made up the bed, she wondered what Fabrice was doing. Her lectures to him about not committing any folly had not been well-received. What she really wanted him to do, with prices rising and food already becoming scarce, was to find a job, any job that would bring in some extra money.

Loud male laughter interrupted her reverie. Coming into the suite was a group of German officers, headed by a large figure in a peaked cap. She realised that this could only be Hermann Goering. A hard-faced soldier with a machine-pistol shoved her unceremoniously into a corner.

Goering and his entourage strolled through the suite. Goering's voice was by far the loudest, his laughter ringing out regularly. She knew enough German to understand his exclamations of '*Schön!*' and '*Wunderbar!*' as he inspected the fittings, paintings and frescoed ceilings.

He came into the Marie Antoinette suite, his large ruddy-cheeked face lighting up as he looked around. '*Wunderschön,*' he sighed, '*absolut bezaubernd.*'

Olivia stood stock-still in her corner, hardly daring to breathe as the Reichsmarschall, the second most powerful man in the Nazi hierarchy, looked around. Monsieur Auzello was with him. The Reichsmarschall was a tall, extremely fat man with a rather high quacking voice.

Suddenly, he noticed Olivia. 'Oh, what a beautiful Aryan girl,' he said in unexpectedly good French. He took off his peaked cap, tossing it on to the bed, and came over to Olivia, smoothing back his sandy hair. A pair of bright blue-green eyes stared down at her greedily, and a laughing mouth, like the entrance to a funfair, opened wide. 'What's your name?'

'Olivia Olsen,' she stammered.

His eyebrows rose. 'Swedish?'

'Y-yes, sir.'

He turned triumphantly to the officers who had gathered around him to inspect this curiosity. 'You see? I knew I could not be mistaken!' He turned back to her. 'The Nordic blood is instantly recognisable. It is pure gold. And the purest Aryan blood is inevitably found in Sweden.' And he followed this with a rattle of Swedish.

Olivia's mind froze. Like everyone in her family, she spoke Swedish. It had been a compulsory subject at the Swedish American school, where they had read the novels of Selma Lagerlöf year after year. But all she felt now was ice running down her spine. Her mouth opened without making a sound. Goering stared at her expectantly. Suddenly her brain kicked into action, and she realised he had merely asked her how old she was.

'Twenty-three, *min herre*,' she heard herself say faintly in the same language.

'And where do you come from?'

She recalled her new passport. 'Stockholm.'

He half-closed his eyes and flared his nostrils, as though inhaling some rare perfume. 'Unmistakeable,' he murmured. 'How long have you worked here?'

'A year.'

'We shall see you promoted to director yet.' A large gloved hand descended on her shoulder. 'You are responsible for these rooms?' he asked.

Thankfully, the Swedish words were flowing to her brain now. 'I and the other chambermaids, sir.'

'No, no, no,' he said, wagging his finger in her face. 'I will have no other chambermaids. You alone, Olivia Olsen. Now. Show me the bathroom.'

Olivia took him to it, her legs feeling like jelly. There was only one bathroom in the suite, beautifully panelled in walnut. However, the Reichsmarschall was unimpressed. He glared at the bath. 'Absurdly small. This will never do.' He turned to Monsieur Auzello, who was hovering anxiously on his other side. 'This room falls far short of the others.'

'But – but, Monsieur—'

'It will have to be completely renovated,' he trumpeted. 'I shall arrange for a bath of the correct proportions to be delivered. You will see to it.'

Auzello sighed. 'Of course.'

Goering's fingers were gently kneading Olivia's shoulder. 'My first wife was Swedish,' he said in a dreamy voice, quite unlike the one he had just used. 'My beloved Carin. She, too, was born in Stockholm. You have heard of her, of course.'

'Of course,' Olivia replied, alarmed that he would probe her for more details. She had no idea what he was talking about.

'You remind me a great deal of her,' he went on. 'In her youth, of course. Not at the end. No, not at the end.' His voice tailed away. He stared at the inadequate bath for a while, lost in thought, then swung round to his entourage. 'Lunch, gentlemen! The table calls!'

The generals trooped out, leaving Olivia feeling as limp as a piece of boiled macaroni. Auzello hissed in her ear, 'What's wrong with you! Don't you know how to smile?'

'Sorry?'

'Smile at him! You look like you've swallowed a toad!'

'He frightens me.'

'He frightens everybody,' Auzello snapped. 'Get the rooms ready. He's sleeping here, one night at least.'

'Yes, Monsieur Auzello.'

'And make sure you are the only one who is found in here. We must not displease him in any way. See that he has everything he wants.' He hurried after his Teutonic guests.

Shaken by the entire episode, Olivia finished the room. A suite of this size was generally done by at least two, and preferably three maids. She was compelled to whizz around like something in a cartoon to get everything even half-done. While she worked, huge bouquets of flowers were brought in, and the drinks cabinet was stocked with a giddy collection of liqueurs and spirits.

Marie-France hurried in. 'Are you coping?'

'Just about,' Olivia panted.

'I hear Goering pinched your cheek.'

'At least he didn't shoot me.'

'Keep it that way,' Marie-France advised as she flew off.

⁂

Having missed a month hadn't concerned Olivia greatly, but when the second month was underway, with no sign of her period, she could no longer ignore the high probability that she was going to have a baby.

She'd anticipated that this day would eventually come, and had discussed it with Fabrice from time to time. Now that it was here her feelings were a lot more powerful than she had anticipated. There was a kind of joy, but it was overshadowed with apprehension.

They had taken few, if any, precautions. Fabrice was not opposed to the idea of children, only bored by what he called the outdated bourgeois concept of marriage. But as Olivia lifted her dress and stared at the as yet flat span of her stomach, she realised that they had done something very serious indeed.

They had been far too casual. Love and desire had blinded them to reality.

This was not a good world to bring a new life into. There was danger everywhere. Though she and Fabrice had not been on good terms lately, she adored the father of her child. However, he would have to become more responsible if they were to all survive as a family. He could no longer risk his own life, because his life now belonged not only to her, but to the child they had created.

She knew that over the past weeks he had been secretly writing anti-Nazi pamphlets. These, badly printed on an underground press, were furtively circulated around Paris. They looked pathetically amateur. The black ink came off on your fingers, which was how she knew what he was doing: Fabrice's hands and fingers were constantly stained black.

She didn't believe they even had any effect. The high-flown rhetoric in them was absurd when matched against German steel; but that

95

didn't stop the Nazis from taking them seriously. They hunted down the authors of such publications relentlessly and dealt with them ruthlessly.

Fabrice could no longer be involved in this kind of resistance, no matter how strongly he felt about the Nazis. Her baby was going to need a father. And nothing was more important than that.

Wednesday was the night of the week she had dinner with Marie-France and Fabrice at their house, and she didn't want to tell him the news in front of Marie-France. She would have to keep her counsel until after the meal, when they were alone.

The meal was better than usual. Meat had become very scarce in the past months and had almost vanished from the butchers' stalls. Marie-France, with her long years of service at the hotel, was able to acquire leftovers from the kitchen. Tonight she had brought home half a chicken and a bag of mandarins and peaches. She and Olivia ate the delicious scraps hungrily, but Fabrice seemed to have no appetite.

'Have something, chérie,' his mother urged.

'I don't want anything that's been touched by the Nazis,' he said.

Marie-France snorted. 'Compared to what others are eating in Paris tonight, this is a feast, my son.'

'It's tainted meat.'

'It came from the soil of France and it was prepared by French hands. Wasting it is a sin.'

But he refused to be tempted, and sat smoking, with his chair half-turned away from the table.

At the end of the meal there was a special treat – the last inch of a bottle of cognac, slipped into Marie-France's bag by a friendly sommelier. They shared this in tiny glasses while Olivia and Fabrice played a game of backgammon. Olivia felt the alcohol ease her anxiety, at least temporarily. They had settled into a kind of truce.

'Olivia is a favourite with the top guests,' Marie-France told Fabrice proudly. 'They all insist on her. Thank God for her strong back and clear head. I don't know what we'd do without her – all the others are so stupid, or so old. The guests want to see a pretty face and a ready smile, and there are very few of either around these days. Goering took a shine to her today.'

Fabrice looked up sharply. 'Goering is at the Ritz?'

'Yes,' Olivia said, 'and no, I'm not going to put a bomb under his pillow.'

'What did he say to you?' Fabrice demanded.

'He said I reminded him of his first wife.'

Fabrice threw up his hands. 'My God. The holy patron saint of the Nazis.'

'Was she anything like me?'

'There's a superficial resemblance, I suppose. She and Goering were part of Hitler's innermost circle. She died young, and the whole of Germany went into mourning. Her life story sold a million copies. Goering's built a huge temple in the woods, called Carinhall, and had her buried there.'

'He got quite sentimental when he mentioned her name.'

'Don't forget, his sentimental bombs obliterated Warsaw,' Fabrice retorted, 'his sentimental Stukas strafed our troops, and anyone who disagrees with him is herded into his sentimental concentration camps.'

It was getting late. Part of the mutual agreement they had all made was that she would not sleep with Fabrice under Marie-France's roof, and it was time she made her way back to her attic. The Germans had imposed a curfew between nine in the evening and five in the morning, and as they made their way back to her home the streets were empty but for a pair of gendarmes, who stopped them to check their papers. The French police were already cooperating fully with the German occupiers, under the terms of the armistice. Fabrice submitted sullenly to having his papers inspected and his pockets searched.

'Bastards,' he muttered as they were allowed to move on. 'They're no better than Nazis themselves.'

They reached her apartment and went upstairs together. She made him sit on the bed beside her and took both his hands in hers. She looked into his eyes.

'My darling, I have something to tell you.'

He had been irritable all evening, but now he smiled. 'We're going to have a baby.'

'How did you know?' she asked in surprise.

'I was joking.'

'I wasn't.'

His smile faded. 'When women say "Darling, I have something to tell you" in novels, it always means they're pregnant. So I thought—'

'This isn't a novel. And I am pregnant.'

He stared at her for a moment. Then a look of delight spread across his face. 'You're not teasing me?'

'Fabrice! Of course not.'

He hugged her tight. 'This is the best news in the world. Why, it changes everything!' He drew back with shining eyes. 'I feel like a new man!'

Olivia seized her opportunity. 'It *does* change everything, my dear – and you *will* have to be a new man. You can't keep on with your underground newspaper. If the Nazis caught you, you'd be sent to a concentration camp. Or worse. And you have more than yourself to think of now.'

For a moment, she thought he was going to argue. His forehead creased into a frown. Then he nodded slowly. 'You're right, of course.'

She felt relief flood through her. 'So you'll give up your writing? You won't publish any more pamphlets?'

He twisted his shoulders restlessly, then laughed. 'You have my word, Olivia. I'll even get a proper job and start bringing home some real bacon.'

A lump rose in her throat. She looked down at his hands, with their oily stains of printer's ink. She felt a huge love for this man who was the father of the child inside her womb. 'I know how hard it's been for you,' she said in a low voice. 'I know you've found it hard to bear. I'm sorry for the things I said. But perhaps this is the best thing that could have happened. Maybe this is what we both needed. A new start. New hope.'

'Yes!' He, too, was on the brink of tears now. 'Does it mean we can't make love any more?'

'No,' Olivia said, putting her arms around his neck and drawing him close to her, 'it doesn't.'

☀

The Ritz was now completely full. Guests who had been unceremoniously ejected from the Vendôme side of the hotel had scrambled for any remaining rooms on the Cambon side. Germans had entirely occupied the Vendôme side, which had turned into a kind of officers' club for senior Luftwaffe staff. With little to do but administer a conquered city, these air force officers spent their time eating, drinking, shopping (the franc was so heavily devalued against the Reichsmark that the most expensive luxuries were affordable to them) and conducting alliances with any Frenchwomen willing to cooperate.

The latter – some hurrying along, shamefaced, some boldly applying fresh lipstick – were a feature of early mornings for Olivia. She passed several of them in the corridors this morning as they made their way out of the Ritz. She greeted them all courteously. She did not feel it her place to judge anybody.

The memory of last night's lovemaking warmed her. Fabrice had been so tender with her. And now that he'd agreed to give up the anti-German pamphlets and get proper work, she felt buoyant again. Times were hard, but there was a future somewhere ahead.

They still hadn't told Marie-France. She would go to a doctor first, and get confirmation, before they broke the news. Then they would celebrate.

The back end of the hotel was bustling with preparations for breakfast. The corridors were rattling with harassed waiters pushing trolleys of coffee and pastries, cursing under their breath as they got in each other's way and occasionally ran their wheels over the gleaming boots of the soldiers who stood guard outside certain rooms.

'It's not as bad as it looks,' Marie-France told Olivia in the dressing room. 'Some of them have brought valets to take care of their uniforms. That takes some of the work off us.'

Monsieur Auzello poked his head round the door. 'Goering's asked to be woken at seven thirty,' he said. 'They'll have his trolley ready at seven twenty-five. You'll go in with the waiter, Olivia. For God's sake, remember to smile.'

Olivia bared her teeth.

There were four armed guards outside the entrance to the Imperial Suite. One of them searched the elderly waiter's trolley carefully, lifting the silver domes on the plates of food, and rifling through the piles of newspapers, as though he might have concealed a dagger among them.

They were finally admitted. The waiter wheeled the trolley arthritically through the darkened apartment, navigating the piles of luggage that stood everywhere, while Olivia pulled the drapes open. Of all the bedrooms in the suite, Goering had chosen the Marie Antoinette. As she opened the curtains on place Vendôme, he sat up, a large figure in the dainty little bed, wearing a mauve silk bedjacket. He was evidently wide awake, his ruddy cheeks freshly shaved and powdered, his pale eyes gleaming.

He pointed a meaty finger at the waiter. 'Get that disgusting old skeleton out of here.' As the wretched old man fled, he went on, 'In the mornings I like to have women about me. Plenty of time for men later in the day. What have you brought me, my dear?' he demanded greedily.

She pushed the trolley to his side. 'There's coffee, sweet and savoury rolls, pastries, ham, sausage, pâté, croissants, cheeses, preserves, fresh fruit—'

'Very well, very well.' He rolled his bulk to one side, making the bed creak plaintively, and began laying the dishes all around him on the exquisitely stitched coverlet. 'Put that painting on the chair, where I can see it.'

Olivia turned. In the light of day, she saw that there were five or six paintings propped against pieces of furniture. The works were superb, Old Masters of the highest quality. The Reichsmarschall had spent a busy twenty-four hours since she had last set eyes on him.

The painting he was indicating now was an oil study of a child, whose vividly alive face peered out of a seventeenth-century lace collar. As Olivia picked it up in obedience to Goering's command, she gasped out loud.

'It's a Rubens! A portrait of one of his daughters!'

'Clara Serena,' Goering said with delight. 'So you know something about painting!'

'I've studied a little,' she said.

He took a great bite of his roll and a gulp of coffee, his jaws masticating with energy. His eyes twinkled. 'What do you think of my taste?'

She surveyed the haul of paintings, dumbfounded. 'They're wonderful. These must have come from some of the finest private collections in Paris. I've never seen them in the galleries.'

'We'll get to the galleries later,' he said. 'One step at a time, my dear Olivia.' He waved a croissant at her. 'So you love beautiful things? Of course you do. The superior soul turns to beauty as a flower turns to light.' He grabbed the newspapers and sorted through the pile, reading swiftly, his eyes darting across the headlines with sharp intelligence. 'These democratic rags will be taken off the streets,' he said, tossing an issue aside contemptuously.

While he read, Olivia moved quietly around the room, moving the paintings to less precarious positions, folding the clothes he had carelessly discarded on the floor. The telephone at his bedside rang several times. The resulting conversations were short and brusque until the last, which was extended. From the repetitions of '*Mein Führer*', Olivia realised he was talking to Hitler.

A secretary came in, followed by a number of officers, until the apartment was crowded with uniformed figures. Judging that Goering had finished with his breakfast, Olivia quietly loaded the trolley with the remnants and pushed it through the throng. She was covertly studying the dishes, wondering what she could pilfer to take home, when Goering's voice trumpeted after her. 'Don't forget! I want nobody else working in this room!'

Seeing a dozen hard-eyed Germanic faces turn her way in surprise, Olivia tucked her head down as she made a rapid exit.

Unrelenting work drove all thoughts from Olivia's head through the remainder of the day. There was no time for a rest or a bite to eat; all that was required were a strong back and strong arms. But shortly before knocking-off time, she met Marie-France, already dressed, running down the stairs with a white face.

'What's the matter?' Olivia asked, alarmed by her expression.

'Fabrice has been arrested,' Marie-France said in a low voice. She seemed to have aged ten years in a moment. 'I'm going to the police station.'

Olivia was already unfastening her pinafore. 'I'll come with you.'

Marie-France stopped her. 'No. Finish your work and go to your studio. Wait for me there. Don't say anything to anyone.' She hurried away down the stairs.

Olivia felt as though the walls had fallen in on her. She stood stunned on the grand staircase, unable to think for a while, hoping this was a nightmare from which she would awaken. She felt a deep ache fill her womb, where her unborn child was growing. They should have fled from Paris like everyone else, she thought dazedly. They should have buried themselves deep in the country, in some obscure village where nobody could find them, and kept a few hens and grown a few potatoes until this was all over.

But perhaps it would never be over, and perhaps there was nowhere one could hide from the hard-faced men with the hard eyes who had taken possession of France.

Ten

'The issue of the Jews,' Otto Abetz said, signalling his staff for another tray of champagne, 'is a delicate one, but one that must be resolved quickly. Don't you agree?'

Arletty accepted the crystal flute that was offered her. 'Resolved in what way?' she asked expressionlessly.

Abetz, the Nazi ambassador to France, was in full military uniform for this gala occasion, which was being hosted at the German embassy. Behind him a huge floral display in red and white roses formed a giant swastika. Despite the warm night outside, the air within was refreshed by the carved ice swans that held caviar and other delicacies. Artfully concealed fans blew on these gastronomic works of art, conveying cool air, together with a certain fishy smell, around the crowded room.

Ambassador Abetz himself had a cold, arrogant face with bulging pale eyes. 'You cannot be unaware,' he replied, 'that the French cinema has been entirely infiltrated by Jews. They own the studios, they direct the films, in short, they control everything.'

'You know yourself it's true, Arletty,' Coco Chanel said. She could hardly fail to be here tonight. The German embassy was full of French men and women from the highest levels of society: aristocrats, entertainers, artists, financiers. 'The Jews run the show.'

'Are you proposing to send our best film producers to a concentration camp?' Arletty asked.

Abetz's voluptuous mouth curled in an indulgent smile. 'We cannot tolerate things as they stand. What we propose is the revitalisation of the French film industry through a new, Aryan film company. It is called Continental. It will report directly to Reich minister Joseph Goebbels. We will make several films a year for the domestic market.'

'Just like that,' Arletty said dryly.

'Just like that. We Germans do things *just like that*, as you may have noticed.' There was a burst of male laughter. 'But it is our intention to steer away from the depressing – and may I say sordid – subjects that have been chosen by French directors of late.' He smiled, showing tombstone teeth. 'We will be concentrating on what the public like best: light comedies, farces and musicals.'

Arletty's voice was harsh. 'I have spent the past fifteen years playing light comedies, farces and musicals. I don't intend to go back to all that.'

'We are putting together an offer, Mam'selle Arletty, which we hope you will find appealing. Five films for Continental, with guaranteed top billing and full artistic control, for a fee of two and a half million francs.'

There was a silence. Chanel watched Arletty's face avidly, but it was masklike. Two and a half million was an unheard-of sum. But Arletty's quick mind was assessing the offer. The Nazis didn't want Arletty the cynical, free spirit of *Le Jour se Lève*: they wanted a tame Arletty, simpering and flirting in shallow comedies, designed to take the audience's mind off the realities of German occupation. An Arletty who was not dangerous, or common, or sexually volatile, or any of the things she really was.

And after five films of that sort, everybody would have quite forgotten the smouldering alley cat of *Le Jour se Lève*. She would be a spayed tabby, sleek, clawless and no danger to anyone.

And that was how they wanted the French cinema to be. Sleek, clawless and no danger to anyone. She kept her expression noncommittal. 'Let me think about it.'

'Don't think too long,' Ambassador Abetz said with a thin smile. 'The clock is ticking.' His eyes swept up and down Arletty's slim figure, clad in a mint-green silk evening gown. 'And no one stays young for ever.'

This was a veiled insult – Arletty had turned forty-two in May – but also a threat. If she didn't take this carrot, the stick would be that she would get no other work. The Nazis were putting a stranglehold on film production. Nothing was going to be done without their approval. And those of whom they did not approve would end up unemployed, or worse.

A string orchestra had been playing popular pieces of Mozart and Haydn. It now launched into a Strauss waltz. A few couples, evidently chosen for their elegance, glided on to the dance floor. Everyone turned to watch them.

Arletty took advantage of this distraction to excuse herself from the group and walk away. Chanel came after her, taking her arm.

'You could have shown more enthusiasm. They're offering to make you very rich.'

'I know what they're offering to make me.'

'They like you.'

'Well, I don't like them. *Sordid?*'

Chanel's monkey face lit up with amusement. 'You can't deny that you've played some rather sleazy roles, my dear.'

'That's who I am. I'm sleazy and sordid, and French to the bone.'

'Don't you know how lucky you are? You'll have it all – money, status, all the star roles.' She gestured at the bright, crowded room. 'Look at these people. They've all accepted what the Nazis are offering.'

'I see a lot of geese with the feeding tube stuffed so far down their throats they're unable to vomit.'

'Do you mean me? Do I look miserable?' Chanel was wearing a Seville-inspired ensemble, all polka dots, ruffles and black lace. Since Franco's victory in Spain, supported by Hitler, everything Iberian was very fashionable among the Nazi elite. She put her lipsticked mouth against Arletty's ear. 'And you'll have something even more precious: *protection*. We're inside the magic circle. You don't want to be outside the magic circle. Outside the magic circle, the wind blows cold. One could even freeze to death. But I don't see your friend the Duchess here tonight.'

'If you think she'd set foot in this place, you don't know Antoinette.'

'She's very foolish to offend the Germans at this point.'

'She'll offend the Germans at any point, I assure you.'

'Are you still so close?'

'She's my best friend.'

Chanel's dark eyes looked into Arletty's, her pupils dilated by naughtiness, or perhaps something more. 'I love to think of you together, getting up to all sorts of mischief. It makes me feel quite funny inside.'

'You're a voyeur.'

'I like a place in the front row. She is my favourite client. And you are my favourite actress.'

'How kind of you,' Arletty replied dryly.

She was unable to leave before the end of the reception, which was at two in the morning. By then, many of the guests were extremely drunk, the women dishevelled, the men louche. The ice swans had melted into shapeless monsters, their contents mangled.

The Germans had provided a chauffeur-driven Mercedes, which took her back to the Lancaster, where she was staying for the time being. The gleaming official vehicle, with its swastika pennants, passed unchallenged through the checkpoints, defying the curfew. Arletty stared out of the window at a beautiful, lifeless city, whose outlines were silvered by a bright full moon.

The hotel was smart yet discreet, situated just off the Champs-Elysées. Her high heels echoed in the empty marble lobby. When she went to collect her room key at the desk, where the elderly night porter was fast asleep, it was missing from the hook. She knew who would be waiting for her in the room.

Antoinette d'Harcourt was sitting on the balcony, a cigarette in one hand and a glass of brandy – evidently not her first – in the other.

'What are you doing out here?' Arletty asked.

'Looking at my country,' Antoinette said in a thick voice, indicating the sky.

'The moon?'

'I moved there when they took my other country away. I saw you arrive. Nice German car. Nice German flag on the hood. Did you have a nice German time?'

'You should have been there,' Arletty said, taking off her shawl. 'Your absence was noted.'

'The women of my family embroidered the Bayeux tapestry.' She gulped at the brandy. 'We were dukes of Harcourt when these Huns were eating acorns in the forest.'

'So you've told me,' Arletty replied. 'The situation has changed somewhat since then.'

'But I have not.' Antoinette had the bottle of cognac at her side. She slopped three fingers of the spirit into a glass and held it out to Arletty. 'Have some disinfectant.'

Arletty noted the blackened opium pipe next to the bottle but didn't comment. She took the chair next to Antoinette and accepted the drink. 'The Germans want me to make five films for them. Half a million per movie and full artistic control.'

'After Judas took the silver, he hanged himself and his bowels burst out.'

'It's not quite the same thing.'

'You can see the thing any way you want.'

'I didn't say I was going to accept.' Arletty drank. 'Don't be sad. You used to love life, Antoinette.'

'It's not life I love, it's you.'

'But you never laugh any more.'

'A spring is broken in the music box.'

Arletty inhaled the fiery bouquet of the cognac. 'Chanel was there tonight. She says that if we don't join the magic circle, we won't have any protection.'

'Chanel is a collaborator. Someone's going to put a bullet in her one of these days.'

Arletty drained the glass, giving up further attempts at discussion. 'I'm going to bed.'

She went into the room, undressed, took off her make-up, and got under the blankets. After a while, Antoinette followed. She got into bed beside Arletty, fully clothed. Arletty could tell she had been crying. They did not touch one another; to Arletty's relief, Antoinette did not want to make love, and was soon asleep, wet sobs mingling with her snores.

❀

Olivia heard the creak of the stairs at three a.m. and darted out of her studio. It was Marie-France. Olivia had been praying Fabrice would be with his mother, but Marie-France was alone. She was exhausted, and couldn't speak at first, just sat in the chair that Olivia gave her, breathing unsteadily and drinking from a cup of water.

'I didn't see him,' she said at last. 'They wouldn't let me, though I waited for hours. And then they said the Gestapo have taken him.'

Olivia felt her guts twist into painful knots. 'The Gestapo!' Her legs wouldn't support her any longer. She sank into the chair opposite Marie-France. 'Is it about his writing?'

Marie-France nodded. 'They raided the printing press. One of his friends betrayed him.' Marie-France's face, usually plump and round, was haggard. 'When they caught him, they found the ink on his fingers.'

Olivia put her hand to her mouth in horror. 'Oh God.'

Marie-France had run out of words. Olivia put her arms around her, and the two women clung together. 'They'll see that he's harmless,' Olivia said at last, making it a prayer. 'They'll see that he's just young, with no malice towards anyone.'

'That's what the sergeant at the police station said. I'll go to the Gestapo headquarters tomorrow and see what I can do.'

'I was dreading that this would happen.'

'So was I,' Marie-France said wearily. She pressed the heels of her hands into her eyes. 'I have to sleep, Olivia. It's still curfew. I only got here because one of the gendarmes walked with me. Can I sleep on the floor?'

'Don't be silly. We'll share the bed.'

They lay beside each other in the dark, each occupied with her own thoughts. Since the Occupation, Montmartre had been a ghost town at night, the silence only broken by the barking of dogs abandoned by owners who had fled Paris. The full moon tonight was making them howl incessantly. It sounded to Olivia like the lamenting of lost souls.

There was little sleep for either of them. They arose, silent and drawn, at four-thirty and prepared to go out, Olivia to work, Marie-France to Gestapo headquarters. Olivia made coffee on the spirit stove. Sugar had vanished from the shops since the arrival of the Germans, as had milk, and the 'coffee' was made from burned acorns, but it was all they had.

On the stroke of five a.m. they hurried out of the house to be sure of getting a place in the lines for the trams. The light of day seemed cruel, glowing on the swastika flags that hung everywhere in the occupied city, like bloody bandages on a casualty.

She parted from Marie-France in the street. There were black shadows around Marie-France's swollen lids. Her lips were dry and cracked.

She seemed to be dying in front of Olivia's eyes, and Olivia knew no way of consoling her.

She suddenly felt that her whole adventure in France had been an adventure up to this point, an adventure she hadn't taken very seriously, but which had all the while been very serious indeed, without her realising.

She and Fabrice had both been playing at a game of life, a game of love. But now the game had ended, and his life hung by a thread, and she was pregnant with his child. She felt as though youth were melting away from her, along with those hazy dreams she'd lost herself in, while real life was going on just beyond their little backwater.

She stood in the crowded tram, dread curled like a snake at the pit of her belly. She could only imagine what Marie-France was going through. Hoping for pity from the Gestapo was futile. Yet that was exactly what she was praying for – a glimmer of pity, a shred of understanding that a spirited young man might want to express his feelings when his pride had been trampled. Then she recalled the things Fabrice had said in his articles – calling patriotic French men and women to arms, urging them to resist the Nazis by all means. She felt sicker than ever.

She thought of Goering's laughing mouth, the jolly face like a carnival mask. Had he really taken to her enough to do something for Fabrice? She recalled Fabrice's words about Goering's concentration camps. If she could arouse a flicker of interest in him, it might save Fabrice.

But bitter disappointment awaited her at the Ritz. Goering had departed for Germany in the night. When she went into the Imperial Suite, it was full of workmen installing a new giant-sized bath and connecting extra telephone lines. There was no recourse there.

She considered speaking to Monsieur Auzello, but rejected that course. There was only one person with sufficient authority to possibly help.

Madame Marie-Louise Ritz, now in her early seventies, and a widow since 1918, was a figure whom Olivia had often seen but never spoken to. Since her husband's death twenty-two years earlier, Madame Ritz had been the owner of the hotel. Severely clad in black, invariably hatted and gloved, she was a small, formidable presence seen in the dining room or the salons, treated with the utmost deference by the staff. She was spoken of as exacting, even severe, and her displeasure was the greatest misfortune that could befall anyone who worked in the hotel; but Olivia had never heard her say a word to anyone. Her instructions were delivered to Monsieur Auzello in her private apartment at the top of the hotel, under the mansard roof, and percolated down from there.

Since the arrival of the Nazis, however, Madame Ritz had not been seen at all. Nowadays, she kept to her own quarters. What she thought of the new guests who paid the derisory rate of twenty-five francs a day and lived like kings, nobody knew. She had been persuaded to keep the hotel open, and open it certainly was, but she no longer made a daily passage through the public areas, her sharp eyes seeing everything.

Olivia now hurried up the stairs to the fourth floor, her heart in her mouth. She made her way to the door of Madame Ritz's apartment, and knocked. The knock was answered by a barrage of furious yapping from within; and when the door was opened, two small bristly dogs shot out, snapping at Olivia's ankles and making her skip.

'What is it?' a dour-faced woman in the uniform of a maid asked.

'I have to see Madame Ritz,' Olivia blurted out.

The woman looked her up and down disdainfully. 'If you have some difficulty with work, speak to Monsieur Auzello.' She began to close the door.

'This is a personal matter,' Olivia pleaded. 'And it's terribly urgent.'

Something in her face and voice made the woman pause.

'Who is it, Emilie?' a querulous voice asked from inside the apartment.

'One of the chambermaids. She says it's urgent.'

'Well, let her come in.'

Grudgingly, the maid admitted Olivia. She entered the apartment with the dogs nipping at her legs.

In contrast to the gilt and velvet of the hotel, the apartment was unexpectedly homely. It was crowded with small pieces of furniture, on each of which stood collections of German and oriental china figurines. The long row of windows opened on to a terrace, which was so full of pot plants that the world beyond could hardly be seen. It was hot up here, the air thick with a vegetable smell from the forest of greenery.

Madame Ritz herself was seated at a little desk, with a pen in one hand. As Olivia approached, she capped the pen and uttered a command. To Olivia's relief, the dogs stopped their assault on her ankles. One hopped into Madame Ritz's lap and the other retreated under her chair, from where it bared its teeth at Olivia like a miniature dragon.

'You are the American girl,' Madame Ritz said, not making it a question. Olivia nodded, surprised that the old lady, who had never, to her knowledge, even glanced her way, should know who she was, and her true nationality.

'Yes, Madame.'

'Well?' Madame Ritz asked shortly.

Olivia's story burst out of her. She was trying not to break down in front of the severe, black-clad presence. Madame Ritz's eyes watched her shrewdly. It did not take long to explain the situation.

'And what is it you are asking me to do?'

'To speak to the German authorities, Madame. Fabrice isn't just my fiancé, he's Marie-France Darnell's son, and Marie-France has worked for you for twenty years. She's at the Gestapo headquarters at this moment—'

'I know where Marie-France is at this moment.'

'And what Fabrice did was harmless—'

'I know what Fabrice did,' Madame Ritz cut in, 'and I very much doubt whether the Gestapo will see it as harmless.' She spoke with the throaty accent of Alsace. 'They shoot people for less.'

'Can't you speak to them?' Olivia pleaded.

One of the little dogs had started growling, aroused by the raw emotion in Olivia's voice. Madame Ritz quieted it with a wrinkled hand on which a single ruby ring gleamed. 'I have already spoken to them. To be frank with you, my words had less to do with saving your foolish young friend than with preventing you and Marie-France from arrest – and from losing your jobs.'

Olivia was taken aback. 'I don't care about my job! I would give up anything to save Fabrice.'

'It is not very wise,' Madame Ritz snapped, 'to tell your employer that you don't care about your job.'

Olivia tried to master her ragged breathing. 'I'm sorry. I'm very grateful to have work. And I have been a good worker, Madame Ritz.'

The white head inclined in acknowledgement of that. 'But your country may soon be at war with Germany. Hiding behind a Swedish passport may not save you. You should have left Paris long ago.'

'I love Fabrice.'

Madame Ritz studied Olivia in silence for a while, stroking the wiry coat of her dog. 'You young people,' she said at last. 'You make a game of life, skipping on the edge of the cliff. And when the knees are broken and bleeding, you call for someone to pick you up and tell you everything will be all right.'

'We've both been stupid. I promise that we'll take everything a lot more seriously from now on.'

'You mean, if your young man emerges from this with his hide intact. But I fear that he may not emerge from this with his hide intact, and you should prepare yourself for that eventuality.'

'Madame Ritz!'

'I repeat, I have said what I could say, and have done what I could do. It is now time for you to think of your own hide, Olivia.'

The use of her first name was a dismissal. Madame Ritz put her little dog on the floor. Both animals began yapping again and making little rushes at Olivia's ankles. She had no option but to curtsey to her employer and make a retreat, the dogs becoming bolder as she approached the door, until they had driven her into the corridor. The door closed firmly in her face.

As she went back down the stairs, crying, she encountered Monsieur Auzello making his way up. He put a hand on her shoulder. 'She knows everything that happens in this hotel,' he said quietly. 'She will do what she can. The best thing you can do now is get on with your work.'

Olivia nodded and tried to swallow the great, cold stone that filled her chest.

Eleven

At fifty-seven, Coco Chanel had conquered yet another of the powerful and worldly men she collected.

She had met him in the south of France during her tedious exile. His name was Baron Hans Günther von Dincklage, but his friends called him Spatz. He'd flattered her with his eyes and words, and she had responded without coquettishness. It had been swift. Each had seen in the other something to be desired and had wanted to seize it without delay. Neither of them was young any longer. Neither enjoyed deferring satisfaction. Within a week, Spatz had been in her bed, where his assiduous attention to her pleasure had confirmed her initial impression that he was someone who belonged in her life.

Handsome, cultured, aristocratic, von Dincklage knew how to dress, how to order a meal in a good restaurant, how to make love. He spoke several languages fluently. She found him charming in the extreme. His fund of funny stories and fascinating anecdotes made him excellent company. He was, in short, the perfect companion.

She was not blind, on the other hand, to the fact that Spatz had been a German secret agent ever since 1918, when he had returned from the Russian front a decorated Hussar; nor that he was a committed Nazi, completely devoted to Adolf Hitler's vision of a German-dominated Europe; nor that he was a personal friend of Joseph Goebbels and was now a senior propaganda officer.

Coco was certainly not ashamed of those things. On the contrary. They were considerable advantages. The fact that his requirement to be associated with the highest echelons of French society dovetailed with her requirement to be shielded from the discomforts of the Occupation seemed to her the happiest of coincidences. In times like these a woman needed such a shining knight at her side.

And Spatz von Dincklage's power was effortless. It took no more than a telephone call to the German High Command in Paris to arrange her return to the hotel she loved.

The old apartment on place Vendôme, of course, was no longer available, being occupied by General von Stülpnagel. But Spatz secured her a large suite on the Cambon side, which was reserved for French friends of the Nazi regime. The rooms were really very charming, quiet and convenient.

The suite was discreet too. Here, one could show oneself gracious to the new arrivals, and arrange charming little candlelit suppers for influential Nazis without being seen by the common people of Paris, who might not sympathise with such overtures to the conquerors – especially since the abundant food available to occupants of the Ritz's 'Guest Section' would have raised the eyebrows of those who were facing daily hunger.

'I think we'll begin with six dozen oysters,' Coco said to the chef who was standing obsequiously by. Spatz adored them, and they had an impressive effect on his libido.

'We have several barrels fresh from Arcachon, Madame. They are excellent.'

'And then, an *escalope de foie gras* with some fresh green peas *velouté*.'

'Yes, Madame.'

Coco tapped her slim gold pen against her false teeth. 'What about a rack of lamb to follow?' she called to Spatz.

The urbane baron was reading a newspaper, wearing a red velvet smoking jacket. His army uniform hung in the closet, but he seldom wore it in Paris. One didn't need a uniform to show one's power these days. He gave her a warm smile, his eyes crinkling in that charming way they had, folded his paper away, and rose from his armchair to join her. 'An excellent idea, my darling. With potatoes Anna and asparagus tips.'

'We'll serve a sorbet to cleanse the palate after that,' she told the chef. 'Lamb is always a little greasy.'

The chef wrote it all down. 'Of course. Sorbet au Montrachet. To follow?'

'German officers like a savoury at the end,' Spatz said.

'We have some veal sweetbreads, Monsieur le Baron.'

'That will do.'

'We'll have them *en cocotte*,' Coco decided, 'with morels.'

'Excellent, Madame.'

'Do we need a pudding, Spatz?'

'None of us are children,' he replied.

'None of us are children, that is true. But something sweet is always nice at the end of a meal.'

'Perhaps we could have some *clémentines givrées*,' he suggested.

'What a clever thought. And with the cognac, a selection of chocolates.' She kissed von Dincklage on his cheek, which was brown and leathery from the summer sun. 'My dear, will you attend to the details of the wines?'

The sommelier, who had been waiting for this moment, glided forward, rubbing his hands together. 'A 1915 Chablis with the oysters,' Spatz said without hesitation, 'a Château Lafite with the lamb – do you have any of the 1929?'

'I am sure there are a few bottles in the cellar, Monsieur.'

'Find them. Then I think a good vintage champagne. The Pommery 1911.'

'Very good, Monsieur.'

Coco left him discussing vintages. Spatz was truly a wonderful find. With such men around one, life was a lot easier. She went to the telephone and called the concierge. 'I want the handsome blonde. I forget her name. You know the one I mean.'

'Olivia, Madame?'

'Yes, Olivia. Send her along at once.'

✷

'She's asking for you,' Monsieur Auzello said to Olivia. 'She wants "the handsome blonde", and nobody else.'

Olivia put her hands to her aching head. 'Can't somebody else go to her?'

'Didn't you hear what I said?' Auzello snapped. More quietly, he added, 'They all want you because you're the only young one left. And it doesn't hurt to be a handsome blonde either. Make the most of it. You might get a fat tip out of it.'

'She's never given me a centime yet,' Olivia replied.

'Smiles earn tips.'

Olivia made her way wearily to the seventh floor. Madame Chanel was with her new lover, the distinguished German who everyone said was a spy. The presence of a senior chef and a sommelier, notebooks in hand, indicated that a little supper in the room was being planned.

Chanel turned to her. 'There you are.' She put on her glasses to stare at Olivia more closely. 'Why the long face, child? You look shocking.'

'I have a migraine, Madame.'

'Well, pull yourself together. I can't have you going around with a face like that. It's bad enough that all the others look as though they've taken poison, like Madame Bovary. I'm relying on you.'

'Yes, Madame.'

Chanel grasped her shoulders in surprisingly strong hands and pulled them square. 'Don't slouch,' she rapped out. 'Straighten your spine.'

Olivia tried to obey. 'Sorry, Madame.'

Chanel's sharp brown eyes probed Olivia's. 'Whatever the matter is,' she said in a quieter voice, 'put it behind you. You're here to work. It will do no good to brood on it. Understand?'

'Yes,' Olivia said.

'We women all have our moments of despair,' she went on, even more quietly, 'our own little whirlwinds. Never let them show on the surface. Face the world. Smile.' Olivia tried to respond to this brusque advice. Chanel turned to her companion, who had been discussing the merits of a seventy-year-old Château d'Yquem with the sommelier. 'My darling, this is the handsome blonde I was telling you about. What do you think?'

The German glanced at Olivia briefly. His eyes were shrewd, his mouth sensual. He seemed to sum her up in a second or two. 'With a little grooming, she will do.'

'Good. Can you wait on table, child? Do you know which side to serve from, how to hold a tray?'

'I – I don't think so.'

'There is no secret to it. I will show you. I am giving a dinner tonight. You will be required.'

'I can't,' Olivia blurted out. She was desperate to get home and get news of Fabrice.

'Don't worry about the curfew. You'll spend the night here.'

'I have to get back home!'

'And what is so urgent?'

'My – my fiancé is sick.'

'He can manage without you for one night.'

'It really is impossible,' Olivia said, her voice rising.

Chanel's eyes grew hard as obsidian. 'I don't like that word, *impossible*. If you want to keep your position in this hotel, I suggest you cut it out of your vocabulary. I need you. I cannot have my guests served by male and female hags.'

Chanel's German lover strolled over to them, his eyes crinkling in a smile. 'What ails your fiancé, young lady?'

Telling them that Fabrice had been arrested by the Gestapo was impossible. 'He has a – a weak chest,' she stammered.

'Doesn't he have a maman?'

'Yes, he does.'

'Then let her look after him for one night. He will be all the happier to see you tomorrow.'

'I will make you presentable,' Chanel said. 'You can't wear those clothes. We'll attend to your hair and so forth. Come to the table.'

The dining room was small and intimate, just big enough for the oval table and its eight chairs. Olivia tried to concentrate as Madame Chanel explained the basic rules of serving at table. 'When you offer food, hold it low enough that the guest may serve himself comfortably with his right hand. Take care that you never touch the surfaces from which food is eaten, or the rim of glasses. Silverware is always held only by the handles. When I signal you that a course is finished, remove all the dishes used in that course. Begin with the guest of honour. He will be seated in this chair. Are you attending?' she asked sharply.

'Yes, Madame,' Olivia said, though all she could think of was Fabrice.

'You did me a kindness once,' Chanel said in her brusque way. 'I am returning that kindness now. There is much you can learn from me, if you are not too stupid.'

Olivia nodded. 'I'm listening, Madame Chanel.'

'You don't want to remain a chambermaid for ever, do you? Now let us begin from the top again.'

Chanel did not release her until two hours later to attend to her assigned rooms. Feeling exhausted, Olivia came down the stairs and went to the chambermaids' room. Marie-France was there.

'Is he free?' Olivia gasped.

Marie-France shook her head. 'They won't let me see him and they won't let me wait there. It's better I work.'

'They haven't said anything at all?'

'No.' Marie-France seemed in danger of breaking down. 'Oh, Olivia, it's a terrible place. A terrible, terrible place.'

Olivia held Marie-France, as much to prevent her from falling as to comfort her. After a while, Marie-France gathered her strength and raised her head from Olivia's shoulder. 'Are you all right, Olivia?'

'Madame Chanel wants me to serve at table in her suite tonight. I've told her I can't do it, but she won't listen.'

'Do whatever she asks,' Marie-France said. 'There's no way you can help Fabrice. Don't annoy Chanel or her friends. They are powerful.'

'Are you sure you're strong enough to work, Marie-France?'

'I am strong enough to do this,' she replied quietly. 'But I have lost one child. If they take the other, I will go mad.'

'Don't even think that,' Olivia said. Marie-France's face had become skull-like, her eyes sunken. But there was no option other than to face the day's work, and pray for mercy.

Madame Chanel's dinner party was going well. The six guests, all in the uniforms of senior German army officers, had eaten and drunk with great appreciation. Their voices had grown louder, their laughter more unrestrained, as the empty bottles gathered in the kitchen. Now they were enjoying a pause.

From the end of the table, Chanel signalled to Olivia. Olivia was forcing herself not to think of Fabrice or Marie-France because it was impossible for her to do her work if she did. She began gathering the Sèvres dishes from in front of each guest. Suddenly, a hand clamped on her wrist. Startled out of her trance, Olivia looked down at the aquiline male face.

'This one is a treasure, Coco. Where did you find her?'

'This is my handsome blonde. You approve?'

The grip on Olivia's wrist tightened as she tried to remove it. 'She has distinct possibilities. What's your name, girl?'

'Olivia Olsen.'

'A Swede?'

'Yes, sir.'

The man's face, framed by the crimson-and-gold tabs on his collar, wrinkled into a grin. 'Good Aryan stock, then.' He was drunk, his eyes bloodshot and his cheeks flushed. 'Are you married?'

'No, sir.'

His other hand was now on her buttocks, squeezing. 'Then you must breed with me. Come to my room after supper.'

There were shouts of laughter from the other officers. 'You're past it, Walther,' someone jeered.

'You will see if I'm past it,' Walther said, still grasping Olivia's wrist and kneading her backside suggestively. 'I have five children at home. A couple of bastards won't come amiss. And I've earned a bit of fun. What do you say, Olivia Olsen? Are you ready to spread your legs?'

Chanel frowned. 'You've had too much to drink, Walther. Leave her alone.'

The officer, offended, released her with an angry laugh. Olivia collected his plate and moved round the table to gather the rest. Chanel, dressed in a spectacular red-and-black gown with a huge diamond brooch on the shoulder, touched her hand sympathetically for a moment. She took the dishes to the kitchen.

The *ris de veau en cocotte* had now arrived from the restaurant in individually baked china pots. She carried them through carefully and set them down before each guest. The lids had been sealed with a ribbon of pastry, which had baked hard. The Germans attacked these and opened the pots. The rich steam, flavoured with the intoxicating, earthy aroma of the morels poured into the room. Olivia, who had eaten nothing all day, felt a wave of nausea.

'Do you foresee any difficulties with the so-called Resistance?' Chanel asked. 'Everything seems very peaceful and happy so far.'

'The French are poltroons,' someone said contemptuously. 'Trust me, they won't raise any difficulties. The Poles fought like tigers. So did the Dutch. These people are sheep.'

'They know what we did in Warsaw,' the officer named Walther said, helping himself to more wine. 'I was there. Between Goering's bombers, our artillery, and the explosives we used afterwards, there's nothing left but rubble.' He laughed shortly. 'If the Parisians prove difficult, we'll do the same here. We'll cut down your Eiffel Tower for scrap metal.'

There was laughter and a clatter of silverware as they began work on the truffles. Chanel beckoned to Olivia and put her mouth to Olivia's ear. 'I won't let any of them touch you, child. But stand up straight, and for God's sake, smile.'

The truffles were disposed of, the plates cleared. The *clémentines givrées* followed, sweet little mandarin oranges that had been frozen, the flesh pulped and made into an iced meringue. The discussion had turned to the first year of war. All of the guests had seen action in various parts of Europe; all were filled with the complacency that comes with victory and a full stomach.

'You gentlemen are lucky.' It was Spatz von Dincklage who spoke, from the head of the table, opposite Chanel. 'An officer posted to Paris has only two battles to face: getting the best tables at the restaurants and getting the prettiest women into bed.'

More laughter followed. Glasses were raised in a toast to their hostess, who accepted the tribute gracefully. Chanel had the knack of being captivating. Approaching sixty as she was, she appeared to be a third of that age this evening. It wasn't just a question of lighting, or of skilful make-up.

Olivia, who had helped her prepare for tonight, knew that there was no cosmetic trick. It was something integral to the woman herself, an energy that lit her from within. It was hard to believe that this brilliant hostess was the same creature she'd found gibbering and toothless in her own mess last summer. Chanel had become a bewitching siren, whose dark eyes glowed alluringly in the candlelight, the focus of attention for every man in the room.

She knew how to amuse, how to flatter; her remarks were clever, witty, pithy. She exuded worldliness and a sensuality that Olivia was certain the Germans were finding new in their experience. She was quintessentially sexy, quintessentially French.

Boots and belts creaked as the officers leaned back and relaxed over cognac, coffee and *friandises*. The atmosphere was mellow. The bottles were set on the table, cigar smoke thickened the air, and at last Chanel indicated that Olivia could withdraw.

***

The hotel was stirring into life the next morning, the corridors beginning to rattle with breakfast trolleys. Olivia made her way to the chambermaids' room, where she changed into her uniform. There was no sign of Marie-France, and nobody had heard anything from her. Olivia's stomach was hollow. She realised that she had eaten almost nothing since Fabrice's arrest. She was feeling weak, but the thought of food made her gorge rise.

She got her trolley ready and set off down the corridor. As she turned the corner, she was confronted with a large, square, familiar figure.

It was Heike Schwab.

Heike smiled tightly. 'So. You did not expect to see me again.'

'No, I didn't,' Olivia said blankly.

'Do you know what they did to me?' Heike asked. 'They put me in a camp with the scum of Germany, up in the mountains. If I did not have Jews and communists to beat, I would have frozen. I beat some of them until they no longer cared about the cold. But I am back. Monsieur Auzello was very surprised to see me, I can tell you. His eyes opened wide, so.' She stretched her eyelids open mockingly. 'He had no choice but to give me my old job back.'

'I'm very pleased for you,' Olivia replied wearily.

'Things have changed, eh?' Heike put her powerful arms akimbo. 'It is all very strange. The flags have changed in Paris. The guests have changed at the Ritz. And Heike has come back.'

'I was sorry about what they did to you. It wasn't right.'

Heike studied Olivia in silence for a moment. 'You are sorry now. But you did not lift a finger then.'

'There was nothing I could do.'

'I will find ways in which you can make it up to me,' Heike said, nodding grimly. 'You may be sure of that.'

At last, she stood aside and let Olivia push her trolley past. Just down the passageway, one of the waiters, encountering Olivia coming the other way, pulled a face at her. 'You know who's back?' he muttered.

'I've just seen her.'

'Watch out for that one,' the man said out of the side of his mouth. 'She's poison.'

With all the dreadful things that had happened lately, the return of Heike was another blow on an already bruised place. She knew that Heike could make serious trouble for her, and that she would need to tread very carefully around the German. But she had more than Heike to worry about right now.

She got through the morning with a sustained effort. At around two in the afternoon, she saw Marie-France arrive. But before Olivia could go to her, Marie-France had slipped into Monsieur Auzello's office, closing the door behind her.

Olivia waited nearby, her heart racing. At length, Marie-France emerged from the manager's room. Olivia hurried up to her, taking her arm.

'Is there news?' she asked.

Marie-France nodded. 'Yes, there is news. The Gestapo say we may go and collect him now.'

Olivia's heart surged. 'They've released Fabrice!'

Marie-France seemed very small and very old. 'No, Olivia. Fabrice is dead.'

⁂

The Gestapo headquarters were not far from the Ritz. The building was a grand one, located on avenue Foch, the severe neoclassical façade draped with a huge swastika flag, the portals guarded by goose-stepping stormtroopers.

In the back of the hearse they had hired, Olivia wept non-stop, but Marie-France said almost nothing. Contrary to her statement that the death of her son would drive her mad, she seemed to be rigidly in control of herself.

They were directed to the side of the building, into a courtyard whose iron gates clanged shut behind them. A guard told them to wait in the hearse. After twenty minutes a middle-aged man in a black Gestapo uniform with riding boots and a swastika armband emerged from the building with a clipboard. He signalled them to get out of the hearse.

'Sign,' he said in guttural French, thrusting the clipboard at Marie-France. Marie-France scrawled her name where the gloved finger indicated.

The officer detached some papers. 'Death certificate. Permission for burial.' His cold eyes looked at them. 'No funeral is permitted. Burial must take place within twenty-four hours. The only information permitted on the grave marker is the individual's name and dates. Understand?'

Marie-France nodded silently.

The man turned on his heel and went back into the building.

Marie-France had said this was a terrible place, and Olivia soon understood why. Screams of terror or pain suddenly came from the building. They lasted for several minutes, the sounds of a soul in unbearable torment, and then they were abruptly silenced.

Olivia had to retch. There was nothing in her stomach, but it heaved nevertheless, doubling her over. When the spasms eased, she got back into the hearse and muttered an apology to Marie-France. Marie-France seemed not to hear or see anything.

Again, they waited. Time passed like the passage of a slow, iron train. It was now late in the afternoon and the courtyard had fallen into shadow. There was no more screaming. Even the sounds of the busy avenue beyond the high walls were muted. Olivia was conscious of the weight of the unborn child in her womb. Did it know its father was dead? How was she going to face the future with a baby and no Fabrice?

Perhaps her heart would simply break, and she would not need to live any longer in this world. She would go wherever he had gone. If there was an afterlife, they would be together. If not, there would at least be no more pain. And she knew that the pain of this day was numbed by shock, and that there was an ocean of pain still to come in the months and years ahead of them.

At length they were roused by a harsh command. The hearse driver and his assistant opened the back doors. Two soldiers emerged from the building carrying a wood-and-cardboard crate between them. It seemed too small to contain a human body, too small to contain everything that had been Fabrice. They thrust it unceremoniously into the back of the hearse, then indicated the gate, which was beginning to swing open. They drove out, under the crimson-and-black flapping of the swastika.

As the hearse made its slow way to Montmartre, Olivia laid her hands on the cheap cardboard of the coffin. Marie-France was peering with swollen eyes at the papers she had been given, trying to decipher the German script.

'They say he died of a heart attack,' she said in a dry voice. 'He was twenty-six.'

The box was laid in the front room of Marie-France's house. The hearse drivers had promised to return with a decent wooden coffin just after curfew lifted the next morning, but for now, it was all they had.

Marie-France unfastened the metal staples that held the lid down, and they looked inside.

Fabrice was naked but for his undershorts. The body that Olivia had loved, that had been so alive, so elegant in every movement, was now a broken thing. The pale skin had become the map of a strange world, continents and islands of blue and crimson mapping a voyage of pain. There were sunken places where ribs had been broken, promontories where what had been done internally had pushed against the skin, making peaks.

Olivia gave a cry of horror and pity. Marie-France was silent for a while, looking down at her son.

'Help me take him out,' she said at last. 'We must wash him and dress him. Can you manage?'

'Yes,' Olivia whispered.

His skin was shockingly cold to Olivia's hands, his limbs heavy. What had killed Fabrice became evident as they manhandled his body out of the box. His blonde hair was soaked, and his head lolled back as they moved him, bloody water spilling from his mouth.

'They hold their heads under water,' Marie-France said dispassionately, 'and beat them with rubber hoses so that they are forced to take the water into their lungs. They drowned him.'

Olivia was sobbing. 'Fabrice, oh Fabrice.'

'It was a mercy,' Marie-France said in the same flat way. 'They didn't know his lungs were weak. It saved him from worse.'

The pain he had gone through was unthinkable. And while Fabrice was being tortured and murdered, she had been serving foie gras to Nazis. She had helped Coco Chanel fill the bellies of German officers with the finest food in France, while French families went hungry. Watched them swig vintage champagne and Bordeaux, while the lungs of the man she loved had been agonisingly filled with water. He had been pulped and choked while the men around that table had laughed at the people they had conquered, made a joke of their weakness, mocked their humiliation.

She felt something alter in her. Something changed from freezing cold to burning heat. It rose through her body, drying her tears, making it possible for her to lift Fabrice's lifeless body in her arms and prepare him for burial.

As she sponged his broken body, she felt a sudden dark ache in her womb, and cried out. Marie-France looked at her. Olivia shook her head and went to the bathroom. She knew what she would find as she undressed.

She was bleeding, and that hope, too, had died.

Twelve

Dinner at the de Chambruns was always interesting, Arletty thought sarcastically. While the rest of France was starving, Josée gave her guests hand-decorated menus on which the opulent dishes had playful names. There were Périgord truffles cooked in sherry, wittily described as *Morceaux de charbon au gazole*. Lobster, pheasant and sole also appeared under amusing titles. These days, to eat well and abundantly was itself a sign of power, of belonging within the magic circle. To joke about it, when 1941 had brought starvation to France, was *la cerise sur le gâteau*.

And then, of course, there were the guests, chosen as wittily and carefully as the menu. Arletty looked around. A sprinkling of entertainers, some heavyweight Vichy politicians, and a dazzle of German military brass; all signalling the same power, the same belonging. It was what the gossip columnists called a glittering occasion. Arletty, however, was sickened by the parties and the obsession with clothes, food and drink.

Filming of *Madame Sans-Gêne* had been postponed. It was beginning to be likely that the film would never be made. And, tiring of her coyness, Continental had finally given the big contract to Danielle Darrieux, an actress twenty years younger than Arletty.

In this second year of the Occupation, France was becoming a bitter country. Food was scarce, fuel scarcer. Over the winter, people had died of cold and malnutrition in Paris. In Paris!

And as the populace grew resentful, the Nazi grip had grown crueller. Members of the Resistance were being rounded up daily and imprisoned or shot. There were reprisals against families, sometimes against whole villages. Brutality now characterised an occupation that had once been touted as a humane *entente cordiale*.

Arletty's own life within the magic circle had been detached from these realities, but they existed nonetheless. And beyond France's borders, the world war had broadened in scope. There was hardly a nation that was not involved, either already crushed under the Nazi boot, or struggling desperately to escape from it.

Britain had fought off the impending Nazi invasion in what they were calling the Battle of Britain, saved by her young and gallant fighter pilots; but now London and other cities were being pounded nightly by the Luftwaffe's heavy bombers. North Africa was being devoured by Rommel. Most of Scandinavia lay under German control. Hitler was a bottle of black ink that had been knocked over, and his dark stain was spreading inexorably across the map of Europe.

'You don't like truffles?'

The question came from the German officer seated beside Arletty. She realised that she had been gazing bleakly at her plate. Josée's truffles of Périgord had been served *en papillote* with their sherry sauce. Her own expensive, fragrant black nugget sat untouched in its nest of parchment, waiting for her to unwrap it. 'I don't have much of an appetite,' she said. 'You can have mine, if you want.'

'This is my first experience,' he replied. 'If I don't like it, eating yours would double the discomfort.'

'But if you do, it will double the pleasure.'

'True. I'm not sure I understand the French cuisine, myself. It appears to be based on a holy trinity of truffles, foie gras and caviar, and I don't think I like any of those.'

She turned to look at him. This, of course, was one of Josée's German soldiers with the beautiful blue eyes. She couldn't remember his name, though she'd been introduced to him earlier. His eyes were certainly very beautiful, and his uniform, that of a Luftwaffe officer, was very smart. He was smiling at her in a way that – had she been ten years younger than he, instead of ten years older – might have made her heart flutter.

'What *do* you like?' she asked.

'To tell you the truth, I don't know.'

'You don't know what you like to eat?'

His smile was boyish, charming. 'I'm still forming my opinions about almost everything.'

'Unusual for a German,' Arletty said dryly. 'Most of you have very well-established opinions.'

'That's only possible if you swallow the opinions of others whole and convince yourself they're your own. Which, of course, is what most Germans do. Speaking for myself, I'm in no hurry to form opinions. Having an opinion suggests you've stopped trying new things. And I hope I will never lose my delight in trying new things.'

Interested in this younger man despite herself, Arletty studied him more closely. An excellent example of the master race, to all intents: athletic, extremely attractive, speaking perfect French. His uniform was replete with the ribbons and emblems of his rank. But she was inclined to forgive all this for a certain melancholy humour that lurked in his eyes and for the way his ears were pointed, like a faun's.

'What new things have you tried lately?' she asked.

'Well, I tried a man for theft and black-marketeering this morning.'

'You're a lawyer?'

'A judge.'

'You are very young to be a judge,' she commented.

'I quite agree. I'm not yet thirty-three.'

Arletty was almost forty-three, but did not say so. 'Then I suppose I should congratulate you on your advancement.'

'Oh, my jurisdiction only applies within the Luftwaffe,' he said. 'The fellow I tried this morning was a Luftwaffe cook. He was selling potatoes and cabbages to French civilians.'

'What was his punishment?'

He scratched his cheek reflectively. 'It was within my power to send him to the front. Had he been dealing in truffles, foie gras and caviar, you may be sure that I would have done. But there was something disarming about potatoes and cabbages. I confined him to barracks for a month. I learned afterwards that he has a wife and two children in Linz. It would have been a shame to put a family man like that in the way of British bullets. You can see that some good came from my slowness to form an opinion.' He picked up his knife and fork. 'Are we going to eat these truffles or not?'

'I think we must do our duty.' Arletty unfolded the *papillote*, releasing the intoxicating, earthy aroma of the truffle within.

'The French cuisine certainly has some very odd aspects,' her companion said, following suit. 'They served us a Camembert cheese at the Ritz that would be banned under the Geneva Convention.'

'You dine at the Ritz?'

'I have rooms there.'

It was a certain indicator that he had power and connections at the highest level. Only the most senior German staff were billeted at the Ritz. 'That must be very comfortable,' she said with a touch of irony.

'Apart from the cheese trolley. It's a branch of the Resistance all on its own. It makes its way round the restaurant, flooring German staff officers right and left.'

She smiled despite herself. 'There is a certain barnyard smell to ripe French cheese. But without moulds, there would be no Roquefort or Camembert, no Burgundy or Bordeaux.'

'Ah, yes, *la pourriture noble*, the magnificent putrefaction.' He put the truffle into his mouth whole and chewed it thoughtfully.

'What do you think?' she asked, watching the expression of his eyes turn inwards.

'It's like a clod of earth,' he said at last, 'dug from the grave of a Renaissance princess who died of a surfeit of mushrooms.'

'Is that good or bad?'

'Oh, good, I think.'

'Then you shall have mine,' she said, ladling the morsel on to his plate.

'What are you two talking about?' Josée called from the end of the table. 'I see two heads very close.'

'Mademoiselle Arletty has undertaken to guide a poor Teutonic barbarian through the mysteries of the French cuisine,' he replied.

Josée shook her dark curls. 'Is Hans-Jürgen pretending to be an ingénue, Arletty? Don't believe a word of it. He's the most sophisticated man you are likely to come across.'

'Is that true?' Arletty asked him.

'Not at all. I'm an innocent, looking for someone to educate me.' As he spoke the words, his eyes looked into hers with unmistakeable warmth. She felt a tingle in her belly.

'I'm not a schoolmistress,' she retorted.

'And I'm not a schoolboy.'

'I'm sorry, I didn't catch your name.'

He clicked his boot heels under the table. 'Major Hans-Jürgen Soehring.'

'That's rather a mouthful.'

'You may call me Hans-Jürgen.'

'Still rather a mouthful. I shall call you Faun.'

He cocked his handsome head on one side. 'Why Faun?'

'Because your ears are pointed, like a faun's.' She didn't add that he had the face of a young satyr – or that there was something magical about him, like the supple, alarming creature created by Nijinsky.

'Very well, I accept. And I shall call you Doe, because your eyes are large and lustrous, like a doe's.'

Embarrassed by this retort, Arletty shrugged, and aware of being rude, turned her back on the German and engaged the man on the other side of her in conversation. Her heart was beating fast, and she felt a little breathless. She was too old for such flirtations. She was certainly too old for the invitation she had seen in those deep blue eyes. There were enough difficulties in her life without the addition of a German Adonis ten years younger than herself, asking her to 'educate' him. She felt her cheeks flushing as the implications of that remark came home to her. She cleared her mind with an effort and devoted herself to the grateful old senator beside her for the rest of the meal, saying nothing further to Soehring.

After supper, too, she avoided him, making sure she was at the other end of the room, concealed behind a barrier of military uniforms and silk gowns. But at the end of the evening, he emerged from the crowd and bowed courteously over her hand. She hadn't realised until now how big he was: very big, broad-shouldered and powerful. He towered over her.

'I was enchanted to meet you tonight,' he said. 'I did not get a chance to tell you how much I admire your work. Especially *Le Jour se Lève.*' Again, those blue eyes looked into hers, with the warmth of a summer afternoon in them. 'I travelled a hundred kilometres to see an uncensored version.'

He meant the version that showed her naked breasts. Arletty laughed shortly. 'I hope it was worth it.'

'Your performance was one of the best I've seen. I watched it twice in a row.'

'Once for each breast?'

'And I may go back a third time.' He leaned forward slightly and lowered his voice. 'I hope you understand that not all Germans are monsters.'

He clicked his heels and made his way out, accompanied by a fellow Luftwaffe officer.

Josée de Chambrun took Arletty's elbow with a sly smile. 'This is exactly what I had hoped for,' she murmured in Arletty's ear. 'I couldn't be happier!'

'Don't be silly,' Arletty said. 'I'm not interested in that young brute.'

'Brute? What are you talking about? He reads Goethe and writes the most exquisite poetry. He speaks five languages fluently.'

'He's a Nazi.'

'They all have to be Nazis, my dear. This one is very different. Why do you think I put him next to you at dinner?'

'I hope you're not expecting *Romeo and Juliet*, Josée. You will be sorely disappointed.'

'It's high time you got away from Antoinette. And Hans-Jürgen is very interested in you. He's the most beautiful man in Paris. Grab him quickly, before someone else does!'

'I'm not so desperate that I need to grab any man,' Arletty retorted.

Josée turned to face her. 'Listen to me. You've already let another actress snatch the Continental contract from under your nose. Don't lose Hans-Jürgen or I shall never forgive you.'

Arletty shook her head. 'You are incorrigible.'

'He's very powerful. He answers directly to Goering. He can do great things for you.'

'You said that about Antoinette.'

'Antoinette is finished. Forget her. She belongs to yesterday. He is of today.'

'I think I am somewhat stuck in yesterday myself.' Arletty kissed Josée on the cheek. 'Good night, meddling gypsy. Find someone else for your Nazi poet to play with. I'm going home.'

Reichsmarschall Hermann Goering had been a guest of the Ritz for several months now. Extraordinarily, considering the war that was raging, he was on long leave, said to be recovering his strength after an illness. Whatever the illness was, it was a very strange one, for the Reichsmarschall continued to eat huge, rich meals, both in the hotel restaurant and in the privacy of his suite. He was especially fond of the best Bordeaux wines, which he drank by the bottle. He had requisitioned a large part of the 120,000 bottles in the Ritz cellars for his personal use, and they had been specially marked with his seal. At least, as Monsieur Auzello said, this prevented them from being pillaged by other German officers.

The Reichsmarschall had become sluggish in his habits. Olivia had even heard other high-ranking Nazis joking about Goering's laziness, though never in his hearing. The only activities that seemed able to rouse him from sleeping and eating were his 'shopping trips', regular forays to plunder the Louvre of its art treasures or to secure the artworks of hapless French Jews. These activities were all he seemed to be occupied with, taking up his afternoons. It was said that he was crating up thousands of artworks and shipping them back to Carinhall, where he was setting up a magnificent museum of his own.

Where he had been an early riser, he was now fast asleep every morning when Olivia entered the Imperial Suite, which she did at ten a.m. on his specific orders. He still preferred the Marie Antoinette bedroom, although his bulk, under the influence of *haute cuisine*, was now growing almost too bloated for the dainty bed.

He was sprawled on the coverlet this morning, still in his uniform, one boot on, one boot off, snoring loudly. Nobody had helped him to undress the night before. He had simply collapsed in a drunken stupor. Sometimes the Imperial Suite was filled by several people, secretaries and adjutants, who occupied the other bedrooms. But sometimes, as today, the Reichsmarschall drove everyone away with curses and was completely alone in the grand chambers. His valet, Robert, slept in the servants' quarters in the gallery and did not appear until summoned.

Olivia approached the bed and looked down at the swollen, sleeping face. She had a vision of Fabrice's body in that cardboard box, broken and dumped like garbage. Rage and grief, undiminished by the passing of months, rose up in her.

She had the feeling, which she had been getting more and more lately around German officers, of being part of an explosive combination: that the man lying asleep before her was a flame, and that she was a can of gasoline, and that it would take only the slightest movement to spill her volatile essence and set off a ballooning fireball of destruction.

Her eyes dropped to the belt around Goering's fat belly, where there was a dagger with an ornate gold-and-silver handle, one of the gewgaws the Reichsmarschall was so fond of; but she knew the blade was sharp tempered steel. She had seen him slicing open letters with it.

She could take the weapon from its sheath in a moment and plunge it into his breast, striking an extraordinary blow against the entire Nazi regime.

For a moment, Olivia held her breath, imagining the feel of the blade piercing Goering's flesh, feeling the hot spurt of arterial blood across her arms.

Or there was Goering's revolver, on the floor next to the bed, a Smith & Wesson, as he had proudly told Olivia, purchased in Hamburg before the war. She could pull it from its embossed holster and—

She recalled Fabrice, on the day of Hitler's visit to Paris, saying he wished he'd had a gun or a knife. But perhaps she could find a better way of striking back.

Pushing down her emotions, she touched Goering's shoulder. 'Herr Reichsmarschall,' she said quietly. 'It's ten o'clock.'

Goering groaned and stirred. Olivia turned away from him and began tidying the room. As usual these days, it was in disorder: a chair lying on its side, empty bottles and half-eaten fruit tossed into the

Napoleonic fireplace, with its golden sphinxes. Papers were scattered across the Empire desk, many of them headed with the eagle and swastika of official Nazi documents. One or two even bore Adolf Hitler's odd, crooked signature, which she had learned to recognise. She studied the papers, trying to decipher the German.

'Olivia.'

She turned away from the desk to look at Goering, who was struggling to sit up. He looked dazed. 'Herr Reichsmarschall?'

'Bring me Vichy water.'

She opened a bottle of the sparkling water and brought him a glass. He fumbled for the morphine pills that always lay in a bowl on his bedside table and swallowed two or three.

'I was having a dream,' he told her, 'a beautiful dream. About the old days. About the Führer. When we were close.' Goering was often maudlin in the mornings, inclined to be weepy until the pills kicked in. 'He no longer speaks to me. Himmler, Bormann, Ribbentrop, Goebbels, those bastards, they don't let me near him. Once, it was always me at his side, through thick and thin!'

Olivia watched him as he struggled to unfasten his belt and unbutton his tunic. This man, large in every sense, had laid waste to Europe and was now in a kind of exile, sleeping in the bed of a beheaded French queen, groping for his drugs from the moment he awoke.

She helped him up. He made his way to the toilet, groaning. She opened the drapes. It was a rainy morning, place Vendôme glistening and grey, the swastika flags hanging limp on the grand buildings.

Goering emerged from the bathroom in his singlet and shorts. 'Hitler blames me for not destroying the British army at Dunkirk. He blames me that the invasion of Britain could not be accomplished because we lost the Battle of Britain. But my Luftwaffe was bled almost to death! All those pilots killed, all those machines destroyed! How can we ever make up those losses? Yet it was he who willed all this.' Once again, he was reaching for his pills. He seemed to have an almost limitless tolerance for them. 'I never wanted this war, Olivia. You must know that.'

Olivia went to get his breakfast trolley, which the waiter had left in the next room. He could abide to see nobody but her when he woke up. She had become more nursemaid than chambermaid to him.

She pushed the trolley to his bedside. It was laden with the delicacies he demanded: cold roast goose, smoked duck, ham, pastries laden with cream and fruit, croissants and brioches.

'You don't believe me?' he demanded angrily. 'You think I'm a warmonger, as all the papers say in Britain and America.'

'I don't think anything, Herr Reichsmarschall.'

'I never wanted this war. I told the Führer we could accomplish everything without a war. He was furious with me. The Führer, because of his nature, needs war. He needs to smash things in order to reshape them. That is the artist's soul in him. But some things, when smashed, can never be reshaped.'

He began cramming food into his mouth. The great, jowly jaw was like a shovel, scooping up fuel to feed a fire that always demanded more.

She went about her business, silently ordering the room, developing the idea that had occurred to her. There were so many documents strewn about this room. Some of them must be important. Some must contain vital information – to the right people.

There was a knock at the door. She opened it to let in Goering's French tailor, a cadaverous man whom Olivia thought of as a kind of Don Quixote, tilting against the windmill of Hermann Goering's bulk, always accompanied by his much shorter assistant, loaded like a donkey with garments. Altering the Reichsmarschall's elaborate uniforms was a weekly ritual, necessitated by his constantly changing vital statistics as he alternately ballooned after overeating, or managed to shed a few pounds by starving himself.

Goering stood with his arms outstretched as the man measured him, discussing various garments that would be needed for the summer:

white dress uniforms in lightweight linen, three dozen silk shirts with diamond studs, pairs of trousers ample enough to contain his belly.

The arrival of the tailor was followed shortly by an influx of German staff officers with briefcases. They trooped around Goering's bed, saluting. One began giving him the morning briefing, reading from a sheaf of documents.

An officer, noticing Olivia, pushed her roughly towards the door. 'Out.'

Olivia had taken her decision. Leaving the suite, she walked swiftly towards Monsieur Auzello's office. On the way, she encountered Marie-France.

Marie-France's hair, once so rich and dark, had grown grey over the winter. Her skin was dry, her eyes sunken. She greeted Olivia with the flicker of a smile, but her eyes were empty. When the Gestapo had killed Fabrice, they had killed his mother too, although her body kept coming to work and doing its daily duty.

She had left the house in Montmartre and moved in with a sister in the neighbourhood of the Paris Nord station, meaning that she and Olivia saw each other only at work these days.

'Are you all right?' Olivia asked.

'I'm fine,' Marie-France said.

'Are you eating enough?' The question did not really require an answer. People no longer invited one another for supper, since food had become much too scarce to share, and each household hoarded what it could, but Olivia could see that Marie-France's uniform hung on her shrunken frame.

'I eat very well, thank you.' Again, that flicker of a smile. 'My sister is a very good cook, you know.' Her eyes were looking through Olivia, rather than at her, seeing something far beyond. 'Fabrice always said that I was the better cook. But then, you know how affectionate he was to me.'

'Yes.'

Marie-France turned away. 'I must get on with my work.'

Olivia watched the small figure shuffle away, like the ghost of something that had once been alive. The murder of Marie-France was another reason to rage against the Nazis, another reason to strike.

She knocked on Auzello's door, and was admitted. The managing director of the Ritz was standing behind his desk, as always. He seemed incapable of sitting. His energetic constitution would probably not permit such a relaxed pose. He glanced at Olivia impatiently. 'What is it?'

She closed the door behind her. 'Monsieur Auzello, I want to do something.'

'Do what?' He had already resumed reading the sheaf of accounts in his hands.

'You know that I'm the first to go into Goering's room each morning. I wake him up and serve his breakfast.'

'Well?'

'He talks to me. He tells me things. About Hitler, about all the top Nazis. Things that could be useful to the Allies.'

Auzello looked startled. He dropped the papers he was holding, walked swiftly to the door, and opened it, looking out to see if anyone was listening. Finding nobody there, he shut the door and took Olivia's arm. 'What do you mean?'

'I want to pass information to whoever can use it.' She met Auzello's eyes squarely. 'You know the right people for me to talk to.'

'Me?'

'You promised we would return to the battle,' she replied. There were rumours, breathed in the strictest confidence among the staff, that Monsieur Auzello knew people in the Resistance. His military background and the fact that his effervescent wife, Blanche, was American made that credible. But his proud face, with its hooked nose and bristling moustache, was stony.

'If one of our employees was caught doing what you propose, the Ritz would be seized immediately and placed under military command.

We would all be sent to a concentration camp. And should any of our German guests be harmed – or God forbid, killed – I truly believe that Hitler would burn down all of Paris – all of France!'

'I don't plan to kill anybody,' Olivia said quietly. 'I just want to do my part.'

'Olivia, this is not your war.'

'If you'll excuse me, that's a foolish remark, Monsieur Auzello.'

'Your Swedish passport will not protect you if you fall foul of the Nazis. You, of all people, know what they would do.'

'I, of all people, have a reason to hate them,' she replied. 'They murdered Fabrice, and they destroyed Marie-France. I lost the man I loved and my best friend. I have to hit back at them in some way.' She clenched her fists. 'Or one of these mornings, I'm going to take Goering's pistol and blow his brains out as he sleeps.'

Auzello looked taken aback at the savage note in Olivia's voice. 'Please do nothing of the sort.'

'Then put me in touch with somebody who can use the information I get,' she retorted.

Not waiting for an answer, she left the office. The looming figure of Heike Schwab was in the corridor outside. Everywhere she went, Heike seemed to be following her, a hulking shadow.

'What are you talking to Auzello about?' she demanded now, blocking Olivia's path.

'None of your business.'

'Everything here is my business,' Heike retorted. 'Do you want me to put your name on a list? You know I report to the Gestapo.'

This claim, which Heike often made, could not be verified; but everyone suspected it was true. Occupied Paris was a murky world of spies and watchers; and the Ritz, with its extraordinary concentration of senior Nazis, was watched with special intensity.

'You can tell them what you like,' Olivia retorted. 'I've done nothing wrong.'

'Then why were you in the office with Auzello?'

'If you must know,' Olivia said grimly, 'I was asking him for a raise. I can't manage on the money they pay me.'

'And what did he say?'

'He said no.'

Heike stepped closer to Olivia. 'You could move in with me. Two can live as cheaply as one – especially as I have a German ration card. I can get double the meat you can, double everything.'

It was not the first time that Heike had made a suggestion of this sort to Olivia. Olivia had learned that the chambermaid who had been fired, creating the vacancy that she herself had filled, had been a 'special friend' of Heike's. That accounted for Heike's initial hostility. But if Heike thought Olivia was going to make up for it by taking the 'special friend's' place in Heike's bed, she had another think coming. 'I'm fine where I am,' she said briskly.

Heike's face soured. 'You should understand your position. I know your little secret, Olivia. Without someone to look after you, you will find yourself in a concentration camp soon.'

The news that America had just signed the Lend-Lease policy into law, giving material assistance to the British and the Free French forces, had made it almost inevitable that America would soon be in the war. It had been greeted with rage by the Nazi press, and by a stepping-up of military activity all over France. 'I'll take my chances,' Olivia replied.

'Ja? See how your friend the Reichsmarschall likes you when your country is an enemy.' Heike was jealous of Goering's preference for Olivia, and furious that, although she was a German, the Reichsmarschall couldn't bear the sight of her. 'I am watching you,' Heike called after Olivia's retreating back. 'And I see everything. Never forget that, my Yankee friend.'

It was two days before she heard back from Monsieur Auzello. He walked into the laundry room where she was disposing of the linen into the chute.

'There is a vineyard by your lodgings in Montmartre,' he said in a low voice.

'Yes,' she said in surprise.

'Be in the hut at four o'clock on Sunday. Take your painting equipment.' He took her arm in a fierce grip. 'And for God's sake, be careful. Do you understand?'

'Yes, Monsieur Auzello. And thank you—'

But he was already walking away.

Her heart lurched as she turned back to the chute. Her tank of gasoline was approaching the flame at last.

She knew the hut he meant: half-ruined, overgrown with vines, it stood neglected among the terraces, a secluded place where tools were kept.

Olivia had the feeling, as she went about her work, of having taken the first, small step on a path that had no return, and perhaps no safe arrival either.

Thirteen

Josée de Chambrun and her charming husband, René, entered Coco Chanel's apartment at the Ritz with gratifying exclamations of delight at Coco's latest acquisition.

'Is it a Poussin?' Josée asked, standing before the large vivid-toned painting that had been mounted in pride of place in the salon.

'Even better,' Coco said smugly. 'It's a Le Brun.' She fitted a cigarette into her amber cigarette holder. 'It's three hundred years old.'

'It must have cost a fortune,' Josée said.

Coco glowed as she recalled her deft manoeuvring. 'As it happens, I picked it up for a song. A gentleman of the Hebrew persuasion, eager to divest himself of his art collection before departing France.'

'What a find!'

'It's a masterpiece,' Josée's husband said. 'Congratulations, my dear Coco.' He examined the glowing canvas, which depicted a naked, blonde woman being stabbed to death by soldiers. 'What's the subject?'

'*The Sacrifice of Polyxena*,' Coco replied.

'Aha. The woman who betrayed the secret of Achilles' heel, and who died for it.'

'You're so clever, my dear,' Coco said admiringly.

Count René Aldebert Pineton de Chambrun was indeed very clever. He had practised law at both the Court of Appeals of Paris and the New York State Bar Association. He was clever with law, clever with people, and very clever with money. He had been her attorney and her friend for some years.

Coco ushered them to the sofas. The Sunday afternoon was warm, after a day or two of spring rains, and Paris was steaming. She threw the windows open. Spatz von Dincklage joined them, and it being now around four o'clock, Coco served tea and petits fours.

'Dr Kurt Blanke will join us shortly,' René de Chambrun said, crossing his long legs. 'He is the head of Jewish economic affairs in the German Military Command in France.' A thin man, de Chambrun admired the plate of petits fours that had been set in front of him, but did not take any. 'Specifically, his mandate is to appropriate Jewish assets and transfer them to Aryans.'

Coco's eyes gleamed. 'Exactly the man for us.'

'Exactly the man.' In the 1920s Coco had handed over the production of her famous No. 5 perfume to the Wertheimers. They produced it in vast quantities, giving her ten per cent of the profit. But that ten per cent, which had once seemed generous, and which had made her very rich, had become an ulcer. On her behalf, de Chambrun had hurled lawsuit after lawsuit at the Wertheimers over the years, to no effect. Now, at last, they were in a position to deal with the Jews as they deserved. 'However,' de Chambrun went on, 'Dr Blanke will want to make sure that the Reich also benefits from such transfers.'

Spatz selected a dainty millefeuille pastry. 'She's set aside funds. Haven't you, Coco?'

'Yes.' She paused for effect. 'Twenty million francs.'

Even de Chambrun raised his eyebrows at that. 'With such an amount, I'm sure we can find a way forward.'

It had taken Coco a lot of wrestling with herself to come up with that sum. But, as Spatz had pointed out, it was a sprat to catch a whale. The pursuit of wealth required sacrifices of many kinds. One sacrificed one's principles, even one's humanity, and certainly one had to occasionally sacrifice one's money in order to acquire even more.

Were Chanel to wrest back what she had sold to the Wertheimers, her wealth would become incalculable. The pursuit of incalculable wealth was something de Chambrun understood perfectly. She also knew that he, although a man born to wealth, understood her insatiable hunger, the drive born of childhood poverty and humiliation. And an unusual situation had arisen in France.

'Dr Blanke has a great deal of experience in these matters,' de Chambrun said, sipping his tea. 'I think we may now be close to victory.'

As if on cue, the arrival of Dr Blanke was announced. He entered the apartment in full uniform, even on a Sunday, removing his officer's peaked cap to reveal that he had very pale hair to match his very pale eyes. Unlike the other guests, he did not look at his opulent surroundings or make any complimentary remarks on Chanel's taste.

'Heil Hitler,' he said in a clipped voice, raising his right hand in the Nazi salute.

'Heil Hitler.' The others echoed the salute with varying degrees of military precision.

Dr Blanke was carrying a briefcase on which was emblazoned a red swastika. This he placed on his knees as he sat. He refused all offers of tea or refreshments. Nor was he interested in small talk. He was a busy man, even on a Sunday.

'My client is well-known enough to need no introduction,' de Chambrun said, lawyer to lawyer. 'Madame Chanel is a good friend to the Reich and the Occupation forces.'

Blanke had a thin voice, like someone sawing through tin. 'As I understand it, this is a question of restoring the property of an Aryan citizen, which has been misappropriated by Jews?'

It did not take long to explain to Dr Blanke the details of the case. The Nazi listened, writing in a notebook, which he rested on his briefcase. 'It's a clear case of Jewish embezzlement,' he said finally. 'Restoring the equity to your client would be in line with our policy of Aryanisation. However, there will be costs involved.'

Coco leaned forward eagerly. 'I can put twenty million francs at your disposal.'

Dr Blanke did not seem in any way impressed or surprised. 'This will be payable in advance.'

'There's no problem with that,' Coco said.

Blanke jotted the figure down with a nod. 'I will begin action immediately.'

'But everything will be done legally?'

'I do not understand the question,' Dr Blanke said coldly.

Coco grimaced. She had known the Wertheimer brothers for years. Pierre Wertheimer, the most dashing and handsome, adored her, and had asked her to marry him. 'I don't want anything reflecting badly on me. I just want what is mine.'

Dr Blanke looked up at her with his pale eyes. 'Everything will be done in full compliance with the laws of the Third Reich.'

She wrapped her thin arms around herself, caught in the grip of a sudden spasm of stomach ache. 'Will they be ill-treated?'

'They will receive the treatment that Jews deserve,' Dr Blanke replied.

'But I don't want—' She groaned aloud at the gnawing pain inside. 'I didn't mean—'

'You are wasting your pity on them,' Dr Blanke retorted. 'Think of yourself. You say you want what is yours?'

'Yes,' she burst out. The daemon that had driven her for sixty years was writhing like a dragon. 'I want what is mine!'

'Then leave it to us.' Dr Blanke clipped his briefcase closed. 'We will handle everything. You need not concern yourself with the details.'

Coco's eyes filled with stinging tears. Whether they were of self-loathing at what she had just done, or joy that she was within reach of what she had fought for all these years, she could not say. She was careful not to blot her mascara as she dabbed her eyes with a silk handkerchief.

She knew she would be sick as soon as all these people had left her. But she had what she wanted.

Olivia was carrying her easel, some paints and a canvas board into the vineyard, just as she had used to do before the war. It felt strange to be equipped as an artist once again. Since Fabrice's death there seemed to be no desire in her to express anything except her anger.

Her heart was accelerating as she made her way between the rows of vines. The rain and the warm weather had made them grow lush, the leafy tendrils curling in all directions, turning the terraces into a maze. Although there were other people here – the vineyard of Montmartre was a pleasing green refuge on a Sunday afternoon – they were only voices whose owners were hidden by the luxuriant rows. The choice of this location had been a clever one, she realised. It was an excellent place to meet without being noticed. And it also revealed that whoever had arranged the meeting knew enough about her to know that her presence in the vineyard, where she had made so many paintings and sketches, was in no way unusual.

The hut was near the centre of the steep rambling plot, an old stone structure that was now covered in ivy. She climbed up the path towards it; but as she reached it, she was dismayed to find that a gardener was already there, wearing blue overalls and pumping vigorously at a dented brass spray tank.

She cursed under her breath. This was an unforeseen complication. Until he was well away from the hut, there was no chance of a rendezvous with her contact. She paused uncertainly, her equipment under her arm. The gardener finished pumping and uncoiled the rubber hose connected to the tank. He lifted the spray and with a hiss applied a turquoise mist to the plant in front of him.

'Copper sulphate,' he said in English, startling Olivia. 'Also known as Bordeaux mixture. Controls fungal infection.'

She walked towards him. 'Are you—'

'What do you want to tell me?' he asked, concentrating on the vines he was spraying.

She hesitated. 'How do I know who you are?'

He glanced at her briefly, showing a hard, suntanned face. 'Set up your easel, Olivia.'

The use of her name reassured her somewhat, but she was still suspicious. 'Why?'

'I have a reason to be here,' he said impatiently. 'You need one too.'

'All right.' She set up her easel, put the blank board on it, and laid her paints out on the shelf. She took a stick of charcoal and began sketching his figure with quick decisive strokes. 'What should I call you?'

'Jack.'

'You're American.'

'So?'

'I was expecting someone from the Resistance.'

'You've got me. I'm still waiting to hear what you want to say.'

'I'm a chambermaid at the Ritz—'

'I know all that part,' he cut in. 'You have information about Goering?'

She kept drawing, trying to capture his decisive movements as she relayed what Goering had said to her about his relationship with Adolf Hitler. He listened in silence, moving from plant to plant around her without giving her a chance to get a good look at his face. The metallic but surprisingly pleasant smell of the copper sulphate drifted in the warm air.

'I go into his room every morning at ten. I'm supposed to wake him at ten and give him his breakfast before his staff arrive. But he's hard to wake up. He drinks a lot. And he takes morphine pills.'

'So?'

'There are always papers scattered on his desk. Official documents.'

The man who called himself Jack paused at this. 'What do they look like, these documents?'

'They're usually typed on buff-coloured paper. They have an eagle holding a swastika in the heading. Some are signed by Adolf Hitler.'

'You know Hitler's signature?'

'Yes. He uses a particular shade of blue ink.'

He put the tank on the ground and resumed pumping air into it. At last he was taking her more seriously. She could see it in his body. Crouched over the pump, he reminded her of some hunting animal, a mountain lion perhaps, whose movements had only one purpose. She kept sketching, trying to capture that grim resolution, and to an extent, she had succeeded. She began applying paint to the drawing.

'Do you know what these documents are about?' he demanded.

'I only understand some German, but they look like military orders.'

'What language do you use with Goering?'

'Swedish, mainly. He speaks it quite well. Sometimes French.'

'I'm going into the hut. Follow me in a couple of minutes.'

He strode into the ivy-covered hut. As commanded, she went in after him a little while later. She had no sooner set foot in the dark interior when she saw that he was pointing a gun at her. Her widening eyes saw that the weapon had a silencer on the barrel.

She tried to turn back to the door, but he was far too quick. He blocked her way out so she was trapped. A rattle of guttural German came out of his mouth, questioning, demanding.

She felt her stomach flip over. Had she been betrayed? Had she walked stupidly into a Gestapo trap? She opened her mouth, but no sound came out.

The gun was pointed at her forehead. 'Answer me,' he said, 'or I'll kill you here and now.'

'I don't know what you're saying,' she choked. 'I don't speak German.'

He cocked the hammer with a click. 'Who sent you here?'

'You know who sent me here.' She was fighting for breath. 'What the hell are you doing?'

He was speaking German again, his voice low and menacing. Olivia shrank back against the rough wall of the hut. 'I don't understand what you're saying to me. I told you, I don't speak German!'

His eyes were narrowed. 'You're very friendly with Hermann Goering. Just how friendly? Are you his lover?'

'Of course not!'

'Why did you come here?'

'To offer you intelligence,' she said furiously. 'I'm an American, damn you.'

'You're a Swede. Swedes are indistinguishable from Nazis in this war.'

'Not this Swede. You—' Olivia seldom used profanities, but the shock of what had just happened released a short, sharp succession of four-letter words from deep inside her.

The curses, more than anything she'd said, seemed to reassure him. The gun disappeared back into his pocket. 'If you're a traitor, you'll end up at the bottom of the Seine,' he said quietly.

She put her hand on her thumping heart. 'You nearly scared me to death, you bastard.'

'That's nothing. Do you know what the Gestapo do to spies?'

'Yes, God damn it. They killed the man I loved.'

'He was lucky. Before they kill you, they'll smash your face. They'll tear out your fingernails. They'll wire you up to a generator and electrocute you until you pass out. Then they'll bring you round and start again.'

'Why are you telling me all this?' she asked, feeling sick.

'Because you can still pack up your easel and go home, Olivia. This isn't a game.'

'I never thought it was.'

'Then are you sure you want to move to the next step?'

'I wouldn't have come if I was a coward.'

He unbuttoned his overalls and pulled them down to his waist. His sinewy chest was naked. 'Take your dress off.'

She took a step back in shock. 'What are you doing?'

'We're having sex.'

'Oh no we're not,' she retorted, turning to leave.

'Don't be a fool.' He grasped her arm, pulling her away from the door. 'We need a reason to be here, Olivia. That's the first rule. Always have a bulletproof reason to be where you are, to be doing what you're doing. If someone happens to stumble in here, they won't be left in any doubt what we're up to. Get it? Now, take your dress off.'

After a moment, Olivia obeyed, tight-lipped. She was still tingling with shock. The hut was piled with tools, disintegrating baskets and other rubbish. It was hardly the place she would have chosen for a romantic assignation. But then, this was anything but a romantic assignation.

She hauled her dress over her head and turned to face him in her underwear. He ignored her semi-nudity.

'How long would you say you have in the room before Goering wakes?'

'Five or ten minutes.'

'Could you get into his suite earlier?'

'The guards would notice. They stand in front of his door twenty-four hours a day.'

'Is the room dark?'

'Until I open the curtains, yes.'

'You're going to be using this.' He held out a small camera. 'And you're going to need some light, so you're going to have to open the curtains.'

'How do I do that without waking Goering?' she demanded.

'It's up to you to find a way. This is a Minox. You have to hold the camera exactly the right distance over the documents. You do that by using this little chain. Hook it on here, lower the camera over the target. When the end of the chain just touches the paper, you'll be in focus.'

She took the camera from him. It was tiny and made from aluminium. 'They search everybody going in and out of the hotel,' Olivia pointed out. 'They're going to find this on me sooner or later.'

'Which is why you're going to get the camera into the Ritz, and leave it there in a secure place. You'll bring me the rolls of film. They're very small. They're a lot easier to hide than the camera.'

It had been weeks since she'd spoken English. She'd longed, in fact, to have a conversation with a fellow American; but this was not the kind of conversation she'd had in mind. She was feeling waves of fear ripple through her stomach. She hadn't envisaged herself photographing documents with Goering a few feet away.

She had her first opportunity to study him at close range. He was in his early thirties, she estimated, with the look of an outdoorsman. The flat accent was slightly rural too, and not too different from her own. It had originated somewhere in the plains of Wisconsin, she guessed. His hair was brown, bleached to near-blonde by the sun in places. He was tanned, but not in the way that came from lying on a deckchair. Like his face, his body was hard and somehow threatening. He looked like the kind of farmhand who got drunk in town on a Saturday night and started a fight. The only aspect of him that was in any way out of the ordinary was his eyes, which were grey, intelligent, and very direct.

'Is Jack your real name?' she asked.

He shrugged. 'What does it matter?'

'What does it matter?' Olivia echoed. 'You're asking me to trust you with my life!'

'Jack is my real name.'

He was probably lying. What *did* it matter? She turned the camera in her hands, ashamed of the way her fingers were trembling, but unable to stop them. 'We're not at war with the Nazis. Why are you here?'

'I could ask you the same question.'

'You know why I'm here,' she retorted. 'Answer me.'

'The people I work for believe it's only a matter of time before we are at war with the Nazis,' he said shortly. 'They also believe that we need to be ready for that day.'

'And who are these people?'

'The people who wage wars.'

'The army? Military intelligence?'

The grey eyes turned stony. 'Please concentrate, Olivia. I'm going to show you how the camera works.'

The camera was simple enough to operate. There was a built-in light meter, which indicated whether there was enough light to get a photograph. A frame counter told you when the end of the film had been reached. The apertures and shutter speeds were set by dials. The film came in a tiny canister. There was little else to it. Except what would happen to her if she was caught using it.

Jack was hauling his overalls up. 'That's it. I'm going to finish spraying, and you're going to finish your sketch. We'll meet here again next Sunday, but later this time. Six thirty.' He held up a battered straw hat. 'I'll be wearing this. If I'm not wearing it, you walk on by and don't look back. If I am wearing it, it means it's safe to approach. Understand?'

'Yes.' She pulled her dress on over her head. 'So what am I supposed to do?'

'Photograph everything you think looks interesting. Stay calm. Breathe deeply. Remember, if you don't get clear shots, you're risking your life for nothing. Bring me the spool, even if it's not finished.'

And that was that. Without another word, he left her. There was no pat on the shoulder, no reassuring expressions of encouragement, not even a *good luck*. She was on her own.

Dressed, she sat back down at her easel. He had moved to the next row of vines down. She could hear the noises of the pump and smell the chemical in the air. But everything had changed since she'd entered that hut. She was a spy now.

She was involved, caught up in something that had shifted her place in the world. There was danger everywhere now. She felt invisible eyes on her. The warm afternoon had become oppressive. Nausea was threatening to double her over, a reaction to the intense emotions she'd been through in the past ten minutes.

She stared at her canvas. She had caught something of Jack's purposeful movements in her sketch. Mechanically, she began to block in the colours. She hadn't held a paintbrush in months, and now it was shaking so much in her hand that she could hardly apply the paint.

She just wanted to get home with the camera that weighed so heavily in her pocket. But she forced herself to concentrate on the work, sketching in the curling green tendrils, the man who crouched among them, the glint of his spray pump.

She heard the real Jack grow more distant as he moved down the terraces. When she could no longer hear the clank and hiss, she gathered up her things quickly and made her way out of the vineyard where ten minutes had changed the course of her life.

Fourteen

The Minox camera was small enough to tuck into her underwear as she dressed on Monday morning, pushing it down between her legs so it wouldn't make a bulge. Although the guards at the Ritz sometimes searched her bag, they had never yet searched her body. Nevertheless, she was so sick with nerves as she approached rue Cambon at six thirty that she almost turned back at the last minute. It was only the thought that she was doing this for Fabrice and Marie-France that kept her going.

At the guard post, her documents were inspected as usual, the details written down in the ledger that the soldiers kept. Over the past weeks, they had grown more familiar, occasionally joking with her or making clumsy attempts at flirtation. They had a nickname for her, *Blondchen*. Today, they were in a good mood. One even pressed a slab of German chocolate on her.

'Here, Blondchen. Something sweet for a sweet girl.'

She tried to refuse. But the young soldier would not take no for an answer, and she didn't want a scene. She thanked him, put it in her bag, and hurried on to the staff entrance of the Ritz.

The SS guards who were stationed there were a lot more thorough. They immediately found the chocolate the soldier had just given her.

'These are military rations,' the SS man said icily. 'Where did you obtain this?'

'A soldier gave it to me in the street,' she replied, looking him in the eyes despite her racing heart. She'd been an idiot to accept the chocolate. If they decided to search her, it wouldn't take them a minute to find the camera.

'You may not accept gifts of German military rations,' the SS man snapped. 'You should know this by now.'

'I'm sorry,' she said, dry-mouthed. 'It won't happen again.'

They emptied her bag and rifled through the contents while she waited. But they didn't search her person. They confiscated the chocolate and let her through with a stern warning. She entered the Ritz on trembling legs.

She usually got at least two rooms done before going to Goering's suite, and that meant keeping the camera with her. It was now getting uncomfortable, so she slipped it among the clean linen on her trolley, reasoning that if it were discovered there, she could always deny all knowledge, whereas if it turned up in her underwear, that would be rather more difficult.

At ten sharp, she presented herself at the double doors of the Imperial Suite. She'd had time to calm her fluttering nerves, and by now she was determined to see the thing through with no more vapouring and swooning. Thinking too much about things, and the consequences of things, would be her undoing. She was at her best when she just acted, without thought.

The guards at the door ignored her as she went into the darkened suite. Just inside was Goering's breakfast trolley, left there by the waiter. She pushed it as silently as she could to the Marie Antoinette bedroom, clutching the Minox.

Goering was motionless in the gold-canopied bed. But this was one of the mornings when the room was relatively tidy. For once, the

Empire desk was clear of papers. She looked at the blank expanse of leather in consternation. She would have to wait for a better opportunity. A mixture of disappointment and relief washed through her. She had keyed herself up for this, and now she was frustrated.

Then she noticed the briefcase propped carelessly against one of the legs of the desk. It was unlatched. She glanced quickly at the bed. Goering appeared to be fast asleep, though it was too dark to see his face. She went quickly to the curtain and opened it two or three inches. A blade of morning light pierced the gloom. Goering still hadn't stirred. She knelt by the briefcase and opened it, taking out a sheaf of papers. Checking the meter on the Minox showed there was just enough light to take photographs, with the lens set to its widest aperture.

Swiftly, she laid out the pages of the document on the shaft of light on the carpet and began to photograph them. She prayed that her hands were not too shaky to make the negatives useful. Her heart was clubbing at her breastbone as she took the shots, the little machine almost noiseless, producing only the tiniest of clicks each time.

She had taken twenty or thirty shots when she heard Goering begin to stir in the bed. She grabbed the papers in a panic and stuffed them back into the briefcase, trying to keep them in the same order she had found them. With luck, Goering would have been drunk again last night, and wouldn't notice anything amiss.

'Olivia?' His voice was hoarse, querulous. 'Are you there?'

'I'm here,' she said, straightening breathlessly.

'What are you doing?' he demanded.

'Just tidying up, Herr Reichsmarschall.'

'Come here.'

She went over to the bed, slipping the Minox into the pocket of her apron. He peered up at her. 'What's wrong with you? Are you shaking? You're as white as a ghost.'

'I – had a bad experience this morning.'

'What kind of bad experience?' he demanded, struggling to sit up.

'A soldier gave me some chocolate on my way to work. It was very kind of him' – she was babbling – 'but the SS men at the door found it in my bag – and they were very angry. They threatened to arrest me for having German military rations. I was – I was frightened.'

Goering snorted. 'Those ruffians. I will make sure they don't bother you again. Why, I produce that chocolate myself!'

'Really?'

'Of course. It's manufactured in the *Hermann-Göring-Schokoladenwerken*, part of my industries in the Third Reich. I will make sure you get two kilograms of it.'

'Oh no, Herr Reichsmarschall. I couldn't possibly accept.'

'Nonsense. You deserve it.' Though Goering had grown fond of her, there had never been any impropriety in his behaviour. He spoke sentimentally of his wife, Emmy, and daughter, Edda, in Germany, and clearly missed them. He treated Olivia more like a favoured niece than a hotel employee.

'I don't really like chocolate,' she confessed.

'You don't?' He seemed disappointed. 'Well, perhaps it's just as well. The stuff is full of methamphetamine, to keep the soldiers alert. You probably wouldn't sleep for a week. I'll find something else to make it up to you. And you can be sure I will have a word with those SS thugs of Himmler's. This is the Ritz, not a concentration camp.'

Olivia smiled feebly as she served him his breakfast. She was recovering her poise, but it had been a close thing. The camera in her pocket felt heavier now, a lot heavier, even though she knew that wasn't possible. It bumped against her thigh as she moved. She'd taken a lot of photographs, and there weren't many left on the roll. There might be another opportunity to use it. She needed another roll.

She took the first opportunity of talking to Claude Auzello, this time on one of the dark sets of stairs that connected one part of the Ritz with another. These awkward, twisting passageways were impassable for wheeled tables or trolleys, and therefore the quietest parts of the hotel.

'I thought you were going to put me in touch with someone from the Resistance,' she said in a low voice. 'Your friend treated me like I was a Nazi.'

'He risked his life to meet you, just on my word. You need to show him that he can trust you.'

'Trust *me*? I don't even know who he is.'

'The less you know about him, the better for you – and him.'

Frustrated, Olivia shrugged. 'Well, I need another roll of film.'

He raised his eyebrows. 'Already?'

'Yes.'

'Olivia, don't get caught,' Auzello said in concern.

'We don't know how long Goering's going to be staying here. He could go back to Germany at any time.'

'Still, don't take too many risks. Be careful.'

'We're not going to win this war by being careful, Monsieur Auzello.'

'Nor are you going to win it single-handed. Especially not from a Gestapo cellar.' He glanced around the corner to check that they were alone. 'There is a lot to learn about this business. You'll understand more as you go along. But there is a fundamental rule: we are all connected. If you fall, others fall with you. Under torture, you will betray everyone – including me, and everyone connected with me. Do you understand?'

'Yes,' she said, chastened. 'I'll be careful, I promise.'

He nodded. 'I'll try to get you another roll of film.'

Voices were approaching along the passageway, and they parted.

Later in the morning, she hid the camera in the linen closet, behind some hot-water pipes; but she was going to have to find a better hiding place. Heike, in particular, was a threat. With her Gestapo connections, she had made herself feared throughout the hotel. She was making everyone pay for what she had suffered in 1939 and 1940.

She encountered Olivia in the chambermaids' room at the end of the day, as she was changing out of her uniform.

'What are you up to?' she demanded, adopting her favourite pose, with her fists on her hips.

'I don't know what you're talking about,' Olivia said warily.

'You're up to something. I can smell it.' Heike illustrated her suspicion by pushing her face close to Olivia and sniffing deeply. This was the second time Olivia had been caught in her underwear with someone she didn't like, and she was growing sick of the experience.

'Leave me alone, Heike,' she growled, changing swiftly into her street clothes. 'I've done nothing to you.'

'I see you in holes and corners,' Heike said meaningfully. 'I hear you whispering. One of these days I will catch you. And then we will see.'

Had Heike found the Minox, Olivia wondered uneasily? Unlikely, she decided as she left the hotel. It was simply her bullying way of trying to instil fear in everyone around her.

On her way home, Olivia found that a street she used daily had been blocked off by the police. A crowd had formed at the entrance to the street. People were craning their necks to see over one another. She could hear shouting, and paused.

'What's going on?' she asked a man in a homburg, who seemed tall enough to get a good view.

'Jews,' the man replied laconically. 'They're clearing out a block. Poor bastards.'

'There's nothing poor about them,' a smartly dressed woman beside them commented sharply. 'If they weren't swindlers, they wouldn't be in trouble.'

A light rain began to fall, and the crowd started to disperse, pulling up collars or opening umbrellas. Olivia moved forward to the barricade. She could now see down the street. Three police vans had parked at the kerb outside an apartment building, and several men, hunched under the rain, were shuffling into them. The shouting was coming from the police, who were pushing and shoving the captives into line. In the background, she could see the grey uniforms and helmets of German troops.

'It's not Germans who're arresting them,' she exclaimed. 'It's French police!'

'That just proves they're criminals,' the smartly dressed woman said, now shielded from the rain by a yellow umbrella. 'Now they'll give those apartments to honest French families.'

'What will happen to them?' Olivia asked unhappily.

The woman drew her finger across her throat and smiled by way of an answer.

'What do you mean?'

The woman with the yellow umbrella shrugged, as if to say that Olivia was stupid, and moved off.

'They won't harm them,' a man beside Olivia said. 'They're resettling them.'

'Where?'

'They've built a Jewish city somewhere outside Paris. They'll all be moved there in the end.'

Olivia watched the shabby rows of grey figures disappearing into the police vans. They were ordinary Parisians of the lower class, very far from the top-hatted plutocrats of Nazi propaganda. Standing mutely by were their womenfolk. Some were carrying very young children in their arms. She'd heard rumours that the Jews were being rounded up, but this was the first time she'd actually seen it happening. Wherever they were going, their fate was unlikely to be a kind one. She wanted to cry. But her tears were no use. Only her rage was useful. It showed her that what she was doing was not just for Fabrice and Marie-France. There was a wider purpose, a wider struggle.

The Paris Conservatoire, which had been deserted in the months after the start of the Occupation, was again a hub of the capital's musical life. Tonight's concert, of music by the Romantic composer Emmanuel Chabrier, was just the sort of thing to bring out the most fashionable people from both sides of the great divide.

And the divide, Arletty felt, was growing ever narrower. There were as many field-grey uniforms as silk gowns at these events; and it was becoming more and more common to see them side by side and arm in arm.

'Every cloud has a silver lining,' she said.

Beside her, Josée de Chambrun chuckled. 'You are the most baffling creature. What on earth are you talking about?'

'I was thinking,' Arletty said, 'that the German prisoner of war camps have swallowed the young men of France.' She gave her one-sided smile. 'It's such a consolation that the Germans are here to fill the gap – or half the seats in the Conservatoire would be empty.'

'Oh, now you are being satirical.' They were making their way up the crowded stairs to their box. Josée was wearing a spectacular and very expensive Lelong gown made from several metres of gold silk, so abundant that she was having to hold up the hem. The wearing of such a garment in these days of austerity was – like the giving of lavish suppers – a sign of great privilege and great wealth. Arletty herself was wearing lavender, a colour she suspected didn't suit her, and that now, as she saw herself in the huge gilt mirrors, she felt had a deadening effect on her complexion. 'The way I see it,' Josée continued, 'this is a historical process that has happened many times over the course of the centuries.'

'Do enlighten me,' Arletty said.

'Didn't the same thing happen when the Romans conquered Gaul under Julius Caesar? At first we fought them, and then we assimilated them. We learned their language, accepted their laws, put their gods on our altars. And thank heavens we did.'

'Thank heavens,' Arletty echoed.

'Or we would still be running around with bare behinds.'

'*You* might be running around with a bare behind. I wouldn't put it past you. I should skin a bear and make sure my behind was covered.'

'You would have to be careful the bear didn't skin you and stick your hide on his behind. But let me continue with my history lesson. The same thing happened a thousand years later with the Norman Dynasty. Those conquering blonde Vikings and the Frankish wives they took gave rise to the modern French race. Superior new blood once again, you see.'

'I do see. And so these Germans are the new Romans?'

'Exactly. In a generation or two, we will have assimilated them, and they will have assimilated us, and we'll be part of the master race of Europe.'

'And all our children will be called Hansel or Gretel.'

They had reached their box. The attendant bowed deeply to Josée and pulled aside the heavy velvet drape to admit them. They were the first to arrive in the box, and went to the edge of the balcony to look down. The murmur of the auditorium rose up to them on a wave of perfume and cigarette smoke, laughter and chatter. The hall was almost full, a hive teeming with Paris's busy bees, idle drones and dangerous wasps. The painted and gilded theatre was as gay as ever – apart from the large glowering German eagle that had been fixed over the stage.

The members of the orchestra were coming on to the stage and taking their seats. The hooting, scraping and plunking of tuning-up began.

Josée, who knew everybody in high society, and all of their doings, gave Arletty a running commentary. Everyone she knew seemed to be doing wonderfully well under the Occupation. Working together with the Germans (she abhorred the term *collaboration*) was as deeply beneficial as resisting them was injurious. It was good for France, good for Germany, good for Europe. It made one healthy, wealthy and wise.

'If only you'd agreed to work with Continental,' Josée sighed. 'Turning down all those wonderful pictures, one after another! You'd have been rich beyond your wildest dreams.'

'I prefer sleeping peacefully to having wild dreams,' Arletty replied calmly. 'Anyway, the scripts they sent me were stinkers. Whatever you say about the master race, their taste in films is abysmal.'

'I never imagined you'd be such a snob.'

'I'm an egg who would rather be hard-boiled than turned into a soufflé.'

Josée giggled. 'Not sure I get the metaphor, darling.'

'A hard-boiled egg is resilient. It will last for days. You can boil it on a Wednesday and take it on a picnic on Sunday. Whereas a soufflé deflates even before you can get it out of the kitchen. It's just froth and can never fill your stomach.'

'Meaning?'

'Meaning I consider myself a serious actress. Not a soubrette.'

Josée leaned even further over the balcony to peer into all the other boxes. 'Antoinette isn't here tonight. She never usually misses an occasion like this. Have you seen her lately?'

'No.'

'Nor have I. I do hope she isn't up to some stupidity or other.'

The velvet curtain was pulled aside and the rest of their party trooped into the box, led by the German ambassador, Otto Abetz. He was not in uniform tonight, but in a bow tie and tails, though nothing could soften the grim arrogance of his expression. He greeted Arletty with icy lack of interest but warmed enough to kiss Josée de Chambrun's hand.

Abetz was followed by two of Josée's oldest friends, the marquis and marquise of Polignac. Melchior de Polignac was spry and jolly, as well he might be, having inherited the Pommery champagne fortune as well as having had the foresight to be notably pro-Hitler well before the war, and to now be among the Germans' favourite Frenchmen. His charming blonde American wife, Nina, dramatically dressed in bright yellow and still a great beauty in middle age, was carrying an ice bucket containing two bottles of the family champagne, which she assured them was better than the stuff served at the bar.

Behind them came more German diplomatic staff: Ernst Achenbach, benign-faced and beaming behind his round spectacles, but said to be quietly rounding up hundreds of Jews as hostages; and Rudolf Schleier, Consul-General of the Reich in Paris, a plump and smiling man sporting a Hitler moustache, who was said to be able to smell a Jew through a brick wall, and who was whispered to be planning to purge France of every last drop of Semitic blood.

They were accompanied by their well-nourished wives, in Paris on shopping trips. With the French franc worth nothing, and luxury stores only open to Germans, such visitors acquired trunk-loads of furs, silk and jewellery. The substantial German ladies were resplendent tonight in recent acquisitions.

'I'm surprised there's anything left in the shops at all,' Arletty commented dryly. Josée hushed her with a frown.

The last arrival was in immaculate uniform, as usual; and as soon as he came into the box, Arletty instantly regretted the lavender gown more acutely than ever. Hans-Jürgen Soehring's deep-blue eyes found hers, and his smile of pure happiness struck her to the heart.

He settled into the seat just behind her and leaned forward. 'I hoped you would be here tonight,' he murmured. 'I've been thinking about you a great deal.'

'And I about you,' she heard herself say. Strangely, she hadn't realised that it was true until she'd said the words; but it *was* true. Her thoughts had circled around him for days. It was as though she had, while walking along a lonely beach, seen a beautiful shell lying in the sand, but had passed it by; and now, on her return, there it was again, waiting for her to pick it up in her fingers. She felt her heart beating fast enough to make her breathless.

'I love your smile,' he said.

'I like it too. Where would I be without it?'

Josée, seeing them talking, leaned over. 'My dear Hans-Jürgen, I have a very important question for you. Which do you prefer – a boiled egg or a soufflé?'

'Oh, that's easy. A soufflé is charming, but a boiled egg is a much more substantial thing. You know where you are with a boiled egg. And not many people know it, but there is a considerable art to boiling an egg.'

'What a clever answer,' Josée said, smirking at Arletty. 'I hope you like your eggs very hard-boiled indeed.'

Darkness fell over the auditorium and the audience settled into an expectant silence. Applause broke out as the conductor appeared. The first strains of music poured richly out.

In the darkness, Arletty felt his hand settle on hers, light and warm. 'I wish the lights had stayed on a little longer,' he whispered. 'I can't take my eyes off you.'

She didn't answer, but her hand, as if of its own volition, turned under his, so that their palms met. Her slim fingers curled through his. His responded with strength, holding her tight.

The music was ravishing, tender and irrepressibly French, tugging at the heartstrings. His mouth was close to her ear. 'I cannot tell you how much I long to kiss you. It makes my head swim. When you look at me in that way, with your lids half-lowered, and your smile all to one side, I can barely resist taking you in my arms in front of everybody and covering you with kisses.'

Part of her was ready to scoff at his words, spoken in such perfect French; but a larger part of her was vibrating like the strings of an instrument under the bow; an unaccustomed vibration, which she had almost forgotten she was capable of. She moved her head very slightly, just enough for her cheek to touch his mouth.

'Doe,' he whispered. 'My Doe. Your skin smells of jasmine.'

She couldn't recall being as happy as this since her youth. She was drunk with it, speechless with it. She kept her head still, feeling his warm breath on her neck, feeling the deliciousness of it crawl down her back, across her hips, along her thighs.

The first half of the concert passed in a haze, so swiftly that she was not even aware of the time going by. At the interval, everyone left the box to circulate, to see and be seen. Only the two of them remained, looking at one another in a manner that was both dazed and vividly aware.

'I feel as though I've been struck by a thunderbolt,' he said, passing his hand across his forehead.

'How did you know the answer to the egg question?'

'Oh, I guessed at once what you must have said to Josée.'

'You're very intuitive.'

'I feel as though I have known you all my life.'

She smiled wryly. 'That's only because you've seen me in my shower – on film.'

'If I thought it was just that, I would run a mile. I've never wanted affairs.'

'But you've had them?'

He leaned forward to light the cigarette she had taken out. 'Not like this.'

Arletty laughed a little unsteadily as she exhaled smoke. 'Are we having an affair?'

'I must see you.' His face, refined and sensitive, was intense. 'I must see you, away from Josée and her arch smile, away from everybody.'

'Very well.'

'Dine with me. At the Ritz. We can talk there.'

She hesitated. To be seen dining in public with a prominent member of the Occupation forces was very different from going to a 'mixed' dinner in a private home. It was a step that might have repercussions. But then a surge of pure exhilaration washed all those reservations away.

She was in a golden bubble with Soehring, and the diaphanous walls contained all her happiness. She couldn't bear the thought of bursting it. It didn't matter that he was a German, or a soldier, or that he was ten years younger than she. 'All right.'

'I will call you.'

'I'm staying at the Lancaster. Room 308.'

The others were already coming back into the box. Josée de Chambrun floated over to them in her gold silk gown. 'What are you two talking about so earnestly?' she enquired, wearing what Soehring had just called her arch smile.

'We were deploring the death of the Romantic movement,' Soehring said, 'and telling one another how charming the music of Chabrier is, compared to the complications of Schoenberg.'

Josée laughed. 'Well, you Nazis have chased him off to America, so you needn't worry about him any more.' She settled down between them with a rustle and looked from one to the other. 'I must say, you two go so very well together. One of those magical combinations, like strawberries and cream.'

'Or mayonnaise and boiled eggs,' Arletty suggested.

Abetz had now arrived and began to talk to Soehring in German. Josée leaned over confidentially to Arletty. 'You're going to need a place.'

'Am I?'

'Hotels are all very well, but they're so public for lovers.' Arletty raised her eyebrows at that, but Josée pressed on regardless. 'I have the most gorgeous apartment for you. It belongs to a delightful American friend who left France when the war started. She'd be only too pleased to rent it to you.'

It was late by the time Arletty got back to the Lancaster. The party had gone for a late dinner after the concert, and they had been joined by several others. There had been a lot of noise, a lot of laughter and drinking. There had been little further opportunity to talk to Soehring. She almost couldn't bear to watch him with others, beautiful as he was;

to see his attention directed anywhere except at herself aroused a fierce jealousy in her.

Jealousy! In a heart that had always been so cool, so undisturbed in its courses! She'd been in foreign beds, but none of it seemed to have touched her. And now to see him smiling at another woman, with those pointed faun's ears and those melancholy eyes, tore at her.

She was half-undressed when the telephone rang. She picked it up.

'I wish I was with you,' his husky voice said in her ear.

'I wish that too.'

'Are you undressed?'

'In my underwear.'

'God help me.'

'You will be disappointed, Faun.' She looked at her legs in their black silk stockings. 'I am no longer young. And they tell me I am thin and gawky.'

'Who has told you that?'

'Those who have seen me.'

His voice grew rough. 'I can't bear to think of you with anybody else.'

'I suffer from the same sickness. Don't worry. I'm alone.'

'Shall I come to you?'

'No.'

'Don't you want me?'

'Yes, I want you. But I'm going to dream about you. Mad, silly dreams that I won't want to wake from.'

'Doe…'

'My Faun.'

'I love it when you call me that.'

'You're more than a faun. You're the god Pan. You have his face. I'm sure you have his horns, too, somewhere about you.'

'Are you really going to be mine?'

'You will have to wait and see.'

She replaced the receiver. Once again, her breathing was quick and irregular. The things they said were so banal. They had been said a million times before, by a million lovers; and yet their spell was so erotic and potent that she could hardly be still. His voice was echoing in her ears, husky and full of longing. The room felt unbearably warm. She walked quickly on to the balcony to cool down. The moon had not yet risen, and in this blacked-out city there was no danger of being seen by anyone. She was merely a shadow among shadows.

She reclined on the chair and lit a cigarette, her last of the evening. God help her. God help them both.

Slowly, she spread her thighs, as though accommodating a lover. She felt the night creep between them, the cool air licking at her hot skin, an invisible caress that was unbearably delicate.

She let her head drop back and closed her eyes, the cigarette falling from her fingers to burn itself out on the marble tiles.

Fifteen

Olivia had had little to do with Blanche Auzello, Monsieur Auzello's wife, and it was a surprise to be sent to her room by one of the waiters.

Madame Auzello's antagonism to the Nazis was no secret. She even had the dubious distinction of having been arrested by the Gestapo; but so powerful had been her charm – or perhaps her effrontery – that whereas she had been taken away in a truck, she had been returned to the Ritz in a Mercedes-Benz.

She was in her mid-forties, a vivacious bottle-blonde, with sad eyes emphasised by the kind of make-up that had been fashionable in the Jazz Age, and a large pouting mouth that was always heavily lipsticked. She was slim, wearing American wide-leg slacks with buttons up the hips, a garment Olivia instantly envied with a sharp pang.

'Come in, kid,' she said, as Olivia peered round the door. 'Let me get a good look at you.' Taking Olivia by the arm, Madame Auzello led her to the window, and slipped on a pair of gold-rimmed spectacles to inspect her closely. She nodded. 'Yup. Authentic Aryan stock.'

Olivia, who was getting rather tired of this appellation, grimaced. 'I'm American, the same as you, Madame Auzello.'

'Oh, I know *that*. Don't get in a snit. Be grateful for blonde hair and beauty. Both are gifts these days. And call me Blanche.' She took off her glasses and tapped them on her chin, still looking at Olivia speculatively. 'Goering likes you, so I'm told.'

'Yes. I don't know why.'

'I do. You're his type. Just like the first wife, what was her name? Carin? Men tend to fixate on a certain type of woman, though maybe you're too young to have learned that yet. They seldom look below the surface. Maybe you haven't learned that either.'

'I'm learning,' Olivia said grimly.

'I'm a Jew. Did you know *that*?'

'No.'

'Born to Isaac and Sara Rubenstein on the Lower East Side. I sleep like a mouse in a cat's ear, you can imagine. How come you haven't hightailed it back to the States?'

'I was in love.'

'Ah. That was my problem too. Claude wanted me to go in 1939, but I wouldn't leave him. Even though he's a cheating, two-timing son of a bitch.'

Olivia was startled. 'Monsieur Auzello?'

'This is your morning for learning new things, huh?' Blanche said drily. 'Yup. *Monsieur* Auzello has a Thursday night appointment with his regular mistress. He insists he needs it for his mental health. Monogamy depresses him.'

This was a new view of the stern and military manager of the Ritz.

'I'm very sorry.'

'I pay him back from time to time, but tell you the truth, I don't really enjoy infidelity. I'm just a faithful Jewish *balabusta*, I guess. You know what a balabusta is?'

'No,' Olivia confessed.

'Doesn't matter. You're asking yourself why I'm telling you my life story. It's so you know you can trust me. And I guess I have to trust you. I heard what happened to the boyfriend. I can understand how that would make you want to hit back.'

'As hard as I can,' Olivia said bleakly.

'Me too. I hate the sons of bitches.' She reached into the pocket of her enviable slacks. 'So. This is what you want, right?'

Olivia blinked at the little film canister between Blanche's finger and thumb. 'You know Jack?'

Blanche looked amused. 'Is that what he told you his name is?'

'I guess it's not Jack?'

'He told me his name was Guillaume. Jack is as good a name as any. I have no idea what he's really called. What a hunk, huh?'

'He's not my type.'

'Did he step on your toes?'

'He's not very sociable.'

'He's a pistol, I'll tell you that. He doesn't have to be sociable. But you can trust him.'

'Who does he work for?'

'Uncle Sam, that's all you or I need to know.' She dropped the film canister into Olivia's palm. 'Be careful of the stunts you pull. Don't go too far. Slow and steady, as the turtle said to the rabbit.'

'Thanks.'

'You know, kid, after all this hoo-ha is over, you should go to Hollywood and get into the movies. You have the looks. You'd be a natural if you learned to smile more. I was getting into the movies when I was your age, back in the Twenties. Then I met Claude, and I threw it all up for love and staying home Thursdays while my husband schtupps his girlfriend. Ah, it could be worse. I get to live in the Ritz, right? And trust me, Claude wouldn't be manager if it wasn't for all the hard work I do.'

'Do I come back to you when I need another film?' Olivia asked.

'Boy, you're all business, aren't you? Not much small talk in Olivia Olsen. You need to relax a little. Look like you're having fun. The Nazis like people who look like they're having fun. Long faces make them suspicious, you know what I mean? And never look scared. Nazis are like mean dogs. If they think you're scared, they'll come after you.'

'Sorry.'

'Don't be sorry. Just take my advice. If you look miserable you're going to draw the wrong kind of attention to yourself. Get me? Lift your eyebrows. Don't frown. Drop your shoulders. Pick your chin up. Don't go around looking like you have a tommy-gun in your pants. Smile at everybody. If they challenge you, smile. If they yell at you, smile. If they insult you, smile.'

Olivia tried with an effort to obey these instructions. 'Okay.'

'That's more like it. You're even more of a doll when you clear the thundercloud off your face. Remember: in this world, appearances are everything. Be what they want you to be. You'll go far.'

Olivia reflected that it had indeed been a morning for learning things. She'd warmed to Blanche and she recognised that her advice was good. The Germans were always relaxed around smiling people, suspicious of grim ones. Since Fabrice's death, she'd almost forgotten how to smile. She would have to learn to wear one again, even if it was a painted smile.

Sometimes a painted smile was the only one you had.

⁂

'What are you doing?' a German voice rapped out coldly.

Olivia felt that her heart had stopped beating. This room was one where she regularly found scattered documents. It was often littered with bottles, as well as traces of female visitors, sometimes even syringes and empty pillboxes. Today she had come across a sheaf of aerial photographs showing the results of the bombing of London, together with detailed notes. She was so intent on the papers in her hand that she hadn't heard the Gestapo officer come into the room.

'I'm just – just tidying up,' she stammered.

The man advanced on her and snatched the papers from her hand. 'I'll have you shot for this,' he shouted, seeing what it was she had been studying.

She backed away. 'I wasn't doing anything wrong. I need to clean the room.' But the Minox was in her pocket. If he found it, she was dead. 'I'm very sorry I picked them up! They were just lying there—'

'You will answer for this at Gestapo headquarters.' The man's hand was on the holster of his pistol. 'Empty your pockets.'

Olivia was too paralysed with shock to move. At that moment, Goering's security chief, Soehring, came into the room. 'What's the matter?' he demanded.

The Gestapo man swung round. 'I caught this woman rifling through secret papers!'

'Is this true?' Soehring demanded.

Olivia tried to get her voice under control. 'I have my work to do,' she said shakily. 'I have to tidy up the things guests leave around.'

Soehring examined the photographs. 'Where were these?' he asked.

Her mouth was dry. She pointed. 'Scattered on the desk.'

'The officer who left them there should face a court martial,' Soehring said.

'Never mind that,' the Gestapo man snapped. 'She should not have touched them!'

'I know her,' Soehring said. 'She's Goering's pet Swede. She's trustworthy.'

'She must be interrogated!'

'She understands nothing of these things. Tell this officer to come and see me immediately.' Soehring glanced round at the champagne bottles and lipstick-stained sheets. 'I have a few words to say to him.'

'But the maid—'

'The maid has done nothing wrong,' Soehring said, turning to Olivia. 'Get out. And the next time you find military papers scattered around, call me.'

'Yes, sir.'

Olivia hurried from the room on rubbery legs, leaving Soehring to deal with the Gestapo man. She felt shaken to the core. That had been a close thing.

Being 'Goering's pet Swede' had saved her life. And thank God, in this second year of the Occupation, the general mood among the occupying Germans was one of complacency. Luftwaffe officers in Paris seemed to regard their main duties as looking smart and having fun. Even Major Soehring, whose intervention had just saved her, was a handsome young playboy whose main concern was seeing that the Reichsmarschall's champagne was cold enough.

The carnage taking place over London, with bombers shot down and dozens of airmen lost each night, seemed not to affect the happy crew who had the good fortune to be billeted here.

Olivia suspected that this attitude was a direct result of the life led by Goering himself. Disconnected from reality, apparently out of favour with his adored Führer, he wallowed in the pleasures of the flesh; and his staff took their cue from him. But it was a long time before she stopped trembling.

On Sunday evening she returned to the vineyard to keep her appointment with Jack. It was full summer and there was warm sunlight on the terraces, making the vine leaves glow like jade.

To her alarm, there were two German soldiers in the vineyard, rifles slung over their shoulders, walking slowly between the rows. She almost turned back. But watching them, she decided they were more interested in the vines than in anything else. She walked past them. To judge by what she could understand of their conversation, they were inspecting with interest the little bunches of grapes that had begun to set.

She reached the hut. Jack was outside, in faded jeans and a check shirt, sharpening a pair of secateurs. He was wearing the battered straw hat, so she judged it was safe to approach.

'There are two soldiers close by,' she greeted him.

'Yeah, I know.' He was intent on the blades and the whetstone. 'They're from the Mosel area. One of the wine-producing areas of Germany. They think their vines are superior to anything in France.' He glanced up at her. The grey eyes were sharp. 'So they haven't caught you yet.'

'They're not going to catch me,' Olivia retorted. 'I'm not stupid.'

'Good to know,' he said laconically. 'Come into my parlour.'

She followed him into the hut. He stripped off his shirt.

'Do we have to go through this charade every time?' she demanded. 'Or do you just like showing off your muscles?'

'I like not being shot,' he replied. 'Get your dress off.'

Angrily, she hauled off her dress. She found this part of their encounters demeaning. This time she had at least taken care to wear new underclothes, rather than the faded things she'd had on the last time. She handed him the three film canisters she'd shot.

'Huh.' He seemed interested, if not delighted. 'Not just a pretty face. You've been a busy little bee.'

She smiled at him brightly. 'Gee shucks, thank you, kind sir.'

'Nice yokel routine.'

'I've been advised to use it when bumpkins say stupid things to me.'

'Okay, I won't say stupid things to you.' He weighed the canisters in his hand. 'Is it worthwhile developing these? Chemicals are hard to find, and if they're just blurry shots of hotel rooms, we can skip it.'

'I risked my life to take those pictures,' she said icily. 'They're as good as I could get them. If you don't develop them, you're not going to see me here again.'

'Fair enough.' He pocketed the spools. 'Where did you hide the camera?'

'Behind some hot-water pipes.'

'How hot?'

'Hot enough to keep people from sticking their fingers in there.'

'That's also hot enough to spoil the film,' he said. 'Clever idea, but don't leave the camera there too long while it's loaded.'

He was about to go on when they both heard the scrape of boots outside the hut, and a German voice. Unhesitatingly, Jack took her in his arms and kissed her. She was too surprised to react, which was just as well, because the door swung open and the soldiers peered in. Jack held her tight, his mouth pressed against hers, not letting her move. After a moment, there was laughter from the Germans and a ribald comment. The door slammed shut again and they heard the boots marching away.

At last Jack released her. She backed away, wiping her mouth. There were angry tears starting to come to her eyes. He saw them. 'Don't get mad,' he said. 'That was necessary.'

She shook her head without replying. He would never understand that she was crying for Fabrice. Fabrice had been the last man to kiss her, and that had been almost a year ago. To be kissed again under these circumstances was terribly painful.

'I'm going to need more film,' she told him. 'Can't you give me a dozen?'

'A dozen?'

'I can use a dozen a week.'

'Take it easy. Risks are just not worth it. I don't want you to have more than one or two spools to deal with. It'll tie your life up in knots. And there's more chance of one going astray, and being found by the wrong people. Blanche Auzello will always have a new spool for you. You can trust her.'

'I'm doing this because I want to,' she replied thinly. 'Because I *need* to. Don't tell me not to take risks.'

He grunted. 'I'll say one thing for you: you've got moxie. But it's my job to keep you alive. And to teach you your business.' His hard, tanned face gave little away. 'We'll take a look at these. If they're any good, we'll find more work for you.' He started pulling on his shirt.

'Is that it?' Olivia demanded.

'We'll meet again in three Sundays. Same place, different time. Twelve noon. Hat on, it's safe. Hat off, walk on by.'

Olivia began buttoning up her dress. 'You still don't trust me.'

'I trust your good intentions,' he replied. 'I don't trust your tradecraft.'

Once dressed, they left the hut. The two German soldiers were nowhere to be seen. The sun was now low, and the sky was taking on a golden tinge.

'Remember what I said.' He was already back to sharpening the secateurs. 'Don't take chances. So long, yokel.'

'So long, bumpkin.'

She walked out of the vineyard. She felt lighter without the films in her pocket. She devoutly hoped the photographs would come out well. He'd spoken of 'we', so there was evidently an organisation behind him, of unknown size and power. That was reassuring. But she felt she was being kept at arm's length, and that annoyed her. She was burning to see results, to get somewhere; taking baby steps was frustrating.

It was a twenty-minute walk to Montmartre cemetery, where Fabrice was buried. She walked fast, trying to burn off her frustration. It was evident everywhere that the Occupation had taken a firmer grip, put down deeper roots. The French road signs had been replaced with German ones, the streets had been renamed after Nazis. Checkpoints had been erected every mile or so. Soldiers patrolled everywhere, filling the cafés and taking photographs of each other in front of the sights.

Bare walls were plastered with Nazi posters, some spewing hate against communists and Jews, or warning of the grim penalties for resistance, others urging friendship and mutual cooperation between occupied and occupier. The tone they took reminded Olivia of the benevolent ogres in the Swedish fairy tales she'd been told as a child, who put children on their knee, but whose laughing mouths could open wide and bite your head off.

And everywhere, the swastika flew, draped on Paris's most iconic monuments. You never got used to that. Olivia still saw people with tears in their eyes as they stared at the Arc de Triomphe, decked in the crooked cross of Hitler's Germany. That produced a daily shock that didn't go away.

She reached the cemetery and hurried to the plot where Fabrice was buried. It had been a couple of weeks since she'd visited it. She'd hoped she might see Marie-France here, but she had missed her: there were fresh flowers in the vase that was fixed in a ring on the bare little plaque that was all the Gestapo had permitted.

Olivia stood looking at the name chiselled in the marble, which was already streaked with soot. Next time she came, she would bring a brush and scrub the stone clean.

She was thinking of a young life cut short, a life that should have been lived; of children they would have had, things they would have made together, good things, things that would last.

'I'm sorry,' she whispered. She was not quite sure what she was sorry for: having missed last Sunday, the black streaks on the marble, the man who had kissed her in the vineyard, the fact that she was alive while Fabrice was dead.

She hadn't said anything to Marie-France about the camera or her meeting with Jack. Marie-France had enough to cope with. Adding a worry just wasn't fair.

She kissed her fingers and laid them on the stone before leaving.

Laszlo Weisz, her old teacher, lived not far from here. There was just time to look in on him on her way home.

As always, rue Lepic was littered with dirty carrot tops and cabbage leaves from the street market. Old people were gathering these scraps. Olivia knew it wasn't just tidying up: this refuse was going into soup pots. The spectre of starvation was stalking Paris.

She rang the bell. After a long while, she heard shuffling, and Laszlo's face peered cautiously out of the iron grille. His eyes flickered into life as he recognised her. But as he swung the door open, she saw that he was thin and drawn, his back stooped.

'I don't go out much these days,' he told her. 'The streets aren't safe any more, between the *apaches* and the Germans.'

'Do you have enough to eat?'

'I'm lucky. I have neighbours who do some shopping for me, and the girl who comes to clean brings me eggs from her family in the country.'

But he was pitifully neglected-looking. 'Have the Germans bothered you?' she asked.

'They came around and put my name on a register. They seemed to only be interested in able-bodied men, and they told me I was not able-bodied, with which I agreed. They also kindly informed me that my work was degenerate.' He gave a hollow smile. 'I regard that as one of the highest accolades I've received in a lifetime of art. But I'm afraid they'll come back one day.' He took a yellow leaflet out of a folder and passed it to her. 'I collect these.'

It was in the form of a comic strip entitled 'The Cancer Killing France'. It began with hook-nosed foreign Jews arriving in France, taking control of the country, gleefully filling their pockets with money and starting the war for their own ends. Now wealthy, they seduced the wives of men dying or being captured in battle. The story ended with the Jews being expelled from the country and grateful French citizens shaking hands with the Germans.

'I'm sorry,' she said, handing it back to him. 'That's vile.'

'There are several variations,' he said, carefully putting it back in the collection. 'The drawings are very effective, don't you think? Some artist, just like you and me, has done them.'

'The Occupation can't last for ever.'

'No, but it will last longer than my lifetime.' He laid his trembling hand on her arm. 'I'm reconciled to that. But you, Olivia – you should leave now. There's nothing to keep you here any longer. Fabrice is dead. Forgive me for not using any of the customary euphemisms.'

'You don't need to use euphemisms. I've just come from his grave.'

'If he were alive, he would tell you to get out. Your country may soon be in the war against Germany. And then what will you do?'

'I will fight,' she replied quietly. 'I'm fighting now. I'm not going to run away.'

The curfew was fast approaching, and she had to go. Quietly, she put money on the table where he would find it. Laszlo felt like a bag of bones when she hugged him. She left him leafing through his collection of anti-Semitic propaganda, as though some answer lay there, and ran up rue Lepic towards Montmartre.

Sixteen

Arletty felt, rather than heard, the silence that followed their entrance into the Ritz grill. She was used to being recognised in restaurants, but this time the recognition was of a different kind. As they passed, the ripple of silence washed along with them. People stopped talking to look at her, and then at the man in uniform beside her. Then their expressions changed, and they lowered their voices to whispers.

Not that there weren't other French women seated with men in German uniforms. One of the larger tables was occupied by three such couples, already far advanced enough in champagne to be laughing loudly. The women were young and pretty, the officers old and ugly. It was the kind of spectacle that made one shrug.

But Arletty knew that she was different from them, that her presence here with Soehring was different from other presences. The walls of her golden bubble shivered for a moment, and she felt a cold breath on her skin.

Then Soehring took her arm. The bubble steadied. The golden glow returned to surround her.

Paul, the suave *maître d'hôtel* of L'Espadon, steered them unobtrusively to one of the most secluded tables, in the corner of the room. Here, they could not be observed by other diners, unless the two women at the table next to theirs were prepared to turn unashamedly and look over their shoulders. It seemed that the two women, both dressed in the height of fashion, were prepared to indulge in such boorish curiosity. Her bubble shivered once more.

'You've gone pale,' Soehring said as they took their plush seats opposite one another. 'Are you uncomfortable?'

After the extraordinary intimacy that had arisen so swiftly between them at the Conservatoire, she suddenly felt almost shy with him. 'Perhaps we shouldn't have come here.'

'Aren't you happy to be with me?'

'I'm enchanted to be with you. Only—'

'Only what?'

'You know what.'

He leaned forward. 'Ignore them. They have nothing to do with us, or we with them.'

The effect of his gaze was to obliterate all her misgivings. Or almost all of them. 'I represent something for them.'

'*La belle France?*'

'I'm not arrogant enough to assume that. But something. And they don't like to see me—'

'With me,' he said quietly, as she once again didn't finish her sentence.

'With a member of the occupying forces.' She smiled. 'Who also happens to be so god-like.'

'Devil-like, you mean, perhaps.'

'Between gods and devils there's little difference. But the pointed ears undoubtedly indicate a certain infernal affinity.'

'Let them stare. Nothing can spoil this occasion for me.'

'Or for me. I'm very proud to be seen in the company of such ears. Josée tells me I should regard you as Julius Caesar, here to civilise the Gaulish barbarians.'

'I think it's rather the other way round. I'm here to be civilised by you.' The waiter gave them the menus, and they chose to share a Chateaubriand and a 1900 Saint-Emilion. 'I wish we had met under other circumstances,' Soehring said once they'd made their order. 'I detest this war. All war. I saw enough of it in Spain.'

Her eyes dropped to the campaign ribbons on his tunic, the Iron Cross on his pocket. 'You were in Spain?'

'Yes, with the Condor Legion.'

The name was one that struck dread. 'Did you do terrible things?'

'Terrible things were done.'

'But not by you?'

'I was a part of it. I cannot say my hands are clean of blood.'

She raised her eyes to his. 'Aren't you a Nazi?'

'Oh, I joined the Party in 1938. That was rather late for my career, but just in time for the war. My father advised me to join much earlier. I should have listened to him. He's a very wise man, a career diplomat.'

She laced her fingers and rested her chin on them. 'Tell me about yourself.'

'It's a tale of disappointments,' he replied. 'As a young man, I fancied I would make my fortune in South America. Alas, I showed no talent for business, and came back poorer than when I left. I was chosen to represent Germany in the equestrian events at the Berlin Olympic Games of 1936, but I had a stupid fall at the last minute and broke my arm. I had to watch as my team went on to make a clean sweep of the gold medals. I've written poetry, but so far the publishers have declined to print it. Chastened, I have settled down to exercise law.'

'You're deliberately making yourself sound tragic to arouse my sympathies.'

He had an engaging grin, which showed his excellent teeth. 'You're too sharp for me.'

'Now tell me the real story.'

'You mean the other half? Very well. I was born in Istanbul, where my father was posted. I received a solid classical education as a boy, and aside from my foolish adventures, I studied law in Berlin, Leipzig, Grenoble, Clermont-Ferrand, Paris and London. I speak English,

Spanish and French, as well as passable German. I joined the Luftwaffe in 1937 because I was getting bored with life, and had the good fortune to attract the attention of Hermann Goering during the Spanish war. It's thanks to him that I have the rank of Major, and this posting.'

'You are the Aryan superman we have all heard about.' Her tone was only half-ironic. 'And you are barely thirty.'

'I'm thirty-two.'

'Do you know how old I am?'

'I hope that doesn't matter to you, because it doesn't matter in the slightest to me.' His eyes never left her face. 'You are the greatest actress of the age. I am the one who is at your feet.'

'I hope you plan to rise somewhat higher.'

His eyes widened for a moment, then he threw back his head and laughed. 'You're very direct.'

'I don't know how to be anything but direct.'

'And have you had so many lovers, then?'

'They've mainly been women.'

He looked startled. 'Women? I was talking of romantic affairs.'

'So was I.'

'But then you are a—'

'No, I'm not that.'

'I don't understand!'

'You don't need to. It doesn't threaten you.'

He seemed disconcerted. 'And how do you think you'll like being with a man?'

'My dear Faun, there's nothing a woman can do that you can't do just as well. And you have something extra besides.' His confusion had amused her and allowed her to resume the role of the sophisticated older woman. She was once again in control of herself, teasing, ironic. 'You made a journey of a hundred kilometres to see the uncensored version of me. That's what I intend to continue giving you.'

Their Chateaubriand arrived, the richly tender fillet sliced into rounds, oozing bloody juice. Perhaps as a tribute to Soehring, the dish had been served *à l'Alsacienne*, with braised sauerkraut in a timbale and tiny shavings of ham. The venerable wine was uncorked and tasted with great ceremony, and they began to eat.

'Of course,' a woman's voice said from the neighbouring table, 'she plays trollops and tarts in her films. What can you expect of a woman like that?'

Her companion answered, 'Oh, quite. There's a reason she got those roles. It just rather puts one off one's food to see it in real life.'

The raised, drawling voices were intended to be heard. Arletty grew very still. Soehring lifted his wine glass to his lips. 'They come here especially to insult people like us,' he said. 'They think it patriotic. In the meantime, their husbands are doing business with Berlin, and making a fortune.'

'I can't bear that sort of woman,' the first voice was saying, growing even louder. 'It turns my stomach.'

Soehring put down his napkin and turned in his chair to face the women. 'I wonder whether you are aware,' he said in his impeccable French, 'that insulting the German army is an offence punishable by a minimum of five years' imprisonment? Although in your case, if you say one more word, I will make sure that you don't see the light of day for ten.'

A horrified silence followed as Soehring turned calmly back to his food; and shortly afterwards, Arletty saw the women, their faces as white as sheets, hurrying out of the restaurant. They had left their food half-eaten.

Arletty felt a strange whirlwind of emotions. She was sickened, yet excited – ashamed, yet exhilarated. Soehring's power was casually brutal, and that made it thrilling. As a working-class woman, she had been vulnerable to insults and slights all her life, no matter how celebrated she had become. But now, with Soehring at her side, nobody would dare slight or insult her again. Her position in the charmed circle, as Josée de Chambrun called it, was assured.

He glanced at her. 'I hope they didn't upset you.'

'If you were ten years older,' she replied in a low voice, 'perhaps you wouldn't have acted in that way.'

'But I am not ten years older,' he said with masculine calm. 'I am as I am. And anyone who wounds you will have me to deal with.'

She placed her knife and fork together on her plate. 'Let's go to your room.'

Heading towards her first rendezvous with Jack in three weeks, Olivia was both nervous and excited. By now he would have developed the photographs she had taken, and would be able to tell her how effective she had been. It would be deeply satisfying to see the sceptical expression wiped off his face, but to the same degree humiliating to see it turn to open scorn.

The door of the hut was ajar when she arrived. She peered in, to find him sitting at a makeshift table made out of an old wine barrel. Laid out on it were a bottle of wine, two ripe peaches and what looked like a quiche.

'Sunday lunch,' he said laconically, waving her to an upturned bucket that was to serve as her chair. 'I hope you like *tarte de brie.*'

'I'm always hungry,' Olivia replied, taking her seat. 'I'll eat anything. What's this all about?'

'A little celebration.'

She examined his expression. 'You mean the pictures were okay?'

'They were better than okay.' For the first time since she had known him, his face broke into a smile. It was like sunlight passing over a rocky mountain. 'They were damn good.'

She flushed with pleasure. 'Really?'

Jack passed her the wine bottle. 'Almost every shot is perfect. Have a drink.'

'Thanks!'

'How did you keep your hands steady?'

'I didn't think about it.' She swigged from the bottle, feeling the rough wine slide down her throat. 'The whole thing is easier if you don't think about it.'

'Yeah.' He was slicing the *tarte de brie* with a clasp knife. 'A lot of things are like that.'

She ate hungrily, talking with her mouth full. 'So what do the documents show? Anything valuable?'

He watched her with something of the pride of a ringmaster watching a performing seal eat sardines. 'Some of it is very valuable: Luftwaffe signals about aircraft production and crew training. Estimates of the success of the bombing campaign against Britain – which, by the way, are completely out of whack. Reports on new aircraft types they're developing.' Jack took the wine bottle back from Olivia and drank from the neck. 'The extraordinary thing is, he's not answering any of it. Berlin are going crazy with him.'

'I've heard his staff complaining that he won't talk to anybody except art dealers. And he's a complete drug addict.'

Jack nodded. 'You've given us a fascinating insight into Goering's position in the hierarchy. He's even weaker than we thought. Goebbels, Himmler and Bormann are all jockeying for position, and they want to edge him out of favour with Hitler. They're persuading Hitler that the Luftwaffe can't be counted on, that Goering is a failure. It means that they're going to rely on their air power less and less. And that information is priceless.'

Olivia basked in his approval. 'I told you I would need more film.'

'Agreed. But there's a limit to what Goering's correspondence tells us. He doesn't handle the most important stuff himself – he's too busy with his art collection. Most of the real dope you've given us has come from his staff. I need you to concentrate on them.'

'They're a lot more of a challenge,' Olivia said cautiously. 'Goering's in a dream most of the time, but they're a lot more alert. I nearly got caught the other day.' She told him about the furious officer who had threatened to have her shot.

He didn't seem impressed. 'You survived, didn't you?'

'It was close.'

'The problem is, you can't rely on these men to leave their documents lying conveniently around for you to photograph. You're going to have to open briefcases and look inside. You're going to have to open desk drawers and valises.'

'That won't be easy,' she said unhappily. 'I don't have much time. And they lock everything.'

'Every lock can be picked. I'm going to teach you how to open just about anything with some basic equipment. If you know what you're doing, and learn to work fast, you can be in and out in two minutes.'

Olivia's warm feeling of achievement was being stripped away by a cold wind. 'I think they're already suspicious of me.'

'I can't show you all this stuff here,' Jack went on as though she hadn't spoken. 'Too many eyes around for a lock-picking class. And we'll need to refine your photography skills as well. I'll come to your studio later this week.'

'Is that safe?'

'We're lovers now,' he replied. 'I think we've established that.' He studied her expression. 'You can say no if it frightens you.'

Olivia took another swig of wine. The course he was suggesting was going to expose her to a lot more danger, and demand a lot more courage. But she had set her feet on this path willingly. She'd wanted to hit back at them for Fabrice, and what she'd done already had given her some satisfaction; but she was starting to realise that every hill climbed revealed a vista of further hills to climb. If she backed out now she would be betraying Fabrice and the promise she'd made to herself to avenge him. There was a long way to go before she would call it quits.

She nodded. 'Okay. I'll do it.'

'Good,' he said. 'We'll meet at your studio on Wednesday evening. I'll be waiting for you when you get back from work.'

She felt a pang of grief as she remembered that it had once been Fabrice who waited for her to get back from the Ritz. 'Right.'

'Take the wine and the food,' he said, rising. 'You're going to need your strength.'

'Is it true?'

Arletty looked up from the table in the Ritz bar, where she had been reading *Paris-soir*. She hadn't seen Antoinette in weeks, and her friend had changed. She was thinner, paler. Her hair looked wild, and her burning eyes were fixed on Arletty. 'If Dr Goebbels says it's true, then it must be true,' Arletty replied with light irony. 'Sit down. You look like you need a drink.'

'Is it true you've taken that Nazi as your lover?' Antoinette demanded, refusing the invitation to sit.

'I thought you were talking about the war news.' Arletty indicated the front page of her newspaper, emblazoned with announcements that the Germans had just begun a vast invasion of Russia along a front that stretched from the Arctic to the Black Sea.

'Don't prevaricate,' Antoinette said in a savage voice.

'It's hardly a prevarication,' Arletty replied laconically. 'The big war is surely rather more important than little Arletty.'

Antoinette stamped her foot furiously. '*Answer me!*'

People around the room were turning to look at Antoinette. Frank Meier, the venerable barman of the Ritz, came gliding out from under the graceful frescoes of hunting scenes that were painted over his bar.

'Good evening, Madame d'Harcourt,' he said smoothly, 'such a pleasure to see you here again after so long. May I offer you a glass of champagne?'

'I don't want anything,' Antoinette snapped.

But Frank, well-practised at defusing situations in his bar, had already pulled out a chair and was ushering the duchess into it. Antoinette had no choice but to subside into the leather seat. 'I'll send your champagne over,' he murmured, 'on the house, of course.' He slipped away.

Arletty stared at Antoinette's strained face, well aware that most eyes in the room were watching them intently. 'You don't look well,' she said quietly.

'I am asking you for the last time: is it true?'

'Yes, it's true.'

Arletty saw the colour drain from Antoinette's face. Antoinette pulled off one of her brown gloves and raised it to strike Arletty in the face. Arletty made no attempt to protect herself from the blow, but looked back steadily at Antoinette.

Antoinette lowered the glove and started to cry. 'How *could* you!'

'I had no choice in the matter,' Arletty replied. 'I've fallen in love.'

'In love! With a man ten years younger than you, a Nazi officer!'

'So it seems.'

'You've not only betrayed me – you've betrayed your country.'

'I've never had a gift for patriotism. As you once informed me, women of my class don't have the same loyalties as women of yours.'

'Are you loyal to *anything*?'

'I think loyalty is overrated. People use the word when they want you to put their interests above your own. A loyal dog, a loyal employee, a loyal wife, a loyal Frenchwoman. None of these are categories I've ever aspired to.'

'My God! I feel that I've never really known you.'

'Perhaps you never have.' One of Frank's white-coated team brought a glass of champagne to Antoinette, who gulped at it. When he'd cleared away the ashtray and left, Arletty went on, 'I love you, Antoinette, but you don't own me. I'm not your property. And may I point out that you left me before I left you.'

'I left you to fight for the Resistance!' Antoinette exclaimed.

'For God's sake, lower your voice,' Arletty replied, 'unless you want to end up in the Gestapo cellars.'

'You've already destroyed me. I don't care what happens to me.'

'It's a little late for resistance, in any case. If you hadn't let the Germans in, there wouldn't be any for me to sleep with.'

'Is that your excuse?'

'I don't need an excuse, my dear.' Arletty took the silver-bound soda siphon that stood on the table and squirted a little more soda water into her cocktail. 'One Sunday in Courbevoie, when I was twelve, I came home crying from church. At confession, the priest had been asking me questions. Did I play with myself, had I taken my knickers off for a boy, that sort of thing? My father was furious. He took me back to the church and dragged the priest out of the confessional by his collar and shouted in his face that if he ever asked me such things again, he would break his neck. He was a little red-haired man – the priest, I mean – and he cringed like a dog.' Arletty swirled the drink in her glass. 'I learned on that day that a priest is just a man with a dirty mind. And so is God.'

'You're disgusting!'

Arletty shrugged. 'I'm honest. Church, government, country, it's all a racket. The whole of France is opening its legs to the Germans. At least I'm enjoying it. And I'm glad, at least, that you didn't hit me in the face. A black eye would have spoiled my evening.' She looked over Antoinette's shoulder. 'You'll be able to meet my Nazi. Here he comes now.'

Antoinette spun round in her chair. Soehring was not in uniform tonight, but in an evening suit, which was just as well on this occasion,

Arletty thought. He looked, to her eyes at least, extraordinarily striking, though he was frowning a little uncertainly as he came to their table.

'Antoinette, I would like to present Hans-Jürgen Soehring. But I call him Faun, because I found him wandering in the forest, abandoned by his mother, so I licked him all over and brought him home. Faun, this is my friend Antoinette d'Harcourt.'

Soehring bowed formally but did not take a seat. Antoinette was looking up at him with a stricken face, her expression an odd mixture of hate and awe. 'I suppose I can't compete with this,' she said in a low voice.

'There's no question of competition between friends,' Arletty replied.

But Antoinette had risen to her feet. 'I wish you joy of one another,' she said bitterly, and hurried out of the bar.

Soehring watched her leave with a thoughtful expression. 'I guessed at once who she was when I saw her from the door,' he said. 'Perhaps I should have turned back and gone away again.'

'It had to be faced,' Arletty said, 'and now it has been faced. She'll accept everything in time.'

He took his seat. 'I doubt that. She's very passionate about you.'

'And I am very passionate about you.'

His dark-blue eyes were still troubled. 'There's so much about you that I'll never know.'

'I'll answer any question you ask me.'

He shook his head. 'You won't. You're full of secrets.'

'That's not true. I'm an open book.'

'But your past—'

'Never look back at the past,' she cut in. 'It will seize you by the throat like a mad dog.'

'That's hardly reassuring.' The waiter arrived, and Soehring ordered a vermouth. 'I don't like to hear about mad dogs in your past.'

'You're surely not jealous?'

'I know I shouldn't be—' He looked even more troubled. She couldn't bear to see him upset. She took his hand in both of hers and raised it to her lips.

'There is nothing to be jealous of, Faun. You see how happy you make me.' She looked into his eyes. 'And look at me now, kissing your hands in public, throwing my reputation to the winds for you.'

'Forgive me. You make me ashamed of myself. I'm not as self-controlled as you.'

'Your lack of self-control is one of the things I love about you.' She smiled at him with unmistakeable erotic meaning. 'When you call my name in bed, and tremble and bury your face against my body, then I know you're completely mine.'

His cheeks flushed for a moment. 'You make me feel things I didn't know were possible.'

She loved his shyness, which came at odd moments, between the cracks, as it were, of his male self-assurance. His moments of fierce jealousy, too, charmed her. Antoinette's jealousy had been cloying, insufferable. His was a rare perfume offered at her altar, to be savoured. She couldn't say why.

'I don't need to tell you what you do to me. You can see it. I'm like a garden that hasn't felt rain in years. And now I'm drenched with you, and my skin has turned into a carpet of flowers.'

He smiled, his eyes dancing with pleasure. He picked up the copy of *Paris-soir* she had been reading. 'You've seen this latest exploit of the Führer's.'

'Yes.'

'He has thrown the war away.'

'Are you serious?'

He tossed the paper down. 'I'm not a military genius, like Adolf Hitler,' he said ironically, 'but even I know that no one can fight a war successfully on two fronts. Hitler assumes our power is limitless. But we're overstretched already. Germany can't win now.'

'You don't seem too perturbed.'

'I can only think about you.'

They were going to the theatre. She collected her wrap from the cloakroom, and he his scarf, and they walked out into place Vendôme. The shortage of gasoline in the city had made taxis almost extinct. Horse-drawn carriages had taken their place, emerging from half-forgotten stables all over Paris, like ghosts of the *Belle Époque*. He could have ordered a staff car, but they both found the carriages, the horses and their ancient coachmen charming.

The fiacre they had ordered was waiting for them outside the hotel. A Ritz doorman held the door open. They climbed on board and settled in their seats. As they clattered away on the cobbled streets, he looked out of the window and pointed to Mars, a red spark in the haze over the darkened city. 'That's where the war is taking place,' he said. 'On another planet, among strange beings with whom we have no kinship, who have to do things we can never understand, and never want to understand.'

Seventeen

Marie-France was carrying a large vase of red flowers down the passageway. 'Can you help me with these, chérie?'

'Of course,' Olivia said, putting down the armful of sheets she was carrying. She took the flower arrangement from Marie-France. Marie-France led her to a room that was being prepared for a guest of the Japanese ambassador. The flowers were red roses and deep-pink hydrangeas, making a vibrant accent in the room's muted colour scheme of cream and silver.

'Aren't they pretty?' Marie-France said, setting the flowers on a console. 'Such vivid colours. I have to tell you something. Can you spare me a moment?'

'What is it?'

'I'm leaving the Ritz.'

'Oh no, Marie-France!'

Marie-France concentrated on arranging the flowers. 'I've been thinking about it ever since Fabrice was killed. I can't do the work any more. It's not just that I feel tired all the time – I can't stand seeing them every day, laughing and swaggering, while he lies dead. I can't bear to hear their language spoken. I have to go.'

'I understand,' Olivia said sadly. 'How will you survive?'

'We're leaving Paris, my sister and I. We're going back to the country. You don't need much money there. We'll keep a few hens, grow a few rows of vegetables. Remember our dead.' She stepped back from the flowers and turned to Olivia. There were tears in her eyes. 'I will miss you.'

Olivia was crying too. She embraced Marie-France. 'I'll come and visit you.'

'Yes, of course you will, and you'll bring me all the news of the great hotel and the great city, and I'll tell you about the caterpillars that are eating our cabbages.' She patted Olivia's cheek. 'You will be housekeeper here when I am gone.'

'There are lots of people with much more experience than me,' Olivia said, blowing her nose.

'But none with your intelligence and your gift with people. I'm going to make the recommendation to Monsieur Auzello myself.' Marie-France had aged even further in the past months, her hair now almost white and her once-proud back stooped. 'If you and Fabrice had been blessed with a child, there would be something for me to do, Olivia.'

Olivia winced. She'd never told Marie-France about her brief pregnancy. 'I'm so sorry.'

'I feel I am wasting the last years of my life uselessly. I want peace.'

'I hope you find it.'

'I see the anger in your eyes,' Marie-France said, her voice sinking lower. 'I know how hard it is for you. You will find someone else.' She raised her fingers to Olivia's lips to silence Olivia's rejection. 'You *must* find someone else. This war can't last for ever, and you have a life to make.'

Olivia made her way sadly back to her abandoned pile of linen, thinking how bereft she was going to be without Marie-France. Olivia could see how exhausted she got lately. Leaving Paris and going back to the little village in the Auvergne where she had been born would at least give her tranquillity, though nothing could restore the happiness she had once had. The longing for a grandchild that she'd just expressed was especially pathetic. Nothing was going to help that, either; she had now lost both of her children, and her sister had never married.

Olivia took the linen to the laundry room to put it into the chute. As the spring door closed behind her, she felt a stunning blow on the back of her neck.

She staggered forward against the sink, the sheets spilling from her arms. Too dazed to even cry out, she grabbed the cold stone of the sink to keep herself from falling. Her first shocked thought was that one of the German guards had found the Minox, which she had hidden behind the hot-water pipes in this very room. But when powerful hands swung her roughly around, she saw that her assailant was Heike Schwab.

Heike was bigger and stronger than she was in the normal course of events, but after that first, devastating blow, Olivia felt like a rag doll. Heike was breathing heavily. She pushed her hot, sweating face up against Olivia's.

'You think you can ignore me?' Her fingers were grappling at the buttons of Olivia's dress, trying to get at her breasts, her breath reeking in Olivia's nostrils. 'You think you can ignore *me*? I will show you that you are not Miss Perfect!' This was nothing to do with the camera. Olivia realised instantly that it was sexual in nature. It was a rape.

Heike used her weight to pin Olivia against the stone draining-ledge, which was digging into her spine. Olivia tried to call for help, but Heike clamped one large hand over her nose and mouth, cutting off her air.

Desperate to breathe, Olivia clawed at Heike's face with her nails. But Heike ducked her head like a boxer and pressed harder into Olivia. She had a terrifying certainty of intent. She knew how to brawl, knew the brutal techniques of subduing an opponent. Her other hand was thrusting up Olivia's dress, trying to get into her underwear. 'I will show you that you are not Miss Head-In-The-Air, Miss Touch-Me-Not.'

Olivia felt that she was blacking out. With a last spasm, she bit the fingers that were suffocating her. Heike cursed sharply, releasing her for a moment. Olivia staggered away from her attacker, making for the door; but Heike grabbed her from behind this time, clamping a brawny arm around Olivia's throat. Through the roaring in her ears, Olivia could hear Heike's ragged breath as she resumed her assault. Olivia reached out for something, anything, she could use as a weapon, her fingers encountering a heavy copper jug. But it slipped out of her hand and fell on to the tiled floor with a clatter.

Heike had chosen her moment carefully. It was late in the afternoon, a time when most of the rooms had already been done, and most of the staff were elsewhere. There was little chance of anyone hearing the commotion, or coming into the laundry room and finding them by chance.

Heike's arm was like a python around her windpipe, choking the life out of her. Her free hand was trying to plunder Olivia's private places. As she felt she was losing consciousness, Olivia remembered the pencil she always carried in her pocket to note guests' preferences. It was no more than a few inches long, but it had a sharp point. She groped for it, and with her last vestige of strength, punched it into one of the heavy thighs that were clamped against her.

The python around her neck instantly uncoiled. Heike jumped back with a crash. Gasping painfully for breath, Olivia tried to orient herself in the direction of the door, and escape. But as her vision cleared, she saw that Heike had stationed herself in front of the door.

'Get out of my way,' Olivia said, clenching her fists.

'Don't tell anybody.' Heike's voice had changed. It had become small and quavering, like a little girl's. She groped at her thigh, where Olivia's pencil was still stuck in, and pulled it out. Then, startlingly, she burst into tears. Through the hands that were covering her face, she blurted out, 'Please don't tell anybody. I'm sorry. I'm so sorry.'

'Get out of my way!'

'Forgive me!' Burly as she was, Heike seemed to have shrunk into something smaller, weaker. It was a transformation that was almost physical, as well as emotional. She held out her hands to Olivia. Her face was wet with tears. 'Forgive me, please. I'm sorry, I'm sorry!'

But Olivia was still afraid that Heike was a threat, despite the extraordinary change from aggressor to supplicant. She tried to get around the German. Heike put her back against the door, her hands behind her. 'I won't touch you again.' She spoke fast and low. 'I know you're up to something. I don't know what it is, but I can tell. I watch you every moment. I never take my eyes off you.'

'I'm not up to anything!'

'It doesn't matter. I won't say a word to a soul. Just love me a little, Olivia. Just a little!'

'Love you!'

'Only a little! That's all I ask. Olivia, I love you so much!'

Reaction had set in. Olivia just wanted to get away. 'What you did isn't love.'

'I know that. I was mad, a beast.' She started hitting herself in the face with her fists. 'A beast, a beast! I have always been a beast.'

'For God's sake, stop doing that to yourself.'

'I can't stand it when you ignore me, I can't bear it, Olivia. Only say you love me a little, and I will be happy.'

Olivia tried to find an adequate response. 'You've got the wrong person. I'm not made that way. I don't want to live with you. I've told you that.'

Heike's shoulders sagged. 'Then just say you don't hate me.'

'I've never hated you.'

'Even now?'

'You haven't made me feel very good,' Olivia said grimly.

'I swear I will never treat you like that again.' She wiped her swollen eyes. 'You are so beautiful. You're an angel, and I know I'm a devil. I've done horrible things, things I'm ashamed of—'

'I don't want to hear anything, Heike. I just want to go now.'

Silently, as though recognising that there was no more to say, Heike stood aside at last.

Olivia pulled the door open and ran from the laundry room on shaky legs.

Jack had lined up a number of locks on the table in her studio. Each was different, as he had explained, but all worked on the same principle. They could all be opened, using one or two simple tools, even in some cases a pair of bobby-pins, or a pair of fine nail scissors, which could be carried with her everywhere. The locks commonly used on briefcases were especially vulnerable.

'They're more for show than real security,' he said, showing her one that had been removed from its leather backing. 'You have to be especially careful not to leave scratches on these, especially if there's gold plating. Somebody who's watching out for signs like that won't miss even the smallest mark. So you should cover the lock with—' He glanced at her face. 'Are you listening?'

Olivia braced herself. The thought of telling him what Heike had done to her was repugnant; the experience had shaken her badly, and left her feeling disgusted and ashamed. Yet it was a situation that could jeopardise her security, as well as his, and everything they hoped to achieve. She had to face talking about it.

'Something happened to me yesterday,' she said quietly.

He put down the lock he was demonstrating and folded his arms. 'Go on.'

It didn't take long to explain the background, or the events in the laundry room; but though she tried to keep her narrative factual, reliving it was difficult enough to bring on the shakes again, and make her want to throw up with nerves.

He listened carefully as she talked. When she ground to a halt, he was silent for a while, his eyes searching her face. At last he said, 'I'm sorry that happened to you. It's going to take you time to get over it.'

'It's no big deal,' she said, giving him a tight smile.

'We both know that's not true.'

'Well, I don't want it to be a big deal. I had to tell you because—'

'Did you sleep last night?'

'Not very well,' she admitted.

'You're exhausted. I can see it in your face.'

'Please don't feel sorry for me,' she said with a shaky laugh. 'I might just start crying.'

'Go ahead and cry if you want to.' He started to gather up the locks and tools. 'We'll do this another time. Tonight isn't the right time for a lesson.' He reached into the rucksack he'd brought with him and took out a flask. He uncorked it and held it out to her. 'Drink.'

She regarded it warily. 'What is it?'

'A taste of home. Wisconsin farm whiskey.'

'You mean hooch?'

'Now you're just being insulting.'

'So long as it doesn't make me go blind.' She swigged from the flask. The whiskey was strong yet surprisingly smooth, with a taste of grain and malt. 'Oh, that's not bad at all.'

'There's a few barrels more of that in an old red barn, waiting for this war to be over.' He drank after her. 'It's made from corn, barley, wheat and rye that grow in the fields right next to the barn. The barrels are Missouri oak, charred inside. The barn gets hot in the summer and freezing in the winter. I like to think you can taste all the seasons in every sip. Starts out with cold, wet winter and leaves you with summer in your mouth.'

'Your farm?'

'My father's. He's not as young as he used to be. I just hope he's still sitting on the porch when I get back.'

The whiskey, or perhaps it was thinking about home, had brought the tears dangerously close. 'What are we doing here?' she asked.

'I know what I'm doing here. I hope you do too.'

'People keep telling me this isn't our fight and that I should go home.'

He passed the flask back to her. 'One of the documents you photographed was a message from Adolf Hitler to Goering about the development of a strato-bomber. He's talking about a plane that can take off from western France, climb to an altitude of twenty miles and reach New York with ten thousand pounds of high-explosive bombs.'

'They're thinking of attacking the United States?'

'If we don't carry the war to them, they'll carry the war to us. Europe was just the start. Now they're taking Russia. They're not going to stop, Olivia. So it doesn't matter where you go. The war's going to be there. That's why they're calling it the Second World War.'

'Pass that hooch back,' she commented, reaching for the flask.

He wandered around her studio, looking at her paintings. 'You're really good,' he said, in his typically flat way. It was the first time he'd shown any interest in her artwork.

'Not good enough to sell any.'

'Get these in a fancy gallery, they'll go for big money. You have talent. Everything's a question of context. A diamond in the gutter looks like any other pebble. In a jeweller's window, it looks a million bucks.'

'Well, thank you for the homespun wisdom.'

'Other than the rape attempt,' Jack said, turning back to her, 'do you think Heike really knows anything?'

'It's hard to say,' Olivia admitted. 'She accuses everybody around her, all the time. She wasn't a happy person to start with, and a year in an internment camp hasn't helped. She says she kept warm by beating up the other prisoners. I think she may have killed a few.'

He grunted. 'We're going to have to do something about her.'

'Like what?'

'There are only three ways, as I see it. You can give her what she wants—'

'No.'

'Or you can keep going the way you are and hope she doesn't catch you.'

Olivia grimaced. 'What's the third alternative?'

'I'll make her disappear.'

She was startled enough to choke on the whiskey. 'You mean – kill her?'

He shrugged. 'You don't need to know the details. I will fix it so she doesn't bother you any more.'

Olivia stared at him, recalling the cold way he'd threatened that she would wind up 'at the bottom of the Seine' if she was a traitor. His face and tone were as calm as though he were talking about posting a letter. There was a ruthlessness in him that shocked her. 'I don't want that on my conscience.'

'She's a Gestapo agent, by her own admission. An enemy.'

'I don't want you to kill her, Jack.'

'I understand that. But I can't take decisions based on what you want or don't want. She's a clear and present danger to you. You're a valuable asset. It's my duty to protect you.'

'Is that all I am to you?' she demanded. 'A *valuable asset*?'

His grey eyes were wintry. 'I told you at the outset that this wasn't a game. If she's obsessed with you, and watching your every move, it's only a question of time before she catches you. I wouldn't put any faith in her promises that she won't report you to the Gestapo. She will. And then you won't only wish she was dead – you'll wish you were dead too.'

'Damn you,' she said tersely. The warmth imparted by the whiskey had fled. She felt cold all over. She'd begun with summer and ended with winter.

'Is there anything else you need to tell me?'

'Yes,' she said reluctantly. 'Marie-France is quitting. She can't face working with Nazis any more. There's a chance I'll get her job.'

'Housekeeper?' He cocked his head. 'Will that affect your access to information?'

'It might. I won't be doing the beds and cleaning any more. But I'll also have a reason for going into any room at any time. Housekeepers have to check that each room is perfect after the chambermaids have finished – and bring fresh flowers, stock liquor cabinets, that kind of thing. I'd get a bigger set of keys, so I'd be able to go just about anywhere I wanted. And rather than having to rush around early in the morning, I could choose my times to go into a room, when there's nobody about.'

'So you'd be in an even better position?'

'Like I said, it's just a possibility. There will be other people applying for the job.'

'Okay.' He glanced at his watch. 'It's way past the curfew. I'm going to spend the night here. Have you any objections?'

'Like you just said, what I want or don't want doesn't count for much,' she replied tersely.

He shrugged without comment and started getting ready for bed. Olivia watched him as he stripped to the waist and washed himself in the basin in the corner of the room. His body was lean but powerful, with broad shoulders tapering to a lithe waist. She could imagine him with a rifle, killing a deer with about as much emotion as he'd just shown talking about killing Heike Schwab.

Yet, perversely, he made her feel safe. The idea that he was there, ready to kill to keep her from harm, was reassuring; and it was a long time since she had felt safe or reassured. It was something, she decided, like the feeling the farm dogs had given her back in Lindstrom. Big grim animals with sharp teeth, descendants of the wolfdogs the first immigrants had brought from Sweden, they were in no way pets; but you knew that they would let nothing bad come near you, so long as they were around.

While he sluiced under his arms and dried himself off with her towel (no permission asked or given), she got into her pyjamas and climbed into bed. Jack had been the first and only man to kiss her since Fabrice, and now he would be the first and only man since Fabrice to share her bed. There was a bitter irony in that.

He turned off the light and came to the bed. 'Move over, Yokel.'

'Move over yourself, Bumpkin.'

By way of an answer, he pushed her unceremoniously against the wall, and took his place between her and the rest of the world. She felt the bedsprings twang under his weight.

'You're just like a big dog,' she said irritably.

'What does that make you?' he retorted.

She lay in silence, facing the wall, trying not to let any part of her body touch any part of his. Thoughts were whirling through her head. At last she spoke in a low voice. 'Please don't hurt Heike.'

'I can't let you run the risk of being caught,' he replied. 'Don't get sentimental about her just because she claims to be in love with you. She loves you the way a pig loves apples. By the time she's finished loving you, there'll be nothing left of you.'

'She's a woman.'

'Yes, a dangerous woman.'

She was silent again for a while after that. 'I thought you would laugh when I told you what happened,' she said.

'Why would I laugh?'

'I thought you wouldn't take it seriously. I didn't know a woman could behave like that.'

'Anybody can behave like that if they want something badly enough and don't care how they go about getting it. It's what we're fighting, isn't it?'

'I guess it is. But I don't want her killed.'

'Let's not worry about Heike now.' He slid a strong arm under her shoulders, and rolled her over to him so that her head was pillowed on his chest. 'I meant what I said about your paintings. You've got something special. When the war is over, you'll go back to it. And this time it'll work.'

She had stiffened rigidly at his possessive behaviour. But as it became clear that it wasn't a prelude to anything sexual, just an attempt to comfort her, she slowly relaxed. Being held like this was surprisingly comfortable. She could feel the slow thud of his heart against her cheek, feel his strength and warmth sheltering her. She was lulled into a kind of animal drowsiness, with no thoughts; and soon she was fast asleep in his arms.

Eighteen

There was little time for conversation the next morning, though she wanted to keep talking about Heike. It was by now high summer, and the day was already bright and starting to warm up. They both prepared hastily to leave, sharing a cup of ersatz coffee. He left first, with a brief goodbye. The intimacy of the night had gone. From her window, she watched him striding down the hill, his rucksack over his shoulder, until he disappeared among the crowds of workers who clattered to their jobs in wooden clogs.

She had regarded Jack as a manifestation of the war until now, like the sandbags that lined every public building, or the German soldiers who demanded to see her papers every day. She had only been concerned to work with him against the Nazi occupiers. But having spent a night with him, even in the most innocent way possible, she found herself entertaining more human questions. She wondered what his real name was, and who exactly he worked for. Where did he go when he wasn't spraying vineyards or showing her how to pick locks?

He'd spoken of a father and a farm – but was that just a cover story? Was he married? Did he have children? It would be unusual for a man to have reached the age of thirty or more without accumulating some family of his own. If so, where were they? Didn't he miss them? Perhaps Blanche Auzello knew the answer to these questions.

As Olivia came down the stairs in her turn, Madame de la Fay peered out of her doorway like an elderly vulture inspecting a passing antelope for life expectancy.

'You've got yourself a new young man, *hein?*'

'He had to spend the night because of the curfew,' Olivia said defensively.

'So long as you pay your rent, I don't care what you do,' Madame de la Fay said with a carnivorous smile. In fact, since starting work at the Ritz, Olivia had paid her rent in advance every week, and relations between herself and the de la Fays were no longer acrimonious. 'Anyway, about time you took a live man to your bed,' she called after Olivia as she hurried out of the door. 'A dead man is cold company.'

Since the German invasion of Russia had begun, military activity at the Ritz had intensified. Machine guns had been set up facing place Vendôme, and there were now always two armoured cars flanking the entrance. There were more SS officers in the hotel than ever, striding along the passageways, booted and all in black, with the silver death's-head insignia on their collars.

It was already evident that these men, officially tasked with protecting senior Nazi staff, were a private army in themselves, engaged in sinister activities that were whispered about but never referred to aloud. Goering's patronage had protected Olivia from being harassed by them at first, but she sensed that they were now in the ascendancy. Their commands were barked louder, and with more authority, and even Goering's staff seemed to fear them.

Blanche Auzello was arguing with one of them now in the salon where she liked to play bridge before lunch. A slight woman dressed in a pale-pink Chanel suit, she made an odd contrast to the midnight-clad

SS officer who towered forbiddingly over her; but her large hazel eyes blazed angrily up at him.

'You can't hang around in here all day,' she snapped. 'You're frightening away my customers. You look like Boris Karloff. All you're missing is the bolts in your neck. How do you expect my guests to relax with you hovering over them?'

'I have my orders,' the man retorted, glaring.

Blanche's party, their game suspended, were looking distinctly nervous at their table, as were all the other patrons enjoying a preprandial drink in the salon. But Blanche was nothing daunted. 'I don't give a damn about your orders. This is *my* hotel, and here are *my* orders: clear out, buster. Or I'll tell Heinrich Himmler what a pain in the ass you're being.'

Blanche's daring was breathtaking. Had the SS man known that she was a Jew as well as an American, her life would not have been worth two cents. But astonishingly, like a Dobermann Pinscher retreating from a yapping Pekingese in pink ribbons, the officer backed away and left the salon.

Olivia hurried up to Blanche before she could rejoin her table. Blanche's eyes were sparkling with triumph. 'That made him turn tail,' she crowed. 'Himmler's arriving here tomorrow. You gotta remember one thing about Nazis – every Nazi is afraid of some other Nazi. Mention the right Nazi's name and you're home free.'

'Blanche, can I talk to you for a moment?'

'Sure, kid. What's up?'

'Marie-France's leaving. I hate to ask – but I'd really like her job.' She lowered her voice to a whisper. 'It would make a big difference to what I can do.'

Blanche looked at Olivia speculatively. 'I get you. And a little extra cash won't hurt either, right?' Before Olivia could reply, a bellboy in brass buttons scampered up to Blanche.

'There's a phone call for you, Madame Auzello.'

'Wait here,' Blanche told Olivia. 'I'll be back.'

While she waited for Blanche, Olivia effaced herself in a corner of the salon. It was one of the most beautiful rooms in the Ritz, panelled to the ceiling in pear wood, with inset bookcases where morocco-bound volumes reposed behind glass. The tub chairs were upholstered in crimson velvet. There was a magnificent Aubusson carpet, woven specially for the room, with flowing floral designs. With sunlight filtering through the arched windows, it was no wonder the spot was a favourite place for wealthy and fashionable women to gather and gossip. For their delectation, glass domes of coloured macarons stood on the side tables, and a steady flow of colourful cocktails was ferried in from the bar.

But when Blanche returned from her telephone call, she was crying. 'Oh, those bastards,' she said through clenched teeth.

'What's wrong?'

'They're rounding up more Jews. Thousands this time. They started at dawn, combing the eleventh arrondissement and all around, checking papers, going into shops and houses. Every Jew they find is thrown into a truck and driven away. God knows what will happen to them.'

Olivia's first thought was for Laszlo Weisz. 'My old teacher lives in the ninth arrondissement. I have to go to him!'

'Easy, Tiger,' Blanche said, putting a hand on Olivia's arm. 'There's nothing you can do for him.'

'I have to go!'

'Stay away from there!' Blanche called after her.

But Olivia was already running out of the room.

The streets were full of German military trucks and the black Citroën cars used by the Gestapo. Among the steel helmets, Olivia could see the kepis of gendarmes. The French police were actively assisting the Nazis in this operation, as they had done before. But this time, as Blanche Auzello had said, the round-up was unquestionably on a larger scale.

215

The groups of shabby men being herded into the waiting trucks were larger. A few carried suitcases or pathetic armfuls of belongings. Many were still in their aprons or other work garments. All had expressions of resignation, as though somehow they accepted the supposed guilt the Nazis had foisted on them, and were weary of it, and just wanted the persecution to be over, one way or another.

She herself was stopped twice and asked for her papers. Both times, she was made to turn back and had to find alternative routes to get where she was going.

Scrambling up a narrow side alley, she found herself on the rue Lepic at last. The market was bustling, despite the large military operations taking place all around. It was a market day, and local housewives were haggling with the stallholders to try to lower the exorbitant prices so they could get the week's supplies for their families. Life went on.

Olivia fought her way through the crowds to number 17 and pounded on the old grey door. There was no answer for a long time; then at last she heard a shuffling footstep from within. But her heart plummeted as the door swung open. It was not Laszlo, but one of his neighbours, the little old woman who helped him with his shopping. Her face had fallen into furrows of grief.

'They came for him early this morning. They spared him before because he was so old. But this time they took him.'

Olivia couldn't hold back her tears. 'Did they hurt him?'

'He went like a lamb to the slaughter. He was even smiling, I think, under that white beard of his. An hour later, they came with a van and cleared out his apartment.' She unlocked Laszlo's door. 'Look what they did.'

Olivia went in. The apartment was empty of furniture. But in one room was a pile of Laszlo's paintings, the wooden frames splintered, the canvases slashed.

'They took all his belongings,' the little woman said, 'even his old clothes, his paints and his brushes. But the pictures they destroyed.

They said they were decadent because he didn't paint things the way they are in real life.' She patted Olivia, who was crying helplessly. 'But I ask you, what is real life? Does anybody know?'

'This is real life,' Olivia said, pointing to the pile of wrecked art. 'Genius put on the garbage heap.'

'Well, now,' the little woman said, 'Laszlo said they would come for him, and he gave me something to keep for you. I have it in my apartment. Come.'

Olivia followed the woman out of Laszlo's home, which was now as dry and empty as a last year's bird's nest blown out of a tree. It felt as though he had never been there at all, apart from the wreckage of his life's work.

The old woman's apartment smelled steamily of the tripe she was boiling on the stove. She opened a cupboard and rummaged in it.

'He said to hide it carefully. He said he knew you would come. Now, where is it? Ah, here it is, right at the back.'

She handed Olivia the painting. It was unframed, quite small, a portrait of a young woman with blonde hair and blue eyes, sitting at a window. It was unmistakeably a portrait of herself, though she couldn't remember ever having sat for him. Perhaps he had done it from memory, or while she was occupied with her own work. It was painted in his free, joyful style, capturing the light, the face of the girl full of hope and innocence.

Through blurred eyes, she could see that he had signed it on the back and had written the title – *La Suédoise*, the Swedish Girl.

Dr Kurt Blanke received Chanel with cold formality.

The meeting on this occasion was at the Hotel Majestic, the immense palace located on avenue Kléber where Coco had once attended sparkling dinners and parties, and which was now the headquarters of the

German military high command. It was here Dr Blanke had his headquarters, and from where he tirelessly administered the confiscation of Jewish businesses, from back-street bakeries to vast business interests spanning the globe.

Dr Blanke had not been a smiling man on the occasion of their last encounter, but he was positively glacial now. When his adjutant showed Coco, Spatz and René into his office, he looked up with a brief flash of his spectacles, pointed to the three hard chairs in front of his desk, and continued writing.

Coco sat in the middle chair, flanked by René de Chambrun and Spatz von Dincklage, who had dressed for the occasion in his Wehrmacht uniform of field-grey, his peaked cap balanced neatly on his knees. De Chambrun was in a pinstriped suit. Coco herself wore one of her own dresses, a froth of cream lace.

From above Dr Blanke's desk, photographic portraits of Adolf Hitler, Hermann Goering and Heinrich Himmler stared down stonily at the three visitors. A large swastika flag was draped on another wall.

For a long time, the only sound was the scratch of Dr Blanke's fountain pen. Coco watched him with intense irritation. She longed to hear the news that she had triumphed over the Wertheimers at last. Finally, Blanke capped the pen, closed the folder and looked up.

'The operation has not been successful,' he said curtly.

Coco almost jumped out of her chair. After all the agony she had been through, all the guilt she had suffered, this was hardly what she had expected to hear. 'What do you mean, not successful?' she demanded.

'Adequate initial enquiries were not made,' the Gestapo man replied. 'The Wertheimer brothers are in the United States. The perfume company is now being held in trust by Félix Amiot, the president of the *Société d'Emboutissage et de Constructions Mécaniques*. Professor Amiot is an Aryan. Businesses administered by him may not be seized.'

'But this is merely a ruse,' Coco burst out. 'A typical Wertheimer trick!'

'Professor Amiot,' Dr Blanke ground on, 'is also the holder of several patents for heavy and light bombers, which are manufactured by his company. He is a close associate of Reichsmarschall Hermann Goering, with whom he is involved in military projects for the Luftwaffe.'

'What!'

'He is now building Junkers transport and bomber planes for Germany.'

'This is intolerable!'

René de Chambrun, who had already seen which way the land lay, leaned over to murmur in her ear, 'Coco, there is nothing to be done. We must be resigned.'

'It's not your money,' she snapped. 'You can afford to be resigned!' Her voice trembled as she turned back to Dr Blanke. 'Are you telling me that Goering is in bed with those Jews?'

Spatz von Dincklage put his hand hastily on Coco's arm to silence her.

Dr Blanke's frown was no less terrible for being the merest inclination of his pale eyebrows.

'I advise you to moderate your language, Madame,' he said.

De Chambrun also laid a restraining hand on Coco's arm, but she shook both men off. 'I came to you for help, and you tell me I have been robbed yet again?'

'Coco,' de Chambrun murmured, 'please be quiet.'

'I will not be quiet,' Coco burst out. 'This is unconscionable!'

Dr Blanke showed a moment of emotion. His dry lips tightened. 'I have been placed in a very difficult situation as regards the Reichsmarschall. I wish I had been made aware of all this before I opened my proceedings. I would scarcely have begun them if I had known I would find myself in opposition to Hermann Goering. I must tell you that there is no chance of success.'

'But you made me a promise!'

'My dear,' Spatz von Dincklage said briskly, 'the Jews have put themselves in an impregnable position. They have the protection of Goering now. There is nothing that Dr Blanke can do.'

Coco thrust her hands out beseechingly to Dr Blanke. 'I gave you twenty million francs!'

'The Wertheimers,' Dr Blanke replied, reopening his folder, 'have put at the Reichsmarschall's disposal an amount of some fifty million francs.'

'Fifty million?' Coco uttered a wail of dismay as it finally dawned on her that she had been outbid, outwitted and outmanoeuvred by Pierre Wertheimer yet again. And she had wasted her compassion on him! 'What about my money?'

'The funds you lodged with the Gestapo have been exhausted. Good day.'

Coco opened her mouth to protest, but no sound came out, much to the obvious relief of von Dincklage and de Chambrun.

René de Chambrun thanked Dr Blanke for his valuable time and von Dincklage threw him a snappy salute. The two men then took charge of their dazed client and steered her out of the Gestapo office without a further word.

As they walked down the stairs, Coco finally found her voice. 'The tears I've shed for that bastard Pierre Wertheimer,' she said through clenched teeth. 'The tears! And he's swindled me yet again!'

'Goering wants to meet you.'

Arletty opened her eyes. 'What for?'

Soehring laughed. 'What a question. Everyone wants to meet you.'

They were lying in his bed at the Ritz, their bodies still entwined after making love. The warmth of the afternoon had brought a sheen of sweat to his skin, but she appeared as cool as ever, despite the passion she had just displayed. She raised herself on one elbow to reach for the champagne glasses that stood on the bedside table. He took advantage of this to kiss her breasts. She nuzzled his damp hair. Her own maternal feelings for him amused her. Never having had a child, or wanted one, she supposed that her suppressed yearnings emerged in this way, in calling him Faun, in wanting to mother him when he was not being her very grown-up lover.

'Does he know about us?' she asked.

'Of course.'

'Relations between Germans and Frenchwomen are strictly forbidden.'

He took the champagne glass from her. 'Forbidden, my dear Doe, but not very strictly. You have only to look around you.'

'There's a difference between an obscure soldier taking a French girlfriend and what you and I are doing. You heard them hissing when we entered the theatre the other night.'

'You imagined that.'

'I don't think I did. Anyway, I'm afraid of Goering.'

'There's nothing to be afraid of. He's been very fond of me ever since Spain. I'm his protégé. I've told you that.' He drank thirstily and held out his glass for her to refill. 'He's invited us to a "five o'clock" in his suite. He will be enchanted with you.'

'I'm not so sure about that.'

'Why are you so sceptical?'

'For the reasons I've already mentioned. In addition, because I am ten years older than you. And notorious in other ways.'

Soehring smiled. 'It's true you are very old and very wicked.'

'And you are just a Faun with wobbly legs, looking for milk at my breasts. If I was your father, or someone who felt fatherly towards you, I should be very suspicious of this strange Doe. I might get my bow and shoot an arrow through her heart.'

'Don't be silly.' He took the glass away from her and laid both glasses on the side table. He climbed on to her, easing his hips between her thighs. He was already hard and eager again.

'How German you are,' Arletty murmured. 'As soon as I talk of hunting, you get aroused.'

'*You* arouse me. Nothing else does.'

She loved the way he desired her, the way nothing could quench his virility for long. He had the insatiability of youth and vigour. It was a long, long time since she had been loved like this – not since her own youth. Other lovers had been more delicate, more skilled in the arts of love, but their lovemaking had been somehow ephemeral. Soehring could be subtle, but not in bed. He was certainly more cultured and better educated than she, but not in bed. He could be melancholy and poetic. But not in bed. In bed, he was rampantly male, and he never failed to take her breath away.

She closed her eyes again and gave herself up to the dominion of this faun, who could rapidly become a rutting stag.

⁑

When Heike came into the room she was cleaning, Olivia instinctively backed away, getting a coffee table between herself and the German. The manoeuvre didn't escape Heike, who sneered.

'You don't have to hide from me any more.'

'What do you want?'

'Nothing. Only to say *auf Wiedersehen*.' She assessed Olivia's expression with her black, piggy eyes. 'Will you miss me?'

'Where are you going?' Olivia countered.

'I am leaving the Ritz again. But this time because *I* choose. And because I have a much better job to go to.'

Olivia tried to keep her face neutral. She could hardly repress her sigh of relief. If it was true, it meant she would neither have to continue in fear of Heike, nor face the prospect of Jack taking action against her. 'I'm happy for you.'

'Oh, yes. You will be able to get up to whatever it is you are doing without me watching you. But sooner or later you will slip. And then we will see.'

'I'm not up to anything.'

'So you say. You did not report me to old Auzello after what I did?'

'No.'

'Why not?'

'It was a private matter.' Heike little knew that she *had* reported the event, and to someone who might have dealt with her more severely than Monsieur Auzello. 'I didn't want to make trouble for you.'

Heike cocked her head on one side. 'Or maybe you enjoyed it – just a little – eh?'

'No, I didn't enjoy it.'

'Maybe you love me – just a little – after all.'

Olivia needed to get off the subject. 'What's the new job?'

Heike paused for effect. 'I am joining the Gestapo.'

'I can see how that would suit you,' Olivia said expressionlessly.

'Yes. It does suit me. I have been a part-time Gestapo agent for a long time. Now they have offered me a permanent position. There is a lot of work. I will have a uniform and a car at my disposal. I think I will enjoy that very much.'

'I'm sure you will.'

'You can come and see me, if you like. Avenue Foch. I think you know where it is.' Heike was smirking. 'But make sure it is a social call, Blondchen. Make sure I never have to deal with you in an official capacity. It would be an experience that I might enjoy – but you certainly would not.' She waved a mocking farewell with her broad palm. '*Tschüss.*'

Olivia felt a mixture of nausea and liberation as Heike departed. It was like a boulder rolling away. Life was going to be a lot easier from now on. Or so she hoped.

Nineteen

'*Le five o'clock*' was one of Goering's favourite events, in part because it was his best time of day – the hour when he had triumphantly concluded his art dealings and was sufficiently buoyed by his pills to have escaped his depression.

The ritual was one that César Ritz had brought back from his time in London, a French version of the English high tea that had become a Paris institution. Goering, of course, loved to host these occasions in his own suite, where he could play the genial host and show off his latest acquisition.

This, luminous in the afternoon light, stood in the centre of the suite on a plinth: a life-size, painted wooden statue of a naked woman with milky skin and flowing red-gold hair. Carved in the sixteenth century, it represented Mary Magdalene, and was said also to resemble Goering's buxom second wife, Emmy. It was an extraordinary object, which Goering had just looted from the Louvre.

It was called, Goering announced to the guests who flowed around it, *La Belle Allemande*, The Beautiful German, and it would be going back to its country of origin to be properly appreciated by the German *Volk*.

Goering's guests were suitably appreciative. Many of the men were in military uniform, the women dressed in fashions currently unattainable to anyone outside the charmed circle, but apparently effortlessly accessible to those within it. They were not a beautiful collection of people, Olivia thought, with the exception of a couple who had caught her eye.

She knew who they were. The man was Major Soehring, who was living here at the Ritz, a Luftwaffe officer with a Puckish face and dark-blue, rather wistful eyes. The woman was a famous French actress, Arletty. Much smaller than he, she radiated a particularly French vivacity. Her beautiful face, on its long stalk of a neck, seemed to glow like a flower. In her films she played amoral, free-and-easy women, and her real-life reputation coincided with that. Her affair with Soehring was already the talk of Paris. Olivia knew that they spent nights together here at the Ritz, dined together, went out together, and did not seem to care what people said about them.

Right now, however, the French actress looked less than comfortable. She and her lover were talking to Goering, who was currently at his fattest, grotesquely resplendent in a white uniform, with the usual collection of medals and orders dangling from his expansive front. He was in a good mood, letting out his great quacking laugh at regular intervals. But Arletty's smile seemed forced and she stood stiffly, with her hands behind her, like a schoolgirl in the headmistress's office.

Goering had co-opted Olivia to hand round tea, drinks and canapés. She was kept busy. The gathering was a lively one. The Germans had made spectacular advances in Russia, taking three hundred thousand Soviet prisoners in the last week, and the military officers present were in high spirits, possibly all the more so because they themselves were in Paris rather than marching towards Stalingrad. They devoured the dainty snacks that Goering had provided, lifting hors d'oeuvres off her tray so avidly that she was kept in perpetual motion.

As she passed by Goering, he put out a large hand and took her arm.

'This is my little Swede,' he said, presenting Olivia to Soehring and Arletty. 'Isn't she a masterpiece? Look at that face! As innocent and pure as a young Madonna by Dürer or Holbein.'

Olivia stood awkwardly holding the tray. Soehring glanced at her briefly with his heavy-lidded gaze and then turned his attention elsewhere, evidently not interested in Goering's Swede, whom he had seen many times before. But Arletty focused on her with curiosity, seeming to be glad to remove her attention from the Reichsmarschall.

'You are certainly very pretty,' she said. 'You should be on the stage.'

'I have no talent for acting, Mademoiselle.'

'How old are you?'

'Twenty-four, Mademoiselle.'

'And you are Swedish?'

'Yes, Mademoiselle.'

'How long have you been in France?'

'Since 1938.'

'And how do you come to be in Paris?'

'I came to train as an artist. But it seems I have even less talent for painting than I do for acting.'

Arletty was wearing a light summer frock printed with poppies that showed off her slim figure. She brought her hands in front of her and Olivia saw that she wore no rings on her fingers, which were lightly freckled. But in lieu of a purse, she was holding a slim, flat compact, which appeared to be solid gold studded with diamonds. She opened it now and selected a cigarette from it. Soehring lit it for her. She exhaled smoke to one side. 'You speak good French.' Arletty's eyes were large and luminous, and also very intelligent. 'Your accent is almost perfect.'

Olivia would have liked to escape, but Goering was still holding her arm. 'The purest racial types are to be found in Sweden,' he said, reverting to one of his favourite themes.

Soehring, who had evidently heard all this before, nodded politely. Arletty continued to search Olivia's face with her eyes. 'So you gave up painting? That must have been hard. To give up one's dreams is painful.'

'Starving is worse,' Olivia replied.

Arletty laughed briefly, showing her perfect teeth. 'Starving is certainly worse. But you must miss your mother and father – in Sweden.'

'Yes, Mademoiselle.'

'I have noticed you before in the hotel,' Arletty said. 'You are too intelligent to be a chambermaid. Find another dream.'

Olivia finally felt Goering's grip on her arm relax, and made a discreet withdrawal. Her tray was empty. She refilled it rapidly from the trolley and began circulating again.

The reception lasted until early evening. *La Belle Allemande* was praised by everyone, and in return bestowed her demure wooden smirk on all who passed by. The trolleys of drinks and snacks were replenished several times. But at length the ruddy hue in the Reichsmarschall's cheeks began to drain away and he showed signs of weariness. He was too heavy to enjoy standing for very long. His hips and knees pained him. The guests began to depart, allowing the evening air to circulate in the Imperial Suite and the slanting sunlight to slip into the vacant spaces.

Olivia saw Soehring and Arletty take their leave of Goering. They left with a large group, emptying half of the room. She went around checking that nobody had forgotten anything, which was one of her duties. A gleam of gold on a chair caught her eye. She recognised it at once as Arletty's gold compact, decorated with a pattern of diamond leaves. She picked it up, noticing how heavy and solid it was, and hurried out of the suite.

She caught sight of Arletty's poppy-print frock among the German uniforms and ran after her.

'Mam'selle! Your cigarette case!'

Arletty turned. 'Oh, thank you.' She took the compact. 'You are not Swedish,' she said quietly as Olivia turned to go. 'I'm an actress, I know accents. You're American.'

Olivia didn't know how to respond to that. 'I—'

'Don't worry. Very few people are able to tell. Where did I leave the cigarette case?'

'You left it on a chair, by the window,' Olivia said.

Arletty grimaced. 'Freud says we do these things deliberately.'

'Mam'selle?'

'He hates it.' She didn't need to say who. Behind them, Soehring was talking to the others. 'It's Cartier, given to me by another man. Long before we met. The man is dead, but his coat of arms is on the clasp.' She showed Olivia the enamelled lock, which bore a family shield. 'And so he cannot bear me to use it.'

'I'm sorry, Mam'selle.'

'It's almost a pound of gold, and very valuable, but that's not why I keep it. I like it because it has memories for me.'

'And that's what he can't bear.'

Arletty raised her wise, sad eyes to Olivia's. A kind of swift, strange complicity had grown between them, as though both had guessed that the other was playing a role, and not a very happy one. 'What do people say about me behind my back?' Arletty asked.

'Some of them are angry, or pretend to be.'

'And they call me a whore and a collabo?'

'Some do. Others say it's nobody's business.'

'Everything is everybody's business,' Arletty said wearily. She lit another cigarette. 'It seems Goering is fond of you.'

'I don't know why.'

'I know why. It's better for you to be Swedish, of course. But you should be careful.'

'I am.'

'I worked as a chambermaid when I was young. The hotel was less grand than this one. I don't imagine you have problems with fleas and bedbugs at the Ritz?'

'It's surprising what pets guests bring with them,' Olivia said diplomatically.

'Well, I can't say I enjoyed the experience much. But one learns a lot.'

'Yes. One does.'

'Darling,' Soehring called, 'we're waiting for you.'

Arletty smiled at Olivia. 'Good luck.'

Olivia watched the actress's slim figure float down the corridor, then went back to her work.

⁂

'What were you talking to that Swedish girl about?' Soehring asked Arletty as they walked towards the garden.

'I forgot my cigarette case. She brought it to me.'

He grimaced. 'That damned thing. You're lucky Goering didn't spot it first. He's quite capable of grabbing a bauble like that.'

'It seems he's also grabbed the Swedish girl.'

'He takes these incomprehensible fancies.'

'There's nothing incomprehensible about it. She's beautiful. And I found her very interesting.'

He raised his dark eyebrows. 'Oh, did you!'

'You needn't say it in that tone.'

'What tone should I say it in?'

'No tone. Goering didn't take much of a fancy to *me*.'

'I think he liked you well enough.'

'No. He didn't like me at all. I could see it in his eyes.'

'Well, you might have tried a little harder,' he retorted.

Arletty paused at the doorway to the twilit hotel garden. The group they were with had commandeered a table beside the fountain and were ordering more drinks. Later, they would dine at Maxim's, a popular restaurant with Germans, and go to a cabaret. Eating, drinking and entertainment were the staples of Paris life, as always for these people.

'Didn't I try hard enough?' she asked quietly.

'You know you were cold with him. He responds to warmth. You can be charming enough when it suits you.'

'Perhaps it didn't suit me.'

'It didn't suit you to be pleasant to the second most powerful man in Germany? When he had specifically asked to meet you?'

'It's a little hard to be warm to a man whose hands are dripping with blood.'

Soehring rolled his eyes. 'Please don't be melodramatic, Doe.'

'And who is gleefully showing off the treasures he has plundered from France.'

'War is war. The Romans took treasures back to Rome from the lands they conquered.'

'And which particular Roman is Hermann Goering? Nero? Caligula?'

Soehring frowned. 'You're trying to provoke me.'

'Of course I am.'

'What for?'

'So you will glare at me, and shout in my face, and drag me to your room by my hair, and throw me on the bed, and spread my legs, and make love to me like a conquering Roman.'

Soehring's face changed. 'Is that what you want?'

'It would be an improvement on the evening that currently unfolds before us,' she said, her knuckles brushing his crotch to make sure her words had had the requisite effect.

'Come on, then,' he said huskily.

Someone at the table spotted them turning to leave and called after them, 'Soehring! Where are you going?'

But they were already making their way up to their room.

The falling yellow leaves of October started to litter the streets of Paris. There was nobody to sweep them up. Able-bodied men were wanted elsewhere, and the elderly were too weak to do it; so they were left to the wind, which blew them from one end of the occupied city to the other.

The previous month had brought a steady torrent of bad news. The Russian campaign was producing victory after stunning victory for Hitler. Kiev had been encircled and captured. Half a million Soviet troops had been taken prisoner. The march on Moscow had begun.

With her newly learned skills, and now appointed housekeeper of one of the most important floors at the Ritz, Olivia was able to get into drawers and attaché cases; but the opportunities for doing so were far fewer. Even though she was now a housekeeper and could move through the hotel unrestricted, she was forced into taking greater and greater risks. Several times she had been actually photographing papers when unexpected visitors had disturbed her. She had only been saved by the automatic assumption that, as a woman and a hotel worker, she was harmless. The Nazi guests of the Ritz seemed to assume that the impeccable service they received indicated they were safe. The Resistance was largely communist-led. Surely purveyors of caviar and fine champagne could be trusted?

The German death grip on Europe was unshakeable, even though the RAF had begun bombing targets in northern France. Collaborationist governments were eager to do Berlin's bidding, whether by committing workers and materiel to the German war effort or throwing their energies into the systematic round-ups of Jews that were being ordered in every town and city.

In Washington, President Roosevelt had condemned Japanese aggression in the Far East as well as offering more support for Britain against Nazi Germany. As a result, the Axis powers had threatened to attack United States naval ships on sight. The entry of America into the war seemed to be drawing ever closer.

Jack, who had arrived at Olivia's studio lugging a welcome load of firewood over his broad shoulder, was in a grim mood.

'I'm starting to think it's time you hightailed it back home, Yokel,' he said, carefully putting a few logs into the old iron stove.

'Not a chance,' she retorted, crouching at his feet and lighting the kindling. 'This is just starting to get interesting.'

Olivia enjoyed their Sunday appointments intensely. He would arrive sometime during the afternoon, collect her films and reports, and then spend the night with her, sharing her supper and then her narrow bed. She never slept better than in his arms, and never felt safer; yet he had never tried to take advantage of their proximity. He just held her close while she slept, and on Monday morning he would leave.

She'd speculated that he must be married, and was staying faithful to a wife, wherever she was; or perhaps that he had a lover; or that she just wasn't his type.

Whatever the reason, it was one of the strangest relationships she'd had in all her young life, and he was certainly the most enigmatic man she'd ever dealt with. She didn't even know how she would respond if he *were* to want sex. He was the only man in her life, after all; and there were times when, to her shame, she couldn't quite remember what Fabrice had looked like any more.

Reticent as he was about his work, Jack was good company. A warmth had grown between them. Since Marie-France had left the Ritz, she had very few people to talk to, and the long stretches between Sundays were hard.

She'd given up asking him where he went and what he did while they were apart. He would never answer. She knew that was for his security as well as hers. But it was clear that he spent a lot of time in the countryside. He often arrived with items unavailable in the city. Today he had brought not only firewood, but wild mushrooms, berries and walnuts. At other times he had come with unlabelled bottles of wine, fruit or eggs. It was an easy guess that he was working with the Maquis, the French Resistance groups who operated in the rural areas, using guerrilla tactics to sabotage or harass the Germans and aid the escape of downed Allied airmen.

They adjusted the stove until a steady crackling showed that it was burning well. Her studio was getting very cold lately, though at least on a previous visit he had repaired the holes in the roof. 'I'm serious about you going home,' he said.

'And I'm serious about staying.'

'You should be back in the USA with a paintbrush in your hand, not a spy camera. Problem is, there are too many people who know you're a Yank. Your old friend Heike Schwab, for one. If Roosevelt declares war on Hitler, or vice versa, she may come looking for you. And Heike hasn't got any sweeter at avenue Foch. They tell me she's taken to wearing a man's uniform and cutting her hair very short. She specialises in interrogations of Resistance women. With torture.'

'You're just trying to scare me.'

'I hope I'm succeeding.'

'If I can't keep working at the Ritz, I'll come and join your Maquis bands in the hills.'

He gave her an old-fashioned look. 'I've told you not to ask me about that.'

'I'm not asking you anything. But I'm not stupid either. I know what you're doing. If I can use a camera, I can learn to use a tommy-gun. Or plant bombs.'

He gave her one of his rare smiles. 'I don't doubt that. But you're far too precious to risk lobbing grenades at German patrols. You're my top asset.'

'Really?'

'Your material goes straight to Washington and London.'

Olivia was pleased. 'I never thought of myself as important.'

'Well, you are.' She was sitting as close to the stove as she could while he prepared a mushroom omelette in her skillet. 'And the last thing I want is to lose you.'

'So what should I do?'

'You wanted to hurt the Germans, and you have. Trust me on that. Rather than risk being interned, go back home. There's plenty you can do there. They'll find work for you, I promise.'

'I'm not a quitter. You should know that by now.'

'I do know it. You're the bravest agent I have. It takes more courage to do what you do, week after week, all alone, than be on active service with a group of comrades.'

'Gee, shucks.' She opened a bottle of red wine. 'Do you look forward to Sundays as much as I do?' she asked.

'Yes.'

'I get so lonely, Bumpkin.'

'It's a lonely job.'

'Sometimes I want nothing more than to be back in Swede Hollow with no worries except keeping the dumplings fluffy. Other times I feel I'm doing something worthwhile here and now, and that the rest of my life is going to be a comedown.'

He dished up. 'Your life isn't going to be a comedown, don't worry.'

She took the plate of food he gave her. 'What do I have to look forward to when this is all over? Marriage and a brood of kids?'

'There are worse fates.'

The omelette was good. He had the knack of making tasty dishes with minimal ingredients in a few minutes. 'Do you have a marriage – and a brood of kids?'

'No kids.'

'But a marriage?' Olivia said, somehow dreading the answer.

He was silent for a long time. 'I had a marriage,' he said at last. 'I wasn't a very good husband. I was only seventeen, and I wasn't ready to be tied down. But that's not an excuse for the way I behaved. It lasted two years, and we were both glad to be out of it.'

'And then?'

'Then I did a lot of stuff I'm even less proud of. Bootlegging, strike busting, poaching, a bit of everything. A judge gave me the option of jail or joining the army. He said the army would straighten me out, and he was right. It did.'

'And then?'

'That's about it, Yokel. You see before you a reformed man.'

'My, it's all gushing out,' she commented ironically. She mopped her plate with a piece of bread. '*My Life in Ten Words*.'

'I'll save the rest up for those long winter nights.'

They finished the meal with the blackberries and walnuts he'd brought. The walnuts were still tightly encased in their hard green rind and had to be peeled. 'I'd love to see where you picked these,' she said, her lips crimson from the berries.

'I doubt it.'

'I haven't been out of the city in two years. What was it like?'

'It was a pretty little country lane outside a village. There were three wounded Germans in the mud. We dragged them into the brambles to finish them off and hide the bodies. That's when we saw the berries.'

'I'm sorry I asked,' Olivia said quietly.

'It would have been a shame to leave the berries.' His grey eyes had a wintry gleam of amusement. 'They're full of vitamin C. Eat them up.'

'I guess I am a little too squeamish,' she admitted.

'Like I said, your courage is a different kind. Anybody can pull a trigger in a fight. Not everybody can hold their nerve for months at a time.'

After eating, they played backgammon, which she'd taught him. He'd picked up the game quickly, and now could put up a good fight, especially if the dice went his way.

'This is the most ruthless game ever invented,' he commented as she knocked two of his pieces out of play.

'The game's harmless. It's me that's ruthless.'

'I believe you.'

She won the game, and the next. To celebrate her victory she did a war dance around him and scalped him with an imaginary tomahawk. He submitted patiently to the indignity. They drank the last of the wine as the heat of the stove began to diminish. She wanted to load in more of the firewood he'd brought, but he pointed out that she was going to need it through the week, so instead they got into bed together though it was only nine p.m.

'Can I ask you something?' she said as they piled blankets on to themselves.

'Sure.'

'You've never tried to put the moves on me.'

'What a dainty way of expressing it.'

'You know what I mean.'

'I haven't heard a question yet.'

'I guess the question is, why not?'

'Wartime romances,' he replied, 'are like the firewood in that stove. They burn up fast, and soon go out, leaving a lot of ash and mess to clear up.'

'You should write poetry.'

'I've already published a slim volume.'

'What's it called?'

'*Pixies and Fairies*.'

She grinned. 'Catchy.'

He turned out the light. 'Are you going to talk all night?'

'Maybe.' Olivia turned the light back on and curled up against him with her chin pillowed on his shoulder. She looked into his face, thinking how completely male he was. 'I'm not *asking* you to put the moves on me, you know. It's just a scientific enquiry. I don't want a lot of ash and mess to clear up either.'

'Wise beyond your years.'

'So you don't have anybody?'

'What does *anybody* mean?'

'Oh, I was thinking of some glamorous Resistance heroine with a beret and crimson lipstick.'

'Nobody like that. Mainly it's male communists who haven't washed in a year.'

'That sounds fragrant.'

'We don't pick them on the basis of their personal hygiene.'

Olivia snuggled up even closer to him. 'Don't you think it's possible to have a relationship without it turning to ash and mess?' she asked. She didn't know why she was deliberately niggling him. Perhaps it was his monumental indifference to her charms that irked her, or a sense of mischief that had been dormant since Fabrice's death, and was only now starting to come alive again.

'It's possible to drop a beautiful vase and not break it. But why take the risk?'

'Is that from *Pixies and Fairies*?'

'It's from the sequel, *Goblins and Gremlins*.'

'I guess you just don't find me attractive.'

'I guess that's it,' he said dryly. He finally succeeded in switching the light off. 'Now can we get some sleep?'

They lay together in the dark. The city was absolutely silent. Even the dogs had stopped howling, having either wandered away or starved to death. There was no traffic, there were no voices in the streets.

'Do you remember when you kissed me?' she whispered. 'When those two German soldiers looked inside our hut?'

'Yes,' he replied.

'That wasn't such a hardship, was it?'

'I survived somehow.'

'Then it wouldn't kill you to kiss me goodnight.'

He hesitated. Then, after a moment, he kissed her on the lips. His mouth was warm and firm. It lingered on hers. She felt herself begin to melt, her head whirling. She slid her thigh between his in deliberate provocation. But before anything else could happen, it was over. He pulled her firmly into a less dangerous position and held her tight.

'I like it when you're wrapped around me, like the skin on those walnuts,' she whispered.

His arms tightened even more. Now she couldn't sleep, and she knew he couldn't either. They were wide awake in each other's arms. Was it possible to have an affair under these conditions, without everything going bad? The problem was, once you had the answer it would be too late to go back.

She hadn't been very smart tonight. Jack couldn't afford to get emotionally involved with her, nor she with him. For both their sakes, this had to be kept professional. There was too much at stake.

Yet how did you stay detached under such huge pressure, when your heart was yearning for a little tenderness, and your body was screaming for release?

※

'I had too much wine last night,' she said the next morning as they got ready to leave the studio. It was her way of apologising. In the light of day, she was embarrassed by the way she'd led him on – or tried to – the night before. 'You must think me an idiot.'

He gave her an unexpectedly warm smile. 'If you weren't a trouble-maker you wouldn't have volunteered for this job.'

As always, he left first. Before he went, he hugged her tight enough to squeeze the breath out of her.

'Be safe, Yokel.'

'You too, Bumpkin.'

And then he was gone.

Twenty

It had happened. America was in the war.

In the last month of 1941, the Japanese had attacked Pearl Harbor. A week later, Germany had declared war on America. America had responded, a sleeping giant awakening and reaching for his cudgel. The world had held its breath for a fortnight; and then Christmas had come.

The bitter weather that had blanketed Paris with snow, and brought further misery to the city's population, made the season all the more enjoyable for the uniformed men and silk-clad women who inhabited the great hotel. They were able to congratulate one another on having a white Christmas; and even a quick stroll across place Vendôme, wrapped in furs purchased at a fraction of their true value, was a delicious adventure.

The Ritz put on a splendid Christmas. At the heart of a Paris that was starving and freezing, there were coal fires in every hearth and tables groaning with food. Orchestras played sentimental German music, there was dancing and there were expensive gifts. General von Stülpnagel supplied a huge yule log, which smouldered in the fireplace in the salon for days. Glittering decorations had been hung in all the public areas, and the towering Christmas tree at the foot of the stairs never failed to bring gasps of admiration from visitors. The ornaments on the tree featured baubles with swastikas. A silver head of Hitler took the place of the star at the top of the tree.

Despite the hard work brought by the season, the atmosphere among the Ritz staff had been one of barely suppressed excitement since Pearl Harbor. Into this darkest and deepest period of the war, light had finally penetrated. Surely the balance of the war had changed! Surely not even Nazi Germany could resist the might of the United States?

On Christmas Eve, they crowded around the radio in the senior staff canteen. Listening to foreign radio broadcasts was now punishable by death, but they had a good hiding place for the set and took care to secure all the doors. The Ritz, Olivia reflected, was full of secrets.

They heard President Roosevelt's speech from Washington as he lit the White House Christmas tree. Winston Churchill, who was visiting him, also made a speech. The drawling, reassuring voices of the two elder statesmen were followed by the strains of the 'Star-Spangled Banner'. People hugged and kissed Olivia, and made a pet of her with little gifts and treats.

The New Year's Eve celebrations the next week were even gayer. The most senior Germans – Goering, Himmler and Bormann – all returned to Germany, and the atmosphere among the remaining Nazis, however distinguished, was like that of children at a party whose parents had left.

Arletty's impish lover, Major Soehring, slid all the way down the banisters from the fourth floor, a considerable feat of athleticism, given the number of sharp turns; but then, he had been an Olympic horseman and skier.

Luftwaffe officers in full uniform fought duels with baguettes and competed with one another to drink bumpers of champagne. The restaurant was so crowded that the dancing couples were able to do little more than cling together in the crush, wearing the party hats the Ritz had given out.

A splendid meal was produced by the kitchen with every luxury the belly could desire. Midnight came with a deafening racket of streamers and crackers and toy trumpets, followed by a rush out into the snow, where a few overexcited spirits fired their Lugers into the air. The ladies shrieked and rushed to get back inside before the bullets could come down again. Most of the staff, having eaten and drunk the leftovers of the feast, slept on the floor in the back end of the hotel, unable to get home.

Life settled back to normal. The entry of America into the war brought no immediate change. Fighting resumed in far-off places; the reality of each day was the hunt for food and fuel. Paris, in the grip of a dark, cold winter, felt like an underground city, cut off from light and warmth. Once again, the old, the very young and the frail began to die, starved or frozen to death.

In the middle of April, just as cherries and magnolias burst into flower in the Tuileries Gardens, Olivia was arrested by the Gestapo.

The arrest was made with practised speed and smoothness, and even a degree of politeness. The two Gestapo men who came for her called her Mam'selle, and asked her to accompany them to headquarters to answer a few questions.

'It will only take an hour or two,' one of them assured her.

They let her change into her street clothes. She was too surprised to be very frightened at first. She kept a clear head, and was able to take the half-finished spool out of the Minox and bury it in the trash. The camera itself she stuffed behind the hot-water pipes, its usual hiding place. Then she was escorted out of the Ritz into rue Cambon with the minimum of fuss. Hardly anyone noticed. Snow was drifting down again, and it seemed to silence what was happening.

It was only when they hoisted her into the back of the truck that she started to feel sick.

There were several other women in the truck. She tried to greet them, but the soldier who was with them pointed his rifle at her.

'No talking. You'll need your breath for screaming, anyway.' He pushed Olivia in with such force that she sprawled on the floor, and he slammed the tailgate shut, leaving the women in semi-darkness.

As the truck rumbled through Paris, the women whispered to each other. Two, a mother and her teenage daughter, were Jews, with the yellow Star of David sewn on to their coats. They had been arrested for trying to take the family sewing machine to relations in the country. The removal from Paris of any property belonging to Jews had been made illegal by a proclamation from the Prefect of Police.

'They're going to open a special department store,' the mother murmured to Olivia, 'where people will be able to buy things confiscated from Jewish households.'

This seemed almost too grotesque for Olivia to believe, but anything was possible.

The other women in the truck were mostly either prostitutes or had been arrested for black market offences. One of them pulled herself up to the tiny, high, barred window and peered out. 'They're taking us to Fresnes,' she said.

There were groans of dismay. Olivia, who had assumed they were being taken to the Gestapo offices on avenue Foch, felt her stomach turn over. Fresnes was the huge Gestapo-run prison in the south of the city where executions took place. There was no chance that she would be getting out 'in an hour or two'.

'Fresnes is the worst,' one of the prostitutes said. 'And it's miles out of Paris. They make you walk back.'

'If they let you go,' one of the others commented grimly. 'They send people to Auschwitz from Fresnes.'

The youngest woman in the truck started to cry. She had been arrested for the crime of infanticide, having just had an illegal abortion, and was still bleeding heavily. Olivia tried to comfort her, hugging her and giving the girl her handkerchief to try to absorb the blood.

The journey took an hour or more. They arrived at the vast prison complex in whirling snow. Heads down, huddled in their inadequate clothing, they were marched to the cells.

Olivia found herself in a solitary cell, the walls naked wet brick and the single barred window too high to see out of. The bed was a straw mattress on the floor. She could see it seething with insects.

Crouching in the opposite corner, hugging herself against the piercing cold, her mind raced. Was this a routine arrest because she was known to be an American? Or had Jack been picked up, and had he betrayed her name under torture? Or was this at the instigation of Heike Schwab, who had always promised that this day would come?

She was at least sure they hadn't found the camera, although it was possible that one of the staff at the Ritz had noticed what she was up to and had reported her.

Could she resist torture? There were so many others whose safety depended on her – Jack, the Auzellos, everyone at the Ritz who had listened to the BBC or made an anti-German remark.

The door crashed open, rousing her from her dark thoughts. A guard came in with prison clothing consisting of a filthy striped uniform and a pair of wooden clogs. He stayed in the cell as she changed into them, with her face to the wall, and then took her own clothes away.

The heavy silence of the thick walls was scratched by tiny, distant sounds of weeping.

※

It was late in the afternoon, and she was shaking with cold, hunger and nerves when the door crashed open again. Two guards marched her down the long corridor. One of the cell doors was open, and an orderly was swabbing up a huge pool of blood. She averted her gaze quickly from the horrible sight.

She was taken to a prison office where a Gestapo officer was seated behind a desk. A guard was standing by with a rubber truncheon, his stony eyes assessing Olivia the way a butcher might examine an animal.

The Gestapo officer was overweight and balding, with round-rimmed glasses in the style of his chief, Heinrich Himmler, whose portrait, with dourly folded arms, decorated the wall over his desk. His fat cheeks looked greasy, as though he had just enjoyed a rich meal, and his manner was unctuous. He beamed at her with phoney charm.

'You are American, Miss Olsen?' he said in English.

'I understand English,' she replied, 'but I am Swedish.'

'Yes, indeed, I have your passport here.' He flipped through it. 'Issued very conveniently one year ago. And yet there is no entry stamp into France. How do you explain that?'

'My old passport expired,' she said, rehearsing the story Raoul Nordling had told her to tell, 'so I had to get a new one here in Paris. They took the old one away from me at the consulate.'

'*Ach so*. That makes everything clear, does it not?'

'It's the truth.'

'So you are not American?'

'No!'

He beamed. 'You need not look so frightened. We Germans do not make war on innocent women. You may admit your nationality without fear. There will be no reprisal.'

'I'm Swedish, I've told you that.'

He clasped his plump fingers and leaned forward. 'In the cellar of this building is a very famous lady. Perhaps you have heard of her? Her name is Madame la Guillotine. She is so beautiful that she has caused many men to lose their heads. If you continue to lie to me, you may find yourself losing yours.'

'You just said you don't make war on women,' she retorted.

'On *innocent* women. But you are not an innocent woman, are you, Olivia Olsen? You are a spy, are you not?'

'I'm not a spy!'

He shuffled through the pile of papers on his desk. 'Two senior Luftwaffe officers billeted at the Ritz report that they caught you going through top secret papers in one of their rooms.'

'That's nonsense,' Olivia said sharply. The strength of her own voice surprised her. The Gestapo man himself seemed a little taken aback by her forthrightness. He blinked at her as she went on, 'I am a housekeeper. It's my job to ensure that rooms are clean and orderly. That means tidying up after the guests. If senior Luftwaffe officers are careless enough to leave top secret papers scattered in open view, then perhaps they should be the ones standing here instead of me!'

'You deny the charge?'

'Of course I do.' She played her trump card. 'I have been cleaning the suite of Herr Reichsmarschall Goering himself. That should show you how trustworthy I am.'

'*Ach so.* We know all about your relationship with Goering. He calls you his little Swede, not so?'

'He has been very kind to me.'

'Yes. But the Reichsmarschall is not a model of caution and security.'

'I'll pass on your comments.'

He smiled even wider. 'Unfortunately, Goering is not here to be consulted. He is currently in the Reich.'

'He'll be back soon. I'll tell him then.'

The man stared at her for a long while, his eyes oily behind the round lenses. 'You are very quick with your answers. Perhaps you don't understand the nature of martial law. I can sentence you to death on the presumption of guilt alone.'

She didn't show the chill of fear his words had given her. 'Why are you threatening me all the time? I've done nothing wrong. I want to see the Swedish consul.'

'What do you want with the Swedish consul?'

'Sweden is a neutral country. You can't keep me here without good reason.'

'I can keep you here for any reason I like, for as long as I like.' He made a brief gesture. 'You will be taken back to your cell now while we compile the evidence against you.'

'What evidence?' she demanded.

But she was already being hustled out of the office, and back along the dark corridor to her cell.

⁜

She saw nobody else for the rest of the day, or that night. Despite her bravado with the Gestapo officer, once she was all alone in her cell she began to be really afraid. The bricks of Fresnes prison breathed a malevolent atmosphere. Here, her individuality meant nothing: she was just one of hundreds who cowered in their cells, awaiting whatever fate the Gestapo decided to dispense. She had never felt so powerless or so alone.

She was fed early the next morning. By now she was crawling with insects. She'd been forced to lie on the straw mattress because the stone flags were too cold to bear, and the resident bugs had soon invaded her dirty prison clothes.

The food was a battered tin bowl of thin porridge that smelled rancid; but she was so hungry and thirsty by now that she licked it clean.

After another two or three hours in solitude, she was summoned to be interrogated once again.

This time, she was shackled. Iron clamps were fastened to her wrists, with a length of heavy chain connecting them. The manacles weighed her soul down even more than her body. They were crushingly heavy.

The fat Gestapo officer, whose name she learned was Captain Kellerman, was behind his desk, as before. The guard with the rubber truncheon was there too.

'I trust your quarters are comfortable?' he greeted her with his phoney smile. 'Any complaints?'

She refused to be provoked by what was certainly an ironic enquiry. 'No complaints,' she replied tersely.

'Excellent.' Smirking, he made a note. 'Let us proceed to the charges against you. You are accused of listening to propaganda from enemy radio stations. How do you reply?'

Olivia's mind raced. The Nazis were obsessed with the BBC World Service, which so often gave news at variance with their own version of events, and the crime of listening to it was severely punished. But there were very few people who didn't occasionally catch a broadcast, one way or another. That he'd phrased it so vaguely suggested he was fishing, hoping to trap her into an admission of guilt, rather than having any real evidence against her.

'Whoever told you that has misinformed you,' she snapped. 'I am not interested in foreign radio stations.'

'Is it not true that there is a short-wave radio hidden in the Ritz hotel that is routinely used to pick up the BBC?'

'Absolutely not. I've never heard of such a thing.'

'Always so quick to answer,' he murmured. 'You have been well trained, Fräulein Olsen.'

'I haven't been trained at all.'

'Your lover, Fabrice Darnell, was a member of the Resistance.'

'Fabrice was just a writer,' she said angrily. 'And he was killed for it by your men. I want to see the Swedish consul.'

'The Swedish consul has washed his hands of you,' Kellerman replied calmly. 'Now that he has been informed you are an American spy he is anxious to distance himself from you completely. He has confirmed that he issued you with a false passport on your urging.'

Olivia felt as though the floor had vanished beneath her feet and she was falling into a dark hole. 'I don't believe it,' she gasped.

His eyes, black and shiny as motor oil, were watching her reaction carefully. 'He has violated international law, and he will be lucky not to end up here himself.' Kellerman tapped the file in front of him. 'I have his confession.'

'That can't possibly be true,' she said, trying to recover her breath, 'because there's nothing wrong with my passport. I'm a Swedish citizen, and I demand to see someone from the consulate!'

He tossed something on to the desk. It was the little sketchbook she always kept in her pinafore. 'You have been making drawings of German officers. These are to be passed to the Resistance, not so?'

'That's absurd. I'm an artist!'

'A chamber pot in one hand and a palette in the other?' he sneered.

'And those are members of the Ritz staff, not German officers. German officers are too ugly to draw.'

He laughed with genuine amusement. 'Very good, very good indeed. You should be on the stage.' The interrogation continued for three more hours, circling around the same questions again and again. She was a liar. She was not Swedish, but American. Her passport was a fake. Fabrice had been an anarchist and a Resistance fighter. She had spied on Luftwaffe officers at the Ritz and passed information to the Allies. She listened to the BBC. She was in touch with the Resistance and gave them her sketches so they could identify German officers for assassination. She would be executed for these crimes unless she confessed.

Her back and her legs began to ache with standing and her mind was dazed. But through it all, she was clinging to the conviction that Kellerman didn't know any of the real stuff. He hadn't mentioned Jack. Nor the Minox. Nor Madame Auzello. She tried not to even think of them, in case she somehow blurted out the names in her exhaustion.

But clinging to her story, that she was a simple Swedish chambermaid, was growing increasingly difficult. Every now and then, Kellerman would slip in a question about America – asking her if she had seen such-and-such a movie, or knew such-and-such a jazz band – which would reveal a knowledge no Swedish chambermaid would have.

Kellerman's unctuous manner slipped away as the interrogation proceeded. The questions grew sharper and more impatient, until at last he seemed to lose his temper. 'This will end badly for you,' he said grimly. 'Take her back to her cell.'

※

The carriage rumbled over the cobblestones, swaying gently. The horse was ancient and the coachman half-asleep. Arletty and Soehring were largely silent. The evening had not been altogether a success. She had taken Soehring to a party at the home of a celebrated Parisian play-wright. The playwright had talked for an hour with Soehring, whose fluent French, sparkling conversation and high level of culture had enchanted him. He had taken Arletty aside and asked, 'But who is your captivating companion, my dear?'

On being told that Soehring was a member of the Occupation forces, the playwright had turned pale and drawn back from Arletty in a rage. 'You had no right to bring him here!' he had said, loud enough for everyone to hear.

They had left early, and not even the drinks they'd subsequently had at the stylish bar at Le Meurice had managed to lift their spirits. They were on their way home now, Soehring sulky and Arletty irritable.

As the carriage crossed the bridge, she opened the gold Cartier compact and took out a cigarette. Her smooth cheeks were lit for a moment by the flame of her lighter. She closed the compact with a snap.

'How I hate that damned thing,' Soehring growled.

Without a word, she opened the window of the carriage and flung the compact over the railing of the bridge. There was a gleam of gold in the night, and then it was in the river.

Soehring lunged to the window as though he could somehow stop the compact from sinking to the bottom of the Seine. 'Are you mad?' he exclaimed.

'I don't want anything between us,' she said calmly.

'It was worth thousands!'

'I hope you weren't expecting me to take it to the pawnbroker. That would be beyond me, my dear Faun. It's gone now.'

'You do such crazy things!' He peered at her dark silhouette, still disconcerted. 'I never asked you to do that.'

'I want no more hours to be wasted in fighting,' she replied. 'We don't know how many hours we'll have.'

Soehring settled back in his seat. 'I suppose now is as good a time as any to tell you.'

'Tell me what?'

'I've asked Goering for permission for us to marry.'

She was silent for a moment. 'I wish you had asked me before Goering.'

He ignored the tone of her voice. 'Goering was happy. His wife is an actress too, you know. Apparently she admires you very much. He congratulated us, and promised to talk to Hitler as soon as possible.'

'Hitler!'

'Yes. The Führer himself has to give permission for German officers to marry non-German wives.'

The glow of her cigarette put red glimmers in her eyes. 'You've made a bad mistake.'

This time he couldn't miss her tone. 'I thought you'd be happy.'

'I have no intention of marrying you.'

He was startled. 'Why not?'

'I'm not made for marriage. I've told you that.'

'I love you, Doe!'

'And I love you.'

'I want to spend my life with you. Isn't that what you want?'

'I see it the other way. I never want to lose you.'

'Don't worry, Hitler gives permission from time to time. It's just a question of catching him in a good mood.'

'Hitler will deny the request. You will look like a fool. Worse, you'll have made Goering look like a fool. They'll recall you to Berlin. We'll never see each other again.'

Soehring laughed. 'You can be so pessimistic at times. It'll all be all right, you'll see.'

Arletty looked out into the dark-blue night. 'I wish I had my compact back now.'

Twenty One

The next day, Kellerman took a new and ominous tack: Hermann Goering.

'Tell me about your relationship with the Reichsmarschall,' Kellerman demanded. 'You woke him each morning, not so?'

'Yes.'

'You were always the first in his bedroom? He refused to have anyone else?'

She was drained. Cold and hunger had worn her down. The incessant questions battered her. She didn't know how much longer she could keep back the truth she so desperately needed to hide. 'Yes. I've told you that over and over again.'

'How exactly did you wake him?'

'I spoke to him gently. Sometimes he was already awake when I came in.'

'Did you wake him like this?' Kellerman was holding up a photograph of startling crudity, showing a fat man and a blonde woman performing a vulgar sexual act.

Olivia grimaced wearily. 'That's disgusting.'

'There was no such intimacy between you?' Kellerman was spreading out more pornographic photographs on his desk, showing the same couple in a variety of positions. 'Like this, for example? Or like this?'

'No!'

'He didn't call you his darling? His little Swede? He never asked you to do this? Or this?'

'Never.' She tried to turn away from the photographs, but Kellerman slammed his hand on the table like a pistol shot.

'Look at the photographs, damn you! Admit that this was what you did with Goering!'

'You should be ashamed of yourself for waving this filth at me,' she said, her voice unsteady.

But through her exhaustion she was feeling a flicker of hope. The more Kellerman hammered on this, the more obvious it was becoming that it hadn't occurred to him she was using the time in Goering's suite to photograph secret documents. His imagination was far more banal than that.

No. What he was after was some evidence of sexual impropriety between herself and Goering, some whiff of scandal that he could transmit to his boss, Heinrich Himmler. Anything Himmler could do to further tarnish his detested rival in the eyes of Hitler would be gold.

All the rest – accusations of spying, references to Fabrice and clandestine radio sets – all that was just to soften her up.

She met Kellerman's eyes. 'Goering never behaved in that way. Not once. For you to suggest that is not only obscene, Captain Kellerman. You're playing a dangerous game.'

'You talk to *me* of danger?' he said incredulously.

'The Reichsmarschall loves his wife and his little girl. He always behaves like a perfect gentleman. He would be astonished if he were to hear your allegations. Astonished and very angry indeed.'

She held the Gestapo man's eyes until the oily gaze slid away. Kellerman's face was as smooth as ever, but she could sense his displeasure. He made a curt gesture. 'Take her away.'

The guards hustled her back to her cell. She had taken a huge chance talking to Kellerman like that. It would be nothing to him to have her shot, as men and women were shot every day in the courtyard. The only thing stopping him would be his fear of what Hermann Goering would do when he learned his little Swede had died at the hands of the Gestapo. Her life depended on which was stronger, his malevolence or his fear.

The wooden shoes had rubbed her feet raw, and made her stumble. As they marched down the corridor, a group of women prisoners was coming towards them, all shackled together. There wasn't much room in the narrow space for them all to pass, and some jostling took place. As the guards cursed and pushed the women around, Olivia felt a swift hand thrust something into her palm. Her fingers curled instinctively around the round hard object.

She kept whatever it was concealed in her fist as they unshackled her and pushed her into her cell. The door crashed shut and the lock engaged.

When she'd heard the boots march away, she opened her fingers and looked at what she had been given – a walnut, still encased in its hard green skin.

She collapsed on to the bed and cried a few tears. Jack had somehow sent her a message. It was as though she felt his strong arms around her, just for a moment, telling her that she was cared for, that she hadn't been abandoned.

⁕

The days passed in dreary monotony. She didn't see Kellerman again. But nor was she released.

Routine came to shape her life. It took the place of her thoughts, her personality, her identity. You became a grey nothing, washed to and fro by the grey tides of a grey sea each day. During the few opportunities Olivia got to talk to other prisoners, she learned that about half of them were there for having had abortions, or for carrying them out. The rest were imprisoned on charges of prostitution or black-marketeering. All were especially female crimes, into which women had been forced by the desperation the war had brought.

Olivia had lost count of the days when one morning her cell door opened to reveal a portly figure in a pinstriped suit, with a solemn rubbery face. It was Raoul Nordling.

The Swedish consul had his hat in one hand and a briefcase in the other. 'Good morning, Miss Olsen,' he said in Swedish as she slowly rose to her feet, not sure if she was dreaming or not. 'Can you come with me, please?'

She limped along the corridor between Nordling and the German guard. Her feet were raw from the sabots, her legs weak with hunger. 'Am I getting out?' she whispered shakily to Nordling.

'We will see about that,' he murmured back. 'Let me do the talking.'

They arrived in Kellerman's office to find the fat Gestapo captain waiting for them. He was all smiles today, greeting Nordling affably and calling Olivia 'Fräulein Olsen'. They were both allowed to sit, a first for Olivia in this office.

The conversation that ensued was mainly in German, which Nordling spoke fluently. She couldn't have followed much of it, even if her mind hadn't been so tired.

At last, Kellerman turned to her. 'You are to be released.'

She thought she must have misheard. 'I'm sorry?'

He produced an official form and placed it in front of her. 'This is to be filled out before you can be discharged. Write "yes" or "no" in the requisite blocks, please. Have you been ill-treated?'

Olivia hesitated, then saw the dark eyes of the Gestapo man fixed on her. She wrote 'No'.

'Have you received adequate food and water?'

She wrote 'Yes'.

'Have you been allowed to have adequate fresh air and exercise?'

Again, she wrote 'Yes'.

There were several more questions, each one giving her an opportunity to make a complaint of one kind or another. Nordling and Kellerman watched her stolidly as she filled out the form the way she knew she was expected to. She doubted whether she would see the light of day again were she to give her jailers anything but a clean report.

She signed her name at the bottom. Kellerman filed the papers away. 'I hope we meet again,' he said. 'With your permission, I will keep your sketchbook. You show some talent.'

Angered by his fake politeness, she started to argue, then thought better of it. There was nothing to incriminate her in the drawings, and getting out of this place was far more important. 'With pleasure,' she said ironically.

He raised his hand in the Nazi salute. 'Heil Hitler!'

He led them to the next room. Olivia's own clothes were laid out on a chair. She couldn't quite believe that any of this was happening, even as she changed into her old garments, which were now loose on her. Her sturdy frame was a lot thinner than when she had arrived.

'Thank you,' she said quietly, turning to Nordling as they were led through the maze of passageways to the exit. 'If you hadn't arrived, I'd have been finished.'

'I've been trying to get you out ever since I heard you'd been arrested. They wouldn't let me see you. Now they seem to have lost interest in you. Of course, the charges were all nonsense. I'm sorry you've had this experience.'

'They told me you had admitted giving me a false passport.'

'I hope you knew that was a lie.'

'Yes.'

But the truth was, she hadn't been certain of anything. Two weeks as a guest of the Gestapo had all but dismantled her self-confidence, her sense of who she was.

'You must be starving,' Nordling said. 'May I take you to lunch?'

'I'm not presentable, but thank you. I just want to get home and take a bath. They didn't let me wash once.' The vision of the huge bath at her studio, with its claw feet and enamel worn through to the metal, was immensely attractive – followed by a night in her own bed.

None of it seemed real to her until they walked out of the gate of Fresnes prison and into a cold, blustery morning.

Nordling's official Volvo was waiting for them, conspicuously flying the Swedish flag on its hood. As they drove away, Olivia sank back into the leather seat and closed her eyes.

I am Olivia Olsen, she told herself. *I am Olivia Olsen. Nobody can take that away from me.*

※

She wanted to get back to work right away, but Monsieur Auzello insisted she take time off to rest.

'The Ritz is quiet. We can manage without you while you get your strength back. We know what you've been through.'

Indeed, everybody in Paris had some idea what a spell in a Gestapo prison was like. Arrests were becoming more and more common as the Germans clamped down on the populace they had conquered. Hundreds of people were arrested each week for common crimes of black-market shopping, showing disrespect to the Nazis, or disobeying the curfew.

The Resistance had made some daring attacks on German officers in Paris, usually in Métro stations or other crowded places. They had managed to assassinate a naval attaché and an army officer. But the reprisals had been savage: dozens of arrests and twenty hostages shot.

She tried to recover from her ordeal. Nightmares woke her constantly. She could not shake off the cruel things she had witnessed in Fresnes; they haunted her. She longed to see Jack and prayed he would come on Sunday.

※

She heard his footstep on the stairs on Sunday morning and flew to open the door. As always, he was carrying something, this time a large duffel bag. His clothes were the same as always too, the faded denims of an agricultural worker. But she'd never been so glad to see his tanned, masculine face or feel the jolt of meeting his grey eyes.

He hugged her tight enough to squeeze the breath out of her, then stepped back to examine her. His face didn't change, but the expression in his eyes did. 'Damn,' he said quietly.

'Am I really hideous?'

'Pretty bad.'

'Ever the diplomat.'

'Mama taught me to speak the truth.' He led her to the window and studied her by the pale light. 'Did they hurt you?'

'Nothing compared to what I saw done to others. I think they went easy on me because I'm supposed to be Swedish. I know I look a mess.'

'You're still a golden girl.'

The simple words made her feel a hundred times better right away. 'I hope that bag is full of eats. They didn't feed me very much.'

'Some of it is clothes. I'm staying a week.'

Olivia blinked. 'Really?'

'If you'll have me, that is. You need looking after.'

'Oh, I do,' she agreed earnestly. 'I really do.'

In a more serious mood, she told him about the interrogations, and what she thought Kellerman had been looking for. 'I don't think they had any idea about what I've really been doing. They were only interested in getting some dirt on Hermann Goering. It was very strange telling them what a perfect gentleman Goering is. But I think it worked.'

'You're right. The whole thing smells of Himmler.'

'I was very lucky, Bumpkin.'

'Yes, you were. I was worried sick about you.'

'I would never have betrayed you,' she said. 'No matter what they did to me.'

'I know you wouldn't.'

'I haven't got anything to betray, anyway.' Her voice was sad. 'You're just a guy called Jack who comes every Sunday to pick up my films – and

I know that's not even your real name. I could tell them everything I know about you, and they would still have no idea how to find you. You share my bed, but you're a complete stranger.'

'I'm sorry it has to be that way,' he said quietly. 'One day it won't have to be like this.'

'Do you know why I call you Bumpkin? It's because I can't bear to call you Jack, when I know it's not your name. Bumpkin is *my* name for you. It's the only part of you that's really mine.'

He touched her hair. 'I'll tell you my name if you want.'

'No. I don't want to know anything that will put you in danger.'

They stared into one another's eyes for a while, thinking the thoughts that couldn't be spoken. Against her will, she felt the tears welling up in her eyes. He cradled her in his arms while she cried silently.

At last she pushed away from him and dried her cheeks. 'Don't worry, I won't do that again. I just had to get it out of my system.'

Jack went to his duffel bag. 'I hope you eat rabbit.'

'I'll eat any damn thing you like.'

He put the rabbit to stew on the stove and unpacked his belongings. Watching him hang up his few clothes and settle himself into her studio filled her with a ridiculous happiness. The blues that had hung over her since her release had finally begun to lift.

As though picking up her mood, he glanced at her over his shoulder. 'Playing house,' he commented ironically.

'I love playing house.'

'Been a long time for me.'

'Don't be scared, I'll be gentle with you.'

He examined her feet, which had suffered from the wooden clogs in Fresnes. 'I'm going to get these splinters out before they get infected. Sing out if I hurt you.'

'I like a man at my feet.' But she winced as he tended to her wounds and disinfected them. 'I was scared in there, Bumpkin. Sometimes there was screaming all night. I'm never going to forget it.'

'No. You never will. But you'll get over it, and that's the important thing.'

The rabbit stew was the best meal she'd eaten in weeks. The food made her sleepy, so he tucked her into bed. She wouldn't let him leave, holding on to his hand.

'Give me something to dream about.'

'Like what?'

'Tell me about the red barn.'

'What's so fascinating about the barn?'

'Just tell me.'

'Okay, if it makes you happy. It was built by my great-grandfather in 1855. He didn't believe in nails much, so most of it is jointed or dowelled. He painted it with a mixture of cow's blood, linseed oil and rust. The iron in the rust and blood keeps mould out of the wood. It also gives it that red colour. We don't use blood any more. But we still use iron oxide paint.'

'What's it like inside?' she asked sleepily.

'It's like a barn inside.'

'Wiseacre.'

'Don't you have barns?'

'Yes. But they're not red. And they're not timber – they're modern galvanised iron. And I want to hear about *your* barn.'

'Well, I guess it's like a church, if you want to see it like that. High and vaulted, with posts and beams and rafters and trusses. Great-granddaddy was quite an architect, and he had a lot of wood to use. These days, barns are mostly metal, like you said, but in those days it was timber. It has a gambrel roof – that's in two steps – covered with cedar shingles. In the hot weather it smells sweet, of cedar and grain and linseed oil.'

'I can just smell it.'

'It's very strong. It stands up to just about anything summers and winters can throw at it. It'll be standing there a hundred years from now, just the same. If I have any grandkids, they'll be painting it with rust, just like I did.'

As she slipped into sleep, she felt his hand caressing her hair.

It was the first night she'd slept without horrible dreams. She woke to find him brewing coffee on the stove.

'Is that real coffee?' she said, sitting up and sniffing.

'Yep. Donated by the German army.'

'My God, what a treat.'

'Only the best for you, ma'am. How are you feeling?'

'Better.'

'Good. My magic is working already.'

They went out at mid-morning, just to stretch their legs and get some fresh air. Spring had now taken hold of the city. The tired old legend of springtime in Paris had been given new life yet again. Daffodils bloomed in yellow swathes, rosebuds nodded in the breeze. After months of dreary greyness, greenery and blossoms were everywhere.

They found an old woman selling fruit from a little basket, wild strawberries and a few apricots covered in leaves. They bought everything she had. They had intended to take their prize home, but somehow they ate it along the way, and kept going, all the way to the Seine, which flowed green and strong under its bridges. The air off the river was moist and spicy.

They walked and talked under the plane trees and elms, which were in full leaf along the banks. Or it seemed to her that they talked; later, she realised that it was she who had done almost all the talking. He had listened. In any case, the war seemed far away. If you didn't look at the German soldiers or the swastikas, there had never been a war at all. There were just the two of them, seeing the city and each other through new eyes.

When she started to get tired, they sat on a bench near a bridge where the river chuckled around stone stanchions. It was here that they kissed for the first time – kissed spontaneously, like lovers, rather than as strangers.

Like everything else that day, it felt completely new, something she had never done before; and yet it was achingly familiar, like a recurring dream that had come true after so many years.

He was sure and gentle, holding her in his arms, not hurrying her, allowing her to explore the bliss of the moment.

'You taste of wild strawberries,' he whispered.

'You taste of apricots.'

By the time they got back to Montmartre, they were wrapped tightly around one another, not just physically, but organically, with no more need for words.

Their lovemaking was slow at first. They undressed and explored one another's bodies. Each had a secret garden: hers was a triangle of golden hair, through which ran a crease, and in the crease were pink cyclamens; his was a tulip on a solid stem, eager for her touch. Both were capable of giving and receiving intense pleasure.

Careful assessment gave way to passionate commitment. With racing hearts and panting lungs, they entwined, kissing, caressing, demanding; until she pulled him on top of her, and they possessed each other completely.

Afterwards, her body still ringing like a great bell that had been struck, she looked up at him and asked, 'That wasn't just to make me feel better, was it?'

'No,' he said. 'I'm in love with you, Olivia.'

Twenty Two

The film was to be called *Les Visiteurs du Soir*, The Night Visitors, and Arletty was to be paid a hundred thousand francs for her role. She was cast as Dominique, a beautiful temptress sent by the devil to sow despair and snatch men's souls. She would play opposite the enigmatic Alain Cuny, who would be her male counterpart from hell, and the diabolical Jules Berry, who would of course play *le diable* himself.

This would be her second film for Marcel Carné, who had directed her in *Le Jour se Lève*, the film that had shot her to stardom. He was regarded as one of the most brilliant directors in France, so brilliant that the Nazi administration was prepared to turn a blind eye to his open homosexuality.

After a spell without work, it was a coup for Arletty. Shooting would start at the end of the summer. She and Soehring were celebrating with a champagne dinner at one of her favourite restaurants, Voisin on the rue Saint-Honoré. Voisin was expensive, chic and discreet. He had never been before. She had asked for the *cabinet particulier*, the private room where waiters only came when summoned by a bell. Here they were insulated from comments and insulting stares. Here one could make love between courses, if one wished.

But Soehring was subdued tonight. He showed little interest in the famous menu and drank morosely, answering her gay chatter with monosyllables. The cosy room, with its carved panelling and gilded sconces, failed to enchant him.

'Faun,' she said at last, leaning forward and covering his hand with hers, 'I'm like a little, lost animal without you. Tell me what's wrong.'

He raised his eyes to hers. They were cloudy, not the limpid, Germanic blue that she loved so much. 'I've heard from Goering.'

'About us?'

'Yes.'

'About this foolish request of yours?'

'Yes.'

'Hitler has turned you down, of course.'

'Yes,' he said a third time.

Arletty lifted his champagne glass and held it out to him. 'Drink, my poor Faun. I've told you already, I will love you for ever, but I won't ruin your life by marrying you.'

He took the glass and drank obediently, then set it down again. 'I'm afraid there's more.'

'What more?'

'I daren't tell you.'

'Then it must be very bad indeed,' she said lightly. But her lids were lowered over her eyes now. 'Courage, my dear. Tell me the worst.'

'They want me to give you up. Or they will withdraw me from Paris.'

Arletty was silent for a while. 'What do they say about me?'

'Nothing.'

'You're lying. Because you don't want to humiliate me. But I am not easily humiliated. They say that I'm too old for you.'

'Yes.'

'What else?'

'They say that you're a seductress. That you've put a spell on me.'

'A spell?'

'The exact phrase they used was *eine sexuelle Hörigkeit*.'

'What does that mean?'

'A sexual enslavement.'

'Oh, la-la.'

'They say that I'm neglecting my duties and bringing my rank into disrepute. They say our affair is damaging relations between Germany and France.'

'Even more than the Gestapo's tortures and executions?'

'Don't be angry, Doe.'

'But I *am* angry,' she said. 'I told you this was a bad mistake. You should have consulted me first.'

'I was mad with love. I still am.'

She sat back on the plush banquette. 'What are we going to do now?'

'I can't give you up. I can't live without you. We'll just have to be more careful from now on.'

'Eyes follow us wherever we go, Faun. How can we hide what we are?'

'We'll be discreet. You can't come to me at the Ritz any more. We'll get a place somewhere else.'

'Josée de Chambrun offered me an apartment on the quai de Conti. She said it was very secluded. I can ask her if it's still available.'

'I'm so sorry.'

She lit a cigarette. 'Odd how life imitates art, isn't it? I'm cast as a demonic enslaver in both.'

'And nobody wants to give us room to breathe, neither your people nor mine.'

She gave him her radiant smile. 'Let's not be gloomy, my darling. Tonight is ours, at least. Let's drink to each other.'

She saw him respond to her beauty, as he always did. But as she swallowed the champagne, it tasted sour in her throat, and she knew that she had lost him. It was only a question of time.

It was a summer of love. After that glorious week together, Olivia had returned to work at the Ritz, but nothing had been as before. She was changed. The focus of her life had been avenging Fabrice. It wasn't any more. She had struck back at the Nazis as best she could, and had only just escaped the same fate as Fabrice. Something had lifted from her, a sense of obligation, a loyalty to a man she had loved, but who had now been dead for two years.

There was another man in her life now, and a new focus. She lived for the weekends, when she would see Jack. The time in between was grey nothingness. She did her work, photographed documents wherever possible, and only became herself when he arrived.

They made love with abandon. Their passion was a garden that grew ever more riotously the more they watered it. He was her man, and yet he was her stranger, someone about whom she knew less than almost anyone else in her life.

Her darkest fear was that she would wait for him one weekend and he would not come. He would vanish from her life without a trace, without a word, and all she would know was that he had suffered in some cellar and died against the firing squad wall. She dreaded that so much that she could only bear to approach it in nightmares.

He never talked about his war, which somehow made it worse. She had no idea of the violence and danger he must go through when he wasn't her lover. There were whole dimensions to Jack that she knew nothing about – and might never know anything about.

In the warm days of early autumn, she had a week's leave.

'Let's get out of Paris for a few days,' he said. 'I know a place where we can be safe and quiet.'

'Together?' she said incredulously.

Jack smiled. 'Yes, together.'

She was overjoyed. The village was called Saint-Benoît-du-Sault. They took the night train from Paris, and the first coach from the station. It dropped them in the village square. The sun was just rising, and a luminous mist hung over the hamlet. Carrying their bags, they clambered down a steep hill, through the sleeping streets. The half-timbered houses had changed little since the time of Molière and Racine, when they had been built. The place had the charm of somewhere that time had forgotten, or which lay under a spell, as in a fairy tale.

They passed over a stone bridge. The river below was still summer-shallow, dotted with little islands, where clumps of irises grew and swans floated serenely. They met two young girls carrying pails of milk, who giggled at the sight of strangers.

'Don't worry, they won't say anything,' Jack told Olivia. 'They know how to keep their mouths shut. They're not fond of the Boche around here.'

The house was right at the end of the lane, a stone cottage in a small orchard of apple trees. The boughs were laden with ripening yellow fruit. The house itself was covered in briar roses. The flowers hung heavily, wet with the mist, their scent of musk hovering in the air, and the thorny stems trailed across the windows and the old oak door.

'Oh, Jack, this is heavenly!'

She put her arms around him, pressing her face to his chest, inhaling his familiar scent. His arms closed around her in return. He pressed his mouth into her hair. 'Let's go in. They promised to leave us some breakfast.'

The main room of the cottage was small. As Jack went around opening the shutters, the morning light flooded in on country simplicity – a pine table, an iron stove, some wicker chairs.

'Fresh bread, butter, eggs and coffee,' he said with satisfaction. 'That'll do for starters.'

Olivia prepared a cafetière while he made the food. Everything was scrupulously neat and clean. The rough whitewashed walls were bare.

The aroma of the coffee was rich and strong. As it bubbled, he fried two eggs and cut two slices of bread, buttering them carefully. He moved with a precision that gave her a deep pleasure to watch. Playing house with him was one of her great joys.

It was a year and a half since she had first met him, and a lot had happened in that time. She'd once thought him unapproachable. She knew now that he had the ability to close his face, like shutting a door, making himself impossible to read. That gave him the ability to pass through checkpoints like a thousand others. But with her, his expression opened, and he became quite different; he took on a beauty of his own. She only owned part of him, but what was hers was hers completely. She knew that he had nobody else. She could tell by the way he made love to her.

She polished off the fresh eggs and mopped up the traces with the crusty country bread. She hadn't realised how hungry she was. They set out to explore their domain.

There was a vegetable garden at the back of the cottage, with artichokes, beans, courgettes, peas and much else, all laid out in straight rows, the climbing plants tied carefully to supports. They set about gathering a basket of vegetables.

While they were busy, a girl came into the garden, as timid as a young fox. She was pretty, with long red hair, and she was carrying a basket, which turned out to contain some bottles of wine and four partridges. She and Jack talked quietly. She shot Olivia a few inquisitive glances, but for the most part her eyes were fixed adoringly on Jack. And indeed, he was rather god-like, Olivia thought, with his shirt sleeves rolled up to show his tanned and muscular arms.

'She must be one of the ones whose mother hasn't locked her up yet,' Olivia commented when the girl had slipped away again.

'She's just a kid.'

Olivia smiled. 'If I was sixteen, I'm sure I would look at you just like she does. You're obviously a hero in these parts.'

'Like I said, they hate the Germans round here.' They walked to the river and watched the swans. Olivia had saved some bread crusts. She threw these to the swans, who hurried over and clustered at the bank to gobble them up, hissing and honking, their long white necks vying with each other for the delicious morsels. 'Look how beautiful they are,' he said admiringly. 'I'm surprised they haven't been eaten yet.'

'Nobody would touch them. There has to be some France left for when the Nazis leave.'

As if on cue, they heard the rumble of military vehicles. A German convoy was passing through the village. Through the trees they caught glimpses of the grey vehicles with their black-and-white crosses. Their engines pumped a diesel haze into the blue sky. Olivia and Jack sat in silence until the noise and the stink had faded.

'I hate them,' she said quietly.

'A lot of them are going to leave their bones here,' he commented flatly.

They went back to the cottage. He made a meal of the partridges with artichokes, followed by fruit from the orchard. Afterwards he led her up the uneven stone stairs to the single bedroom. It had a floor of old clay tiles and a ceiling of oak beams. In the centre was a four-poster bed, made up with fresh linen. There was a vase of roses on the table and a hand-painted pine cupboard.

'This is so pretty,' she said. 'Whose house is this?'

'Ours for as long as we want it.' He took her in his arms. 'I miss you so much when we're apart. I've dreamed of this for weeks.'

'Me too.' They kissed, their mouths swiftly becoming passionate. Their need for one another was overwhelming. He pulled off his shirt, and she ran her hands over his lean body, pulling him closer against her. She drew him down on to the bed with her.

⁕

Afterwards, they lay together in a reverie. The place was lost in deep tranquillity. There was hardly a sound to be heard beyond the thick stone walls. There was only the soft whisper of their breathing and the dancing of dust motes in the slanting light from the high windows. After the stress and noise of Paris, this was like being suspended in amber.

They hardly had need of words, but still they came.

'Do you remember the day we met, in the little vineyard?' she asked.

The colour of his eyes deepened. 'How could I forget?'

'You were so rude to me. But I've never forgotten that afternoon. It was so exciting.'

'I was suspicious because you were far too beautiful to be true. I thought you must be a German spy.'

'Well, there's a double-edged compliment if ever I heard one.'

In the evening they opened a bottle of the wine the red-headed girl had brought. The bottle had no label, but contained a velvety pinot noir. They toasted each other in thick green-glass tumblers. There was no electricity in the cottage. The oil lantern cast swooping shadows on the walls. They finished the rest of their midday meal and went back to bed to finish the rest of their love, this time more slowly, drawing out each other's pleasure to an almost unbearable pitch, before yielding to the exquisite release of experienced lovers.

She awoke in his arms the next morning, her head pillowed on his broad chest. She felt heavenly. She hadn't been as calm as this in years. She opened her eyes and saw that, outside the window, there was a sky the colour of a robin's egg.

Jack's hand brushed her tumbled hair. 'I can feel your eyelashes on my chest,' he said.

Cat-like, she nestled against his warm body and smiled up into his face. 'You're the handsomest man I've ever known.'

'Even first thing in the morning?'

'Well, you could do with a shave, it's true.'

He kissed her lips lingeringly. 'And you are so beautiful, you make my heart ache.'

The days passed with awful speed. They ate in the local bistro, where everyone discreetly left them alone, yet gave them warm smiles. He swam in the river, though he couldn't tempt her to join him; she was content to dip her feet in the cold water. They walked, talked and made love, leading a life of more normality than they had known in years.

It seemed that they had hardly arrived when it was over and they were walking back to the bus station in Saint-Benoît-du-Sault. The ancient yellow *autobus* arrived wheezily, but on time. Leaving the village was almost too painful to bear.

Rattling back to Paris on the crowded train, which was full of German soldiers, she thought about the past years. Losing Fabrice had left a huge hole in her life. That wound had healed now. She had grown and matured in that time. But what if she were to lose Jack too? Could she survive that?

And was this a forever love – or one of the wartime affairs that Jack predicted always turned to ash? The countryside, clad in autumn colours, flitted past the windows of their carriage. Her body was still warm and tender from Jack's lovemaking. Only time would tell.

The premiere of *Les Visiteurs du Soir* was a gala occasion. The film had been keenly anticipated, not least because the plot, with its devils sent from hell, was whispered to be an allegory of the Nazi occupation. There was an excited crowd outside the Madeleine movie theatre, cheering the stars as they arrived in their big, flashy cars. A row of German soldiers had been posted to keep order, as at all public events these days, but the crowd ignored them completely. This was a wholly French occasion: a French movie, made by a French director, with French stars. It was proof that France was still alive.

But the cheering fell silent as Arletty and Soehring got out of the limousine. She was in a silver lamé sheath and a white mink cape. He was in full Luftwaffe uniform.

The cameras flashed, making her dress sparkle, but there was no sound from the crowd as the couple walked arm in arm into the theatre along the red carpet. It was a silence more of disbelief than disapproval. Though she and Soehring had been lovers for over a year, the relationship had not been common knowledge outside the smart set who frequented the Ritz and had boxes at the Conservatoire.

For most of the ordinary men and women who had turned out on this cold December night, seeing their beloved Arletty on the arm of a Nazi officer was a stunning shock.

There were no catcalls or boos. There was no time for that. The couple had passed into the thronged lobby of the Madeleine before the crowd had recovered from their astonishment.

She looked beautiful tonight, and she felt beautiful. Nothing mattered to her except being here on the arm of the man she adored. His presence was important to her. She knew it would be a slap in the face for some of her public, but she didn't care. She had wearied of hiding and running, of concealing her emotions. Tonight was her triumph, and she wanted Soehring at her side.

And the film was a coup. Sumptuous, occasionally grotesque, it was set in a castle in the fifteenth century, complete with dwarves, minstrels, lords and ladies. By the interval, nobody in the theatre was in any doubt that *Les Visiteurs du Soir* was a masterpiece, one of the highest achievements of the French cinema. Her own role, as the she-devil Dominique, sent to capture a man's soul, was mesmerising.

Even Antoinette d'Harcourt, who came up to her in the lobby, looking like a ghost, acknowledged the greatness of her acting.

'I had to come and see it,' she said. 'I'm glad I did. You are wonderful in this part, Arletty.'

Arletty kissed her on both cheeks. She hadn't seen Antoinette in months, and her old friend appeared unwell and exhausted. 'Have you forgiven me yet?' she asked Antoinette.

'I'll never forgive you,' Antoinette replied. She hadn't said a word to Soehring, or even glanced at him. 'But I will always love you.'

'Are you still driving your ambulances?'

'I am still involved,' Antoinette replied, 'until your German friends decide to stop me.'

Arletty smiled. She was too excited to be brought down by Antoinette and her dramas. She talked gaily to the reverential crowd that had gathered around her, praising her co-stars, extolling the charms of Vence, where the film had been made, telling anecdotes about the difficulties of making such an elaborate film in wartime, with so few materials for costumes and props.

'And there was a pig at the villa where I was staying – a four-legged pig, I might add, and a pig unknown to the authorities – who showed his superb taste by eating my swimsuit.'

On a wave of laughter, and with the bell ringing, she led the way back into the crimson-and-gold auditorium for the second half.

The audience's exclamations of admiration or pity died down as the film reached its climax. They sat spellbound. Satan, played by Jules Berry, strutting and snarling in a black uniform, punished the disobedient lovers by turning them to stone. In complete silence, they watched him gloating over his handiwork. And then, just audible on the film's soundtrack, came a steady, rhythmical thud. It was the beating of the lovers' hearts, still alive deep in the stone.

Enraged, the Hitlerian devil lashed the statues with his riding crop to silence those obstinate hearts, but in vain. The hearts kept beating in unison. As Satan faded away on a scream of fury, the audience rose to their feet, cheering until they were hoarse. Tears were streaming down many faces.

The image of the imprisoned lovers, still alive and faithful to one another under cruel imprisonment, was as clear a metaphor for the Occupation as could be. The applause lasted a full fifteen minutes. Flowers were thrown, bouquets were presented. Even the Germans in the theatre seemed to have been affected and were clapping their gloved hands approvingly. Perhaps so long as the beating hearts remained imprisoned, they could tolerate a little antipathy.

'France will not forgive you,' a voice said quietly in Arletty's ear as the crowd finally moved to the exit. She turned in surprise. The man was a stranger, well-dressed, with dark hair and a pale face. 'You have been sentenced to death, Arletty. You will be killed – and soon.'

Arletty cried out in alarm. The stranger had already turned away and was making his way quickly through the throng of furs and uniforms.

'What's wrong?' Soehring demanded.

'That man threatened me!'

'Who?'

She pointed at the man's retreating back. 'Him!'

Soehring and others chased after the man, but he had vanished as swiftly as he had materialised and couldn't be identified. Nobody else had noticed the exchange or heard the menacing words.

Arletty tried to recover her poise, laughing the incident off as a prank. Her dazzling smile was one of her best assets; she could summon it up effortlessly, whatever she was feeling inside. It convinced everybody. But she was trembling. And as she walked out of the theatre, the waiting crowd once again fell silent, a silence that she felt more keenly than any insults. She glanced at the rows of expressionless faces that watched her. How many of these people held hatred for her in their hearts? How many would willingly plunge a dagger into her back?

Perhaps Antoinette could tell her whether the Resistance had really sentenced her to death. But Antoinette, too, had disappeared.

Arletty tried to forget the encounter during the party that followed. It was a lively affair, hosted by the director, Marcel Carné, at his home in Montmartre. Many of the actors and crew were there, as well as critics, poets, composers and other members of Paris's creative circles. Soehring was notable as the only German in uniform.

There was another German officer present, although he was in evening dress: the dashing Spatz von Dincklage, who had accompanied his companion Coco Chanel to the film. The two Germans stood rather awkwardly together, holding their drinks. Though each spoke perfect French, and was capable of talking brilliantly on almost any subject, they were largely ignored by the Parisians.

'Did you enjoy the film?' Soehring asked von Dincklage politely. The men were not friends, though they treated one another with the courtesy of fellow officers and fellow guests at the Ritz.

'I found it rather hostile to the Reich. Almost anti-Nazi. But, of course, your Arletty was magnificent, as always, my dear boy.' Spatz von Dincklage was some dozen years older than Soehring and inclined to patronise him. He paused delicately. 'I understand you will be leaving Paris shortly.'

Soehring grimaced. Of course von Dincklage, with his convoluted spy network in both the German and French communities, knew everyone's business. 'Yes, so it seems.'

'Still,' von Dincklage said encouragingly, 'a little active service always looks good on one's résumé. And it ensures that one does not forget that one is a soldier, after all.' He smirked with the confidence of a man who knew very well how to avoid being sent to the front. He was unlikely ever to do anything to threaten his stay in Paris. 'Does she know?' he asked, indicating Arletty, who was deep in a discussion with Coco Chanel on the other side of the room.

'Not yet. I don't know whether I should tell her or leave it to the last minute.'

'In my view, bad news is best given as early as possible. And without any attempt to soften the blow.'

'Thank you for your advice,' Soehring replied dryly.

'And if you will allow me to say so,' von Dincklage went on, 'this unfortunate situation would never have arisen if you hadn't approached Goering with a request to marry her.'

Soehring gave von Dincklage a bitter look. 'It's a bit late for that.'

'Forgive me. I feel sympathy for you. You and I have much in common.'

'Except that the Reich approves of Chanel, whereas it disapproves of Arletty.'

'Everything can be handled, if one knows the right way to go about it.' Spatz lit a cheroot and puffed at it with satisfaction. 'I wish you had come to me, my dear boy. I could have explained how best to handle this.'

Soehring grunted. He now had only a few weeks left in Paris. Perhaps the odious von Dincklage was right, and telling her right away was the best approach.

On the far side of the crowded room, Arletty and Chanel were talking in low voices.

'I was threatened at the movie theatre tonight.'

'By whom?' Coco asked.

'I don't know. A young man with a strange face. He said I had been sentenced to death and would be killed soon. Then he disappeared.'

Coco studied Arletty with her sharp dark gaze. She must be sixty years old, Arletty guessed, but had the gift of looking ageless in the right light. 'Your first time?'

'Yes. You mean it's happened to you too?'

'Many times. There's a list. Made by the Fifis.'

'The Fifis?'

'They're calling themselves *Forces Françaises de l'Intérieur*. The FFI. Boys in espadrilles with guns from 1914.'

'Are they dangerous?'

Coco shrugged. 'Any boy with a gun is dangerous.'

'Who is on this list?'

'Me. You. Anyone they choose to call a collabo. Naturally, anyone who is successful is right at the top. They hate the rich. And it's easier to frighten a woman than a six-foot stormtrooper.'

'He managed to frighten me,' Arletty said.

Coco studied Arletty speculatively. 'What will you do if the Germans leave France?'

The question was a pointed one. The tide of war had turned against the Axis powers. The Russian campaign had turned into a nightmare for the German army, now pinned down by snow and ferocious Soviet resistance. Allied bombers were making raids on German cities. In the Far East, the mighty Japanese navy was being steadily worn down by the Americans.

'I haven't thought about it.'

'Now would be a good time to start thinking about it.' Chanel's cheeks hollowed as she sucked on her cigarette.

'What will you do?'

'Churchill will protect me,' Chanel said confidently. 'He's been in love with me for years.'

'I don't have such useful lovers,' Arletty said ironically.

'You could go to Germany with Soehring.'

'I don't think so. I'll stay and face the music.'

'The music may be very unpleasant.'

'I'd be no good anywhere else. My heart is French, even if my *cul* is international.'

'How is he in bed?' Coco asked.

Arletty found the question insolent, but Chanel was too powerful to offend. 'We're very happy together,' she replied neutrally.

'Spatz is good. But I need more than one man. I have a big appetite.' Chanel chuckled, glancing at the two striking German officers.

'Luckily, Spatz understands me. He even likes to watch – if my playmate is a woman. Ah, by the way: your friend Antoinette Harcourt has been arrested by the Gestapo.'

Arletty felt cold. 'I've heard nothing.'

'It's being kept quiet because of who she is. Spatz knows all about it, of course. It seems your little friend has been very unwise.'

Arletty felt ill. What a terrible evening this was turning out to be. 'Can Spatz do anything for her?'

Coco's eyes, usually darkly brilliant, softened with pity at Arletty's expression. 'No, my dear. There is nothing to be done. They are interrogating her. If she is clever, she may come out again. If not—' She touched Arletty's arm compassionately. 'Then things must take their course.'

Arletty and Soehring got back to their room late, around three a.m. 'There's terrible news, Faun,' she said as soon as the door was closed. 'Antoinette has been arrested by the Gestapo.'

'That was inevitable,' he replied with a shrug.

'But you must do something for her!'

'There's nothing I can do.'

'Faun, I know you are jealous of her – but those brutes will tear her to pieces. She's so frail. Please, my darling. I'm begging you. Help her!'

His face was hard. 'There's nothing I can do, damn it.'

'Faun, please! Goering will listen to you!'

Soehring pulled off his shirt. She loved to see his body, so strong and youthful, and all hers to possess. 'I'm not on Goering's staff any more. I've been called up on active duty.'

Arletty became very still. 'I don't understand what you mean.'

'They're sending me to the front.'

She didn't move, with the zipper of her dress half-down, her loosened hair hanging to her shoulders. 'When?'

'Soon.'

'Can't you speak to someone? Get it changed?' The inane words were coming from her mouth, but she wasn't aware of speaking them. Someone much less wise was asking these questions. She herself was still frozen within.

'There's nothing to be done,' he said heavily.

'How long have you known?'

'I found out today.'

'You're lying.' She slipped out of her dress and hurried into the bathroom, slamming and locking the door behind her.

She saw his silhouette appear at the frosted-glass pane of the door. 'Doe!'

'No. Don't come in.'

'Please don't lock the door. Say what you want to me, but don't shut me out.'

'Go away.'

'Please.'

She had finally found her tears, and was crying bitterly over the basin, her knuckles white as she gripped the porcelain rim. She felt as though she were breaking apart, piece by piece. The architecture of her own self, which she had been so carefully putting together since Courbevoie, was no longer holding together. And when everything slid into rubble, all that would be left was a skinny, crying, red-headed child on the bank of a stagnant canal.

Twenty Three

Hermann Goering was paying another visit to the Ritz.

He arrived with his entourage of lackeys and hangers-on, like a Renaissance prince; but he was now a prince in decline. Olivia could see that he had put on even more weight. His gaudy uniform was strained across his great belly. His tailors could no longer keep up. And yet his face was gaunt, his jaws prominent, his eyes sunken in dark clefts.

He greeted Olivia like a long-lost niece, taking her hands in his and calling her his little Swedish girl. She wondered whether he'd heard about her arrest by the Gestapo, and the attempt to compromise him. It was probably best not to mention it.

She brought him tea and cake in the afternoon. He was alone in the suite, sitting at his desk with piles of papers around him. All she would need was ten minutes with the Minox and nobody around; but she was unlikely to get them. Major Soehring, who had been responsible for Goering's security, had now left Paris. The careless old days were gone. The new chief of Goering's security was an SS man whose eagle eye missed nothing.

'Stay,' Goering commanded, heaving himself away from his desk and sinking into an armchair to enjoy his tea. 'Talk to me for a while, child. Cheer me up.'

'What can I tell you to cheer you up?' she asked, standing obediently in front of him with her hands folded demurely.

'Something to distract me from all this.' He waved his hand at the documents scattered all around. 'I tell you, Olivia, I wish you and I were in Sweden now, walking together in the mountains, with nothing to worry about.'

'Is it all bad news?' she asked.

'Terrible,' he said shortly. 'The Führer asks the impossible of me. He expects me to send fighters to shoot down the American bombers. I have none. They've all been destroyed.'

More pastries went into the shovel of a mouth. 'What do you tell him?' she asked quietly.

'Nobody says no to Hitler. But the bearing factory at Schweinfurt was smashed, so we can't build engines. The oil refineries have been set alight, so my planes have no fuel. The assembly plants have been pounded – the Focke-Wulf works, the Messerschmitt plant, all crippled. They are reducing our cities to rubble. And there is nowhere in the Reich they cannot reach. We have brought our great nation into ruin. Future generations of Germans will judge us for that.'

He didn't seem too perturbed about all the other nations that had been brought to ruin by the Nazis, but Olivia didn't comment on that. What he was telling her was perhaps more valuable than any photographs she could take. She was committing it all to memory as he talked. 'Is it impossible to defend Germany?'

'Do you know how many fighters we can put in the air against the Flying Fortresses? No more than one thousand. One thousand! That's barely enough to protect a couple of large cities! Four-fifths of our fighters are needed at the front. With only one-fifth left, how can I stop the Americans? Yes, it is impossible.'

He ate and drank for a while in silence, staring hollow-eyed into space. 'It will all be behind us soon,' he said, seeming to brighten. 'When Hitler is out of the way, I'll take charge. I can talk to Churchill and Roosevelt in a way he can't. They'll trust me. I'll be the leader of a new Germany, a Germany to be rebuilt and made strong again.'

She realised that he was serious. He imagined that all his vast crimes would be somehow forgotten after the war, leaving him untouched by guilt. It was incredible; yet the way he was eating showed how disassociated from reality he had become.

She reported this conversation, and much else that Goering had gone on to say, to Jack on Sunday. She'd made notes immediately afterwards, so she wouldn't forget any of the details. He read through the notes carefully, and then burned them in the stove. He had a steel-trap memory that forgot nothing.

'You did well, as always,' he said, as they got into bed. 'That'll make interesting reading in Washington. They'll be glad to hear the bombing has been so effective. The Luftwaffe has always been the Nazi's weakness. It seems Goering was so anxious not to disappoint Hitler that he let him think there were more planes and pilots than he could possibly get together. It was their Achilles' heel from the start.'

'He thinks he's going to take Hitler's place.'

'A palace coup?'

'That's what he was hinting at.'

'Interesting.'

'I'm sorry I couldn't get any photos.'

'Please be careful, Yokel.' He held her close. 'I can't lose you again. Don't take chances.'

She nestled against him. 'There aren't many chances to take these days. Security's a lot tighter now that Major Soehring's been replaced. They say he's been sent to the front. And demoted to private.'

'Because of this affair with Arletty?'

'Yes. She'll be heartbroken without him.'

'I don't have pity to waste on collaborators,' Jack retorted.

'I like her. There's something very special about her. People can't help falling in love, you know.'

'With an enemy?'

'Soehring's not a typical Nazi.'

'Well, wherever he is, he's busy killing Americans. So, yes, he is a fairly typical Nazi.'

'I wish I was like you. I can't see things in black and white. To me there are just shades of grey.'

He kissed her lovingly. 'Yeah, you even have a soft spot for Hermann Goering, don't you?'

'I once thought about stabbing him with his own dagger while he was sleeping.'

'You're a bloodthirsty Yokel sometimes.'

After they had made love, they lay together dreamily, lost in bliss. Their bodies were now so accustomed to one another that separation didn't leave them just alone, it tore something that had to knit together again every Sunday.

'The Resistance have put Arletty's name on a list,' Jack said after a while.

'What kind of list?'

'They'll kill her if they can.'

'Oh no,' Olivia said, feeling cold. 'She doesn't deserve that. Can't you stop them?'

'It's their decision, not mine. She's more than just a woman who slept with a German. She was their pin-up. The essence of everything French. They see what she did as the worst kind of betrayal.'

'What about the French generals who surrendered to the Nazis in 1940?' Olivia retorted. 'What about the French police who do everything the Gestapo tell them? And all those French millionaires making deals with Germans at the Ritz? Are you telling me those aren't the worst kinds of betrayals?'

He smiled at her passion. 'I didn't say it was logical. It's a gut reaction.'

'It just isn't fair.' Olivia raised herself on one elbow to look at her lover. 'What are they planning to do?'

'They'll lure her out into the streets at night and shoot her.'

'And that will make everything all right?'

'It'll make them feel better about themselves, I guess.'

'That's disgusting,' she snapped. 'She's a defenceless woman.'

'This is a crucial year, Yokel. The war is finally turning our way. Anything that raises the morale of the French will help when the invasion finally starts.'

'Murdering Arletty isn't going to raise anyone's morale! It'll shock the whole country.'

He stroked her cheek. 'I love you when you get yourself good and mad.'

She pushed his hand away. 'Don't patronise me. Tell your Maquis friends there are a hell of a lot of other people they should kill first.'

His face was compassionate. 'Sweetheart, I don't think you realise how much they hate women like Arletty. They feel she's cuckolded them with the enemy. She won't get any pity from them.'

Olivia got up and went to the balcony, wrapping her gown around her nakedness. It was early evening. The uncertain spring weather was cold. The sky over the faraway outline of Sacré Coeur was glowing crimson as the sun went down, giving her the impression that, if she could only read those colours, which no paints could ever capture, some mystery would be revealed to her, some explanation for the stupidity and ignorance of men.

They feel she's cuckolded them with the enemy. What abysmal immaturity. Did they think all women belonged to them, like the cows in the French fields? What did men expect of women? That they should think and act as men did, and sacrifice all their own nature to the gods of war? And yet be ready with legs open when men were ready to be comforted, and be soft and pliable, and tell them how clever they had been at killing and maiming?

Arletty represented something that went beyond France, something beautiful and quintessentially feminine, a great artiste who knew how to portray the feelings only women had, and which men could not grasp at.

The rich complexity of women's nature didn't matter a damn to them. They just didn't care. The only quality they wanted in women was that nursery-school gold star of being *good*. And if a woman lost that gold star, she was fair game. She could be 'lured out into the street and shot'.

Destroying Arletty would leave the world infinitely poorer. But by doing so they could put all the blame for their own cowardice and failure on her. On a woman. The eternal Eve, whose fault it was that paradise had been lost.

She thought of everything she herself had been through in the past four years, the losses she had endured, the dangers she had run every day, the risks she had taken and the parts of herself she had lost. And for what? She felt sick of it all. She wished she had tears, but she'd run out of them long ago.

Jack came up behind her and put his arms around her shoulders. 'I've upset you,' he said quietly. 'I'm sorry. War stinks.'

'This one's gone on too long,' she replied in a brittle voice.

'Yes, it has. And it still has a ways to go. You have to hold yourself together, Yokel.'

'Tell them to lay off Arletty.'

'I'll try, but I can't guarantee anything.'

'They'll listen to you.'

'I doubt it. They don't take their orders from me. My job is just to help them make life difficult for the Krauts.'

'They're not killing Arletty to hurt the Germans. They're killing her for fun.'

'Maybe you're right,' he said.

'If they hurt her, you can forget about getting any more information through me. I'll never pass on another word. You can tell them that.'

Jack turned her to face him. He looked into her eyes and saw that she was serious. 'Okay,' he said. 'I will tell them that.'

'Tell them we're fighting for a better world. Not a worse one.'

'I'll tell them that too.'

'I mean it, Bumpkin.'

'I know you do.' There was something new in his expression now, a look of respect. 'Now come back to bed. It's cold.'

They closed the shutters on the flaring sunset and went back to make love again.

⁂

As though the conversation had somehow conjured her up, Arletty appeared in the Ritz hotel the following week. She took one of the small rooms on the rue Cambon side, with an enamelled stove and a window that had the street as its only view.

Olivia had the room prepared with special care, putting a vase of gay yellow daffodils and white spring lilies on the console. She got a message at mid-morning to say that Arletty wanted to see her. She went to her room and found her lying on her bed, looking tired.

'Are you unwell?' Olivia asked.

'I have some nausea.'

'Would you like me to call the house doctor?'

'No doctor.' Arletty indicated the chair at her bedside. 'Sit and talk to me.'

Olivia settled into the chair beside Arletty. The actress was as beautiful as ever, but her face was drawn. Her flawless skin was pale. She must, Olivia guessed, be missing Soehring very much. The depth of the love between them had been evident for all to see. 'Is there anything I can get you? Some tea?'

'I'll be all right.' She glanced at Olivia with her large, lustrous eyes. 'I threw it into the river, in the end.'

Olivia knew at once what she was talking about. It was as though they had resumed their conversation from almost two years earlier. 'Did that make him happy?'

Arletty smiled tiredly. 'He was shocked. It was Cartier, you know. Gold and diamonds.'

'Yes, I know.'

'I suppose I wanted to shock him. Some men are sunny when they're in love. Others are stormy, like spoiled children, full of tantrums and jealousies. Hans-Jürgen was like that. I wanted to punish him for badgering me about the thing. But when women punish men, we usually hurt ourselves more. And it didn't really upset him. He took it as quite a compliment, once he got over the surprise. I wish I had it back now.'

'I wish you'd given it to *me*.'

Arletty laughed. She had an earthy, unaffected laugh, not the silvery tinkle of the women who came to take *le five o'clock* at the Ritz. 'I wish I had too. This is what I'm reduced to now.' She took the blue cardboard packet of Gitanes from her side table. 'Do you smoke?'

'I gave up. I couldn't afford it.'

'Then I won't tempt you.' She lit one for herself and blew out the match. 'He didn't like me to smoke because he hated the taste of tobacco in my mouth. But nobody tastes my mouth now, so it doesn't matter, does it?'

'I'm sorry.'

Arletty smoked in silence for a while, staring into space. 'I'm pregnant,' she said at last. 'With his child.' She glanced at Olivia. 'You say nothing.'

Olivia was thinking of her own lost child. 'I don't know what to say.'

'Nor do I. Except that I can't keep it.'

'Does he know?'

'No.'

'I suppose you've considered it a lot.'

'Not really. I try not to consider it at all. There's nothing to be done. I'm in the middle of shooting a film in Nice. *Les Enfants du Paradis*. It's huge. I've never had a better part than Garance. I can't lose it.'

'I understand.'

'And I may never see him again. The Americans might kill him. Even if he comes back, I'm too old to be a mother. I'm forty-five. Can you see me presenting him with a baby? Pushing a pram around Paris?'

'So you'll terminate?'

'I'll have an abortion, yes. That's why I'm here. Nobody can know about this. It's bad enough that they are calling me a whore and a collabo. If they knew I was pregnant they would stone me.'

'You'll need someone with you.'

Arletty swung her slim legs over the edge of the bed and sat up. 'I suddenly find I have no friends. I used to be the most invited woman in Paris. Now I'm the most shunned.' She went quickly to the bathroom, and Olivia heard her being sick. She went in to help Arletty, passing her a towel when she'd washed her face.

'I'll go with you if you like,' Olivia said.

Arletty dried her face. 'Thank you. I hoped you'd say that.'

'Have you made all the arrangements?'

'Yes. I've got an address. The doctor is said to be reliable. I'm going first thing tomorrow.'

'I'll get the day off.'

Arletty nodded. 'Have you ever had an abortion?'

'No.' Olivia hesitated. 'I thought I was pregnant once. Then the father was killed by the Gestapo, and I lost it.'

'You had a miscarriage?'

'I believe so. Either way, it was all over,' Olivia said bitterly.

'Perhaps it was for the best.' Arletty was not the sort of woman to give – or ask for – sympathy.

'Perhaps it was.'

'I knew there was something. I could sense it in you the moment we met.'

'You're very perceptive.'

'I am an actress. I feel things that are beneath the surface.' Arletty exhaled smoke. 'This will be my second abortion. I was your age the first time, back in the Twenties. He was a White Russian prince. That cigarette case was his parting gift to me. Life is strange, don't you think?'

'Life is strange and sad.'

'I'm not sad. I'm as happy as a lark all day long.' But her eyes were heavy.

Olivia felt sorry for her. Apart from being illegal, 'the operation' was fraught with danger. Everyone had heard of cases where it killed the woman; and the moral condemnation that followed if it were discovered would destroy an actress's career. 'You're brave, Madame,' she said gently.

'Please call me Arletty. Everyone does. It's not my name, but I like it.'

'All right.'

'You've changed since I last saw you,' Arletty said, studying Olivia's face. 'You've turned into a woman.'

Olivia smiled. 'What was I before?'

'A beautiful child.'

'I suppose I've learned a few things.'

'Has the war been hard for you?'

'It's hard for everyone,' Olivia replied, reflecting on how odd it was to be so at ease with Arletty, when their lovers were fighting on opposite sides of the great conflict.

'Not for everyone. I have friends who have done very well out of the war. War suits certain classes of people.'

'It doesn't suit me,' Olivia replied.

'But you stayed in France – when you could have gone home to America?'

'I was in love,' Olivia replied simply.

'Why did the Gestapo kill him?'

'He printed anti-German pamphlets.'

'That was not so wise. And now you have someone new?'

'Yes.'

'And is he sunny or stormy?'

'He's not jealous, if that's what you mean. He doesn't brood about things. He's a man of action.'

'In the Resistance?' Arletty guessed shrewdly. 'Forgive me, you mustn't answer that. Do you love him?'

'Very much.'

'And he loves you?'

'He says he does.'

Arletty stubbed the cigarette out. 'Good. At least you chose the right side, unlike me.'

Olivia rose. 'I'd better get back to my work.'

Arletty held out her hand. 'Thank you for being with me.'

Her handshake was cool and firm. Olivia left her lying on the bed, staring into space.

Twenty Four

Olivia had arranged to take the next day off, so that she could be with Arletty. She didn't go into work, but waited for Arletty to meet her on the opposite side of place Vendôme. It was the warmest day of the year so far, and the rising temperature had made the river steam, causing a fog that percolated through the streets, making everything imprecise, like an out-of-focus scene in a movie.

She saw Arletty walking quickly towards her, and was struck by how small and slight the actress was. With her lively gait and her thin arms held elbows-out, she looked almost like a marionette being operated by some jerky puppeteer. For some reason, that thought filled Olivia with a rush of affection and pity for the older woman.

Arletty kissed her briefly on both cheeks. 'Shall we go?'

'I'm ready.'

Arletty was wearing a plain brown check dress, with a scarf tied around her hair, and was carrying a large bag. She wore no make-up. But the pale face, on its slender stalk of a neck, was hard to disguise. It was beautiful enough to be easily recognised if anyone were to take a second look.

She took Olivia's arm in a nervous grip and they walked to the rue Saint Honoré, where a plain little Simca car was waiting for them. They got in. The driver set off without turning to look at them.

Olivia had assumed that Arletty, being who she was, would have arranged to visit some sleek, discreet establishment. To her surprise, they drove along the misty Seine into the factory suburbs of Courbevoie, past the rows of drab yellow houses, the looming chimneys, the railway lines.

'This is where I grew up,' Arletty said.

'You must have had an interesting childhood.'

'I was one of those.' Arletty was looking at a group of shabby children playing on a street corner. 'Every afternoon after school I used to go and work in a fishmonger. I hated everything about it. The smell you could never get rid of, the scales that got everywhere, the way your hands got torn up. Fish are resentful creatures. They don't like being gutted and filleted. I still have the scars.' She looked down at her fingers. 'The oysters would just lie there, waiting to be opened and eaten, but the crabs were always trying to walk away. I made up my mind early to be a crab and not an oyster. That's what I like about you. You're a crab, not an oyster. One good thing about working in a fish shop – you learn to talk there.'

'To talk?'

'*La gouaille* – you know what that is?'

'That's what they call it at work when someone answers back.'

'It's more than answering back. It's an attitude, being ready to defend yourself. Especially if you're a woman. Make people laugh, make them blush. That's how I got out of Courbevoie. And now I'm back again.' She turned to stare out of the window of the Simca. 'I had my first abortion here. The old hag died years ago. It wasn't a very nice experience. What was your childhood like?'

'I grew up on a farm. There wasn't much place for *gouaille* there. My mother would have slapped our faces. I thought my childhood was boring at the time – just rolling fields and staring cows.'

'I envy you.'

'I envy you. Nothing prepared me for this. If I'd developed a bit of *gouaille*, I'd have managed better.'

'You don't seem to be doing too badly,' Arletty said dryly. 'I'm worse off than you, at any rate.'

They had arrived in a mean little street that ran alongside a railway station. The house where the Simca had stopped was huddled in an overgrown garden. Sagging green shutters blocked the windows. The walls were flaking pinkish paint, like a diseased body shedding skin.

'This doesn't look good,' Olivia commented.

'It's the place,' Arletty said flatly, getting out of the car.

They went to the door. They were let in by a girl of about twelve in a dingy pinafore, whose nose was running copiously. The interior was dark and smelled strongly of some strange chemical. The child led them into a kitchen where a very fat man in a rubber apron was filling rows of little brown bottles with a pipe. The smell was sharp enough to make Olivia cover her mouth and nose with a handkerchief.

The fat man turned to them, lifting his glasses on to his domed, hairless head. He smiled widely. 'My own mixture,' he said, indicating the hundreds of little bottles. 'An abortion in twelve hours.'

'What's in it?' Arletty asked.

'Amphetamines, quinine, strychnine, mercury.'

'Does it work?'

'Who knows?' the man replied, shrugging. 'There's only one sure way, and that's my line of business.' He gestured at Olivia. 'Your daughter in trouble?'

Arletty shook her head. 'No. It's me.'

The fat man peered closer at Arletty. 'You're a little old for this game. Sure it's not menopause?'

'I'm sure.'

He wagged his finger at her. 'I recognise you!'

'No, you don't.'

'You're right. I don't. And you don't know me.' He burst out laughing, his belly jiggling under the rubber apron. 'I don't exist. Have you got the money?'

Arletty held out a thick envelope. When he tried to take it, however, she held on to one corner. 'They told me you're a doctor.'

'Oh yes, I was. Until they struck me off.'

'What for?'

He tugged impatiently at the envelope. 'What the hell does it matter? Do you want my help or not?' By way of an answer, Arletty released the packet. He counted the money carefully and pushed it into his pocket. 'How far along are you?'

'About three months, I think.'

'So. Are you ready?'

'Yes.'

'Then come.'

He waddled into a side room. Arletty, now very pale, turned to Olivia. 'Will you go with me?'

Olivia nodded, and followed. She was feeling sick to her stomach. That a woman like Arletty had to resort to a creature like this, in a place like this, was obscene.

As though reading her thoughts, the fat man sneered at Olivia. 'Why that face? People are guillotined for what I do. They call it murder, infanticide, treason against the state. I risk my life to help others.' The room had been set up as a crude surgery, with a table in the middle covered with a dirty and bloodstained cloth. Olivia desperately wanted to get Arletty out of there, but Arletty was already undressing, as the fat man directed. Olivia could see by her face that she wouldn't be talked out of this.

The little girl was apparently the man's assistant, and was already preparing a few instruments on a steel tray. Olivia could only pray that they were sterile, or at least clean.

Arletty clambered on to the table and lay down. The man examined her cursorily. 'More like four months, I would say.' He set to work between her slim white thighs.

Olivia saw Arletty's hand groping for hers. She took it, standing as close as she could. Arletty's eyes were shut tight. She was trembling all over.

The operation was so brutal that Olivia could barely watch. Arletty clenched her teeth in agony. As the pain increased, her nails dug into Olivia's hand. Olivia stroked her hair in a futile attempt to comfort her.

At last the fat man withdrew the instruments and tossed them back on to the tray. 'That ought to do it. It will be over by tomorrow. You can get up now.'

Arletty was too shaken to get off the table without Olivia's help. She swayed on her feet, almost falling. There was blood spattering the linoleum floor.

'For an extra hundred francs I can let you have these.' He was holding out a handful of unclean-looking crepe bandages.

'I brought my own,' Arletty said in a shaky voice, digging in her bag.

The fat man smiled sourly. 'Ah. You've been this way before.'

Arletty tucked a wad of fabric into her underwear and dressed.

'What will happen now?' Olivia asked him as Arletty groped her way out.

'She'll start to miscarry. When the bleeding stops, it'll all be over. But don't come back here, whatever happens.' He thrust his face close to hers, grinning ferociously. 'Not even if she dies. Understand?'

'Yes.'

'Unless, of course' – he jiggled with laughter – 'you find yourself in the same boat as your mother one day.'

By the time they got back to the Ritz, Arletty was bleeding heavily. Olivia somehow got her to her room without drawing too much attention and put her on a pile of towels on the bed. The amount of blood was frightening. She was going to need an ally in the laundry.

'Have you got five hundred francs?' she asked Arletty.

Arletty silently pointed at her bag. Olivia took the money and hurried to the laundry. One of the laundresses, Berthe, was a capable, taciturn woman always in need of extra money for her large family. Olivia gave her the five hundred francs.

'The guest in room three-oh-nine is going to need her towels boiled, but nobody must know. Can you help?'

Berthe nodded briefly. 'Yes, Olivia.'

'Come in an hour.'

The laundress arrived in Arletty's room an hour later with a canvas bag to take away the bloodstained towels and replace them with fresh ones. She made no comment as she worked.

'She'll be discreet,' Olivia said when Berthe had left. Arletty was lying motionless in her bed gown, her face white.

'Can you light the stove?' she asked. 'I'm so cold.'

It must be the blood loss that was making her cold on this warm day, Olivia thought. She lit the enamelled stove and shut the window. The room became stifling, sickly with the smell of blood. She went to sit beside the actress.

'You should try to sleep now, Arletty.'

'Hold my hand.'

Olivia held the slim, cold hand. 'Are you in a lot of pain?'

'It will get worse.' She squeezed Olivia's fingers. 'What are you doing all this time at the Ritz, child? Are you a spy?'

Olivia hesitated. 'I didn't set out to be one.'

'But your lover, this man of action – he persuaded you?'

'No. It was my idea.'

'Did you spy on Soehring?'

'No, I didn't do his room. But he almost caught me once.'

There was the ghost of a smile. 'My Faun is no fool.'

'Your Faun?'

'That's what I call him. Don't you think he looks like the god Pan?'

'He's very attractive.'

'They say he's in Italy now. Have you been to Italy?'

'Never.'

'It's very beautiful.' Arletty broke off with a sudden cry, sitting up in the bed and clutching her belly.

'What is it?' Olivia asked anxiously.

'It's coming.'

'What's coming?'

Arletty cried out again, gritting her teeth. Olivia realised with horror that she was going into labour. 'Should I call a doctor?'

'No!'

'At least let me get a nurse.'

'No. I don't want a nurse. They all talk. I have to go through this alone.'

The next hours were dreadful. Arletty was largely silent, and Olivia marvelled at her stoicism. Bit by bit, the miscarriage went on its agonised way.

Olivia heard a tap at the door. She opened it cautiously to find Monsieur Auzello outside.

'Is Madame Arletty ill?' he asked in concern.

'She has the grippe.'

'I'll go in to see her.'

'No,' Olivia said sharply. 'She doesn't want to see anyone.'

Auzello was taken aback. 'We should call the house doctor.'

'She insists on seeing nobody. Please respect her wishes, Monsieur Auzello.' She closed the door in his astonished face.

Arletty turned her wan face to Olivia as she returned. 'Tell me about your spying.'

'I can't.'

'Your secrets are safe with me.' She laid her hand on her womb. 'As I hope mine are with you.'

Olivia used a damp cloth to wipe Arletty's sweating forehead. 'I just use my eyes. If I see anything interesting, I pass the information along. That's all there is to it.'

'Faun thinks the Germans will lose the war.'

'Even Goering thinks that.'

When Olivia went out to get some beef tea for Arletty, she found Coco Chanel in the corridor. 'How's Arletty?' Chanel asked.

'She has a bad cold.'

'I've had a couple of those bad colds myself,' Chanel said dryly. She offered Olivia a little black bottle. 'Give her a teaspoon of this in a glass of water.'

'What is it?'

'Tincture of opium. Laudanum. Old-fashioned, but it works. It'll make her sleep.'

Olivia pocketed the little bottle. 'Thank you.'

'You'd think she'd be past the age of getting *bad colds*.' Chanel shook her head. 'Poor bitch. Is she bad?'

'She's not good.'

'Do you need my help?'

'Thank you, Madame Chanel, but she doesn't want to see anyone.'

Chanel patted Olivia's arm. 'If it all gets too much for you, call me.'

By evening the bleeding hadn't stopped. Berthe had changed the towels three times already, and Arletty was frighteningly weak.

'I have to get back to the set,' she muttered restlessly. 'I'm holding up filming.'

'You're the star,' Olivia said gently. 'They'll wait for you.'

'It's my greatest role.' Her haunted eyes held Olivia's. 'I have to finish this film. They'll forget everything I ever did unless I finish it.'

'They'll never forget you.'

'Yes, they will. They'll forget it all, because I'm a collabo. But they won't forget Garance.'

Arletty was feverish now. She seemed completely exhausted. Olivia thought it was time for Coco's little black bottle. She measured a teaspoon into a glass of water and gave it to the actress. Arletty made a face as she drank, then slumped back on to the pillows. She hadn't cried yet, but now two tears slid out from under her lids. 'I always took woman lovers because I didn't want this ever to happen to me again. And now it has. What a fool I am. I'm so tired, Olivia.'

The laudanum took effect quickly. Arletty sank into sleep. Olivia covered her. But she knew it wasn't safe to leave yet. She made a bed for herself on the sofa and tried to get some rest.

The bleeding continued through the next day, although the contractions had finally stopped. Olivia gave Berthe another five hundred francs to pay for the discreet clean-up. Arletty remained stoical through it all, and the two women talked quietly. It was a relief to them both to have another woman to talk to – neither had the luxury of female friends who could be trusted.

Today, Arletty was intensely melancholy. For the first time, she talked about the child she had aborted. At one point she asked Olivia whether the baby had been a boy or a girl. Olivia didn't know what to answer because she couldn't bear to look too closely. To Olivia's relief, Arletty answered the question herself.

'Of course it was a boy. Soehring would only have made a boy. My first was a girl.' She looked at Olivia with her big, tired eyes. 'I don't regret it. I'm not made to be a mother. I'm too selfish.'

'They say motherhood changes that.'

'I don't want to be changed. I like the way I am. I like being selfish. Or what the world calls selfish. It's only the selfish women who get by. The rest are trampled.'

'I don't think they're all trampled. Can't we have children *and* a career?'

'Not me,' Arletty said tiredly. 'Maybe you. You'll make a good mother. You're not like me.' Her thoughts took another turn. 'How will he survive the war, my poor Faun? He's just a chocolate soldier, you know.'

Olivia smiled. 'He looked big and strong to me.'

Olivia spent a second night with Arletty. The next day, the actress insisted on leaving, though she was clearly far from recovered.

'You need to rest more,' Olivia urged. 'You should see a doctor.'

'I have to get back to Nice. The weather will be hot there now. It'll fix me up in no time. Do I look very haggard?'

Olivia studied Arletty's face. 'You've never looked more beautiful,' she said truthfully.

Arletty smiled and laid her hand on Olivia's cheek. 'Ah, you are a darling. You're better than any doctor.'

Olivia helped her pack. She was taking the afternoon train back to the south of France, where the film crew waited for her. Before she left her room, she turned to Olivia and took both her hands. 'Thank you,' she said simply.

'I'm glad I could help.'

Arletty slipped something on to Olivia's finger. Olivia looked down and saw that it was a ruby ring, set with a single superb stone. 'A drop of my blood,' Arletty said. 'Hide it until the war is over, and then wear it in memory of me.'

'I can't accept this!' Olivia exclaimed.

But Arletty was already leaving. She didn't look back.

⁂

Olivia called one of the chambermaids, and together they stripped the room and got it ready for the next occupant. She wanted to make sure there was no trace of what had taken place in it over the past days.

By the time they had finished, the room was immaculate, concealing its secrets as discreetly as did all the rooms at the Ritz.

Olivia glanced around one last time before closing the door. Like a beautiful woman, the room bore no trace of its sorrows; it remained inviting and serene, as though no tear had fallen and no drop of blood had ever been shed in it.

※

The city of Nice was hot. The huge set that Marcel Carné had built for *Les Enfants du Paradis* baked in the sun. It was a miracle, this set – eighty metres of nineteenth-century townscape, every detail perfect. Nobody knew how Carné had managed to acquire the hundreds of tons of wood, plaster, nails and paint required to build it at a time when obtaining a hammer was almost an impossibility.

But it had been done somehow. Meticulous, tyrannical, inspired, Marcel Carné had triumphed over the obstacles of the Occupation yet again, and the cameras were rolling.

The scene was set in Garance's dressing room. Her face shaded – but not hidden – by a veil, Arletty sat at her dressing table. 'Little Baptiste' was being played by one of the child actors on the set, six-year-old Jean-Pierre Belmon. He was a sweet, gentle child who'd had no difficulty learning his quite long lines, and who delivered them with a luminous innocence that contrasted exquisitely with Arletty's haunted shadows.

The silence on the set was absolute as they spoke their lines. The cameras moved in for tight close-ups at the climax of the scene.

'You are a kind little boy,' she said.

'Are you married?' the child asked.

'No,' Arletty replied quietly.

'Then you don't have a little boy?'

The ache in her womb suddenly became unbearably sharp. 'No,' Arletty replied after a pause, even more quietly, 'I don't have a little boy.'

'Then you're all alone?'

Arletty paused again. Behind the veil her eyes glistened wetly. Her reply was just loud enough to be picked up by the boom microphone over her head. 'Yes. I am all alone.'

Twenty Five

The siege of Leningrad had been lifted at the end of January, and Hitler's campaign in Russia had ended with catastrophic losses of men and equipment. After years of toeing the Nazi line, the French newspapers were accustomed to putting a pro-German slant on every story. But little could be done to make any of this sound good.

From the BBC, they had heard that much of Hamburg had been destroyed in terrible firestorms caused by incendiary bombs. Mussolini had been deposed and was now being sheltered by Hitler. After a fierce battle for Sicily, the Allies had landed on the Italian mainland and had already fought their way far up the peninsula. The ferocious struggle for Italy was drawing ever closer to the borders of France and Germany.

'The invasion may start as early as the summer,' Jack told Olivia. He was filled with a suppressed excitement lately, his body seeming to hum like a building that housed a dynamo. 'The Partisans are playing a hell of a big part in Italy. It shows us what we can do here in France.' He put his arms round Olivia. 'We need all the information you can get, Yokel. It's vital that we know what they're thinking.'

'I'll do what I can,' she promised.

And all this week she had been gathering everything she could. It was no longer as easy a task as it had been two or three years ago. Security was far tighter now. SS men were everywhere in the hotel. The old German assumption that the staff at the Ritz were above suspicion had faded into history. Even Monsieur Auzello had been arrested and questioned over several days at the Cherche-Midi prison. Everyone coming to work or leaving again was subjected to a rigorous search, meaning that Olivia had to be imaginative in concealing the film reels she took to Jack. It was just as well, she reflected, that the things were small, but they were still horribly uncomfortable.

The Germans had taken to posting a guard outside every room that was being cleaned. The men would look into the room every few minutes to make sure nothing untoward was going on. All rooms were locked by the guards once the cleaning was done and the keys handed over to the security officer on each floor.

However, Olivia, with her set of master keys, was still able to get into the rooms at odd moments, and occasionally, as today, she met with a stroke of luck – a briefcase, emblazoned with the eagle and swastika of the Luftwaffe, lying beside the bed. The room belonged to an air attaché, and the briefcase was likely to contain something interesting.

Olivia locked the door and set to work swiftly. The briefcase was secured with two straps, but the lock was of the familiar design that Jack scornfully referred to as 'Mickey Mouse', and which he had long ago taught her how to pick. A few seconds with her little nail scissors, and the briefcase was open.

It was packed with grey folders. She carried them to the window, got out the Minox, and began to take photographs with the efficiency of long practice.

Even with her limited understanding of German, it was evident that she had hit pay dirt. The folders contained summaries of aircraft concentrations, numbers and types within the Forbidden Zone, the area of France along the coast that was known as the Atlantic Wall, where an Allied invasion from the Channel was most likely to begin.

The maps and columns of figures were priceless, laying out the proposed response to attacks at various points where the Nazis anticipated landings. This was exactly the kind of information Jack had wanted.

She knew he would be delighted. She forced her hands to stop shaking with excitement as she worked.

Then her blood froze.

The door was being unlocked from the outside.

It could only be a German. Nobody else had the key. Her first thought was to protect the Minox, with the photographs she had already taken. The room had a small balcony, which overlooked rue Cambon. Without thinking, she tore open the door and tossed the miniature camera into the trough of geraniums that stood there. She had just time to slam the door again, and was standing with her back against it, the picture of guilt, when the door opened.

The SS guard who entered was young, as they all seemed to be these days, dressed in black from head to foot, with the silver skull and crossbones at his collar. He looked at Olivia blankly for a moment. '*Was machst du hier?*' he demanded. Then his eyes flicked to the opened briefcase on the desk and the folders laid out next to it. '*Spion!*' he shouted, and rushed at her.

Olivia tried to run around him, but he punched her full in the face with his gloved fist.

The events after that were a confused blur. Being hauled up off the floor, her face numb and her mouth full of blood. The corridor milling with people shouting in different languages. Being dragged downstairs between two SS men.

Monsieur Auzello's appalled face appearing briefly among the German uniforms, and then being shoved aside.

The handcuffs clamping her hands behind her back.

The cold air striking her face and the pain starting to take over from the numbness.

Being shoved into the back of a truck.

And then, for the second time, jolting off towards a Gestapo prison.

Her last stay at Fresnes prison had been horrible. She knew that this time it was going to be far worse. Her head was splitting. The right side of her face was swollen from the SS man's punch. It was difficult to keep her thoughts together during the long drive. She was alone in the truck, apart from a stolid infantryman with a rifle.

She was hauled out of the truck to face the familiar, looming hulk of the prison. Frightened and in pain, she wasn't sure she would be able to walk, but in the event it didn't matter. Two Gestapo men took her arms and carried her through the gates between them, her feet barely touching the ground.

The smells and sounds of Fresnes overwhelmed her. She was back in this dreadful place again, back in the darkness.

They didn't take her to her old, verminous cell, but to the communal toilet, a stinking chamber of white cracked tiles and rusty plumbing. She knew what was going to happen here.

They made her strip naked and took away her clothes. Then they shackled her wrists to an iron pipe. She waited, shuddering with the cold. Two Gestapo men came in with rubber truncheons. Without a word, they started the beating.

The first blows were shockingly violent. Later, they were numbing, but she still screamed each time, her voice echoing off the tiles. They worked with the thoroughness of long experience, alternating from side to side, covering her body from head to foot.

When they had finished, a third man came in with a hose. The jet of icy water blasted her out of her numbness, hammering into her body. They washed her clean and then took her to her cell.

This one was different from last time. It had no window, and the ceiling was so low that she could barely stand upright. Lying on the floor were the familiar striped prison clothes.

Somehow, battered as she was, she got the garment on while they watched. They slammed the door and locked it.

At first she thought she was in complete darkness; but as her eyes adjusted, she saw that a thin blade of light washed in from under the door, just enough to show the insects that shared her quarters.

Her body now wore the same map of pain as Fabrice's had done. And one day it would end up tossed into the same cardboard coffin.

She curled up in a corner like a kicked dog, and tried to sleep.

※

The pain didn't really start until hours had passed. She'd thought it couldn't get any worse, but it seemed to take time for her body to work out what had been done to it, and make the nerves transmit the damage. Soon it was unbearable. She couldn't find any position that didn't hurt. Every movement made her gasp. Using the bucket that served as her latrine was especially cruel. At least they had spared her face. The rest of her felt like jelly.

They brought her a plate of food: a cup of water and the rancid gruel she remembered from her last time here. She forced herself to eat and drink, knowing she would need all her strength.

After that she was left alone for a day, as far as she could tell. It was hard to tell how much time elapsed. As an opening gambit, the beating had been masterful. It had shown her exactly how helpless, how vulnerable she was. It had shown her what she could expect from now on. And the fact that it had been conducted without a single question, without a single word in fact, had told her that they were very sure of getting what they wanted out of her. It could only get worse from here on.

The door opened. Grey light poured in for a moment, then was blocked by the shadows of the men who had come for her. She tried to shrink away. They hauled her to her feet and dragged her out of the cell.

Every muscle felt torn as they marched her down the corridor. There were other prisoners being moved around, but nobody looked at her, and she looked at nobody.

She was taken down a long flight of stairs and into a cellar. The room contained a large furnace. As she came in, the door of the furnace swung open, revealing an orange blast of flame.

Terrified that they were going to thrust her into it, Olivia screamed and crouched down on to her hunkers. They hauled her upright again.

Someone was chuckling. She raised her head slowly, fearfully.

The rotund figure of Captain Kellerman, with his Heinrich Himmler spectacles gleaming, was standing in front of her.

'So. Here we are again. As I had hoped.' He slapped the wall of the furnace with his riding crop. 'This is the main boiler for this wing. Your work for this morning is to feed it. Yes? And in the meantime, we will have a little discussion.'

'I am a Swedish citizen,' she said shakily.

'Let us not go through that stupid rigmarole again. Your double-dealing friend Nordling will not be coming to rescue you again, you can be sure of that.' He jerked his head at one of the guards, who pulled over a large box. 'Here are some things that need burning. You may begin.' The guards seized her shoulders and pushed her to the furnace door. The ferocious heat poured out, enveloping her in pain. By the orange light, she saw what it was they wanted her to burn. The box was filled with rectangular shapes. Her paintings. They had been to her studio and had collected all her work.

'These paintings are degenerate,' Kellerman said. 'We confiscated them when we searched your premises. They must be destroyed. Proceed.'

She stood, dumbfounded, until Kellerman suddenly lashed out with the whip. It cut across her shoulders, making her gasp. 'Proceed,' he repeated.

Blindly, she took the first canvas and pushed it into the fire. Being so close to the flames was terrifying. Her face and hands were scalding.

'Why were you in Hauptmann Wolff's room, looking through his papers?' Kellerman asked.

Olivia could see her first painting in the flames, the frame twisting, the canvas bubbling and flaring into oily gouts of fire. She tried to concentrate on the answers she had prepared.

'I was looking for money. The price of food is so high—'

The crop cut across her shoulders again. 'Continue your work.'

She took the next painting. It was the one she had made of Jack in the orchard. But she mustn't think of Jack now, or she might blurt out the truth. She threw the painting into the furnace.

'You were not looking for money,' Kellerman said. 'You will have to do better than that.'

'It's the truth. We all steal what we can from the guests these days. If we didn't, we'd starve.'

Kellerman indicated a painting with his whip. 'Now that one.'

It was one of her best works, a larger study of a Montmartre street, made during her first weeks in Paris. She pushed it into the fire, trying to avoid getting too close. The furnace claimed the painting gleefully, consuming it in a crackle of coloured spurts.

'If you were looking for money, why did you have all the folders laid out on the desk?'

'I – I was looking for spare paper.'

'Spare paper?'

'To draw on. There's no drawing paper to be had in Paris. I hoped there might be some blank pages I could steal.'

'Do you take me for a fool?'

'No.' Her mind was groping after the logical conclusion of his questions – that they hadn't yet found the Minox. Could such a simple ruse have worked? It seemed it had – for the time being, at least. So long as they didn't have that, she could keep spinning a yarn. If it occurred to them to search the flowerpots, and they found the camera, it would all be over for her.

'Give me that one,' Kellerman commanded, pointing with his whip. It was the portrait of her that Laszlo Weisz had left behind. Silently, she handed it to him. He studied it, his lip curling. '*La Suédoise,*' he said contemptuously, reading the inscription on the back. 'A hopeless daub. Painted by one of your friends?'

'My teacher,' she replied in a low voice.

'Ah, yes. The Jew. We know all about him. He is no longer with us, I'm glad to say.' He handed back the painting. 'Burn it.'

Olivia had been able to hold back her tears until this, but now she started crying. She pushed the portrait into the flames. She could feel her face swelling with the heat, the tears drying as soon as they were shed.

She knew what Kellerman was doing – trying to break her, reduce her to nothing. Somehow, she had to find some core of strength and cling to it.

'You were not looking for money or spare paper,' he continued. 'You laid out those documents so you could memorise their contents. Who were you going to pass the information to?'

'I don't speak German! I had no idea what was in them.'

'You were memorising the figures and maps.'

'No, that's not true. I don't understand military stuff.'

'You are lying.'

As the interrogation proceeded, Kellerman selected her canvases, sometimes making disdainful comments on them, before giving them to her to burn. Her months of work, her vision of Paris, and of herself, were being incinerated.

'Admit the truth,' Kellerman said at one point, 'and you can go back to your cool cell. I'll have water sent to you. You can rest.'

She shook her head. 'It's not true.'

The questions were repeated again and again. Who was she passing information to? Was there an American or British agent in the Ritz? Or was it a Soviet? Had she stolen papers in the past? Which papers had she stolen? How long had she been spying?

Her repeated denials grew weaker as exhaustion set in. The heat was making her faint. Her hands and face were blistering. Whenever she staggered, one of the guards would thrust her back to the furnace, or Kellerman would hit out with his riding crop. Blinded by the furnace, she could hardly see what she was doing any more.

At last there were no more canvases to be burned. Everything she had painted in Paris had been cremated. She was unable to move. She simply stood with her head hanging down, mumbling denials: 'No, no, no.'

'You spent months making these hideous things,' Kellerman crowed. 'Strange how quickly they burned to ash, isn't it? It's an act of cleansing. Of purification. You will be taken back to your cell now. It's a pity you have not chosen to be cooperative. The next interrogation will be far harsher.'

She was so broken and so burned that she could only shuffle as the guards thrust her back down the corridor. At a narrow opening that looked down on the central courtyard, they jerked her to a halt. They turned her to face the opening and thrust her face against it.

In the courtyard down below, a row of German soldiers in winter greatcoats faced a woman who stood against a pockmarked wall. On a command, the soldiers raised their rifles to their shoulders, aiming at the lone woman.

Olivia didn't know quite what she was looking at for a moment. Her mind refused to engage with the images. She was focused on the snow that gathered on the soldiers' shoulders and helmets. The reality dawned on her suddenly, and she tried to look away, but she was too late. At another command, a volley rang out. As the smoke cleared, she saw that the woman was now slumped in the chains that secured her to the wall, her long hair hanging over her face. An officer strode forward, taking his pistol from its holster. He held the gun to the woman's head. There was a single shot.

Then the guards were shoving Olivia, stumbling and crying, back to her cell.

☙

Despite his threat, she didn't see Kellerman again the following day, or for several days in a row thereafter. She was left isolated in her cell, nursing her blistered hands and face. The torture had become a blur in her mind, which was merciful in one sense, but an added torment in another, because she couldn't remember what she had said. Had she let drop some hint about Jack? About the Minox? She simply couldn't remember. But each time she heard the crash of a door open, her body would jolt in terror.

The blisters on her face and hands slowly dried and scabbed. Her skin felt tight. For an hour each day she was marched, shackled to six other women, around the courtyard, in a parody of exercise. It took place at exactly the same time each day, as did everything else in the prison, from mealtimes to slopping-out. Absolute silence had to be maintained, on pain of a stunning blow with a rifle butt.

One day the exercise took place immediately after an execution. They were marched silently past the clear-up detail, an old man who swabbed the blood off the walls and cobbles, and two others who dumped the shattered body unceremoniously into a barrow and wheeled it away. A couple of the women in the exercise party started crying. It was a fate that awaited many of them.

There were at least two executions each day. Even more frequent were the screams of women being beaten or otherwise tortured. It was common to see prisoners with battered faces, some of them beaten until they were unrecognisable, staggering around the prison yard. The guards would hammer a woman to pulp, and then scrupulously insist she take morning exercise. Routine could not be disobeyed on any account. It was an insight into the extraordinary mentality of Nazism.

All around Olivia were women being shot, tortured, beaten. Why was she being left alone? Had they lost interest in her? Or were they planning something even more horrible for her?

She grew weaker on the starvation diet and the filthy conditions in her tiny cell. She dared not think of Jack, for fear that allowing the man she loved to enter her mind might make her blurt out his name, or divulge the secret relationship she had with him.

Instead, she tried to remember every detail of the paintings she had been forced to destroy.

She spent the lonely dark hours reliving the brushstrokes, the shades of paint she had mixed, the arrangements of line and colour she had composed. The fact that she hadn't painted in three years gave the exercise a special poignancy.

She would paint those canvases again one day, she vowed. But not the same. This time, she would make them better. She would improve everything. The mistakes she had made would be rectified. The unnecessary details would be removed. The places where she had strayed from the truth of her vision would be made fresh again.

She would emerge from this a stronger and better artist in every way. One day, she would have a new studio, a new vision. And in it, she herself would be a new person.

One particularly icy morning, her door was unlocked. The hinges squealed as it was opened. As always, the light, dim as it was, hurt her eyes. They adjusted slowly, and she saw a burly figure standing in the doorway, fists on hips. There was something familiar about the outline.

Then she realised who it was. It was Heike Schwab.

※

They had gone down to Josée de Chambrun's country estate to see the horses exercised. It was very cold, frost riming the trees around the paddock and sparkling on the grass. The colours of the landscape were muted browns and russets, the sky low and heavy. Both Arletty and Josée were wrapped in furs. Spring seemed to be still a long way off.

The horses were led out of the exercise yard, where they had been warming up. Arletty couldn't suppress an exclamation of pleasure as they appeared, a row of skittish masterpieces prancing in line, their eyes rolling, nostrils arching as they puffed out clouds of steam. A heady wave of their chocolatey smell washed over her. The grooms took off their blankets and socks and began saddling them.

'They're so beautiful,' she said to Josée, who was watching the animals intently.

'Yes, they are indeed. Ah! See that one?' She was pointing to a big bay stallion, who was kicking up his heels as he was led along. 'That's Tiberius. He'll be three this year. We're going to enter him for the Prix de l'Arc de Triomphe. Come along.'

As they approached, the splendid horse caprioled, froth spattering from his mouth. Arletty, who was rather afraid of horses, hesitated. Josée took her arm firmly. 'Don't be silly.' She slapped the horse's neck with her gloved palm. 'Isn't he magnificent?'

'You're very lucky to have him.'

'Yes, aren't I?'

'And to have all this.' Arletty's eyes wandered across the fields and woodland that stretched for acres all around them, all of it de Chambrun property.

Each animal was now mounted by a jockey in a roll-neck jersey, wiry men perched atop the highly strung animals, which shied away from each other as they were forced unwillingly into an untidy bunch.

'Are you going to help Antoinette?' Arletty asked.

Josée shrugged. 'She's been very foolish, and now she's paying the price for her folly.'

The jockeys were having to rein back their mounts. The instinct to race was becoming overwhelming. Josée leaned perilously over the rail to get a better view. 'Let them go!' she shouted.

The animals exploded into motion. Arletty hadn't expected the gallop to be so wild. The sight was unforgettable, primal. The pounding of the hooves was deafening. Almost immediately, the horses were in full gallop, manes and tails streaming, long legs stretching out and devouring the turf.

'Tiberius is in the lead!' Josée yelled as they receded around the bend, her binoculars to her eyes.

'You haven't answered my question,' Arletty said quietly in the lull while the horses were out of sight beyond the trees.

'What question was that, darling?'

'Whether you're going to do something for Antoinette.'

Josée let her field glasses drop and lit a cigarette. 'And what do you propose that I do for Antoinette?'

'Your father is head of the Vichy government. You could ask him to intercede.'

'There's an old saying: never come between the lion and his prey.'

'I thought she was your great friend.'

'She was your great friend too, darling. Why don't you do something for her?'

'I would, if Soehring was still here. But he isn't. And I'm not exactly in vogue with the Nazis any more.'

'I assure you that Antoinette is in it up to her neck,' Josée drawled. 'There's no pulling her out now. When she isn't smuggling Resistance men in her ambulance, she's smuggling butter and cheese. And when she's not smuggling, she's consorting with every undesirable in France. Besides, she's a notorious lesbian.'

'You were only too glad to introduce *me* to her,' Arletty retorted.

'Well, of course I was, darling. You know how much innocent pleasure I derive from mixing and matching people. I thought it would be an amusing interlude for you. Wasn't it amusing?'

'You're disgusting sometimes,' Arletty said tersely.

Josée, quite unoffended, burst out in a merry laugh. 'Oh, I know I am. I'm a wicked creature and quite reprehensible. But please don't ask me to intercede for Antoinette. It's none of my business. She got herself into this pickle, let her crawl out of it. If she can.'

The horses had now come round the clump of trees. The group had stretched out. They entered the straight and began their final gallop. As they thundered past, Josée waved her arms and yelled in exhilaration. Arletty couldn't tell who had been in the lead, but Josée was convinced it had been Tiberius. She called out to the grooms.

'Who won?'

They shouted back, some saying it was Tiberius, some giving other names. Josée turned to Arletty. 'What fools they are. Who do you think won, darling?'

'What does it matter?' Arletty said tiredly. 'They're all your horses anyway.'

Twenty Six

Heike had altered.

Olivia recalled Jack telling her she had started dressing like a man and cutting her hair short. But she was not prepared for what she now saw. Heike's face had somehow become heavier. Her hair had been clipped around her ears and her thick neck, like a man's, leaving only a dense crop high up on her crown. Her body, too, was heavier. She strained her black Gestapo uniform of tunic and riding breeches. But the prominent bosom she'd once had was strangely absent. Her figure was that of a man, rather than of a woman.

Heike had taken Olivia to an interrogation room equipped with a desk, chair and metal rings on the walls, to one of which Olivia's wrists had been shackled. She dismissed the guards, so that they were alone in the room.

'I told you this would happen,' Heike said. Even her voice was deeper, rougher. 'I knew you would be caught sooner or later.'

'I haven't done anything wrong.'

'Do you think I have changed?' Heike asked, ignoring that.

'You look – different.'

Heike smirked. 'In what way?'

'You look stronger.'

'I am stronger. Stronger in every way. I have changed. Let me show you.' She was unbuttoning her tunic as she spoke. She pulled it open to reveal her chest. Instead of breasts, there were two diagonal scars.

'What happened to you?' Olivia asked in shock.

'I had them removed.' Composedly, Heike took off her uniform and put on a vest and shorts, like a boxer. Her limbs were powerful, the fat wobbling whitely over heavy muscles. 'I never wanted them. And with my new work, they just got in the way. The German doctors have been giving me hormones. The results are very satisfactory. I have developed my muscles. I box with the men now, and they're afraid of me. I have no tedious female symptoms. But there was nothing to be done about my breasts. So I dispensed with them.'

'What have you done to yourself?' Olivia whispered.

'You're surprised, Blondchen?' Heike laughed. 'I'm sorry I wasn't here to welcome you when you arrived. I was busy with some Resistance people. They give me the women to deal with. The male interrogators tend to be too squeamish.'

'I hadn't noticed that,' Olivia said in a low voice. She felt sick.

Heike came up to her and took a fistful of Olivia's hair, jerking her face up. Her hot, dark eyes stared into Olivia's. 'You spat at me the last time I tried to kiss you. Eh? You ran away. But now, if I want to kiss you, you will not be able to run. What do you say to that?'

Olivia tried to fight away, but Heike's strong fingers were knotted in her hair, and now tightened painfully to keep her immobile. Her other hand pushed up under Olivia's shirt.

'I still like breasts,' she said, as her fingers explored and squeezed. 'Just on other people.' She burst out laughing. 'Your face is a picture. You should see yourself.' She looked closer at Olivia. 'That fool Kellerman has roasted you like an apple on a stick. He is an amateur, pretending to be an interrogator.'

She went to the desk and came back with a white glass jar. She unscrewed the lid and dug out a dollop of the contents on her broad finger. As she smeared it on Olivia's face, Olivia caught the smell of cold cream. She squeezed her eyes shut. The stuff stung at first, then cooled and soothed.

'Whatever else I do to you,' Heike said, rubbing the cream in, 'you can be sure I will leave your face till last. I like to look at a pretty face while I work. When I smash your face, you will know that the end is near.'

Olivia heard her screw the lid back on the jar, and slowly opened her eyes. Heike had gone back to her desk and was sitting on one corner, flicking through a folder.

'They were stupid enough to let you go last time. The meddling Swede arrived, and Kellerman lost his nerve. I never lose my nerve. When I start something, I finish it. We have plenty of leisure time to get to know one another.' She closed the folder and came back to Olivia. Her smirk had vanished. Her eyes were narrowed, like a boxer's. 'So let us start at the beginning. You and I both know that you were not born in Stockholm. Where were you born?'

❦

Olivia emerged slowly from an exhausted sleep on the floor of her cell. Her body ached dully from head to foot. The beating Heike had given her had been expertly delivered. Heike had used her fists, not a club. She had worn boxing gloves, and she had worked Olivia over with the precision of a boxer, careful to break no bones, but battering her ribs so that each breath she took hurt like a knife, pounding her kidneys and liver until they were bruised and throbbing.

Chained to the wall, all Olivia had been able to do was spit and curse, using the vilest words she knew. But Heike had enjoyed her resistance, and Olivia had soon been in too much pain to curse.

What had made the punishment especially disgusting had been Heike's unabashed relish in every detail of it, and her expressions of tenderness in between blows and questions: the hot mouth that had covered hers, the intimate caresses.

There had been little point denying that she was American. Heike knew that very well. She'd yielded all the information Heike had demanded about her place of birth, her education, her arrival in France.

But she had stuck to her story about the documents. She'd insisted that she was a thief, not a spy. That what she 'had been up to', in Heike's words, was simply systematically pilfering money from guests who would never notice it was missing.

Heike hadn't believed a word of it, but Olivia had somehow found the strength to keep repeating it again and again. She had managed to lock the truth into a kind of vault inside her, vowing that it would never be opened.

'There is no hurry,' Heike had said at last, using her teeth to unfasten the laces of her boxing gloves. 'I am enjoying this far too much to want it to end. We have a long way to go, you and I. Tomorrow we will talk again.'

And now that tomorrow had come.

The clatter of the lock made her shrink into a corner. She wanted so much to be brave and resolute, but her body, with its memory of pain, betrayed her. It shrank into a ball, like a wounded animal. They hauled her to her feet with humiliating ease and marched her down the corridor to her fate.

Heike was in a cheerful mood this morning, smoking a cheroot as she leaned back in her chair with her boots on her desk. She waved Olivia to a seat instead of chaining her to the wall as she'd done before.

'You are tougher than I thought, Blondchen. You resist. Not like the others, who beg and cry after one slap. I like that. I will enjoy breaking you down. I know how to use my fists, eh?'

'Yes, you know how to use your fists,' Olivia said dully.

Heike laughed, dropping her feet to the floor with a thud and rising from her chair. 'Let me show you.'

Olivia got ready to fight back, but Heike was only lifting some photograph albums on to the desk. She stood beside Olivia, kneading the back of her neck with one hand while she flipped through the pages of photographs with the other. They showed Heike in the ring with male boxers, adopting the aggressive poses of a heavyweight. 'I fought all these men. Professionals. I beat them too. I am an athlete, Blondchen. I was born to compete. Did you know that I have gold medals in javelin and wrestling?'

In other albums there were hundreds of photographs of Heike at various sporting events, going back years. Olivia gazed sluggishly at these images of her tormentor lifting weights, throwing the discus, in a bathing suit, in the wrestling ring.

Heike, with her eyes narrowed against the smoke from the cheroot clamped between her lips, gave her a running commentary on her past triumphs through the Twenties and Thirties.

At last she turned the page to reveal a far earlier image, of a slim smiling Heike in a fashionable dress, with long, curly hair.

'This is what I was,' Heike said. 'A weak, pretty fool. Just as you are now. What do you think?'

'You've changed.'

'Oh, yes. When I started to become myself, they called me a freak. They tried to stop me from competing. They wanted to keep me out of athletics. But the Nazis recognised what I was. When they came along, everything changed.' Her grip on Olivia's neck tightened, with the strength of a lioness's jaws. 'Now I am free to be who I want to be. Is that not the most important thing in life?'

She released Olivia at last and put the photograph albums away.

'Come, Blondchen. Let me show you my work.'

She led Olivia through a warren of rooms that adjoined her office. Olivia realised at once that these were torture chambers. It was torture turned into a bureaucratic routine, with the hideous banality of the Gestapo.

Here was the device for tearing out fingernails, carefully made by some carpenter, its number and location stamped on one side, bolted on to a desk so it could be conveniently applied.

Here was the machine for cutting off fingers and toes. Here was the bathtub where prisoners were left to freeze for hours at a time, or had their faces submerged until they drowned, were brought around, and drowned again.

Here was the electrical generator, tastefully housed in marbled brown Bakelite: a wire was attached to the victim's ankles so agonising shocks could be delivered all over the body. Here was the bucket and the stirrup pump, used to pump the guts so full of water that the pain could not be borne.

Olivia was so sickened that she had to throw up halfway through this tour. Heike thrust her head over a basin while she vomited what little was left in her belly.

'I'm going to kill you in the end, Blondchen,' she said casually. 'But before I do, you will experience all of these delights in my company. And many more. Like I said – we have a long way to go together.' Gripping Olivia's hair, Heike stared into her face. 'You know, I don't care what you did or didn't do. It doesn't interest me. So you can say what you like. Nothing will stop me.'

Olivia spat in her face, raging with disgust. 'You're sick,' she said.

Heike wiped the spit off her face with her large thumb. 'One of these days I will ask you whether I should pull another fingernail – or kiss you. And you will beg me to kiss you. I look forward to that.' She was reaching for the boxing gloves. 'And now, let us have a little sport.'

Once again, Olivia was Heike's punching bag. The blows were crueller now, more vicious. Heike selected her targets with care, enjoying her ability to inflict the maximum pain on a defenceless victim. By the time she was done, Heike was panting with excitement, her face a dull red.

'That has given me great pleasure,' she sighed, taking off the gloves at last. But Olivia could no longer walk and had to be dragged back to her cell between two guards.

⚜

Spatz von Dincklage and Coco Chanel were dining together *à deux* in their apartment in the Ritz. Although the food was as exquisite as ever and the vintage champagne chilled to perfection, both were in a sombre mood.

They had recently returned from Spain, where they had been sent on a secret mission on behalf of Heinrich Himmler, chief of the SS. While in Madrid, Coco had gone to the British embassy to meet senior diplomats and to convey various messages from the head of the SS: that Himmler was willing to push Hitler aside and rule the Third Reich himself, in exchange for a truce with the Allies, and an end to the war that was decimating Germany; and that it was in the Allies' interests to join with the Nazis in crushing the Soviet Union.

It had all sounded so wonderful to Coco, ringing in her ears like triumphal music. She would be out of this trap that was closing around her, back on top again.

The humiliation of being told the ambassador would not even see her had been like a kick in the teeth. The mission had failed before it had even begun. A lowly attaché had informed her icily that Britain had no intention of stopping the war now, or of turning on its ally Russia, and had shown her the door. She and Spatz had been sent away with their tails between their legs.

'It's because we were palmed off with little nobodies,' Coco said, picking restlessly at her quail. The little birds had been deboned and cooked in port with raspberries and wild mushrooms. Delicious as they were, she had no appetite. 'If only I could talk to Churchill directly,

Spatz! I know I could convince him. He's been in love with me for years.'

'I don't doubt that, my dear,' von Dincklage said in his carefully modulated tones. 'But I'm afraid it's impossible.'

'Couldn't you get me to London? Put me on a plane some dark night?'

'And parachute you into Trafalgar Square?' Spatz suggested dryly.

'Face-to-face with Winston, there's nothing I couldn't achieve.'

He shook his head. 'Out of the question.'

She pushed her plate away and snatched up the champagne glass. She hated to be thwarted, and with the prospect of the war ending in a very different way from what they had expected two years earlier, she was as nervous as a cat on hot bricks. Her nerves tingled, making eating impossible. She longed for the morphine syringe next to her bed. It would bring oblivion for a night, at least. 'Why is it out of the question?'

'Because we are no longer negotiating from a position of strength,' he replied patiently.

'What do you mean?'

'I mean that the war is lost, Coco. Himmler knows it. Churchill knows it. Only the Führer is able to keep fooling himself that there is any chance of victory.'

She hated to hear him talk like this, so calm and reasoned, as though there were nothing in the world to worry about. 'I was so certain we could negotiate a truce.'

'There will be no truce.' Von Dincklage had enjoyed his quail, unlike Coco, and was now mopping up the sauce with a piece of bread. 'Only a reckoning.'

'A reckoning for what?'

'Don't you know what they have done in the East? The sea of blood they have spilled? Himmler and his henchmen have slaughtered millions upon millions of men, women and children in their wretched camps. There is no possibility of forgiveness. They will all be hanged. Nothing else will appease our enemies. Churchill may be soft-hearted. Stalin is not.'

'But—'

'And I must tell you, my dear,' von Dincklage went on, emptying the last of the champagne into their gold-rimmed glasses, 'that we have made a bad mistake in carrying this message of Himmler's. You may well face a charge of collaboration with the SS.'

Her stomach clenched, as it always did at moments like this. 'You never warned me about that!'

'I still had hopes you and I could pull something off. The way we were received in Madrid demolished those hopes. It was a risk, and we took it. It didn't pay off.'

'If I could just speak to Winston—' she began again.

He cut in. 'My dear, we must think of escaping with our hides intact now. The invasion is a matter of weeks away.'

She recoiled in her chair, a small, shrunken figure in black. 'The invasion?'

'Our intelligence reports a massive build-up of troops along the coastline of southern England. Hundreds of thousands of men. Tanks and armoured cars. Aircraft. Barges. Warships. The only question is where they will choose to land. But they *will* land. And once they have landed, it's all over for us.'

She was appalled. 'This is dreadful.'

'Like many dreadful things, it's inevitable.'

She clasped the goblet in both hands, staring at him over the rim like a frightened child. 'What are we going to do?'

Spatz von Dincklage looked at his lover. He had grown genuinely fond of her over the past years, though he was not a man who let emotions rule his actions. He had chosen her carefully in 1939, knowing she could be useful to the Reich. But her usefulness to the Reich had ended. The trip to Madrid had shown that, if it had shown nothing else.

And the Reich would soon be no more. Germany was going to be bombed to rubble, occupied by British, American and – one shuddered at the thought – Russian troops. Between them, they would quarter Germany like a chicken and pick what meat was left on the bones. Hard times were ahead.

Coco was no longer useful to the Reich, but she possessed something that was still of great value to *him*: her money.

Her vast wealth could ensure a comfortable existence for the two of them after the war had ended. In South America, perhaps. One heard that Panama had an ideal climate. Or somewhere more civilised, like Switzerland. Yes, Switzerland. Insulated from outrage, protected against prosecution, they could live out their lives in comfort and luxury. Let the world say what it would, they would be unmolested in Switzerland. The Swiss understood the value of money.

He would need to explain all this to Coco. The Ritz would be barred to her. Paris would be barred. France would be barred. She would weep the bitter tears of the exile; but the tears of exiles could be comforted by the pleasures of exiles: good food, good wine, a comfortable home, and memories.

He dabbed his mouth with his napkin, rose from his chair, and came to her side. Perching on the arm of her chair, he put his hand on her shoulder.

'Don't look so frightened, Coco. Listen to me. I have something to discuss with you.'

<hr />

A ripple was passing through Fresnes prison. Prisoners were calling to each other through the walls of their cells, ignoring the furious guards who tried to silence them.

Olivia crept to the door of her cell to try to hear what was going on. After days of beatings, her movements were those of an old, old woman.

The whispered messages were garbled, almost inaudible, but at last she caught a couple of words.

'She's dead.'

She didn't grasp the full import of this until the exercise yard. One of the prisoners who was always in their group was named Jeanne, a raw-boned girl of seventeen or eighteen who sometimes relayed the latest gossip. She had mastered the ventriloquist's art of talking while keeping her face completely immobile.

'The Resistance ambushed them on a country road.'

'Who?'

'Heike Schwab and another Gestapo bitch. Our boys threw a hand grenade into their car. Killed them both.'

'Are you sure?' someone hissed.

'Sure. She'll never come back.'

Almost inaudibly, someone whistled a few bars of *La Marseillaise*, until the guard lashed out with his rifle butt. But there were smiles on most faces. All of them had suffered, or were due to suffer, at Heike's hands.

Olivia felt no joy at the news, only a deep shuddering relief. Heike had beaten her every day. She had no doubt that Heike had meant every word of her promise to torment her beyond endurance and then kill her. Whatever else awaited her here in Fresnes, she had been spared that fate, at least.

As for Heike, whatever had happened to her to turn her into the torturer she had become, the mystery had ended on a lonely country road.

And when Olivia got back to her cell, there was something lying on the stone floor.

It was a walnut, still wrapped in its green rind.

Twenty Seven

Arletty had rushed home on hearing the news. As she rounded the corner of rue de Conti, she saw that it was true. The charming little apartment that Josée de Chambrun had found for her, with its views of the river and the Louvre, had been machine-gunned.

Bullet holes scarred the plaster in long ragged lines. All the windows had been shot out. The door was splintered. Even the terracotta pots on the balcony had been blown to pieces, scattering dirt and geraniums.

A stolid gendarme was standing outside the house with his hands behind his back.

'Who did this?' Arletty demanded, shaking with anger.

The man would not look her in the face, but stared disdainfully over her shoulder. 'Patriots, Madame.'

'This is not a patriotic act,' she snapped. 'It's attempted murder! If I had been home, I would have been killed.'

'When they want to kill you, Madame,' he replied in the same insouciant tone, 'they will, don't worry about that. This was just high spirits.'

'What the devil do you mean, "high spirits"?' Arletty demanded.

'Haven't you heard?'

'Heard what?'

At last the man's eyes met hers. They were bright with triumph. 'The Allies have landed in Normandy. They'll be in Paris in a few weeks.

This is no longer your home, Madame. You had better look for another one.'

She pushed past the gendarme and entered her apartment. The bullets that had come through the windows had scarred the walls and furniture within. The place was desecrated.

As she stood staring at the mess, the telephone began to ring. She picked it up, dreading what she would hear.

'Doe.' The voice was Soehring's. 'I'm at the Ritz. Come.'

He had only forty-eight hours' leave. Thirty-six hours of that were needed for travelling from the front and back again. Which gave them twelve hours together. He looked exhausted, and he smelled of war. Even his lovemaking had changed. He rutted blindly on top of her, the expression on his face one of desperation rather than love, his gaze somehow blind, not seeing her but seeing something awful that lay beyond her. She made no sound, even when he hurt her.

Afterwards, he slept for three hours out of the precious eight that were left, while she watched over him; and then he woke in a panic, wild-eyed and shouting in German.

She calmed him. He got up and began pacing around the room naked, smoking a cigarette.

'The war is lost, Doe. It's all *kaputt*. You have to leave France.'

'I'm not leaving,' she replied quietly, watching him.

'The invasion has already begun,' he said impatiently. 'The Allies will be in Paris in a question of weeks. What the Resistance did to your apartment was just the start. They'll put you up against a wall as soon as the Occupation forces leave.'

'Well, at least it will be a French wall.'

'I've got everything ready for you,' he went on, ignoring her reply. 'My family are waiting for you in Baden-Baden. It's so beautiful there. You will love it. The war hasn't touched it – it's still pristine.'

'Faun, stop.'

'My parents will look after you. They know all about you—'

'No.'

'They've already prepared a room for you in Baden-Baden.'

'No!'

'Baden-Baden is the only safe place in Europe,' he said, his voice rising to a bark. 'You'll die if you stay here!'

'You're not addressing your troops now. Don't shout at me. And if I have to die, I would far rather die in Paris-Paris than Baden-Baden.'

'Stop being a little fool.' He grasped her shoulders and shook her so hard that her teeth snapped. 'What do you think I've come all this way for? To make love? Listen to me. You have to get out! They'll kill you!'

She rose to her feet, pushing him away. 'Stop bullying me.'

'You don't know what's coming! You know nothing!'

Her face was white and her eyes were blurred with tears, though she refused to let them fall. 'And you know less. You don't know what I've been through, or who I am. Get it into your thick German skull – I am *not* going to Baden-Baden-Baden-Baden.'

And in the end, it was he who burst into tears, sobbing helplessly while she held his head on her bosom.

※

They had heard the firing squads working day and night, and knew the Gestapo had stepped up the execution of condemned prisoners. But since none of them had been let out of their cells for three days, nobody knew who had died.

In any case, Olivia was too listless to care any longer. She had entered a terminal state of exhaustion and suffering. Months of malnutrition and ill treatment had reduced her to a skeleton of herself. Her once-strong body was so weak that she could barely lift her arms or walk more than a few paces before having to rest.

Since Heike's death, she had become a forgotten woman, buried alive. There had been no further interrogations, only this long, slow death by starvation.

Exercise had ceased in April; the yard was used only for executions. Since then, she had shared a cell with five other women. Two of them had died in that time. The corpses had lain among them until they had started to stink before the guards had removed them.

There were now four of them left.

They spoke little. There was no energy for conversation, and in any case, there was nothing to talk about except the imminence of death. And with no food or water for three days, death hovered over them all now.

The firing stopped at last.

There were new sounds: the revving of truck engines down below, shouts in German, the thudding of boots outside the cells.

'What's happening?' someone asked.

'They're taking us to the camps.'

The roar of the trucks intensified. They could hear the vehicles manoeuvring, doors slamming, horns honking. The sound rose to a cacophony lasting for several hours.

Then, one by one, the truck engines began to rumble away.

'They're leaving,' a voice whispered.

They all raised their heads slowly, listening to the fading noises.

'They can't be leaving.'

'But they are. Listen.'

'What about us?' Olivia asked.

'They've left us in here to starve.'

The four of them shuffled to the door of their cell and listened to the silence. Then they began to bang on the solid wood with bony hands, calling out. They paused. They could hear others now, pounding on their doors or rattling tin cups and calling weakly, a litany of lost souls.

There was no answer.

They sank back down on to the floor of the cell, looking at each other in terror. All were crusty-lipped with thirst already. The heat of August was worse than the piercing cold of winter. They had tried drinking their own urine, but it had been too bitter and had only made them sick.

The high window was no more than a barred slit, but the shaft of light it admitted was their clock, telling the passing of each empty day by the line it cast across the ceiling. They watched it now as the afternoon wore on. A profound silence had fallen over the prison.

At around five o'clock, they heard a noise at their door. It was not the peremptory rattle of the guards, but a tentative scrape.

Then the door creaked open. They raised their thin arms to shield their eyes from the stabbing light. Olivia was the first to stagger to her feet.

The person who had opened the door was a prisoner like themselves, wearing the striped prison garb. She was holding a large ring of keys.

'They've gone,' she said. There was no triumph in her voice, only a kind of wonder. She turned away and moved to the next door.

Slowly, the corridor filled with women, emerging from the filthy cells where they had been kept. Some hugged each other and wept as they recognised friends who, like themselves, had survived somehow. Others shambled aimlessly, not seeming to understand what had happened.

There was a bathroom at the end of the corridor. They lined up at the taps, gulping the water until some of them vomited.

When Olivia had slaked her thirst, she made her way slowly down the stairs to the courtyard. She held on carefully to the rail to avoid falling. Her weakened legs were no longer trustworthy. The one thought in her mind was to get out of the prison shadow.

The yard was full of ghostly figures, men and women milling without direction. The bodies of the last victims killed by the firing squads lay where they had fallen, in heaps against the wall. A few prisoners with sufficient energy found blankets to cover them. But of the Nazis there was no trace. They had departed with such haste that in some offices, uniforms were still hanging on coat hooks. But they had been careful to take their instruments of torture with them.

A cheer went up as the gates of the courtyard began to open. It died away as the prisoners saw the uniformed soldiers lined up outside, weapons at the ready. There was a silence.

Then Olivia recognised the uniforms and the helmets. 'They're Americans,' she said. 'They're Americans.'

The prisoners rushed forward to greet their liberators, laughing and crying, but Olivia just stood there, too drained to either laugh or cry.

※

The force that had come to Fresnes prison was a mixed group consisting of Free French, the United States 4th Infantry Division and a detachment of Paris police. The task of sorting out the Gestapo's political detainees from the genuine criminals was going to be complex. A desk was set up in the yard with a row of officers to attempt to decide each case.

Among the chaos of arguing and shouting, a portly figure in a pinstriped suit appeared. A solemn, round face with a clipped moustache peered at Olivia uncertainly.

'You are Olivia Olsen, I think?' he said.

'Mr Nordling, don't you recognise me?'

The Swedish consul in Paris, Raoul Nordling, looked closer. His face changed. 'I do apologise, Olivia. Of course it's you. Come along with me, please.'

'But my papers are still here.'

'It doesn't matter about that now. I have your United States passport at the consulate. Come.'

Nordling's familiar Volvo, with the Swedish flag on the hood, was waiting for them. He helped her in and sat beside her. As they set off, he was inspecting her curiously. 'I do apologise once again for not recognising you,' he said. 'My eyesight is not what it was.'

'You don't need to be tactful,' Olivia replied. 'I can imagine what I look like.'

'You've obviously been ill-treated.'

'I was tortured.'

'I'm very sorry to hear that,' he said gravely.

'Others had it far worse than me. And the Germans seemed to forget about me after my interrogator was killed by the Resistance.'

'You were in the hands of Heike Schwab?'

'Yes.'

'Oh dear,' he said uncomfortably.

They didn't talk much after that. Olivia stared out of the window as they drove back to the city centre. Bathed in the tender evening light, it was Paris as she had not seen it in four years; the Tricolour flew everywhere in place of the swastika. The Nazi signs were being taken down. The ugly German panzers and armoured cars were gone. In their place were Sherman tanks and Jeeps with a white star painted on their sides. And in place of the Wehrmacht field-grey uniforms and the Gestapo black ones, Paris was full of American khaki.

While she and her fellow prisoners had been lying in the darkness, a pitched battle had been fought for this city. The thick stone walls of Fresnes prison had insulated them from it. But now she saw the evidence all around: burned-out vehicles, bullet holes in walls, street barricades and buildings blown to rubble.

The Parisians themselves were out in full force on this benign August evening. Women in their best clothes were parading arm in arm, throwing flowers to the soldiers. Men cheered the American and Free French tanks that rumbled past in long, seemingly endless lines. The crews perched on the turrets beamed with delight through their masks of oil and dirt.

Nordling's driver steered a skilful path through all this congestion. It was all astounding, but Olivia was somehow isolated from it, as though she were still lying on the stone floor of her cell. She was perhaps too weak to feel much joy at the liberation of Paris, or even at the astonishing fact of her own survival. The light, gentle as it was, hurt her eyes, and the jolting of Nordling's official car made her joints scream in protest.

'Mr Nordling, where are we going?'

'To the American field hospital.'

'I don't need a hospital. I just need to get in touch with Jack.'

He looked at her oddly. 'Your friend Jack can wait. You need medical attention before anything else.'

'But I'm fine. Just a little weak.'

He covered her hand with his own large, soft one. 'Of course you're fine,' he said soothingly. 'Don't agitate yourself, please. We'll just get you checked over. Now try to rest. We'll be there soon.'

⁂

She emerged from an exhausted sleep that had been troubled with nightmares. Nurses were opening the curtains around the crowded ward, revealing that it was early morning. The drugs they'd given her made it hard for her to talk or move. She lay in a kind of haze, inert.

Yesterday was a confused memory of tests and examinations. She could barely remember any of it.

A group of men stood at the end of her bed, some in uniform, some in white coats. They were consulting a clipboard. She couldn't see or hear them very well. Her vision was blurred and her ears were ringing.

'She's suffering from malnutrition and a whole bunch of injuries,' she heard an American voice say. 'Some of her organs seem to be on the point of failure. I'm especially worried about her eyes.'

'Is she fit enough to fly?' another voice demanded.

'Yes, sir, I believe she is.'

'Then we'll send her Stateside right away.'

'There's a problem. She doesn't want to go.'

'She doesn't want to go home?'

'She keeps talking about some man. She claims she's been operating with an OSS agent. That's why she was arrested. She won't leave until she's seen him.'

'She'll leave tomorrow,' the second voice said briskly. 'Contact Colonel Davis right away.'

Olivia struggled to sit up in the bunk. 'I'm not going,' she said. Or that was what she tried to say. There was something wrong with her tongue. It wouldn't obey her commands. She stretched out her hands imploringly to the doctors.

'Nurse!' someone called.

A khaki-clad nurse hurried over to her bedside and adjusted the drip that snaked into her arm.

Darkness swept back over her.

⁕

The next time she was conscious again was hours later, in the mid-afternoon. An American officer was sitting at the side of her bed, talking to her. Apparently, they'd been having a conversation, but she couldn't remember having started it, or what had been said up to this point.

'I'm sorry, could you repeat that?' she mumbled.

'I said, there's a long way to go.'

'A long way?'

'You're in bad shape, Miss Olsen. The best place for you is back home, in an American hospital, where they can get you fighting fit again.'

'But I have to see Jack!'

The man sighed. His name was sewn on his uniform: Colonel Davis. He was in middle age. He had a round hairless head, the top of which was scabbed with sunburn, which he kept scratching in a worried way. 'Yes, they've told me about this Jack of yours. And I promise, we'll do our level best to find him. But there are a couple of things you have to understand. One is that he might have used a dozen field names, and with nothing more than "Jack" to go on, it will be hard to identify him.'

'But—'

'And I have to tell you that OSS don't like giving up the identities of their agents. They're a law unto themselves.'

'OSS?'

'The Office of Strategic Services. That's almost certainly who he works for. Our secret service.'

'Can't you get a message to him through them?' she pleaded.

'Talking to them about an agent in the field won't make them very happy.' He leaned forward, elbows on his starched knees. 'You have to appreciate, Miss Olsen, Paris may have been liberated, but France is still one huge battlefield. The Nazis are going to fight for every inch of it. It's going to take months longer, maybe years, before we beat them. The OSS and the Resistance are working closely with our invasion forces. My guess is that your Jack is fighting somewhere around Rouen right now. There's a hell of a battle going on there.'

The tears burned her eyes, sliding down her cheeks. 'What if he's killed?' she whispered.

He patted her shoulder. 'Don't think like that. We're all in God's care, and we all must trust to God's mercy.'

'Please don't send me back,' she begged.

'It's out of my hands,' he said. 'Miss Olsen, you've been extraordinarily brave. You'll get a medal for what you've done—'

'I don't want a goddamn medal!'

He ignored her outburst. 'Right now there's a Liberator waiting to fly you back to the States. Your family's been advised that you're coming home, and let me tell you, they are going to be very, very happy to see you. Apparently they haven't laid eyes on you in four and a half years. They've been worried sick.' He hesitated. 'There's been a rumour going round that you were dead.'

'Who said that?'

'A woman who was with you in Fresnes. She claimed to have seen you executed by a firing squad. You can imagine how that made your folks feel. Don't you think they've suffered enough? Now, get some rest. You're going home.'

He signalled to the nurse, and despite Olivia's protests, the morphine flowed into her veins again, and she sank back into oblivion.

Since the machine-gunning of her apartment in rue de Conti, Arletty had moved back to her old room at the Lancaster. She'd made no secret of her location or her identity, although friends (including Josée) had urged her to flee France, or at least cut and dye her hair and change her appearance.

She had refused to do any of that. She had simply waited for them to come for her. The weeks had passed. Paris was full of joy. All she knew of Soehring was that his unit was now in Poland, fighting a desperate rear-guard battle against the advancing Russians. She didn't expect to see him ever again.

And at last they had come – three police inspectors and a big, square, black-and-white police van.

'I'm very impressed,' she said coolly as they confronted her in the marble lobby of the Lancaster. 'Do I really merit all this? You know I'm not very resistant.'

'You'll make fewer jokes when you're swinging from the gallows,' one of them said grimly. He produced the handcuffs. Arletty held out her hands. He clamped them on her wrists tightly. 'Léonie Bathiat, known also as Arletty, you are under arrest for the crime of collaboration with the enemy.'

The last Olivia saw of Paris was through the Plexiglas canopy of a Liberator bomber. Her eyes were too full of tears to see much. It was just an Impressionist sketch of sunlit buildings and green grass as the huge plane lumbered on to the tarmac.

The engines began to roar, vibrating the fuselage of the bomber until everything rattled wildly.

They were all pressed back in their seats as it raced forward, propellers howling. The passengers, mostly civilians who were not used to flying, clutched anxiously at whatever supports they could find around them.

The Liberator's nose lifted slowly. The rumble of the wheels ceased. The plane began to climb.

And then there was nothing around them but blue sky.

Twenty Eight

Lausanne was charming at this time of the year. The lake was a vivid blue, the Swiss Alps on the far shore inlaid with seams of snow as the year drew to a close and the weather began to grow cold.

On the terrace of her stylish house in the old town, Coco Chanel fretted anxiously. She had expected Spatz hours earlier. He was always so cavalier about keeping appointments. It infuriated her.

Von Dincklage had applied many times for a permit to live in Switzerland, and had been refused on each attempt. She had sent him money to bribe officials, but none of it had helped. He had been banished from France, and from almost every other country in Europe, forced into a peripatetic existence, relying on the hospitality of various aristocratic relatives.

It was 1946 and nobody seemed to want retired Nazi spies, however urbane and charming they might be.

She herself had passed through turbulent times. Dragged in front of a tribunal to explain her years of collaboration with the Nazis, she had barely escaped imprisonment. Only her friendships with certain highly placed individuals, especially dear old Winston, had saved her. She'd had to get out of France in a hurry. Just as Spatz had predicted.

They wanted to paint her as a traitor!

What did they know about her? They saw her wealth, but they didn't see the desperate poverty into which she had been born. They saw the great fashion house, but they didn't see the orphanage where she had been forced to sew to earn her bread. They saw her German lover, but they didn't see all the men she had submitted to in order to claw her way out of the gutter. They thought 'Coco' was a pretentious nickname; they didn't know that it had stuck to her because she'd lived perilously close to the life of a whore.

She had survived all that, and she had sworn she would never return to those humiliations. She'd sought out strength all her life. She'd clung to the Germans because she'd seen they were stronger than the French. And now the Germans had been routed.

Now, instead of Spatz looking after her, it was she who had to look after Spatz. She had fought hard to get him permission to join her here in Switzerland, even though the hypocritical Swiss looked down their noses at him. As though their vaults weren't overflowing with Nazi gold.

She couldn't have Spatz wandering around Europe from pillar to post, perhaps running out of money at the roulette tables, and perhaps deciding to sell a few juicy secrets to raise cash. That would never do.

Far rather keep him here in the luxury to which he was accustomed, and keep an eagle eye on him.

Besides, she needed the companionship.

Lausanne was as dull as only a picturesque Swiss town could be. One looked at the lake and one looked at the mountains, and that was all the stimulation one had from one week to the next. Why, compared to Paris—

But Paris was closed to her now. There was no going back to Paris. It was better not to think of Paris.

She had prepared a separate bedroom for him in this house, some distance from her own, but close enough to permit visits when required. He would have everything he needed, and they would pass the years, as he had once said, in comfort together.

The sound of an automobile interrupted her thoughts and sent her hurrying down to the garden. Spatz had arrived at last.

He clambered out of the car, long-limbed and distinguished as ever in a dark suit and fawn overcoat.

'Forgive me, my dear,' he greeted her. 'The stupid Swiss police took it into their heads to check *all* my travel documents in Bern. I sat in a waiting room for four hours. Very tedious.'

'Never mind, you're here now,' she said. 'Welcome to Switzerland, my beloved.' They embraced. At sixty-four, she was more gorgon than *gamine*; at fifty-one, he was rather long in the tooth to play the dashing rake. But they made a valiant effort to encompass these roles. After a light lunch, they retired to her bed together.

She noticed, with some irritation, that he kept his eyes firmly closed during the preliminary engagement. She knew she was no longer young, but she was surely not *that* bad. Worse still, he proved unable to rise fully to the occasion, despite all her attempts to ignite his passion.

'Perhaps we should give up the struggle,' she said tartly, wiping her mouth with the back of her hand.

He sighed, rolling away from her. 'Forgive me, my dear Coco. The journey – the long wait at the police station—'

'You don't need to explain. It's nothing.'

But she was irritated, again, by the alacrity with which he dressed and the look of relief on his face.

In the evening they dined in a local restaurant, where the food was expensive, dull and indigestible. Then they went home and sat by the fire, drinking cognac and watching the logs burn.

'While I was in the police station waiting room today,' Spatz said, 'I was thinking of something. Do you remember that play we saw together in Paris in 1944? Something by Sartre, put on by the Comédie-Française – about those people stuck in a waiting room?'

'*Huis Clos*,' she said.

'That was it. *Huis Clos*. What was that all about?'

'Hell is other people,' she replied, a touch grimly.

'I didn't get it then, and I don't get it now. What does it mean?'

'The three people were damned souls, my dear Spatz. And the torture the devil had dreamed up for them was to spend all eternity together in that waiting room.'

'Funny ideas these writers get,' he commented, pouring more cognac for both of them. 'I'm sure the Gestapo could think up worse tortures than that.'

'That's because your imagination is purely German,' she said waspishly, 'while Sartre's is universal.'

'Are you angry with me about something?' he asked.

She lit a cigarette and snorted smoke out of her nose, a favourite habit of her, which had resulted in her nostrils being stained with nicotine. 'Not at all,' she replied briskly.

'You are. Was it my failure of this afternoon? We can have another go at bedtime, if you like.'

'Very kind of you, but no thank you.' There was only one thing she wanted at bedtime. The morphine syringe was already loaded on her bedside table. Obtaining the drug to which she was addicted was no longer as easy as it had once been, but luckily she had found an obliging chemist in Lausanne willing to keep her supplied – for a price. She was already longing for the dark embrace of the drug.

And she *was* angry with von Dincklage. Not just for showing how little he desired her any more, but for bringing up *Huis Clos*, that dreadful play about sinners forced to live for ever with their own and each other's sins. Spatz pretended to be bluff and stupid, but he was neither, and he had known very well what he was referring to: the long years of exile that stretched out ahead of them.

She rose to her feet, her body suddenly prickling all over. 'I'm going to bed,' she announced.

'So early?' he said in surprise.

'Yes,' she replied. The need for morphine was unbearably acute. 'I'll see you tomorrow.'

'And tomorrow,' he replied with a smile, lifting the brandy bottle, 'and tomorrow. And tomorrow.'

She kissed the air above his head and hurried to her room to find oblivion.

Arletty had spent two long, hard years of imprisonment, served in more places than she could remember.

The worst had been the prison at Arras, that terrible fortress where the Gestapo had once tortured and executed members of the Resistance, and which had then been deemed an appropriate jail for collaborators.

The last year had been spent at the chateau at La Houssaye-en-Brie, officially a house arrest with a sympathetic communist couple, but in reality an arid exile in a bleak landscape without friends. She had been made to check in at the local police station every week, cut off from the world so strictly that she had not even been permitted to attend the première of *Les Enfants du Paradis*, her greatest triumph and the peak of her career. It had gone ahead without her.

Her only visits to Paris had been to see her doctor when her health collapsed; or to face the interrogations, the depositions, the accusations, the sneers of lawyers and judges, the often bizarre 'evidence' produced by accusers.

Her fame had become her worst enemy. Some were motivated by jealousy. To others, her face was so familiar that they had seen it in every evil action.

There had even been a man who had appeared from nowhere, claiming he had seen her attending the torture of a Resistance agent and demanding his execution. She'd laughed in astonishment. Then she had seen the faces of the judges. They believed this lunatic. They believed anything of her. She had been an inch from a death sentence.

After weeks of testimony, the man had finally admitted that the woman he had seen was someone else.

She had borne it all with patience and good humour, defending herself with the only weapon she had, her *gouaille*, the ability to answer back and make her accusers blush or laugh.

And at the end of it all, her sentence had finally been handed down: *un blâme*. A reprimand. Nothing more. She was free to go.

She had waited so long to be free.

They said she had got off lightly, the ones who had wanted to see her given ten years or put up against the firing-squad wall.

Lightly? She did not view the destruction of her career, the two years of imprisonment, the dragging of her name through the mud, as light punishments. They had dashed the cup from her lips before she could even drink from it, and she would never get it back. She had fallen from the pinnacle of success to the abyss of despair. That was not something she took lightly.

But it was over now. One shrugged. One showed the world that luminous smile that covered all the pain inside. One picked up the pieces of one's life and tried to resume the journey.

And one prepared to meet, once again, the man one loved.

They had written to one another almost daily through the long months: Arletty a few words at a time in her large turquoise scrawl, Soehring dense pages in his neat black script.

And he, too, had gone through his own purgatory, which the Allied Control Council in Berlin called 'denazification'. He had come through with flying colours. As she had once remarked to the American girl, he knew how to swim.

He, too, was piecing his life together now. He was writing a book of short stories. He had sent her some of them, in which she herself figured, romantically portrayed as a vulnerable young woman with a poetic soul. That had made her smile rather ironically. He had some talent, though she doubted whether he would ever make a living from his writing; nevertheless, she encouraged him, as any good lover would, and he had persevered.

And now, after so many years, they were about to meet again.

Belle-Île was a delightful island in the summer, ten miles or so off the Brittany coastline, a place of rocky coves and turquoise bays. In autumn, it could be a lot bleaker. The summer visitors, many of them artists, were driven back to Saint-Nazaire by the pounding waves and lashing Atlantic gales. It became more like a prison than a paradise. But it was here Arletty had chosen to make her second home. Her second exile.

The little white fisherman's cottage near the sea was equipped with a cavernous fireplace, and it amused her to collect driftwood every day, during her walks along the windy shore, to feed this hungry household god, who returned his thanks with heat and light.

By this fireplace she could sit and think. And wait for Faun.

His letters lately had been full of excitement. He was overjoyed at the prospect of seeing her again. He wanted to marry her.

That was the chief subject of almost every letter: the life they would have together as husband and wife, the new start they would make now that the suffering and the separation were over. He was still the same Faun, her uninhibited lover, bursting to bury himself inside her and possess her utterly.

But she was not the same Arletty. She no longer wanted to be utterly possessed. She was forty-eight. She was an out-of-work actress with a crippled career and a ruined reputation, her wealth used up, her prospects limited. He was thirty-eight, a man with his life still ahead of him.

She couldn't give him the children he would want. The doctor she'd seen in Paris had told her that quite clearly. The last abortion had done irreparable damage. Besides which, the doctor had added calmly, she was too old.

Too old! Such harsh words for a woman to face! Yet she had the courage to face them, and to face him with them. And enchant him with that smile of hers, her dazzling mask of a smile.

She had thrown away her golden casket for him, again and again. It had sunk into the waters of time. But she would never let him sink too. He would be distraught at her refusal. He adored her, and she adored him. That didn't change the answer. It would always be no. She was not a Circe, wanting to enslave her lover and hold him in thrall. She loved freedom too much to sin against it.

But there was still *l'amour*. Love to be made, a season in the sun to be enjoyed, before the final winter. They would have that, at least.

She returned from her walk with an armful of wood, smoothed and polished by the sea. She piled it carefully in the hearth and lit the kindling. The sea salts in the wood burned with magical blue and green sparks that rushed up the chimney and vanished into the blackness.

When the fire was burning brightly, she went to take off her heavy jersey and put on something pretty to greet him in. The ferry from the mainland would have docked by now, and he would be striding across the island towards her.

She had barely finished getting ready when she heard his knock at the door – that impetuous knock of his, demanding and eager. She had wanted to glide to him serenely, like the goddess she was, but her feet betrayed her, and she ran quickly to answer that imperious summons.

She threw the door open. He was there. She had almost forgotten how big he was, how strong and tall and male. One look was enough. She closed her eyes.

'Faun.'

'Doe.'

And then she was lifted in his arms.

Northern Wisconsin was a divine carnival in the fall. Spikes of evergreen punctuated the layered masses of crimson, yellow, orange and gold. The eye was dazzled by the infinite beauties revealed at each bend in the country roads. When they were reflected in blue water, these scenes became too beautiful to believe, living postcards, chocolate boxes and Christmas cards.

Olivia drove without haste through this glorious world that came to life only one month a year.

The past two years had done much to heal her body and mind. There were a few scars on her face. She wore them with pride. Being home again, among her family, had been wonderful. But not easy.

She was grateful for so much. For having survived. That her health and strength had returned. That she was loved. That she was able to paint again, better than before, better than she had ever done.

But much was missing, and she was in search of that much. She prayed she would find it soon, and that her heart would finally be able to soar.

Finding Jack had not been easy. Finding a man with no name, whose very existence was shrouded in secrecy, in the midst of a vast war extending across Europe, could never be easy.

It was only the fact that she herself had an OSS file – complete with a code name, which had rather pleased her – that had even got her a hearing. Otherwise the doors of the secret world would have remained locked to her.

As it was, it had taken her weeks to get anywhere. She had no claim on the OSS. She was neither an employee nor an agent. She had only ever been what the jargon termed an asset. And assets didn't count for much.

After dozens of letters and calls, she'd finally found herself invited to a gracious white building on the shores of the Potomac, where the OSS apparently had its headquarters, and ushered into an office where an urbane colonel in a uniform covered with campaign ribbons had entertained her to a cup of tea.

He'd asked her to tell him about her time at the Ritz, and had listened carefully as she told him the whole tale: how Fabrice had been murdered by the Gestapo, how she'd been determined to avenge his death, how she'd met Jack. She'd left nothing out – not even the fact that she and Jack had been lovers, or the details of her torture at the hands of Heike Schwab and other Gestapo thugs.

From time to time, the colonel had made neat little notes in a pad, but for the most part he had just listened. At the end of it all, he'd leaned back in his chair and said, 'You're a very brave young woman. You deserve to be decorated for what you did. But unfortunately, we don't give out decorations. And you can't tell anyone about it.'

'Don't worry. I can't even tell my family the whole story. You're the first person who's heard it since I came back from France.'

'That's good. But I'm going to have you sign a form binding you to secrecy, anyway.'

'Is that why you asked me to come here?'

'Partly,' he admitted.

'All I want is to find him,' she'd replied. And then she had added with a catch in her voice. 'Actually, all I want is to know whether he's still alive.'

The colonel had nodded sympathetically. 'I can understand that, Miss Olsen. But we don't give out any information whatsoever on agents who are in the field.' He held up his hand as she started to pro-test. 'I don't make the rules.'

'The war's over!'

'The war may be over, but we still have agents in the field. We have new enemies now. A new war to face. Right now, I can't help you.' He'd offered her a tissue to help with her tears. 'What I can promise you is that as soon as it's possible, I'll get someone to pass on any available information.'

That had been nine months ago.

No 'available information' had been forthcoming in all that time. She'd sunk into dismay, and then despair. All across the United States, soldiers were coming home. The country rejoiced as its surviving sons returned from the shattered cities and villages of Europe.

And then there were the sons who would only ever come back in coffins, if at all. So many of them, lying in foreign graveyards, or still unidentified in hastily dug battlefield graves.

Which category did Jack fall into? She didn't know, had no way of knowing. But as the slow months passed, she felt in her bones that Jack was never going to come back. That he had died in some cellar or on a lonely country road. She would spend the rest of her life never knowing, forever grieving.

It was terribly hard not to give up hope. Hope was a torturer worse than Heike Schwab. But she clung on. Giving up hope was giving up on the love she felt for him, the love that had kept her going through the months of suffering and desolation. So she clung to the hope that at least she would find out his fate, and where he was buried.

And at last, a letter had come from the gracious white building on the banks of the Potomac.

It had contained little more than a name and an address. But it had lifted her on soaring wings.

Her first impulse had been to rush to him.

Then she'd remembered her own first months back in the United States. The invisible walls that had still been around her, locking her in. The impossibility of explaining what she'd been through to those who loved her, preventing her from sharing herself with anyone. It had been like going from one prison to another. A year had passed before she'd started to feel in any way like herself.

She'd known that her strange aloofness had puzzled her family, just as her sudden bouts of hysterical crying or anger had shocked them. They'd asked her what was wrong, what they could do to help her. Every time she'd started to explain, the words had frozen in her throat. She didn't want to hurt them by telling them that she needed to be left alone more than she needed their questions. She didn't want to appal them by telling them the things she'd seen and been through. It was better to just stay silent.

Dr Carlblom, the family physician, who had known her since measles and mumps, had done his best, prescribing tonics and sedatives. But this wasn't measles or mumps. The tonics hadn't helped, and she had quietly poured the sedatives down the sink.

It had been a long, hard, lonely road.

Jack would be travelling the same difficult road. He, like she, would be struggling to adjust to an existence that appeared normal, but where he no longer belonged. Throwing herself into his arms and making fresh demands on him would be a bad mistake. Having journeyed the same road herself, she could offer her understanding, if nothing else. But she knew that there was no guarantee he would even want to see her.

She didn't know whether he still shared any of the feelings they'd once had for one another. It had been two years since they had last been together. In that time, he might have forgotten her. Might have found someone else. Might be injured, physically or mentally, and no longer the man she had known. She had no way of knowing.

And for her own sake, she had to restrain herself from throwing herself at him, risking a brutal rejection. She had been patient and methodical up until now. Losing control at the last moment would result in heartbreak.

No. It was far better to dawdle, to approach slowly.

So she had loaded up the Ford and had set off on a meandering route towards him.

The car, an ancient Model 'A' station wagon with wooden sides, forced her to go slowly. It was liable to bust a gut if pushed too hard. Besides, the back was so piled with easels, canvases and boxes of oil paints that any sudden movement would send everything flying around.

Among the artist's equipment in the back of the station wagon were her mattress, sleeping bag and pup tent. When she couldn't find a friendly farmstead or a cheap motel, she slept in the Ford, or out of doors. She ate what was offered, stopped to paint whatever pleased her eye.

Perhaps there would be an exhibition somewhere ahead: a collection of fall paintings in some quiet gallery?

The important thing was that each day brought her a little closer to him. And each day she had to force herself to stop, get out her easel, apply herself to art, so that her mind could remain clear and her heart could slow down – her heart that longed to do nothing more than race to him.

She had left America almost eight years ago, a rash, heedless tearaway looking for something more than her life had offered. She had returned a very different woman. She had fought the Nazis, met famous people, been in a Gestapo prison. She had been petted by Hermann Goering and educated by Coco Chanel. She had been loved by two men, one of whom had died. Arletty's ruby ring was on her finger to remind her of a unique woman. Her experiences had taken her through rage and grief, love and loss, bravery and terror, to a final understanding of herself, of her strengths and weaknesses, her ultimate resilience. She was finally at peace with who she was. She was ready to settle down. Ready to love, and be loved in return.

And at last, she had arrived.

The farm was in a valley, not far from Cedar Falls. She saw the row of silos first, glinting in the sun, and as she came down the hill, the whole place unfolded before her. It was a sweet spot, with fields of corn, barley, wheat and rye around the farmhouse, and a big old red barn that stood proudly beside it.

Olivia drove along the dirt road to the house, admiring the neatness with which everything was laid out. The machinery was far from new, but it was well-maintained and shiny-clean. There were horses, which came to the rail inquisitively as she trundled past, and three or four retrievers who galloped alongside her, barking a welcome. The house itself was snow white, with a shingle roof and a long, shady porch.

An old man in dungarees was sitting on the porch, reading a book and drinking a cup of coffee. He got up as she parked the car, and came over to her, an expression of surprise on his weather-beaten face.

'You lost, Ma'am?' he enquired, touching his hat.

'Well, no. I think I'm found,' she replied.

His expression of puzzlement deepened. 'Come again?'

Olivia got out of the Ford and held out her hand. 'My name's Olivia Olsen.'

'George Merrill,' he replied, shaking her hand politely, but evidently none the wiser.

'I'm an artist.' She pointed to the gear piled up in the back of the station wagon. 'I'm travelling around Wisconsin, making paintings of the red barns. I wanted to ask if you'd kindly give me permission to paint yours.'

He stared at her. Understanding slowly illuminated his lined blue eyes, making them bright. 'Well, now. I think I know who you are.'

'That's more than I do sometimes,' she smiled. 'I met your son in France.'

'I figured that. He talks about you.'

Olivia tried to hide the way her heart leaped into her throat at those words. 'Does he? What does he say?'

'Just that there was a girl he met in France.' He looked her up and down. 'A woman, I guess he meant.'

'Nothing else?'

'Just that she was a painter.'

'He's not much of a talker, is he, Mr Merrill?'

'Depends on the subject. The fact that he mentions you at all is pretty remarkable. I've never known him so quiet. How did you find this place?'

'Oh, I've been nagging the Joint Chiefs of Staff for a couple of years. They finally admitted that your son might possibly exist. And that they might possibly be bringing him home round about now.'

'He got back two weeks ago.'

'That's what I heard. So I thought I'd take a little trip painting barns until I got around to *your* barn.'

'Well, you're right welcome. My son's not here right now, Olivia. He went out early. But he'll be back soon. Since he came back from Europe, he doesn't sleep a whole lot.'

'I didn't sleep much myself when I first got back. And I was pretty quiet too. My family couldn't figure me out. Tell you the truth, I couldn't figure myself out for a long time. I'm just starting to remember who I am.'

He nodded slowly. 'I guess you young people all saw a whole lot of things over there that you can't tell us about. Things that keep you awake at night. Things you can only talk to each other about.'

She studied his wrinkled, tanned face, which was as wholesome as a baked apple. 'I think that's true. One day we'd like to leave all that behind us.'

'I hope you can teach each other how to do that.'

'I hope so too.' She bent down to greet the dogs, who had finally caught up with her, and were seething around her, tongues lolling happily. She was glad of the distraction. She didn't want George Merrill to see the turmoil that was inside her.

'You'll have lunch with us,' the farmer said decisively. 'And I'll get the girls to make up the spare bedroom for you.'

'Oh, I don't want to be a trouble to you.'

'It's no trouble. More like a pleasure and a privilege.'

'You're very kind. Is it okay if I set up my easel over by that clump of trees?'

'We call those hackmatacks round here. You can set up your easel pretty much anywhere you want, Olivia Olsen.'

As he turned to go into the house, she asked, 'Mr Merrill, what does your son like to be called?'

He smiled. 'William.'

'William,' she repeated to herself. 'I like that.'

'Not Billy. Or Bill, or Will, or any of that. Just plain William.'

'I can live with just plain William.'

'I'm glad to hear it,' he replied. He waved his hand to encompass the house, the barn and the fields of grain all around. 'Welcome home.'

She got to work as soon as her easel was set up. She didn't need to think about the composition of the painting or anything else: she had seen this barn enough times in her dreams to know exactly how she wanted the picture to be.

She sketched quickly with a charcoal stick, and began painting right away. She had laid in several tubes of a colour called English Red, made from iron oxide, for just this occasion. She squeezed a fat red ribbon on to her palette and started to blend the shades with her palette knife.

Farm hands were busy around the yard, working on machinery, hauling grain, driving trucks; though some of them glanced at her curiously, none of them bothered her.

Two of the dogs had chosen to keep her company and were dozing beside her, occasionally whimpering as they chased rabbits in their dreams. Suddenly, both dogs sat up, floppy ears pricked. Then they hurtled off down the road, barking joyfully to greet the car that was approaching.

Olivia felt herself start to tremble. She got shivering fits from time to time, the legacy of what she had been through in Fresnes; but this time, the trembling wasn't from fear.

The car stopped, and she saw his tall figure get out. He wore the same faded denims as he'd always worn in France, with a red bandanna at his throat. He stood stock still for a long time, staring at her. Then he walked slowly towards her.

'Hello, Yokel,' he said quietly when he'd reached her.

'Hello, Bumpkin.' She wiped her hands with her cloth and looked up at him, shading her eyes. His grey eyes were steady, his face thinner than when she had seen him last. But he had all his arms and legs, as she saw in one swift glance. 'So they sent you home at last?'

'Guess they got sick of me hanging around.'

'Did you make a nuisance of yourself?'

'Some.'

'You've lost weight.'

'You look pretty good yourself. Got those yokel apples in your cheeks.'

'Do you like 'em?'

'I like nothing better.' Still, he seemed to be hesitating, as though he could not quite believe she was real. 'I was going to come and find you.'

'But I found you first.'

'I wasn't sure you would want to see me. Being as I was the one who put you in harm's way.'

'I'll think of ways you can make it up to me.'

'And I wanted to get myself together a little before we met.'

'Don't worry about that. I'll get you all fixed up – William.'

'Yes,' he said, 'I believe you will, Olivia.'

She indicated her canvas. 'I really just came to paint your barn.'

'It's a long way to come, just to paint a barn.'

'Well, it's a very special barn to me.'

'Would you like to see inside?'

'I've always wanted to see inside.'

He held out his hand to her and she rose to take it.

They walked into the barn together, out of sight of the workers, hand in hand. He'd once described it as like a church, and she could see why. It was high and cool and dim, an intricate yet strong construction of pillars and trusses. The air was scented with cedar. She thought of the Bible stories of her childhood, of the temple of Solomon that was made with cedar timbers from Lebanon. There were other scents too: of linseed and grains, of burlap and bourbon.

'Most of what we produce goes into the silos,' William said. 'It gets sold to the government. This is where we keep our own stores, for the household.'

She looked up. As her eyes adjusted to the soft light, she saw the sacks of corn, barley, wheat and rye neatly piled in the loft, the barrels of whiskey maturing. There were stores here for the seasons to come, nourishment and sustenance for a family, and the descendants of a family, down through the years.

They walked down the central aisle until they reached the stone slab at the end, which supported the wall. She turned to face him.

'Should I have waited longer?'

'No.'

'You're not angry?'

'I can never be angry with you. I can't live without you, Olivia.'

'I can't live without you, William. These have been the hardest months of my life.'

He started to answer, but something caught in his throat, preventing him from saying what he wanted to say.

Instead, he caught her up in his arms and crushed her to his heart as though he would never let her go.

AUTHOR'S NOTE

This novel contains both real and fictional characters. However, the whole book should be regarded as a work of imagination, not history.

The Ritz played a unique role during the German occupation of France. It was the only hotel that accommodated both senior Nazi officers (who gave themselves a ninety per cent discount) and privileged civilians of other nations (who were sheltered there from the rigours of shortages and rationing). As a result, for four years the Ritz was a seething marketplace for the buying and selling of information, art, sex, black-market luxuries and other commodities. It was also the ideal place for the occupying powers to conduct liaisons – officially forbidden – with prominent French women.

Arletty remained a controversial figure in France for the rest of her life. Her smouldering performances in masterpieces such as *Hotel du Nord* (1938), *Les Visiteurs du Soir* (1942) and *Les Enfants du Paradis* (1945) are among the finest in twentieth-century cinema.

She made no attempt to hide her passionate wartime love affair with Major Hans-Jürgen Soehring, and she was charged with collaboration by the *Commission d'Epuration* in 1944. Although she was finally all but exonerated, her career never recovered.

After the war, she and Soehring remained friends. She encouraged him while he struggled to make a name for himself as a writer. His short stories show that he had a considerable, poignant talent. She also encouraged him to marry a young, clever and well-off wife, Analisa Pistor. They had two children. In 1954 he joined the German Foreign Office, like his father, and was sent as consul to Angola and the Congo. He was killed by a crocodile in 1960, at the age of fifty-two, while swimming in the River Congo with his sons.

His widow, Analisa, and Arletty remained friends after his death. Arletty died blind and impoverished in Paris in 1992.

After 1945, Coco Chanel spent many years in exile in Switzerland, much of that time with Spatz von Dincklage. Her couture house stayed closed for fifteen years. She made a comeback in 1954, at the age of seventy. Her first collection received a ferocious mauling from the French press, which had not forgiven her for her pro-Nazi wartime behaviour; but before long she took her place at the top of the fashion world once again.

Her relaunch was sponsored by the very business associate she had fought so many lawsuits with: Pierre Wertheimer. He was one of the many men she captivated, despite her behaviour. They renegotiated their agreement: Wertheimer took over full control of Chanel's perfume and fashion business in exchange for paying her personal expenses and taxes for the rest of her life.

She returned to the Ritz and lived there until her death in 1971 at the age of eighty-seven. Altogether, she had spent something like half her adult life at the hotel.

Dr Kurt Blanke enjoyed a successful career in law and politics in Lower Saxony after the war. His part in the persecution of the French Jews was forgotten until his death, when a street was named after him in Celle. The attention resulted in his Nazi record being uncovered. The street was swiftly renamed.

Hermann Goering was cured of his obesity and addictions by American doctors while in jail. A thinner, more alert Goering was tried at Nuremberg, where he conducted a spirited defence. He was sentenced to hang, but took his own life on the eve of his execution in

1946, using a cyanide capsule, which he had kept hidden in his cell. He was the most senior Nazi to stand trial for the crimes of the Third Reich. Hitler, Himmler and Goebbels all managed to kill themselves before they could face justice. The task of unravelling the vast web of Goering's art thefts, and returning the works to their rightful owners, has taken decades and continues to this day.

The character of Heike Schwab is based on the athlete Violette Morris. Recruited by the Nazis during the 1930s, she underwent experimental hormone treatments, had her breasts removed and dressed in male uniforms. She became one of the Gestapo's most dreaded torturers, hunting down members of the Resistance. She was assassinated by them in an ambush in 1944.

The Swedish consul, Raoul Nordling, helped many people escape from the Nazis. He is also remembered for having persuaded General Dietrich von Choltitz, the German military governor of Paris, to disobey Hitler's direct command to destroy the city's great monuments with explosives as the Occupation forces withdrew. He was honoured in many ways by France and died in 1962 in the city he loved.

Among the people Nordling managed to rescue was Antoinette d'Harcourt, Arletty's close friend and lover, who had been interned in Fresnes prison by the Gestapo. The duchess's alternative lifestyle made her distrusted by both the Germans and the French. She and Arletty met again in the late 1940s, and their friendship resumed to an extent; but like many guests of the Gestapo, Antoinette never fully recovered her health, and she died prematurely in 1958.

Josée de Chambrun and her husband, René, both helped in the legal defence of Josée's father, Pierre Laval, the leader of the Vichy government. Laval was sentenced to death after a brief trial. He was executed by firing squad in Fresnes prison. After the war, the de Chambruns spent their great wealth in purchasing and preserving art. Josée died in 1992; René in 2002.

Claude and Blanche Auzello both survived the war, despite both being arrested and interrogated by the Gestapo more than once. They remained at the Ritz until 1969. However, as retirement approached, and with the prospect of leaving his beloved hotel after nearly fifty years in management, Claude fell into depression. He had kept a handgun in his office since the Occupation. He used it to kill Blanche as she slept, and then shot himself. She was seventy-two; he was in his eighties.

Madame Marie-Louise Ritz remained in control of the hotel until 1961, when she died at the age of ninety-three. She was succeeded by her son, Charles Ritz. After his death in 1976, the hotel went into decline. In 1979, the Egyptian businessman Mohamed Al-Fayed bought the Ritz for thirty million dollars and revamped it, returning it to profitability.

Having fallen short of the French government's coveted 'palace' classification in 2011, the Ritz was closed for a complete renovation, which took four years. It has now regained its place as one of the most luxurious – and most famous – hotels in the world.

The Imperial Suite can be booked for rates well in excess of $10,000 a night. However, bearing in mind the fates of some other occupants of Marie Antoinette's bed – Goering, Princess Diana, Dodi Al-Fayed, F. Scott Fitzgerald, Maria Callas and of course, Marie Antoinette herself – one might be inclined to wonder whether it is a very lucky one.